THE SECRETS OF GASLIGHT LANE

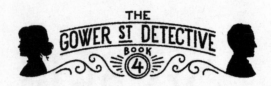

THE MANGLE STREET MURDERS

THE CURSE OF THE HOUSE OF FOSKETT

DEATH DESCENDS ON SATURN VILLA

THE SECRETS OF GASLIGHT LANE

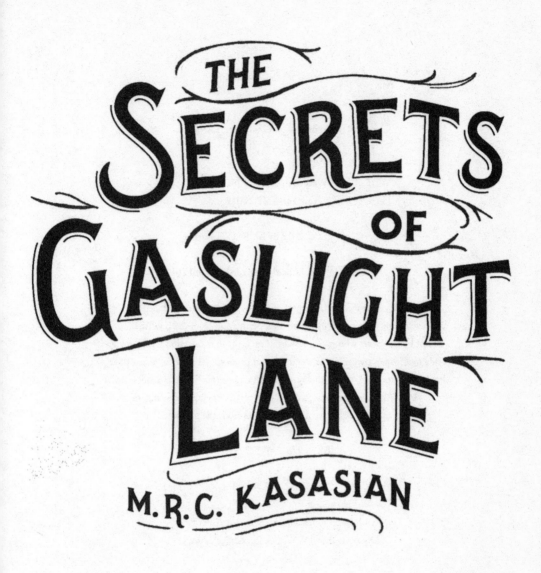

THE SECRETS OF GASLIGHT LANE

M.R.C. KASASIAN

PEGASUS CRIME
NEW YORK LONDON

THE SECRETS OF GASLIGHT LANE

Pegasus Books Ltd
148 West 37th Street, 13th Floor
New York, NY 10018

ISBN: 978-1-68177-358-2

10 9 8 7 6 5 4 3 2 1

Printed in the United States of America
Distributed by W. W. Norton & Company, Inc.

For Mel, Tom and Will
with love

Introduction

I VISITED OUR OLD maid in her new home yesterday and, while we were talking, a bell tinkled in the background. Two rings for tea, she remembered, but was too tired to get up. After I had made sure that she was settled, I took my leave and, on exiting the building, found that Thanet Street had been cordoned off whilst the army dealt with an unexploded bomb.

And so I passed down Burton Crescent – as I still think of it. The elegant curve of buildings was broken at the northern tip by the massive edifice of a house called Gethsemane, the only remaining fragment of what used to be Gaslight Lane.

Terrible things had happened in that building but, with the shockwaves of a near miss, the façade had collapsed into the road and turned the building into a giant dolls' house, its darkness finally exposed to the world. Some of the furniture had been blown into the street or looted but the octagonal table was still there, poking through the dust and rubble.

For a moment I saw Cherry by the fireplace, reading a letter, and I almost called out. But we are separated by a gulf now that I would have to give my life to cross.

The horror evoked by the awful deeds in the area led to demands from the residents for the place names to be changed. And so, in 1908, Gaslight Lane and the Crescent lost their separate identities and were rechristened Cartwright Gardens, in honour of the social reformer whom Sidney Grice so heartily detested.

My guardian regarded this case as one of his greatest achievements, though the world believed it to be a rare failure. But I cannot think of it in such terms.

I pass the firemen unseen, drifting unnoticed amongst ARP officers and weary crowds, for I live in shadows now and the shapes of the past are as real as those of the present. It is as if I am no longer part of this world but have not yet joined the many ghosts still haunting the wreckage of Gaslight Lane.

M.M., 19 July 1943
125 Gower Street

1

The Slaughter of Innocents

ON THE TWENTY-FIRST night of September 1872, almost ten years before I came to London, the Garstang household was murdered. Holford Garstang, his wife Augusta and three of the residential servants were discovered with their throats cut. Their godson, Lionel Engra, was strangled.

The only survivor was Angelina Innocenti, the lady's maid, found in a deranged and bloody state the next morning.

They had lived and died in Gethsemane, an imposing building in the Bloomsbury area of Camden, London. Holford Garstang was a respectable and successful seller of religious tracts and a master of his Masonic Lodge. Augusta came from a long line of ship owners and the merger of their companies created a highly successful export business. The marriage was not entirely one of convenience, however. By all accounts they were an affectionate couple, though their union was not blessed by children. The Garstangs had every reason to anticipate long and healthy lives. They had no reason to anticipate being slaughtered like pigs.

2

————⋯◆⋯————

Over the Point

THE MAN WHO had murdered my father hid a depraved and calculating mind behind an amiable manner. But the mask had shattered when he thought that I was going to kill him, and he was curled in a whimpering ball when Sidney Grice and Inspector Pound found him on the floor in the corner of the laboratory. The prisoner was handcuffed and chained in the guard's van for our trip back to London, and it was only when my guardian went to check on him that I had a moment alone with the inspector.

I edged along the seat until I sat opposite him in our compartment.

'Thank God you are safe,' he said, but made no attempt to move towards me.

'I am sorry that I gave you back your mother's ring,' I told him. 'I have spent too long clinging to a memory. I learned that much from my experiences.'

George Pound touched his brow. 'I wonder what would happen to me if your fiancé could return tomorrow.'

'I cannot answer that.'

'Perhaps it was an unfair question.' He plucked at his forehead. 'But something else concerns me, Miss Middleton.'

'*Miss Middleton?*' After all I had been through, I found I could still be shocked.

'I do not feel I can be more familiar.' He put his palm out.

'It is not just that you prefer a dead man to me but, when we met, I understood that you had little in the way of personal wealth.'

'That was the case,' I confirmed, 'but some of my father's mining shares increased in value.'

'So now you are a woman of means,' he lowered his hand but the palm still faced me, 'and therefore beyond my reach.'

I considered his words. 'If that is the only barrier that stands between us, it is easily torn down.' The train rattled over a series of points. 'When I am of age I can give my money to a good cause. There is no shortage of those.'

Pound looked out at the darkness. 'I cannot permit you to do that.'

I flared indignantly. 'You cannot prevent me.'

'No.' He struggled for words. 'I mean I could not ask any woman to give up her comforts to share a pinched life with me.'

'I had hopes that *you* would be my comfort.'

A ghostly image materialized in the outer corridor window and I slid back. I was in my place when my guardian rejoined us. The world we inhabited kept me there.

Hoping to recover from this personal blow and from the effects of the poisons I had been fed in an attempt to drive me mad, I travelled throughout Britain, accompanied by my true friend, Harriet Fitzpatrick, with whom I became embroiled in the appalling occurrences at Scarfield Manor, the journals concerning which are stored in my banker's vault.

In the autumn of 1883 I returned to 125 Gower Street, but I fear I was of little use to my guardian until that November when, once again, I accompanied him on a case, the details of which must remain confidential. I do not suppose that I shall ever be able to publish an account of the sordid events surrounding the Clerkenwell Publisher.

The Demons of the Night

IT ALWAYS BEGINS *in the same way – I fall into the emptiness, no light, nothing to hold on to, just the falling. If I land, the jolt wakes me up. I take my medicine and try to calm down.*

Then there is the hand over the eyes forcing the head down. I feel the pressure on the nose and brow, every finger, the palm and heel of the hand.

Usually it ends there and I sit up with a jump, but it changes in between. Bits might be added or taken away. There may be an endless corridor, the boards squealing silently or a staircase cracking without a sound under somebody's feet. Something rushes. Is it me or towards me? Something shrinks back. Is it me or away from me? The worst is when it goes on – the whiteness in the moonlight, the thin line widening and darkening. No that is not true: the worst is the whimper and the word when I hear it.

NUTTY.

And then I am tumbling, fighting to escape, unable to run in the treacle air, not daring to think what is behind or before me, boards squealing shrilly, the staircase cracking explosively.

And NUTTY bounces about inside my skull, trying to find a way out. But there is no escape. It hurts. My head hurts. I stumble.

That is when I wake up drenched and choking, my heart hammering in my tight chest. I am paralysed as the shades loom above me but I force myself to breathe, will myself to reach out through those shapes. The tiny glow shines like my guardian angel, my one protection against the demons of the night. I fumble to turn up the wick on the oil lamp that I keep forever burning by my bed. My hand trembles so much that I almost knock the lamp over. The shapes dart around me and away from me, cowering from the light, and the only shadows are those of the furniture. I know them by heart but I still fear them.

Sometimes – and I am deeply ashamed to confess this – I wet my nightgown but I dare not do anything about it. I am terrified to stay soaking in my bed – it feels like hot blood – and yet I am petrified to move out of it; and it cools as blood cools, as we all cool.

Even when I am awake that word whispers close by.
NUTTY.

And then I remember why I fear it so much and my very soul screams out of me. That was not the nightmare. This moment is the nightmare. And this moment will never end.

4

The Sydenham Cyclops

A SPIT OF RAIN hit the glass and burst.

'Twenty-five,' Sidney Grice said.

He had been standing by the window of 125 Gower Street for almost an hour, huffing and breaking off only to limp round and round the central circular table before returning to his vigil.

'What is?' I gave up trying to write my account of *The Sydenham Cyclops* in the journal I kept of our cases.

'The approximate age of the woman standing on the pavement. I cannot see her clearly through her veil.' My guardian spoke over his shoulder. 'But she has just put her spectacles on to read my new professional plate and they are almost on the tip of her nose.' He wiped some condensation off the glass with the side of his hand. 'I have oft observed that as men get older they wear their spectacles lower down their noses since they need them for reading but, because they have become long-sighted they peer over them for general purposes. Young women who are forced to wear eyepieces, however, start with them low so as not to obscure what they imagine to be their alluring eyes, but slowly push them up as necessity overrules their vanity.'

'So at about forty both sexes should be wearing them on the bridge,' I hazarded.

'Forty-five,' he corrected me, 'but, for once, you have grasped the idea. She has set her foot upon the lower step.'

'Should you be staring at her?' I asked and he piffed.

'Of course I should. It is my job to stare at people.' The door-bell rang in the hall and Mr G turned away. 'Molly is disappointingly swift to respond.'

I could just make out her footsteps clumping up the stairs.

'Why *disappointingly*?'

Mr G whipped off his scarlet patch and produced a glass eye from his waistcoat pocket, holding it between his thumb and forefinger like a kindly uncle offering a toffee. 'Because if she were performing her tasks she would be setting them aside before emerging from her lair.' He stretched his right eyelids apart and forced the eye into his socket. 'Whereas the speed of her reactions is more indicative of a guilty start.'

'Even Molly is entitled to rest sometimes,' I said.

'Nonsense.' Mr G limped to the mantel mirror and ran his fingers back through his thick jet hair. 'Her entire life is one of leisure.'

I was about to enquire who he thought performed all the household duties when Molly came in. Unusually – since Sidney Grice often accused our maid of sleeping in her uniform – her apron was brilliant white and uncreased, though her ginger hair, as always, strayed from the clips that fought and failed to restrain it under her crisply starched hat.

'A lady wishes to see you, sir,' she announced, holding out the silver hall tray. 'I told her you aintn't not very well but she said it was urgent.'

'How dare you discuss my health with strangers?'

'But there aintn't not no one else to discuss it with,' she answered reasonably. 'Miss Middleton is too – oh, what's the word?'

'Discreet,' I suggested.

'Boring,' she decided.

Her employer slid the card off, covering it with his hand like a cagey poker player. 'Miss Charity Goodsmile – what a depressingly cheerful name – of 28 West Grundy Street.' He grimaced. 'Not the most prestigious of addresses. I hope she does not imagine that I will lower my fees, though she looked well-enough attired to afford them.'

'She don't talk poor,' Molly put in.

'My memory must be failing.' Her employer rubbed his brow. 'I have no recollection whatsoever of soliciting your vacuous conjectures.'

'Dontn't not worry, sir,' Molly reassured him. 'I'm always forgetting to ask for your change in the grocer's or pass on important messages, and there aintn't not nothing wrong with my brain.'

'Except that it has never been activated,' my guardian told her. 'Show my caller in.'

I closed my journal and stood up as Molly went to collect our visitor.

'Miss Charitable Goodsmell.' Her voice rang out proudly as a slim young woman followed her into the study.

'Smile,' she corrected mildly and Molly bared her teeth uncertainly.

'Get out,' Mr G snapped. 'And fetch us tea.'

Molly flushed, bobbed jerkily and left.

'Mr Grice,' the lady said softly. She was dressed entirely in sable with a gauze veil folded back over her hat. 'It is good of you to see me.'

'Please do not mistake my curiosity for kindness.' Mr G took her hand and bowed, not from courtesy but to examine it closely. She was a striking woman, a good four or five inches taller than either of us, her raven hair and ebony dress contrasting with the pallidity of her skin. Her face was white and unblemished, the only colours being her pale pink lips, the dark thin lines of her eyebrows and long lashes and the lightest wash of cerulean in her almond-shaped eyes.

'Do take a seat, Miss Goodsmile.' He guided her to my armchair and she sat upright on the edge of it.

'My friends call me Cherry.'

'I am saddened to hear that.' He deposited himself into his

armchair opposite her. 'This other woman –' he indicated vaguely – 'is my assistant, Miss Middleton.'

I took her hand. 'How do you do, Cherry? Please call me March.'

I fetched myself an upright walnut chair from the round central table and sat to face the fire with them to either side.

'It must be hard to have lost your father so recently, especially as he was estranged from your mother and you have no brothers or older sisters,' my guardian commented and our visitor stiffened.

'You have done your homework, Mr Grice.' A double row of waves furrowed her brow. 'But how could you have known that I was coming?'

Mr G smiled tightly. 'Until two minutes and fourteen seconds ago I was unaware of your existence.'

'It does not take a detective to see that I have been bereaved.' She touched her veil. 'I am puzzled by the rest of your remarks, though.'

'That is a man's signet ring.' Mr G pointed to the silver chain around her neck with a band of gold bearing a shield hanging on it.

'It could be my late husband's,' Cherry Goodsmile objected and he sniffed.

'You do not wear a wedding ring and, if you had removed it to advertise your re-entry into the marital market – which would be in impoverished taste since you are still in deep mourning – it would also be on that chain.' He watched her closely. 'And if you had a brother or an older sister the ring would have gone to one of them.'

She nodded slightly. 'And my mother?'

Mr G ran his left thumb over his left fingerplates. 'If she had been living with your father, she would have taken it. If she were dead, you would sport her ring as well.'

Cherry Goodsmile looked at him. 'You have a keen eye, Mr Grice.'

My guardian shrugged. 'I see nothing that others cannot. It is paying attention to what I see that makes me observant. My immense genius lies in knowing what to make of such information.'

'Then perhaps you can tell me why I am here?' she challenged, and he inclined his head.

'I can read books, street signs and journals in eight languages, but not minds in any of them.' He sat back. 'Obviously I could speculate that it concerns your father's death, but I dislike being obvious and I hate guessing.'

Molly returned and put a tray on the table between us.

'That's true,' she told our visitor. 'He wouldn't not play "Who's in the Coffin?" last Christmas Day when Miss Middleton was pretending to be what's-his-name Bones-Apart.'

'Napoleon,' I informed her.

'I'm sure it was Bones-Apart,' she mused. 'You did that funny Irish voice.'

'Go,' her employer barked and she left.

'Your guess would have been correct,' Cherry said quietly. 'My father was murdered, Mr Grice, savagely in his bed.'

'Excellent,' my guardian cried, clapping his hands together.

5

Hezzuba Grebe and the Battle of Ruspina

CHERRY GOODSMILE STARED at Sidney Grice and her lips
blanched.

'I am glad you think so,' she remarked bitterly.

'I suspect you are being ironic,' Mr G said as our visitor
grasped the sides of her chair and braced her arms ready to rise.
'But I must tell you that I am immune to sarcasm and sympathy
is not included in my bill of charges.'

'Oh, for goodness' sake,' I exclaimed.

'Human feelings are – as you have probably calculated – Miss
Middleton's department,' he declared unabashed. 'And, if you
want tears, any competent undertaker can provide a team of
mourners. The Irish have a reputation for wailing to great effect.'

'I have not come here to be mocked.' Cherry Goodsmile
jumped to her feet and I stood to let her pass.

'However,' my guardian continued smoothly, 'if you want
your father's murderer discovered – and I think it fairly safe to
assume that you do – so long as you have the money, I can guarantee to do it.'

Our visitor paused. 'How can you possibly make such a
promise?'

'Because I never fail,' he said simply.

Cherry Goodsmile hesitated. 'I do not like your manner.'

'Neither do I,' I assured her, 'but he is telling the truth. I have
only been here twenty months—'

'It feels like eternity,' Mr G mumbled but I ignored him.

'But in that time,' I pressed on, 'he has captured six murderers and a number of other criminals. What he lacks in charm he more than makes up in ingenuity.'

'Have I left the room?' he muttered. 'I do not believe that I have.'

'At least stay for a cup of tea.' I put a hand to Cherry Good-smile's arm. 'I am sure we can help.'

She looked at me. 'You are the main reason I came. This is the only private detective I could find who has a female assistant.'

'Personal,' Mr G snapped. 'I am a *personal* detective.'

'But not personable,' I whispered and she offered a half-smile.

'Nor deaf,' he retorted as she rejoined her seat. He looked at her coolly. 'Now, if Miss Middleton has finished chattering, perhaps you could tell me what has happened.'

I reached for the teapot. 'When was your father murdered, Cherry?'

Our visitor swallowed. 'Three weeks ago, on the fourth of January.'

'The one thousand eight hundred and thirty-eighth anniversary of the Battle of Ruspina and the one thousand and thirteenth of the Battle of Reading,' Mr G interlocked his fingers as if in prayer, 'but generally a quiet day here. There were only four murders reported in London that Friday. Jessie and Jermey Unwin who may well have managed to kill each other with spikes, Paul Devine who was injected with quicksilver and Nathan—'

'Mortlock,' Cherry broke in. 'Nathan Mortlock was my father. He resided in—'

'Gaslight Lane.' Sidney Grice sat up.

'Is that not the site of the Garstang massacre?' I remembered reading an account of the murders when I lived in Parbold and a later version by Trafalgar Trumpington, the unscrupulous hack who had smeared my reputation after our first meeting.

'Garstang,' my guardian breathed, his face alight like the

painting of a visionary. 'A name that is hallowed in the chronicles of felony most foul.'

'You will understand why I use another surname.' Cherry lowered her head. 'Though you might as well call me *Mortlock* now. I doubt there is one man in a hundred who has not heard what befell my great-uncle's household.'

'And if the press are to be believed – which they are occasionally – your father met a similar fate.' Sidney Grice happily stirred his unsugared milkless tea six times clockwise and then in reverse.

'He was found in bed with his throat cut,' Cherry's voice was scarcely audible, 'and strangled.'

'Two methods for the price of one death.' Mr G made a brisk note.

'Who found him?' I asked and, when she touched the ring, I instinctively put a hand to where I used to hang one beneath my dress.

Cherry Mortlock raised her head. 'His valet.'

'And his name is?' My guardian shook his spoon dry.

'Austin Hesketh.'

'That name sounds familiar.' At Cherry's assent I poured milk into her cup and mine.

'He was Great-Uncle Holford's valet.' Our visitor picked at her sleeve.

'And on the night of the massacre he was allegedly visiting his sick mother in…' Mr G flicked through his encyclopaedic brain, 'Nuneaton.'

'I do not think there is much *allegedly* about it.' Cherry brushed her sleeve as if there were a wasp on it. 'The police investigated him thoroughly and a great many independent witnesses testified that he was away from London all that night.'

Mr G lifted his cup and looked at her over it. 'All facts are alleged until I have confirmed them.' He sipped his tea appreciatively. 'Suspicion fell upon your father too, as I recall.'

'I have never understood why.' Cherry's cup rattled in its saucer. 'Admittedly he came into the Garstang fortune, but he spent that entire night locked in a police cell and you cannot have a stronger alibi than that.'

'I can think of fourteen.' Mr G put his cup down, carefully aligning the handle. 'But six might not apply.'

'The Spanish maid survived too,' I recollected.

'Angelina Innocenti.' Sidney Grice put his fingertips together.

'Unfortunately,' Cherry confirmed bitterly. 'She may have escaped justice by pretending to be mad, but never was a girl so inappropriately named. She was no angel and she was certainly not innocent. There is no reasonable doubt that that she-devil committed those crimes and now she idles her life away in Broadmoor.'

'I trust they keep a closer eye on her than they did on Miss Grebe.' Sidney Grice fluttered his long eyelashes.

'Who?' Cherry asked automatically.

'Hezzuba Grebe, the pigeon poisoner of Primrose Hill,' I explained. 'She escaped just before Christmas and the authorities have no idea what has become of her.'

'The average policeman could not find himself in a foot-locker,' my guardian scoffed.

'If all she did was kill birds, why is she in Broadmoor?' Cherry enquired abstractedly.

'Under normal circumstances she might have been commended for reducing a pestilence.' Mr G wound up his watch. 'But Hezzuba Grebe was a cook by profession and fed the birds to her employers. Once might have been an unfortunate mistake, but when twenty-five members of six households which employed her died in less than three years' suspicions were raised.'

Cherry groaned. 'Does any of this have anything to do with my father's death?'

'Probably,' the great detective listened to his hunter watch ticking, 'not.'

'Why are you so convinced that Angelina Innocenti was guilty?' I asked. 'As I recall she never stood trial.'

'Who else could it be?' our visitor challenged. 'Even before my father took extra precautions, that house was impregnable.

Nobody could have got in or out that night.' She tipped half a spoon of sugar into her tea. 'But I have not come to rake over old ground.' Her voice rose. 'My father has been murdered and the police are getting nowhere with their investigations. I want justice, Mr Grice; I want to bury my father and come into my inheritance.' She took a drink. 'I am sorry if that last reason sounds vulgar.'

'Money is never vulgar,' my guardian declared, 'only the people who do not have it.'

This was not the time to argue that I had met some very vulgar people with a great deal of money in our capital city.

'He has not been laid to rest yet?' I reiterated. 'After three weeks? How dreadful for you.'

'Quite so.' Sidney Grice tutted. 'But how wonderful for me.'

'Wonderful?' Cherry echoed in disbelief.

'Indeed,' he concurred. 'There are only fourteen things I hate more than investigating a murder without sight of the corpse.'

Cherry Mortlock inhaled sharply. 'You are talking about my father.'

'We can discuss the weather if you prefer,' he suggested. 'My time is your money, speaking of which...' He pulled out a drawer and handed her a sheet of paper. 'I have standardized my fees and they are listed here.'

Cherry brought a pair of gold-rimmed spectacles out of her satin handbag and, as my guardian had observed, perched them on the tip of her nose. 'You are very expensive, Mr Grice. Charlemagne Cochran does not charge half that amount.'

My guardian blenched at the mention of his hated and despised rival. 'And my cook would not charge you a fourteenth,' he agreed, 'but the result would be the same. If you want to be charmed and flattered, then I suggest you engage him immediately, but Charlatan Cochran would have arrested Adam and Eve for the death of Abel.'

Cherry Mortlock took her spectacles off. 'He apprehended the Regent Street suffocationist.'

My guardian huffed. 'Christopher Focton was no more guilty than you, Miss Mortlock – and I take it you have an alibi for each of those crimes. If he had possessed the means to employ me, I could have saved Mr Focton from the gallows in an afternoon. The real culprit is a Peruvian phrenologist who still wreaks havoc undisturbed in the thoroughfares of Glasgow. But nobody cares much who dies in that city, least of all me.'

She listened to him uncertainly. 'Very well,' she decided at last. 'I will make you an offer, Mr Grice. I shall pay your fees plus ten per cent the day my father's murderer is pronounced guilty in the dock. Otherwise you shall not get a brass farthing.'

'You have appealed to the better side of my nature.' Sidney Grice tugged at his scarred ear. 'My greed.'

'Then we have a deal?'

Mr G pulled out a document. 'You have your Great-Uncle Holford's flair for commerce. Let us hope you do not share his fate.'

'I cannot believe you said that,' I scolded.

'You would rather I hoped that she did?' My godfather tossed the document on to our visitor's lap. 'That is my unorthodox contract. I would particularly draw your attention to the conditions for terminating our agreement as outlined in clause five, and the strict rules of confidentiality.'

'I am sure I can rely on your discretion,' Cherry said generously.

'So am I.' Sidney Grice polished a thumbplate on his lapel. 'And, to ensure yours, the contract forbids the client to discuss anything that transpires between us for fourteen years.' He shut the drawer.

'I shall read it at home.' Cherry Mortlock folded the contract into her handbag.

'Do so, then sign it neatly and return at my earliest convenience.' Mr G leaned towards her. 'One more thing, Miss Charity Mortlock. Be under no misapprehensions. If I discover that you are a patricide I shall not hesitate to inform the police.'

Cherry flared furiously. 'Why on earth would I come to you if I were guilty?'

My guardian shrugged. 'I have referred three clients to the hangman and they all protested the same thing. I should not like you to be the fourth.'

'I should not have thought that you would care,' she retorted sourly.

'I should care intensely.' Mr G's eye slid outwards. 'It is very bad for business.' He leaned back. 'But drink your tea. There are fourteen questions I must ask you.'

'Do all your thoughts come in fourteens?' she demanded.

'They do today,' he replied serenely.

6

---◈━◈◈◈━◈---

The Old Wound and the Beast

C HERRY MORTLOCK CLIPPED her handbag shut and huffed heavily and, for a moment, I thought she would go.

'Tell us about your father,' I urged.

'What would you like to know?'

'When did you last see him?' I topped up her tea to encourage her to stay, but she did not glance at it.

'On Christmas Day.' She sucked her lower lip. 'I called on him to try to make amends.'

'For what?' Sidney Grice reached over and selected a maroon leather-backed notebook from the smallboy at his side.

Cherry clutched her handbag. 'I have such happy early memories of my father. When he was young, he would chatter and laugh for hours. We never had a penny but then – as he would tell us – we never had a care.' She fiddled with the catch. 'All that changed when we moved into Gethsemane. We became rich but the circumstances under which he came into his fortune led to him being ostracized by society. Rumours abounded that he had paid to have his uncle's household killed, and the only attention he received was from sensation seekers. He became nervous and morose. He suffered terrible headaches and would fly into frightening rages.' She hesitated. 'Eventually my mother found living with him intolerable. Her name is Fortitude and heaven knows she needed it to survive in that marriage. Three years ago she left him.' Cherry placed her handbag on the floor.

'She eloped with an Italian sculptor and illustrator by the name of Montanari.'

'Agostino Cristiano Montanari?' Sidney Grice dabbed a grain of sugar off the tray and, noting her assent, added, 'I have long admired his work.'

'But you do not like art,' I objected.

'I loathe art and anything posing as it,' he agreed, without taking his eyes off our guest. 'Where are the happy couple now?'

Cherry Mortlock grimaced. 'In a village on the shores of Lake Geneva.'

'Switzerland.' The very word tasted bad to Mr G. 'A vile country crammed to bursting with unnecessary mountains and superfluous valleys infested with odious lactating ruminants, republicans and cuckoo clocks.' He brought out his Mordan mechanical pencil from his inside coat pocket. 'But I see your mother is not the only one to associate with artists.'

Her head jerked back. 'Now I *know* that you have prior knowledge of me.'

Sidney Grice scribbled a note. 'As you sauntered with great gracility through my study you deposited three specks of partly dried oil paint from the soles of your Andalusian cow-skin boots on to my inadequately polished Hampshire oak floor.' He pointed with his pencil. 'Two Prussian blue and one burnt umber. Where else could they have come from other than a studio?'

And that is when Spirit made an appearance. She must have been hiding under the desk – where she loved to play with the balls of paper my guardian was always tossing towards his bin – because the first I saw was a bundle of white streaking across the room, under my chair and launching itself on to our visitor's lap.

Cherry jumped.

'I am so sorry,' I said.

'I told you to keep that offensive beast upstairs, especially when we have clients,' Mr G scolded.

'I forgot she was here.' I made to shoo her away but Cherry laughed.

'Please do not worry. I love cats.' Her face darkened. 'But my father never allowed me any pets.' She stroked Spirit's back. 'What beautiful hair.'

'We rescued her from a factory where they bred cats for fur,' I said and she winced.

'How savage.' She ran a thumb under Spirit's throat and it was only then that I noticed what extraordinarily long fingers our visitor had. 'Have I annoyed her? She is not purring.'

'Nor will she meow,' I said. 'She is mute.'

'For which you more than compensate,' Mr G informed me and turned to his client. 'When did you last hear from your mother?'

'Not since she wished me a good night the day before she ran away.' Cherry allowed Spirit to nuzzle her knuckles.

'Have you ever tried to contact your mother?' I asked and Cherry paused.

'She knows where I am but I do not have that advantage regarding her.'

'Is it possible that she has returned?' I suggested.

'To kill her husband?' Cherry frowned. 'She was terrified of him.'

'What about the sculptor?' I slid the milk jug towards our visitor.

'I only met him once.' She tickled behind Spirit's ear. 'He was a gentle person. I imagine that is why she fell for him.'

'How pleasant it is to wile away the hours with sterile speculation,' Mr G commented. 'What happened on Christmas Day?'

'You have a talent for getting to the point, Mr Grice.' Cherry exhaled heavily through her little nose. 'I joined an art class last summer, if for no other reason than to escape the oppressive atmosphere at home. My teacher was a painter of the Pre-Raphaelite school, Fabian Le Bon. We fell in love. He is poor. My father violently – and I mean *violently* – disapproved and I left. Maria Feltner, a fellow student, let me share her lodgings in West Grundy Street. That was in October. Fabian had a small but quite successful show in November and was getting several commissions. I hoped that with this knowledge and a little seasonal goodwill, my father would soften his stance.' She patted Spirit's back. 'The only concession he made was to come to the door after Easterly, our footman, could not bring himself to turn me away.' She sighed. 'My father did the job for him and with relish. He slammed the door and left me standing in the snow.' She nibbled her lower lip. 'The next time I saw him was in the morgue.'

'And where was Mr Le Bon while this abortive reunion was taking place?' Mr G enquired.

The mantel clock struck the quarter hour.

'He was waiting in the gardens out of sight.'

I watched Cherry Mortlock closely. 'Did your father ever hit you?' I thought I saw a tic under her right eye.

'Never me.' Our visitor leaned back as Spirit's tail waved under her nose. 'But he slapped my mother not long before she left and he pushed our housekeeper, Mrs Emmett, over when he found a mistake in her accounts. She struck her head on the hearth fender and was knocked unconscious. When she awoke she thought she had had an accident.' Cherry stroked the tail away. 'I am not sure that she has ever fully recovered.'

'How did you learn that your father was dead?' I asked.

'Hesketh sent me a telegram. *Regret to inform you that your father passed away in the night.*' She shivered. 'He made it sound so peaceful.'

'Perhaps it was quicker and less painful than you imagine,' I suggested, 'especially if your father was asleep.'

Cherry Mortlock's shoulders rose. 'It was a bungled killing.' Her shoulders fell. 'My father must have been awake and struggling.' She struggled to compose herself. 'The police told me there were several cuts on his neck.'

'I have seen many cases where the razor has been drawn tentatively over the throat or wrist many times before the suicide steals himself to administer the fatal laceration,' Sidney Grice remarked.

Our visitor closed her eyes. 'His neck was severed to his spine. Was that self-inflicted?'

Mr G tugged his earlobe. 'I was merely observing that there are other possible interpretations of multiple incisions.'

'He was hacked to death,' Cherry cried. 'What more do you want?'

'To apprehend his killer or killers and collect my fee.' Mr G held his pencil horizontally and peered at her under it. 'Who is in charge of the case?'

'Inspector Quigley.' Cherry grimaced. 'A horrid man.'

'I will not argue with that,' I told her. 'The last time I was involved with Quigley he tried to force me to sign a confession for the murder of a client.'

'A great pity you did not comply,' Sidney Grice lamented. 'It would have been evidence of his corruption. But I shall bring him to book sooner or later.'

'He strikes one as being quite thorough,' Cherry conceded. 'But I do not think he has made any progress.'

'He is less incompetent than most of his so-called profession.' My guardian rubbed his shoulder. The old wound troubled him more in the damp weather. 'But he is not as ready as I to tolerate the foolishnesses of the weaker sex.'

Cherry and I exchanged glances.

'Have you seen your father's bedroom?' I asked and she shook her head.

'I could not even bear to go into the house without it being thoroughly cleaned.'

Mr G shot a hand to his eye. 'You have not had it scoured?'

'Not yet,' she assured him. 'Though, when probate is granted and it is my house, I shall do so at the first opportunity. The police have already searched it. Should I leave my home looking like an abattoir?' Her voice rose. 'For heaven's sake, that room must be full of my father's blood.'

Cherry Mortlock's breast spasmed.

'No.' Sidney Grice slapped his notebook shut. 'It is full of clues and you shall not touch anything without my permission.'

'Your...?' Our visitor lifted Spirit and put her gently on to the rug. 'I cannot work with you, Mr Grice. You are the most unpleasant person I have ever met.'

'Give me fourteen days and I shall introduce you to at least one a great deal more unsavoury than I.' My guardian pushed the lead back into his pencil.

Cherry Mortlock blinked twice. 'Very well,' she agreed at last. 'But not a day longer.'

'Is the house occupied at present?' I enquired.

'Hesketh and the other servants are looking after it.' She put her spectacles back on. 'The police have sealed my father's bed-chamber.'

'And may I ask where your father is now?'

'In heaven, I trust,' she replied, 'but his earthly remains are at Snushall and Sons, the undertakers on Gordon Street.'

'Instruct your father's valet to anticipate and admit us.' Mr G sprang up and hurried back to his filing cabinets. 'I shall communicate with you at my convenience.'

Cherry Mortlock looked at me in confusion.

'Are we...?'

'Our business is complete for today.' He opened two drawers at once. 'But you may drink your tea so long as you promise not to distract me with your inane gossip.'

'Well, really!' Cherry Mortlock banged the arm of her chair and got to her feet.

'Farewell, Miss Charity Mortlock alias Goodsmile.' Mr G gave her a cheery wave as I saw her to the door.

'I am sorry about his behaviour,' I said and she took my hand.

'I am sorry for you having to live with him,' she retorted as she stepped outside.

*

'What a delightful young lady,' Sidney Grice enthused when she had gone. 'I am sure we shall get along famously.'

'I do not think she liked you,' I said and he smiled thinly.

'You should know by now, March, that I do not want clients' affection. I want their money.'

'And what do you intend to do with all this money?' I asked in disgust.

'The wealthy do not *do* things with money,' he retorted. 'They *have* it. But that is not all that interests me. This is the most delicious murder that has come my way in months.'

I did not ask whether he had found the death of my Uncle Tolly quite so delightful.

The Nine

THERE ARE NINE *demons. Sometimes they come to me all at once, but usually one at a time and in the wrong order. Eight of them are victims. I see their faces and I know their names. I see their terror and I hear their screams.*

The ninth is their destroyer and I cannot speak his name.

I see him, usually from above, often from behind, and, in the worst dreams, the ones that crush the heart in my breast, I see his face and it is a mask of mine, and their blood stinks hot on my hands.

8

Gouging Eyes and Gauntlets

W E HAD A hurried lunch and it was unappetizing as usual – over-boiled sliced carrots and cold butter beans strewn over whole under-boiled potatoes. Sidney Grice separated the constituents into three piles, sowed lines of salt up and down his fare and tucked in with gusto. He spoke little but occasionally waved his left hand around in an animated discourse with himself. Once he whipped out his pencil and made a note on the tablecloth, but two minutes later he scribbled it out.

'I see,' he said loudly to his carafe, but did not reveal what it was that he saw.

With the tip of my knife I gouged the eye out of an old King Edward, before I broke the silence. 'Where shall we start our investigations?'

A year last May he had balked at the very idea of me being involved in his work, but after the Ashby case I do not think it occurred to him to exclude me, provided I was well enough to accompany him.

My guardian shook a grey cloud of pepper over his plate and the surrounding area. 'Perhaps you would like to answer that question yourself.'

My dissection had exposed a boggy brown crater and I pushed the potato to one side. 'Nathan Mortlock's body,' I suggested, knowing that he would pour scorn on whatever I suggested.

'Justify your decision.'

'The site of the murder has been closed off and the witnesses, including the guilty party, will have rehearsed their accounts by now,' I reasoned, 'but any evidence the body can give us is deteriorating all the time.'

'Quite so.' He mashed his beans with the back of his fork, formed them into a square, shovelled them into his mouth and washed them down with a tumbler of water. 'Come along, March. You cannot spend your entire life indulging in epicurean excesses.'

We went down and, whilst Mr G gave the bell rope three tugs, I turned the brass handle in the hall to run a green flag up outside and summon a cab.

'What on earth is keeping that lumpen sloven?' He lifted his Ulster overcoat from the rack and slipped it on.

'You have only just rung.' I put on my favourite moss-green cape with a matching hat.

'I have told them ninety-two times to keep a kettle constantly two degrees below the boil.' He donned his wide-brimmed soft felt hat and riffled through his collection of silver-topped ebony canes in the old oak stand. 'At last.'

Molly's boots came clattering up the stairs and she appeared, racing down the hall clutching his flask of tea in one hand and a shrivelled apple in the other.

'Two minutes and fifty-two seconds,' he reprimanded her.

'Sorry, sir,' she panted. 'I rememberered what you said about one ring for come immediantely, two for a tray of tea and three for your insularated bottle.' She struggled for breath. 'Only Cook thought she heard four rings and said that could mean two trays of tea or come immediantely four times.'

'Tell Cook that I do not employ her to do anything other than cook.' He snatched the flask from Molly's hands and rammed it into his scratched leather satchel. 'If there is any thinking to be done I will do it.'

'She aintn't got our intelligentness, has she, sir?' Molly said wisely and her employer looked at her.

'Your cognitive incapacity is balanced only by your mental vacuity,' he replied and Molly grinned.

'Don't worry, miss,' she told me. 'He thinks the same about you.'

'I believe he does,' I assured her.

There was a knock on the door and Molly opened it to reveal Gerry Dawson on the step.

'Morning, miss,' he greeted me merrily. 'What is it today – felons or frippery?'

Gerry had been a police sergeant before he was thrown out of the force for being intoxicated on duty and, by his own admission, was on the road to destitution until Mr G helped him get work as a cabby.

'Business,' I told him.

The stink of methane was overwhelming.

'Pity.' He clapped his leather gauntlets. 'There's a new line of dresses from Paris in 'Arrods. Suit you down to a T.'

'Nothing would suit Miss Middleton up or down to any letter of the alphabet, thank you, Dawson,' my guardian told him severely.

'I did not know you followed the fashions, Gerry,' I said as I stepped out. Workmen were digging a hole, piles of wet earth all around and spilling on to the pavement, a heavy drizzle turning the mud into an adhesive sludge.

'I don't.' He put out his canvas-cloaked arm to help me aboard. 'But I 'ave a regular lady from Endsleigh Gardens what goes there every day and she keeps me informed of all the new fancies. What's goin' on 'ere then?'

'A collapsed sewer,' I told him. 'They have to go carefully because it runs next to the water mains and gas supply.'

'Indeed.' Mr G clambered in after me. 'It is quite a three-pipe problem.'

A group of urchins had been playing with a rag ball but they quit their game for the better sport of running after our hansom, chanting.

'Gricey ricey pudding and pie
Killed the girls and made them cry
When the boys came out to play
Gricey locked them all away.'

I laughed. 'I haven't heard that one before.'

But Mr G was not amused. 'A pity they do not expend their energies on something more useful.' He scowled.

'They cannot find work,' I countered.

'One does not *find* work; one *does* it,' he decreed as they fell back.

Two men staggered out of number 129, dragging an upright piano.

'I saw an old man carry one of those on his back in Bombay,' I remarked.

'We mollycoddle our lower orders in this country,' he commented, 'allowing them to lounge about in workhouses when they should be building railways across the wastes of Berkshire.'

We passed the great neoclassical portico of University College to our right and the red-brick turrets of the hospital on our left, before crossing the traffic into Gower Place and turning right again into Gordon Street.

''Ere we are,' Gerry announced. 'Nice quick one for Cleo.'

We could easily have walked but Mr G did not care to mingle with hoi polloi and, when we stepped down, I gave Cleo the apple. In truth she was getting too old for the job, but we all knew that the day she retired would be her last. Gerry had neither the space nor the money to keep her as a pet.

'*Snushall and Sons*,' I read on the discreet highly polished brass sign.

9

The Stone Sarcophagus

SIDNEY GRICE MARCHED through the entrance and I followed him into a dusky, black-draped office, where an elderly male figure sat in a murky armchair. He rose, his movement slow and stately, as I closed the door.

'Crepolius Snushall at your service.' His voice was low and husky and his features so cadaverous that he looked in need of his own firm's attentions.

'Mr Grice and Miss Middleton,' my guardian announced.

'I am sorry for the loss of your loved one.' Mr Snushall bowed deeply, the flicker of four tall, thick candles nestling in his hollowed cheeks. 'May I enquire if I should be merely sad or prostrate with grief?'

'You may be however maudlin you choose,' Mr G told him. 'I have no loved ones and am confident that I never shall.'

The air was perfumed with a haze from the silver incense burner suspended from the ceiling.

'Then the loss is yours.' Mr Snushall addressed me.

'I have already buried all my loved ones,' I told him and he nodded wisely.

'Then you have come to discuss Mr Grice's funeral arrangements?'

'Unfortunately not.' I smiled but Mr Snushall did not.

'It is always advisable to plan ahead.' He fondled his left hand. 'We have a selection of caskets ranging from the splendid to the magnificent.'

'That is as may be,' Mr G said. 'But I shall be laid in the Grice vault in a Purbeck stone sarcophagus carved by craftsmen whose families have been in the service of my family for generations.'

Mr Snushall reeled. 'And you, miss?'

'I shall be buried in Lancashire between my parents,' I told him, 'and the Middletons always have simple pine coffins.'

'Pine?' Mr Snushall parroted as if I had told him we were slung on to dust heaps.

'And donate the difference in price to the quarry workers' welfare fund,' I concluded.

'Welfare?' Mr Snushall turned plum. 'A funeral is no time for *charity*, miss.' His voice soared tremulously. 'A funeral is a time for ostentatious extravagance on a ruinous scale. Why, some of the greatest families in England have been brought to their knees by the duty to express their dynastic griefs, and I am proud to say that Snushall and Sons has been instrumental in ravaging the estates of many an incumbent of both Houses of Parliament.' He pointed at me accusingly like one of the Christmas ghosts. 'A man of substance is not to be carted away like...' he fought for a word fit to express his disgust, '*night soil*.' His nostrils retreated from the stench of his own words. 'What will show the world how deeply you are missed unless huge sums are expended? Who, for instance, will mourn you?'

'My friends, I expect,' I told him, 'and I may have family by then.'

'Friends and family?' He spluttered in disbelief. '*Friends* and *family*? What use is that?' His ears wagged furiously. 'They will be dignified and fight to contain their emotions. Why, when Squire Whitethorn was interred we had fifty paid Cornishmen following his hearse, and they set up such a howl that the rats ran out of Bedford Square, not to return for a fortnight.'

'My family retainers shall mourn my passing,' Mr G said, 'for when I die without issue they shall all be cast out of their homes.'

'I would prefer one genuine tear to a thousand fake,' I said.

'But that is exactly what I am offering.' Mr Snushall held out his hands as if welcoming a favourite daughter. 'Allow me to demonstrate.' He reached up and gripped a thin cord between his thumb and forefinger, and a small bell tinkled far away.

'I do not—' I began, but he put a digit to his desiccated lips and, after a few seconds, the curtains on the back wall parted and a small black boy entered, dressed in black velvet and trailing an enormous matching handkerchief in his right hand.

'Permit me to introduce Master Dorolius Lacrissimus,' Mr Crepolius Snushall said and the boy bowed gravely. 'This lady and gentleman,' his employer informed him, 'have suffered a loss.'

Dorolius looked at us sadly. His lower lip quivered and a fat tear trickled from each of his wide eyes.

'It is a serious loss,' Mr Snushall added, and Dorolius moaned. The tears fell freely now.

'An inconsolable loss,' Mr Snushall avowed, and Dorolius gasped. His whole body shook and his face streamed as he fought for breath. He wrung the handkerchief and water dripped from something inside it.

'Oh woe, alas, alack,' he sobbed. 'Ohh ohhh ohhhhhh.' And Mr Snushall stood by, for all the world a proud parent whose son has just been awarded a great prize.

'Enough,' Sidney Grice rapped. At once the boy quietened and resumed his decorous melancholia.

'Go.' Mr Snushall clicked his fingers and Dorolius bowed again before reversing from our presence.

'We have come to inspect the body of Mr Nathan Mortlock,' I disclosed.

'I am afraid Mr Mortlock has not been prepared to receive visitors yet.' He crossed his arms over his waistcoat.

'We are here to investigate his death,' I continued, and the light dawned.

'Of course.' The undertaker put a silk-gloved thumb to his concave temple. 'Mr *Sidney* Grice. I have heard of you – the man responsible for all those death-club murders.'

'I am not answerable for any of those fatalities,' my guardian growled, and Mr Snushall hugged himself.

'I quite understand if you are sensitive about the matter, sir, especially after you had your other client executed.'

Mr G emitted a guttural snarl. 'Show me the body.'

'And you must be his deranged assistant,' Mr Snushall declared excitedly.

'I often think so,' I conceded.

Sidney Grice raised his cane to point just under Mr Snushall's chin and said icily, 'The body.'

'Make it worth my while,' the undertaker invited him.

Mr G reached into his trouser pocket.

'We are not talking about *coins*, I trust.' Mr Snushall snuffled, and my guardian brought a wallet from inside his coat. Mr Snushall slipped the note inside his buttoned glove. 'This way, please.' He held open the curtain and we found ourselves in a long carpeted corridor lit by a series of oil lamps, the wicks trimmed low. 'We call this the Hallowed Hall,' he whispered as we made our way along it. 'This door leads to the Room of Repose and this the Salon of Sleep.' He drifted to a halt. 'Here we are.'

'Let me guess,' I begged. 'The Hall of Hypocrisy? No, we have already had *hall*.' I tried again. 'The Foyer of Fakery?'

'Room six,' Mr Snushall informed me coldly. 'Shall we go in?'

He pitter-pattered with his fingertips on the woodwork before twisting the handle.

'Why do you knock?' Mr G enquired and the undertaker suspired.

'One should never take the departed by surprise,' Mr Snushall said.

'But the departed have departed,' I pointed out as my guardian and I entered the room.

The undertaker made to join us.

'You have some of my money.' Mr G waved him off. 'But none of my integrity. Go away.'

Mr Snushall opened his mouth.

'You had better do as he says,' I told him, 'or Miss Mortlock might discover that you allowed strangers to bribe you to let them ogle her father's body.'

The undertaker stiffened. 'How do I know that you are not body snatchers or migrant auto-photography mailerists?'

'What are they?' I tried to pretend I had not slithered on a pool of condensation and was merely examining the doorpost that I was clinging to.

'People who take photographs of themselves in different settings and send them to their equally infantile friends.' Mr G pushed me in and took hold of the door. 'Goodbye, Crepolius Jimmy Snushall.' He closed it firmly.

It was a square, windowless room and unadorned. The floor was tiled and the walls and ceiling whitewashed. In one corner was a sink and in another a tall wooden cabinet. In the centre was a granite table with an unmistakeable shape beneath a heavy cotton drape saturated in formaldehyde, its vapours stinging my eyes and catching the back of my throat.

'Take the other corner,' my guardian instructed, and we uncovered the body to its waist.

Nathan Mortlock was laid out on his back. He was a small man, short with skinny arms crossed piously over his sunken chest. His hair was sparse and grey and his skin was blotched. His eyes were closed and his lips had been stitched together.

'Cherry Mortlock was telling the truth about the wounds,' I observed.

The dead man's throat had been slashed so deeply that I could see the open pipe of his trachea above the collapsed tube of his oesophagus, and the bundles of muscles to either side had been sliced through like raw beef, though the wound did not extend, as Cherry had been told, quite so far as his spine.

'The main laceration sweeps from right to left.' Sidney Grice traced the line with a finger just over the wound.

'So we are looking for a right-handed man,' I surmised.

'Or an ambidextrous male or female,' he corrected me. 'As in most cases, whether murder or suicide, the incision runs just under the jaw.' He clipped his pince-nez on the bridge of his nose and leaned over the body, unconcerned by the vapours of embalming fluid rising from it. 'There are five other cuts, four of them quite shallow, but what do you make of this one?'

He straightened up for me to see a neat hole in the middle of the neck.

'It goes through his larynx,' I said. 'The thyroid and cricoid cartilages have been separated and you can see his epiglottis just above the wound. That would be painful if he were still alive, but there are no major blood vessels in that area so it would not have killed him.'

Mr G clicked his tongue. 'So why would anyone cut a throat there? It does not look like a wild hack.'

'I once met an army surgeon who said he had performed an incision like that on a major whose windpipe had been crushed in an accident when pig-sticking. It was to enable him to breathe, but I have never seen it done.'

Mr G hummed three B flats. 'And it is unlikely that our murderer would be trying life-saving procedures.' He rooted about in his satchel for a thin steel spatula, flattened at both ends, and I shivered involuntarily. The first time I had seen him use that instrument was when he inserted it into Sarah Ashby's ruptured heart, as clinically as he now poked one end into the lower cut. 'No blockages.' He turned his attention to the main wound, peering through a magnifying glass and humming contentedly as he prodded about. 'Would you say this corpse has been cleaned?'

'Wiped but not washed,' I decided. 'There would be more blood if he had not been wiped but less if he had been washed.'

My guardian paused and rewarded me with the fleeting lift of an eyebrow.

'Quite so.' He shuffled round the top of the table, scanning Nathan Mortlock's face through the lens as he did so. 'Interesting.' He pushed his spatula up the right nostril, held it up to the light and repeated the procedure with the left. 'Just as I thought.' He wiped the spatula on a cloth from his bag. 'There is no blood in the nasal cavities.'

'And this,' I pointed to two deep ruts running round the neck just under the chin, 'looks like the marks of a rope.'

'Very likely,' Sidney Grice agreed. 'The plaited pattern is clear even to your ill-trained eyes. Turn away, March.'

'Why?'

My guardian coloured. 'Because I am about to uncover him.' He grasped the top of the sheet.

'I have seen naked men before,' I told him, 'alive and dead.'

'Dear lord,' he muttered as I helped pull the sheet down over the dead man's feet. He inhaled protractedly through his long thin nose. 'Have a look at those haematomas.'

Nathan Mortlock's upper arms were marked by large purple bruises.

'Do you think he was beaten first to stop him struggling?' I suggested, but Mr G demurred.

'Who administers such symmetrical injuries in the course of a fight? Mortlock was in his bed and – judging by the wounds – on his back. What easier way to restrain a man than to kneel astride his chest pinioning his arms with your knees?'

'So he was not killed in his sleep?'

'He was alive for quite some time after the attack began,' Sidney Grice said grimly. 'Haematomas like that do not appear instantly, nor do they form post-mortem.' He went to the top of the table and placed his hands over the vault of Nathan Mortlock's head, working his fingers around and massaging the scalp. 'No bumps or depressions, so he was not knocked unconscious first.'

I shrank back. 'So he lay helpless in his bed while somebody hacked at his throat.'

'It would appear so,' Mr G concurred. 'It is a pity they have wiped the body, but the world is ever intent on destroying any trace that a criminal might have left.' He scrutinized the hands with his glass. 'The nails are slightly grubby, indicating that they have not been cleaned. But there are no scrapings of skin, hair or fibres under them, therefore...?' He glanced up at me.

'His arms were under the sheets,' I reasoned.

'Most likely,' he agreed, and went down to the feet again. 'Help me with this.'

I took the opposite corner of the sheet and we walked up, re-covering the body to the armpits. Sidney Grice produced a pair of curved nail scissors and snipped through the sutures, and Nathan Mortlock's lips crept apart in a mockery of the grin of a man who does not quite understand a joke. Sidney Grice ran a finger under the lips and humphed. He pulled Mortlock's jaw down and it hung agape in an unformed scream.

'What sad travesties we become of ourselves,' I mused.

My guardian clucked. 'No facial contusions or damage to the teeth.'

I peered over. 'His tongue has been badly bitten. Why were you so interested in his nose?' I felt a bit queasy but nothing would induce me to show it.

'Because,' he straightened his back, 'if any air had passed through the upper respiratory tract while the throat was being cut, the nose would have been flooded. See where the line crosses over itself just near the left angle of the jaw.'

'So the cord was wrapped twice round his throat and tied,' I surmised. 'But that would not be enough to stop the blood getting to his respiratory tract.'

Sidney Grice clicked his tongue. 'It might, if he were breathing through the incision in his neck.'

'But he would not have been able to cry out,' I realized. 'His breath left his body before it reached his larynx.' I thought about it. 'So these were not frenzied slashings but a deliberate attempt to prolong the victim's agony, while his killer cut deeper and deeper into him.' I went to the sink to rinse my hands. 'I shall never get used to cruelty.'

'Nor I to kindness.' My guardian wrapped his spatula in the

cloth and put it away. 'I see so much of one and so little of the other.' He washed his hands thoroughly, dried them and washed them again.

'What now?' I took a last look at the mound that used to be a man.

'Home,' Sidney Grice announced. 'To rinse the taste away with Molly's attempts at a decent pot of tea.'

On the way out I glimpsed Dorolius polishing the lid of an oak casket in a side room.

'Is that your real name?' I asked.

He grinned. 'It is now.'

'How do you make yourself cry so easily?'

'Simple.' Dorolius Lacrissimus paused in his work. 'First I finks of 'ow Rovers beat The Wednesday. Then I finks of 'ow it was 5–1. Then to get the fountains turned on full,' he winked, 'I recalls 'ow I 'ad a tanner on The Wednesday.'

'Nonsense.' Mr G picked up a brass handle off a workbench. 'He has a tack in his handkerchief and squeezes it in to bring tears to his eyes.'

'Show me your hand.' I looked at the boy's palm. It was dotted with dozens of new and old punctures. 'Oh, you poor child.'

The fingertips had been burned recently, but Dorolius danced away before I could look further.

'People cry all the time.' He took the handle from my guardian. 'But only me what gets paid for it.'

10

Widows' Weeds and Horses' Brains

A HORSE HAD collapsed at the junction of Gordon Street with Endsleigh Gardens and much to my guardian's annoyance I got down to have a look. It was an ageing chestnut gelding with its legs folded under it in the gutter. It must have been a fine animal once, but now the skin sank between its ribs and its haunches were scarred by old and recent lashings.

The driver gave it a kick in the loin. 'Stupid animal – won't get up no matter 'ow 'ard I whip it.'

He was a short man, pocked and scantily moustached.

The horse strained to lift itself, but its head flopped thuddingly on to the kerb.

'You should have tried feeding it,' I berated him.

''Orse what don't work don't eat,' he told me. 'And it ain't worked proper for a munf now.'

A hefty, ginger-haired man in a leather apron was pushing his way through the onlookers. 'Don't worry, mate. I'll finish it off.' He produced a long-bladed flaying knife.

'No!' I stepped between him and his intended victim.

'What?' the knacker's man demanded. 'You goin' to carry it 'ome and put it to bed?'

The crowd laughed and somebody shouted something about *fevva pillas*, but I ignored them and crouched over the creature, loosening the bridle to ease the rusty bit digging into its cheeks. It was chomping wildly, eyes straining, frothing from its mouth and nose, and its hooves slithered helplessly through the muck in a final hopeless effort to rise.

'It would be kinder to end its suffering.'

I looked up and saw Sidney Grice standing over us.

'But they will cut its throat,' I cried.

'Too right I will,' the knacker's man agreed.

Sidney Grice reached into his satchel.

'Get up, you good-fer-nuffink.' The driver unfurled his whip and his arm rose.

'If you use that I shall report you to the police and have you banned,' I vowed. But the contempt curdling his lips was enough for me to know that the driver had no licence to be revoked.

'Stand back, March,' my guardian said quietly, and I saw that he had his ivory-handled revolver.

'But...' I stroked the horse's muzzle and it calmed a little before I did as I was told.

Sidney Grice was always most particular about his appearance but he crouched, oblivious to his Ulster overcoat trailing through the filth of the thoroughfare.

'It is all right.' He patted the animal's neck. It strained up again but he pressed its head down, placing the muzzle on its forehead about halfway between the ears and eyes. 'Sleep now.'

I think we all jumped with the explosion and two horses pulling an omnibus shied, but Sidney Grice slipped the gun calmly away. The gelding fell limp, a neat round hole drowned in the scarlet well of dying.

'It is still breathing,' I whispered.

'A reflex action.' He peeled back the horse's eyelid and touched its eye. It did not blink and I saw that the pupil was enormous already.

'Good aim,' the knacker's man conceded. ''Tain't easy to find an 'orse's brain.' He was already looping a canvas strap round the body.

'Nor that of some drivers,' I muttered, and we returned to our hansom.

'Why are people so cruel to animals?' I asked as Mr G tried to shake some of the mud off his clothes.

He clambered in after me. 'The horse would have suffered no worse a fate than Nathan Mortlock or any of the Garstang family,' he observed.

The gelding was being hauled up a plank ramp on to the back of a cart as we passed.

'And we are supposed to be made in God's image,' I pondered. But Sidney Grice was never much interested in philosophizing.

We turned left into Gower Street. Two chestnut sellers were scrapping over their pitch outside the hospital entrance and one man kicked the other's bucket, spilling charcoal on to the wooden cobbles.

'Some God,' Mr G commented drily, and tossed two coins up through the hatch. The driver caught them deftly and released the catch.

The workmen had gone but the hole was still there, covered with a tarpaulin and surrounded by a heap of earth ringed by a makeshift post and rail fence.

'Interesting,' my guardian said to himself and, before I could ask, poked his cane towards an area of yellow clay. 'There is a set of footprints.'

'There are a dozen sets of footprints,' I pointed out.

'A hundred and three prints made by five different pairs of boots,' he corrected me. 'But only this set goes towards the hole and does not return.'

To me it looked like a muddy field trampled by a herd of cattle, albeit wearing boots.

'I cannot imagine anyone would be sheltering in there.' I looked again and could just about see what he meant – five or six small prints going over the large boots of the workmen. 'It must be half full of sewage water.'

'Pick up your corner.' Sidney Grice stooped to take hold of his end and between us we re-enacted our uncovering of Nathan Mortlock on a larger, heavier, messier scale, foul water spilling over my legs as I heaved back the heavy canvas. The fumes were almost overwhelming.

'My goodness, there *is* somebody in there.' I hesitated as I heard a splash and then a series of them.

'Hurry.' Mr G ran up his side of the hole but I was almost knee-deep in the mud now, my skirts heavy with it and my boots nearly pulled from my feet.

The hole was two-thirds exposed when I looked down and saw a dark shape ploughing through the stinking sludge and into a low arched tunnel.

'It is all right. We will not harm you,' I called.

'We might,' Sidney Grice contradicted me, 'depending upon who you are and your intentions.'

'Come back,' I called in alarm as the figure disappeared.

'Why?' My godfather let his end fall. 'Did you want to play?'

'She could die in there.' I was almost certain I saw a dress.

I stared into the bricked hole as the sounds echoed and faded away.

'Yes.' He stepped back, only slightly muddied by his work, on to the pavement. 'And I hate it when they do that. It blocks the drains.'

I looked and listened for a while longer before I let go of my corner, feeling almost as if I had buried the unfortunate creature in there. And, when I tried to climb out, the clay was so heavy and adhesive that I could not.

'Help me.'

My guardian surveyed the mess that was me.

'I will send Molly out,' he decided.

11

Swallowing Keys and the Unsavoury Snood

THE DUMB WAITER had jammed and Molly was obliged to carry our breakfast upstairs over several trips the next morning. I did suggest that we ate at the table in his study, but my guardian would have none of it.

'The day I concern myself about my servants' convenience is the day I start making and taking them breakfast in bed,' he forecast grimly.

I laughed at my image of that, but before I could respond Molly burst in.

'Oh, I've been up and down those stairs like a haddock,' she puffed, depositing a china bowl on the sideboard.

'There is a certain resemblance around the gills.' Her employer tapped the spout with his fork. 'More tea.' And she drifted tiredly away.

'What do you think that woman was up to in the hole yesterday?' I cracked open my egg. It smelled fresh enough.

Sidney Grice squeezed a slice of toast experimentally. 'She was hiding,' he announced as if that thought were profound.

'From what?' I reached for the salt.

'Or whom,' he added, but did not proffer a theory. 'This toast is an impostor.' He skimmed it into the fireplace.

'Us?' I suggested as my godfather selected another slice.

'Why not?' He crumbled this piece over his bowl. 'We are superb people to hide from.' Sidney Grice dripped prune juice from his spoon into the cloth. 'There was something strangely unfamiliar about that woman.'

'There must be hundreds of thousands of women unfamiliar to you,' I reasoned, delving into my egg.

'Indeed.' He had crumbs over his nose. 'But there was something strange about her unfamiliarity.'

And, with that, the conversation was at an end. Sidney Grice opened his copy of *Devlin's Illustrated Guide to the Dissection of Tree Frogs* at the page he had marked with the leaf of an aspidistra. Where the latter came from I had no idea, for he disliked having plants in the house.

Molly returned wearily with a fresh pot and announced, 'Cook says she's sorry she broke the dim waiterer.' She plonked the pot on the table. 'But she needed a piece of strung to tie up the back door after she swallowed the key.'

'How on earth did she manage that?' I asked.

'She cut it with a knife, of course,' Molly explained, as one might to a simpleton.

'No, I mean how did she manage to swallow the key?'

Molly tutted. 'She just sort of put herself back and dropped it in.'

'But why?'

'Because it was a stupid thing to do,' Mr G interjected. 'What other reason does she need?'

'Well, she was worried in case she ever got hikketyhups –' Molly leaned on the back of a chair – ''cause she aintn't not never had them.'

'But you are supposed to put a key down your back for hiccups,' I informed her and Molly snorted.

'Cook ain't not got no back.' She rocked in mirth. 'Her front goes all the way round.'

'Why do you not just join us for breakfast?' Sidney Grice sniffed. 'You have dominated it so far.'

'No thank you, sir,' Molly declined. 'Me and Cook ate all the good stuff before I brought yours up.' She pinched her chin. 'Only I dontn't not think I was supposed to tell you that.'

'I think you had better go, Molly.' I glimpsed her employer's jutting jaw.

'You might be right, miss,' she agreed, clearing an empty milk jug, and added in a whisper that would have carried to the gallery of Wilton's Music Hall, 'I think you must have upsetted him.'

Molly hurried away.

'What do you know about the massacre of the Garstang household?' Sidney Grice asked as I refilled his cup.

'Only what was in the papers and shockers at the time.'

'Your father let you read about it?' He popped his eye into a velvet pouch. The socket looked much cleaner since he had allowed me to bathe it for him, but the edges were still raw. 'You were a child.'

'My father rarely stopped me reading anything,' I said. 'He believed that the truth never hurt anyone.'

'Leaving aside the scant opportunities of stumbling across anything approaching verisimilitude in the press,' my guardian snorted, 'I could name a sizeable crowd of criminals who have suffered tremendously because I discovered the truth about them.' He plucked a vermilion patch out of his coat pocket and tied it behind his head.

'It was their lies that hurt them,' I argued. 'If they had stuck to the truth they would not have been criminals.'

But Mr G was bored with that conversation. He stood up, his face still sallow from a recent bout of fever. 'Come immediately. We must adjourn to my study.'

I rammed the last corner of toast into my mouth and followed him out of the room. It was always on stairs that my godfather's shortened right leg was most apparent. He bobbed and weaved about like a lightweight avoiding punches, until he reached the hall.

'Do try to keep up,' he urged as I struggled not to trip on my skirts and kill us both.

Sidney Grice hurried to a filing cabinet on the back left and flicked through a row of large brown envelopes.

'Here they are.' He heeled the drawer shut and upended the contents on to his desk.

'What are?' I went over to have a look.

'My records of the 1872 multiple killings.' The leather top was scattered with documents. 'The investigation was led by the unscrupulous and unsavoury Chief Inspector Snood Mulholland, who died, I am delighted to recall, in the Coram Street fire five years and nine days ago, but this should interest you.' He jabbed his finger to the third column of a cutting from *The Times*.

'*The coroner then heard from Sergeant Pound, who was the first police officer to attend the scene,*' I read out before he whipped the paper away. 'I assume that is the man we know as an inspector now.'

'He had only just been promoted from the ranks,' my guardian confirmed. 'So this was his first big case, though I have never heard him speak of it.'

'He must have been a very young sergeant.' I browsed the article.

'George Pound was the bright-eyed boy of Marylebone.' Sidney Grice whipped the paper from my hand. 'Until he besmirched his reputation.'

'But how?' This did not sound like the Pound I knew.

'He raided a house of ill-repute, only to discover two senior police officers availing themselves of its services.'

'I wonder if he could tell us anything that would cast light on this case,' I said.

Sidney Grice leafed through a stack of handwritten notes bound together with red string.

'It is a simple matter to satisfy your curiosity.' He smoothed out a dog-eared top corner. 'Indeed you may get the opportunity today if Pound is there, for we have an appointment with Quigley at eleven o'clock.'

I went upstairs to get ready and smoke out of my bedroom window.

'Oh, George,' I said involuntarily.

After Edward died I never thought I could suffer love again or feel this sort of pain. The cigarette did not make things any better. Nor did it make them any worse.

And afterwards I sucked on a parma violet. It would not fool my guardian but I felt I had a duty to try.

12

The Mad Girl and Lord Alphreton's Son

IT WAS NOT far to Marylebone Police Station, but a wagon loaded with bales of rags had broken its axle on a pothole in Tottenham Court Road and there was hardly room for one vehicle at a time to squeeze by. We were lucky to be there soon after the accident because, by the time we had negotiated it, the whole street was choking with traffic behind us.

'The roots of the problem are idleness and bloated wage packets,' Mr G pronounced. 'If the lower orders were made to walk instead of frittering money on omnibuses we would not have one-third of this vehicular congestion.'

'But you rarely walk anywhere,' I pointed out.

'I am a gentleman.'

A man dressed as a Red Indian, with a dyed goose-feather headdress and bearing a longbow, was balancing cross-legged on a platform on top of a totem pole, and a girl painted crimson, with a frayed headband, was skipping round the base rattling a tin for money, but the only people showing any interest were throwing rubbish from a bin to try to knock the man off.

'So was my father and he walked everywhere,' I pointed out.

A youth in a battered mauve hat lobbed a potato and it struck the Indian on the cheek. The Indian jerked in surprise but stayed in place.

'What are you doing?' my guardian demanded as I banged on the roof with my umbrella.

The road ahead was clear now. There was a cold drizzle in the air, not enough to soak us, but enough to make it difficult to look straight ahead and more than sufficient for the few carefully arranged strands of hair outside my hat to cling limply to my cheek.

'Sixpence if you can knock that mauve topper off,' I called up, and the driver's long whip snaked out. It stung the youth on the nape of his neck, coiled round his hat and sent it spinning into the gutter. The youth yelped and put a hand to the weal that instantly appeared. After a light flick on the horse we trotted on.

The hatch slid open and our cabby leaned over it. "Ow was that for you?'

'Worth a shilling,' I replied and Mr G rolled his eye.

'Why are you always interfering in matters that do not concern you?'

'I do not like bullies,' I told him and he hugged his satchel.

'Neither do I.' We jolted over some raised cobbles. 'But you are inflating the cost of retribution. The driver would have done that for tuppence. He might have even done it for fun – whatever that may be.'

The main hall at Marylebone Police Station was crowded.

'We tried to break up a bare-knuckle fight,' Horwich, the desk sergeant recounted, 'in an old warehouse down Drummond Street, only there was a lot of money resting on Biggs and 'e was winning 'ands down when we arrived.'

'Your gov'ner 'ad tin on Crosby,' a stumpy, snub-nosed man with a busted nose swore. 'Uvawise you'd 'ave stopped it in round eight when Biggs was on the floor free times.'

'The only thing my super would speculate on is 'ow long you're going to be locked up for.' The sergeant acknowledged Sidney Grice. 'Inspector Quigley said to send you straightways to his office.'

We walked down the long corridor. Inspector Pound's office door was closed and I hoped it would stay that way. My wounds were still raw and I was not sure that I could mask the pain if we were brought face to face. His colleague's door, the next one along, was ajar, and Inspector Quigley sat working his way through a neat stack of forms and writing along the top of one of them.

'Mr Grice.' He did not rise and neither man proffered his hand. 'And your mad girl, I see.'

'Do not worry,' I assured him. 'I have not attacked a policeman for over a week now.'

I was pleased to see that the inspector had grown a short beard to hide the mark left when I had stabbed him under the chin with a pen. It did not suit him at all as I hoped to get the opportunity to point out.

Sidney Grice dusted a chair with his gloves and the two men sat facing each other across the desk.

'Gethsemane,' Mr G said, with no preliminary courtesies. 'Gaslight Lane.'

I lifted some files off a rickety stool in the corner and dragged it over to perch beside my guardian.

'What's your interest?' Quigley's hair was oiled flat from a low side parting.

'His daughter has engaged my services.'

I was under the impression that she had employed both of us.

'Miss Mortlock does not think you are making any progress,' I told the inspector and he threw me a malignant glare.

'That woman thinks the entire Metropolitan Police force should put all its resources into one crime,' he retorted acidly. 'But I have five other killings on the go already, including that of Lord Alphreton's son, who takes priority over them all.'

'So a titled man's death is more important than a commoner's?' I demanded and Quigley fleered.

'Of course.'

There was a cold draught on the side of my neck.

'Do you have any suspects?' Mr G ran his fourth finger over the mark of an old mug on the pine top.

'Too many,' the inspector replied. 'Three, to be precise, and evidence against them all.'

'What kind of evidence?' I asked.

The window looked through a cream-painted grille on to the smoke-stained brick wall of the next building, across a blind passageway. The gap was too narrow for a man to pass along, but it served to let in a little light. The top sash had been pulled down six inches, allowing the ceaseless hubbub of London to enter in streams of cold and filthy air.

'It must have been an insider.' Quigley talked on as if I had not spoken. 'Gethsemane is like a fortress, every window barred and every door locked and bolted. Even the loft hatch was secured.'

'No secret panels then?' Both men ignored me.

'Don't even know how the killer got in or out of the room,' the inspector admitted. 'The door was bolted on the inside.'

'So who was in Gethsemane that night?' Mr G traced the loop of an ink stain out to where it disappeared under a clean new blotter.

'All servants,' Quigley told him. 'There's the footman, the maid – she's foreign so she has to top the list – and the housekeeper, who doubles up as cook since the last one left after Christmas. Mortlock's daughter wasn't living with him and the valet was away seeing his sick mother. That's a funny one – exactly the same alibi as he used last time, but it's well supported.'

'Alibis are like iron.' Mr G ran his finger back again. 'The stronger they are, the more likely it is they have been forged.'

'What kind of evidence?' I repeated more loudly and Mr G tugged at his scarred earlobe.

'You had better answer or she will keep asking,' he told the policeman.

'How do you put up with her?' my good friend Quigley enquired.

'I have a well-deserved reputation for tolerance and kindliness,' Mr G responded without a hint of irony. 'So what evidence *do* you have?'

The inspector bent to his right and delved into an unvarnished wooden crate, about the size of a tea chest, from which he extracted a number of boxes and placed them on his desk.

'This belonged to Nathan Mortlock and was found under the bed of Mrs Amelia Emmett, his housekeeper,' he announced, and a dog howled outside. 'No explanation was offered as to how it got there.'

Quigley drew out a scuff-edged sheet of parchment.

'In a box?' I asked.

'Just lying on the floor,' he told me.

'May I?' I held out my hand.

'Not suitable for a lady.' He passed it over, his fingerplates chewed so far back that the nail beds were raw. 'But I can't see any ladies right now.'

'Perhaps you should consult an ophthalmologist,' I suggested, and took the parchment from him. On the back was a dark stain. On the front was a beautifully executed pen-and-brown-ink drawing of a nude kneeling and fastening her plaited hair. 'There is no need to be coy, Inspector. I see a naked female body every time I undress.' I was not sure which of the men looked more revolted, but I stuck to my task. 'It is signed Albrecht Dürer and I think it might be original.'

'Valuable?' Quigley asked.

'I read about one being sold for six hundred pounds,' I recalled and the inspector spluttered.

'That's more than I'm worth.'

'It certainly is,' I agreed, and Inspector Quigley closed his hand, doubtless wishing my throat was in its grasp. 'If Mrs Emmett stole it, she did not make much attempt to hide or look after it.'

I held out the drawing to Sidney Grice, who took it with the air of a schoolboy being presented with a difficult Greek translation and placed it on the desk without comment.

Quigley drew out a length of cord.

'This was found hanging on the back of the valet Hesketh's door,' he announced, and a dog howled outside.

'Was it used in the murder?' I asked.

'Well...' The inspector gave me his *silly girl* look. 'It ain't a skipping rope.'

'Pity,' I said. 'You look like you could do with a bit of exercise, Inspector.'

Mr G ran it through his fingers and passed it to me. It was a curtain pull made of blue, red, gold and green cords and stained with blood.

'It is very thick,' I commented.

'The drapes are long and heavy,' Quigley deigned to explain.

'Can I borrow it?' I recoiled the rope.

'Why?' Inspector Quigley folded his arms.

'To see if it matches the marks on Nathan Mortlock's neck.'

The policeman nodded approvingly. 'No,' he said.

'Show me those keys.' Mr G made a begging bowl of his hands and Quigley dropped a small bunch into it.

'There are two sets.' He scratched his nose. 'The valet has one and these were found in Mortlock's bedside table.'

Sidney Grice clipped his pince-nez on to his thin elegant nose. 'Two of these are Chubb detectors.'

'That's right.' Quigley scratched his arm. 'The lock jams if anyone tampers with it or tries to use the wrong key. This turned easily, so there had been no attempt to pick it.'

'With what power of magnification did you scrutinize these devices before inserting them?' Mr G crossed his ankles.

'I looked at it carefully and there were no scratches.' The inspector's fingers flexed. He had taken to wearing a hefty signet ring, embossed with an intricate Q. It would make a vicious knuckle-duster, I decided.

'Zero magnification then.' Sidney Grice rattled them. 'Even under a pocket glass you might have seen burrs which were invisible to the unadorned eye and would show whether it had ever been used before.'

I held out the rope and Quigley snatched it away. 'There were no burrs,' he insisted.

'What else do you have?' My words filled the awkward gap.

Quigley's thin lips shrivelled as he reached over and dragged a large, flat brown cardboard box out. 'This was found crumpled up in the bottom of the footman's wardrobe, a bloke by the name of Nutter.'

'Oh lord.' Mr G put a hand to his brow. 'If he is the culprit, I will never live it down. The press will be clamouring to know why I did not arrest him on the spot.'

'Pound got enough chaff when he let Harry Lightfingers go for that jewel theft,' Quigley sniggered as he revealed a stained bundle of cloth. 'Obviously worn by the murderer.'

'Examine it,' my guardian commanded and I stood to lift it out.

'It is a man's shirt,' I began.

'You don't say?' Quigley mocked.

Sidney Grice pencilled something in his notebook and shut it. 'Why a man's?'

The cotton was heavy and dried scabs broke from a cracked brown crust as I opened it out.

'The buttons have been removed but the holes are on the left.'

'Good.' Mr G leaned back. 'It is the obvious that is all too often overlooked.'

'And it is thick with blood.'

'Not paint?' My guardian closed his eyes.

'It smells like blood.' I turned the shirt round. 'But it was not soaked during the murder.'

Inspector Quigley put his elbows on the blotter. 'Rubbish.'

'The blood is almost all on the body of the garment,' I pointed out. 'If I cut a man's throat I would expect a lot of it to be on my sleeve – the right in my case.'

'What if he rolled the sleeves up?' Quigley objected as Mr G sank lower into his chair.

'It would be difficult to take the shirt off without them getting smeared,' I reasoned, 'even if you rinsed your arms first. And...' I rotated the shirt for him to see what I meant, 'the stain on the back of the shirt almost exactly matches the front. How would that happen?'

'When the murderer took it off.' Quigley wavered. 'I suppose,' he qualified his assertion.

'If you wore an old shirt and rubbed ink over the front I don't think you would get a perfect copy on the back when you took it off.' I tried not to sound too confrontational, for I knew that we needed this man's cooperation. 'Also, most of the stain is in one area with no droplets.'

Quigley found a partly smoked cigarette in his nib tray. 'If you were close up you'd get a violent gush like from a hosepipe, not a spray like a watering can.'

My guardian stretched out his legs.

'You would expect some peripheral spatter,' I reasoned.

'So what do you think happened?' the inspector challenged and Sidney Grice covered a yawn with the side of his fist.

'I think somebody laid it out flat and poured blood on to it,' I told him. 'Then, when it was dry – or the blood would be all over it – the shirt was rolled up and put in the room where you found it.'

Quigley clacked his teeth but said nothing.

My guardian opened his eyes, the right sticking in a crescentic slit. 'Bravo.'

'I suppose you guessed that straight away,' I said crossly.

Sidney Grice raised the eyelid with one finger. 'I never guess.' He showed us his notebook where he had written in block capitals *BLOOD POURED*.

'So it was all a stupid game,' the inspector growled, the cigarette butt wiggling foolishly with his words.

'I never play games.' Mr G stretched lazily. 'And I never do anything stupid. I wanted to see if Miss Middleton could work something out for herself that you could not.'

Quigley bristled. 'I haven't had a chance to look at it properly.'

He gripped the stub between his lips.

I put the shirt back and pointed at the next item. 'What is in that?'

'See for yourself.' The inspector thrust an oblong silver case at me. It was embossed with a standing lamb overlapped by a cross. 'The Garstang family crest. They were some kind of religious people.'

I hinged back the lid to find an ivory-handled straight razor.

'Where was that found?' Mr G enquired.

'In the possession,' Quigley told him sulkily, 'of Veronique Bonnay, the—'

'Suspiciously foreign maid,' I put in.

'In her bedroom, under the pillow,' he added.

'Is she mentally defective?' I asked, and felt my chair creak beneath me.

'She is French.' The stub split.

Mr G wrinkled his nose.

'Who would hide a murder weapon where it could be found so easily and incriminate her?' I demanded.

'Perhaps she did not have time to find a better place.' Mr G yawned. 'But we have not established that it *is* the murder weapon or that she put it there or, even if she did, that she was the one to use it.'

'Obviously.' The inspector picked a few strands of tobacco from his hairy tongue. 'Which is why she was released after questioning.'

I fought down a shiver, for I had personal experience of Marylebone police cells and Inspector Quigley's interrogation techniques. He returned my gaze scornfully.

Sidney Grice reached across for the silver box. 'Was it in this when it was found?'

'Yes.' Quigley pulled open the top drawer of his desk and took out a leather pouch. 'And it was clogged with blood.'

'You washed it off?' Mr G asked in disbelief.

Quigley unbuttoned the pouch and brought out a flimsy rectangle of paper. 'We had to clean it up to examine it.'

'So you washed off a clue to look for a clue,' Mr G muttered.

'It was just blood.' Quigley took a fresh pinch of tobacco.

'Fresh or coagulated?' Mr G hauled a pink handkerchief out of his pocket.

The smell of grilling meat drifted in, delicious to me, but my guardian – the man who poked around decomposed corpses with relish – clamped the handkerchief over his lower face.

'Coagulated.' The inspector lined up the tobacco and rolled it into the paper.

'How coagulated?' Sidney Grice's enquiry was muffled. 'Did you cut any of the clots open to see if they were hard and dry all through?'

'Of course not,' Quigley jeered. 'We don't do any of your fancy tricks here.' He licked the paper with forced casualness.

My godfather put his handkerchief away.

'More is the pity,' I retorted and the inspector glowered at me.

'I do not need you to tell me my job.'

'Apparently you——' I began, but my guardian put a hand on my arm – 'have your own methods,' I added hastily.

Quigley mouthed something but I could not read it.

'And to think you two did not get on at first,' Mr G remarked drily as he adjusted the angle of his pince-nez and lifted the razor out. 'It has done good service. See how the ivory has worn on the handle? It would take years of use to do that.' He put a thumb to the tang and flipped the blade out. 'Square end. Double transverse stabilizer.'

'They are not called cut-throats for no reason,' I said. 'What a wicked-looking blade.'

'Blades have no moral value for good or bad,' Mr G informed me. 'They can, however, tell us a great deal.' He turned the razor this way and that. 'Sheffield silver steel, the very finest, and engraved by Crispin's – true craftsmen – hollow-ground for maximum sharpness. Whoever used it for its intended purpose was highly skilled at his task.'

'How can you say?' I enquired.

'The blade is seven-eighths of an inch,' he explained, 'which is wide. Barbers use them because they hold more lather and need less rinsing, but it is much more difficult to do the fiddly areas such as under the nose. Most men use a five-eighths for personal shaving.'

'The edge is badly chipped,' I noticed.

'I don't suppose it was used very gently,' Quigley countered.

Mr G extruded a smidgen of lead from his pencil. 'So how many pieces did you pick out of Mortlock's neck?'

'Well,' the inspector shifted uneasily, 'none.'

Mr G printed NONE, in huge letters. 'There were not any in his flesh when I looked and, though the undertakers had sponged the body, they would not have picked flakes of metal out of his wounds.' WHATSOEVER, he wrote underneath, and then !!!

'So where did the pieces go?' I asked, not sure why it mattered.

Quigley shifted in his chair. 'In a frenzied attack they could fly anywhere.'

'If they are to be found, I shall find them.' Mr G looked at his own right palm as if that were the start of his quest. He touched a spread of handwritten papers. 'Are those your records of the case?'

'A rough draft.' The inspector sealed his cigarette.

'Have a copy sent round,' Mr G instructed and Quigley bristled furiously.

'I am not a grocer, Mr Grice. In fact I am not sure why I am helping you at all.'

'It is a moot point who is helping whom, Inspector Norbot Stillith "Sly" Quigley,' Mr G said coolly, 'for we shall both benefit if this case is solved with the minimum delay.'

Far away a child hollered *God Save the Queen* presumably in hope of a patriotic contribution from a passer-by.

'And you can concentrate on placating the nobility,' I reminded him.

Quigley considered the matter. 'Very well,' he decided.

'According to Miss Mortlock, her father's bedroom has been sealed.' Sidney Grice fastened the buckles on his satchel.

'With a padlock.' The inspector rooted through the box and slapped something on the desk. 'It is the only key, so I shall want it back and,' he sneered, 'you needn't think I didn't see you slip that bunch into your pocket.'

'Nothing escapes you, does it, Inspector?' I gushed. 'Except the occasional criminal.'

'Why you…' Like Sidney Grice's kettle, Quigley was constantly two degrees below the boil.

'One last thing.' Sidney Grice made some sort of animal shadow in the gaslight. 'Any chance of a cup of tea?' He did not sound very hopeful.

Inspector Quigley swept his notes into a pile and tapped them straight, 'None,' he said shortly.

NONE, Mr G wrote again, and sprang to his feet. 'Light your cigarette, Mr Quigley, and inhale the products of its combustion deeply. They may do something to you.'

'Go hang yourself.' Quigley flicked ash in my godfather's direction.

'How can I,' Sidney Grice enquired politely, 'when you will not lend us the rope?'

*

There was still no sign of Inspector Pound when we made our exits. Sidney Grice left him a note at the desk.

13

———◆◆◆———

The Stranger in the Parlour

W E HAD A quiet meal as usual. Sidney Grice regarded dining not as a social occasion, but a chance to get more reading done – the papers at breakfast, case notes at luncheon and an informative book with his dinner.

'What is it tonight?' I asked and he stirred through his food.

'Vegetable stew.'

'No, I meant your reading matter.'

'*The Anatomical Structure and Biological Chemistry of Human Hair.*' He raised the book for me to glimpse the cover. 'By Dr R. V. Fourtrees – the only person of intellect to come from Lancashire in the last thirty years.'

'But I come from Lancashire,' I reminded him and my guardian humphed.

'My statement stands.'

I turned back to my book, *Far from the Madding Crowd.* I loved Bathsheba and I envied her – her looks and even her name. How I wished I could have been a proud beauty or even a modest one.

'Do you think the two cases are linked?' I asked as he made a note in the margin.

'I assume you mean the Garstang massacre and the death of Nathan Mortlock.' He sighed and put down his pencil, carefully aligning it with the edge of the table. 'Well, let me see – members of the same family have their throats cut in the same

60

house. I think even you might spot some tenuous connections.'

I speared a large chunk of turnip with the back of my fork and it oozed into the rest of my meal. 'A Spanish maid on both occasions and the same valet with the same sick mother,' I added, trying to decide if I was actually hungry enough to ingest the turnip.

'He could hardly have a different sick mother.' My guardian polished his fork on the tablecloth. 'But, as I have already observed, I do not care for speculation.' He dug into his dinner. 'It is always idle and the fruits it bears are often false.' He pushed a dripping pile of mush into his mouth and chewed it twenty-four times, though it required little if any mastication.

'I am sure that I read about another murder in Burton Crescent,' I pondered.

Mr G groaned. 'I could name another three cases in the last twenty years, but I suspect you are referring to the death of Rachel Samuels, a widow aged seventy-three, who resided across the gardens at number 4 – on the straight side of the D – and expired there on the twelfth of December 1878.'

'Oh yes, that was in a Penny Dreadful I bought at Southport Station,' I recalled. '*The Battering of Burton Crescent*.'

Mr G picked a hair out of his food. 'Where would the dregs of Fleet Street be without their alliterations? What would they have called it if she had been throttled?'

'*The Samuels Strangling*,' I suggested. 'The police never found her killer either, did they?'

He puffed out his cheeks. 'When have the constabulary ever apprehended anyone who was not caught in the act or stupid enough to confess?'

'As I remember it, they arrested her cleaner.'

'Mary Donovan,' he confirmed. 'She was the last person known to have seen Mrs Samuels alive and there were stains on her shawl which might have been blood. Donovan herself admitted they had argued because she had been sent to fetch a haddock and returned with a bloater, but she claimed that a man had turned up in the meantime claiming to be looking for lodgings, and that he was still waiting in the parlour when she left. Nobody was ever convicted and reports of strangers loitering in the gardens late at night sent property prices plummeting so badly that they have not yet recovered.'

'Do you think that case could be linked to this one?'

'I have no reason to suspect that it is or that it is not.' He turned back to his book and I to mine, but Sergeant Troy's showing off with his sword was starting to exasperate me and I was cross with Bathsheba for being aroused by it. I have always admired a man's rapier mind more than his rapier.

'Shall we go to the Crescent tomorrow?' I asked.

My guardian bent a page at the corner. 'If I had wanted constant chatter –' he dropped his book on to the floor – 'I would have taken in an over-stimulated monkey and given it strong coffee.'

'It might have enjoyed the food more,' I retorted, 'but it could not have bathed your eye, nor tended you in your most recent attack of malaria.'

He started. 'Was that you? I thought it was my mother.'

'Your mother has never set foot in this house whilst I have lived here,' I told him. 'You were delirious.'

'But I wrote to thank her and she replied that she had only done her duty.' He moulded his stew into a square, banking the sides with wilted carrots.

'She probably realized that you were hallucinating,' I reassured him.

'Or more likely she was befuddled with diamorphine.' He took out his eye and polished it with his napkin. 'She was so alarmed by having that headache last year that she takes it daily as a precaution.'

'But that cannot be good for her.'

'Nothing is good for my mother.' He scooped up some more stew.

*

I went up to my room for a cigarette and a gin, and I read one of Edward's letters, the first he ever sent me, in which he protested his love. His handwriting was awful – I found out later that he had given himself Dutch courage to write it – so bad that I thought he had expressed the hope that one day he might *worry* me.

I put the letter away and in that act I knew: it was time to stop living with my memories. There was no point wallowing in lost love while I had it now and almost within reach.

Sidney Grice was coming out of his room.

'Why did you take me in?' I asked, in the hope of catching him off-guard.

'An interesting question.' He started down the stairs. 'And one which I have often asked myself.'

'What really happened to my mother?' I called after my guardian and he stopped.

'*He murdered her,*' a dead voice whispered in my ear, but we were still on the stairs when the doorbell rang.

14

The Man in the Meat Safe and the Elephant in the Park

GEORGE POUND HAD not been to the house whilst I was there since I had returned his mother's ring. And I had not seen him to speak to, except for polite greetings on chance meetings, since we had travelled back on that last train from Parbold.

'I got your note,' he told my guardian as he came into the hall.

'Obviously.' Sidney Grice shook his hand.

Inspector Pound rolled his eyes. 'Good evening, Miss Middleton. I trust you are well.'

'I am very well,' I said, 'and I only wish that you could truthfully say the same.'

'You are straight to the point as usual.' Inspector Pound handed Molly his hat.

'Miss Middleton is always straight to disappoint,' she confirmed, missing the hook and depositing his long russet overcoat on the floor.

Pound was grey. I knew that he'd had to take the best part of a month off at the end of the last year, and that his superiors were threatening him with early retirement if he did so again, but he was left with little choice. I had known men in the army with similar problems where a wound kept reinfecting and bursting open, and I did not think that his abdomen had ever fully healed.

'What are you doing?' Molly's employer demanded as she wobbled slowly down.

Our maid paused mid-descent.

'Ladies pick things up without bending their backs.' She tipped sideways against the hall table. 'It says so in that book on ekikette what Pruffelia lent me.'

Ophelia was a maid at number 123.

'I shall restrict my rebuttal of those remarks to three refutations.' Mr G checked his hair in the mirror. 'First, you are not a lady and never shall be. Second, they do not. Third, they employ lumpen maids to pick things up for them. I shall now append my argument with two instructions, both of which you shall obey.' He opened his hand one finger at a time to count off the number for her. 'First, pick up that overcoat. Second, and more importantly, bring tea *now*.'

Molly heaved herself up and hung the overcoat on the rack.

'I aintn't not lumpy,' she muttered as she scuttled off, 'and, if I am, it's his fault for being so kind and overfeeding me.'

We went through to the study where we sat by the weakly shimmering fire, the inspector refusing my offer of my armchair to pull out an upright chair for himself.

'Gaslight Lane,' Mr G announced, as one might address a large meeting, and Pound nodded.

'I thought it might be about that. A very nasty business, from what I've heard, but one of Inspector Quigley's cases as I'm sure you know.'

'You investigated the first deaths, I believe.' I leaned over to stir the coals with the poker. 'The Garstang Slaughters.'

Pound grimaced. 'I was on that case,' he agreed, 'but Inspector Mulholland led the investigation.'

'Mainly from the nearest saloon, if my memories of Snood Mulholland are anything to go by – which, of course, they are.' Sidney Grice brought out his watch and flipped open the lid.

'Mulholland was past his best by then,' the inspector conceded.

I was sure that he had lost more weight.

Mr G wound his watch. 'Some might say he never had a best.'

Inspector Pound did not take the bait, but he hated my god-father criticizing the force of which he was so proud.

'Were you the first on the scene?' I asked and he dissented grimly.

'Not quite. It was Constable Hutching who saw Angelina Innocenti, the Spanish maid, standing in the front window covered in blood. She took one look at him and vanished. At first he thought she must have injured herself, but eventually, when nobody responded to his knocking, he stopped a lorry carrying a telegraph pole and persuaded a bunch of clerks to help him use it as a battering ram. It was a bit of a lark for them, but when he went into that front room and saw Angelina standing holding a cut-throat over the body of the kitchen maid—'

'Kate Webb,' I remembered.

'That's the one.' His cup vibrated on the saucer. 'Hutching took one look and summoned help, and the constable he alerted came to fetch me.' George Pound rested his drink in his lap. 'It was an awful business.' He pinched the bridge of his nose. 'Probably the worst I have ever seen and I was only a young sergeant at the time.' His eyes, once so penetratingly blue, were capillaried around the edges and they clouded with the memories. 'That poor couple and their servants and their nephew.' He rubbed his cheek. 'So sad.'

'Indeed.' Mr G stretched his feet under the low table between us.

'Were you able to rule out theft as a motive?' I wished I could have offered him a real drink.

'Unless you count a bit of curtain cord. Mrs Garstang was having the drapes replaced and there was a coil of it in a spare room. The murderer used about eight foot of it to tie up Lionel Engra, but the rest of it – about twenty foot – went missing,' Pound replied. 'But I can't imagine anybody breaking in just to steal that.'

'If the actions of criminals were limited by your imagination,' Sidney Grice reached behind his chair, 'I might be forced to commit a few crimes myself to give us both something interesting to solve.'

'Perhaps the murderer took the rope to climb out of a window?' I suggested.

'All the windows were still locked from the inside,' Pound informed me. 'And if he had been thin enough to climb up a chimney there would have been soot all over the hearth.'

'Do you think Angelina Innocenti killed them?' I asked.

The inspector breathed out heavily. 'As God is my witness, I do not know.' He lowered his head. 'There was hardly any proof except that she was the only person left alive and the house was impregnable. We got Dippy Smiff, the housebreaker, to see if he could get in without forcing any locks. The chief promised to reduce a murder charge to manslaughter if he succeeded. He tried for six hours, including crawling all over the roof and nearly breaking his neck before the hangman had a chance, but Dippy couldn't see how it could be done. In a real state he was, and then he died of gaol fever before he even got to trial.'

'It is even more fortified now,' I told him. 'But there is something else.' I knew that hesitancy in his manner all too well.

George Pound put a thumb and forefinger in his philtrum. 'From the disarray of her nightdress and the bruising – quite apart from the knife wounds – I thought she had been... interfered with, but the doctor said not.'

Sidney Grice snorted. He had strong views on police surgeons, none of them favourable.

'There was so much blood,' George Pound struggled to whisper his next words and I could hardly hear them above Mr G's throat clearing.

'Do you think it in any way possible that Nathan Mortlock committed the crime?' I asked.

'Well, he had the most to gain.' Pound separated his fingers along the fringe of his moustaches. 'But he had the perfect alibi.'

'No alibi is perfect,' Sidney Grice argued. 'I could produce a dozen men of unimpeachable reputation, including a high court judge, who would swear under oath that I am presently employed breeding camels in Peru if I told them to.'

'How?' I challenged and my guardian clipped his watch shut.

'Because I know enough to ruin them all.' He smiled bleakly at the prospects.

'Mortlock's alibi was more solid than that.' Pound shifted uncomfortably. 'He was arrested the evening before the murders, charged and detained in cell one at Marylebone Police Station until the next morning. I myself saw him being taken to the magistrates' court and it was definitely him – tubby little man with gingery hair.'

'Who arrested him?' I asked, and Pound wrinkled his brow before replying. 'I think it was Constable Dutton – *Mutton*, as he was known. He left the force a few years ago, but it will still be in the records.'

'Look it up,' Mr G instructed and the inspector's mouth tightened.

'If you would not mind,' I added hastily.

'When I get the time.' He glared at my godfather. 'I know that Sergeant Horwich booked him in and out, and I think you have both seen enough of the cells to know that Mortlock could not have wandered off in the night.'

I could not argue with that, having had a highly unpleasant night in them myself. The cells were underground and very secure indeed.

'Was Horwich a sergeant at the time?' I asked and the inspector managed a slight twinkle.

'Horwich was born a sergeant,' he said. 'He can be a bully and sometimes the men need that, but he is as honest as the day is long. If he wrote Mortlock in the station log, Mortlock was there. I would stake my career on it.'

'I would be inclined to agree with you,' Sidney Grice put his hands together in prayer, 'if I were in an agreeable mood.'

'I should like to see that,' I remarked and George Pound chuckled. 'Anyway, you can ask Horwich about it yourself now he's back on duty.'

'We saw him today,' I said, 'but I did not know he had been away.'

'First day back.' Pound puffed out his cheeks. 'His daughters were run over by a carriage. The driver never stopped. The older died two days later on her fourteenth birthday and the younger is crippled and not expected to walk again.'

'May I anticipate Miss Middleton informing us how awful that is by expressing the same sentiment myself,' my godfather said with something approaching sensitivity.

'Don't tell him I told you,' George Pound begged.

I mulled over what the inspector had said about Mr Mortlock. 'So, if Nathan did not commit the murders, that would rule out any motive of revenge or retribution.'

'Ah, there was a time when things were what they seemed,' my guardian reflected dreamily. 'I read about it in a children's book.'

Molly staggered in with a laden tray. 'Cook thought you might like some bread sandwiches,' she announced, plunking it down, and Inspector Pound perked up.

'Tell Cook that she may be as considerate as she likes, but neither of you will be having a half day on Thursday.' Sidney Grice lifted the corner of a napkin to see what lay beneath. 'No matter how much you want to see the invisible elephant trick in Hyde Park.' He let the napkin fall.

'Oh,' Molly yelped, jumping back, almost physically stung.

'It is not a real elephant, Molly.' I tried to console her, but Molly was not fobbed off that easily.

''Course it is,' she reasoned scornfully. 'If it aintn't not real how can it be in the park?'

I shrugged but could think of no reply that would satisfy her.

''Taintn't not fair,' she grumbled. 'They get to see in invisual things all the time.'

'If she slams that door—' Mr G began but his next word was lost in the percussion.

I refreshed our cups.

'I wouldn't mind seeing that show,' George Pound admitted.

There was a time I might have suggested going together, but I only gave us both some milk and said, 'Tell us about the Garstangs.'

15

Yellow Oceans and Pernicious Distillations

THE CITY LAY submerged in fog the next morning –
choking, soaking yellow oceans of it. At nine o'clock it
might as well have been night, for not a ray of sunlight
could penetrate the smothering murk. It even sneaked into the
house, for the drapes felt damp and the windows ran with
condensation as I tried to peer out through them. There was no
hope of our green flag being spotted in such conditions, so I went
to the door and whistled between my thumb and first finger.

Sidney Grice recoiled. 'No lady should ever make such a
cacophony.'

'She should if she wants a hansom,' I responded as a dull clop-
ping came to a halt close by.

'Have a care, miss,' Molly warned as she gave me my hat.
'One of my sort-of cousins went out in the fog and he wasn't not
never seen again.'

'Oh dear, when was that?'

'Ten days short of a forthnight ago.'

'Well, I hope they find him,' I commiserated.

'Oh, I hope not, miss. He slippened off from a work party at
Dirtmoor.'

'Dartmoor Prison?' I checked my hat and marvelled at the
sales technique of the girl who had convinced me that I needed
it. 'What on earth was he sent there for?'

'He is a warden.' Mr G ushered me outside.

Our cab crept along, jolting wildly, as the driver could not spot any craters to avoid them. The two lamps at the front were no more than blurred balls of orange in the saturated air. A sinister quiet had settled on the street, even the careful clump of our horse's hooves on the cobbles was scarcely audible, and there was only the muffled rattle of a few other vehicles and the faint coughs of choking pedestrians breaking through. I wrapped my scarf over my mouth and nose, but it made little difference to the filth I was inhaling.

'How can he possibly know where he is going?' I coughed on a strand of wool.

'He does not,' Mr G asserted cheerfully and called up, 'Left here, Driver.'

We swung round and I steadied myself on the window frame.

The cab rocked and I trod on his foot. 'But how can you tell?'

Our seats tipped violently as the inside wheel hit the kerb, almost throwing my guardian into my lap.

'God, or so the Bible tells us, gave us senses.' He struggled up and straightened his hat. 'But I appear to be the only person who can use them. There is a cross-breeze where the roads intersect. See how the droplets drift to our right?'

'If you say so.' I could hardly see anything and it was an effort even to keep my eyes open; the acid fumes of a million coal fires, trapped in the clouds, stung them so much. 'Therefore we must be in Gordon Street.'

He pulled out the bung from his flask and sipped his tea straight from it. We were being jostled far too much for him to attempt to use his cup.

'As far as I can make out, the air is swirling randomly in every direction now,' I said.

'It gives every appearance of such behaviour,' he agreed, 'though nothing is truly random. It is just that the pattern is too complex for us to rationalize it.' He pushed the cork back into his flask and, for a while, was lost in thought, but then he raised his cane and tapped twice on the roof. 'We are passing Christ the King.'

'So the road bends,' the cabby acknowledged.

'I cannot hear any bells,' I said.

'That is because none are ringing.' Mr G grabbed hold of the strap. 'But if you listen, you will hear a choir attempting to disturb the being they blame for making them.'

I strained my ears and perhaps made out the fading rumble of an organ, but the only voice was the hopeless unseen call of *'Buy my fresh hens' eggs noo lay, noo lay too-day.'*

Something banged into the side of us and I glimpsed a horse, wild-eyed and frothing, as it strained to turn its invisible cargo away from our cab.

'Bleedin' bleeders,' the voice above us cursed.

'Ladies,' my guardian warned as an omnibus overtook us.

'Nearly 'ad us over, that one did,' the driver complained. 'Where the 'ell are we now? 'Dilly Circus?'

'Tavistock Square,' Mr G shouted over the triumphant hoots of the omnibus passengers. 'Straight on.'

A man had died in Tavistock Square. I did not like him but I still imagine him standing forlornly at his window every time I pass number 2. Every death haunts me, for even the most cruel of men was an innocent child once.

A hay wagon loomed to the right and our horse shied.

'Frebbin' dungface,' our cabby yelled. We came to a halt. 'I don't like this, pal.'

'First, I am not your pal,' Mr G retorted. 'If ever I acquire a friend – which I hope not to – he or she will certainly not be you. Second – and rather more urgently – this is a crossroads and, if you stay here long enough, we will become embroiled in a vehicular collision with concomitant jeopardy to our collective morbidity and mortality.'

'You what?'

'If you do not move we shall die,' I explained anxiously.

'But where?'

'Straight on and for goodness' sake keep a lookout,' my guardian urged.

'Can't look awt for what I can't see,' the driver reasoned, but his whip cracked flabbily and we inched forwards again.

A dark shape hurtled from above and burst into our compartment.

'Mein Gott!' Sidney Grice cried as a pigeon, fluttering in confusion, crashed into my shoulder. Mr G raised his hands across his face and shrank back in his seat while I shooed it away. 'Vile, odious, pestilent creature.'

It flapped up and out and was one with the vapour.

'Why do birds upset you so much?' I asked, ever astonished that so brave a man could be so easily terrified.

'They are ugly,' he cupped his eye, 'in ways that you cannot imagine and I shall not describe.'

Mr G pushed his fears downwards with the flat of his hands. 'But some—'

My fog-drowned world shot up and my guardian's collapsed and all at once I was above him, catapulted into the air. I dropped sprawling across his knees, my head banging on the side of the cabin.

'Blimmit!' I yelped.

'Kindly return that speech to the sewer from which it emerged.' Sidney Grice pushed me off him, crushing my hat more in the process than our collision had managed to do.

Our world tipped a few degrees more, paused for what felt like an age, and came crashing down.

'What on earth?' I disentangled myself.

'We have run over something or someone.' Mr G retrieved his eye from a rip in the upholstery.

'It's a woman,' the driver yelled in alarm. 'I can see 'er frock.'

'Open the flaps,' I shouted.

''Twasn't my fault. Can't see the 'airs on me snout I can't.' The catch clicked back and I pushed the double doors open, but my guardian was out before me, running back and crouching over a shape clad in dark velvet.

'Maeve Birchall,' he declared.

I drew close and saw that he was cradling a head, long silver hair streaming over his crooked arm.

I bobbed. 'Is she dead?' I hardly needed to ask. Maeve Birchall's forehead had been crushed almost flat by the wheel and her eyes stared dully.

'Most assuredly.' Sidney Grice picked an ear from the ground. 'She went to the gallows thirty-six years ago, but is largely forgotten now. I assume this waxwork was on its way to storage.'

I breathed in relief. 'I suppose it fell from a cart in all this confusion,'

'Only in some of the confusion.' Mr G floated up.

'Oh fank gawd.' The cabby cracked his fingers as he joined us. 'I don't fink the beak would've taken kindly to me killing *two* ladies in a week.'

An arm dropped off as our driver rolled Maeve Birchall aside. He rolled the figure into the gutter and climbed back on top.

'Drive on.' Sidney Grice drew out a voluminous white handkerchief.

'Gawd.' The driver double-clicked his tongue and urged his horse forward.

'Keep straight.' Mr G wiped his hands, held the handkerchief at arm's length between his thumb and third finger, and let it fall as if to start a duel. It hung, then was whisked away and immediately became one with the fog.

'I shall not forget this in a hurry,' a disembodied man's voice threatened almost in my ear, and further away a woman screeched, 'Mind you don't, for I won't, not ever.'

We trundled on and I began to worry if this journey would ever end.

Mr G closed his eyes. 'Left again, Driver.'

'You sure, guv?'

'This is my city,' Sidney Grice proclaimed. 'I am where I say I am and, whilst you have the delight of my company, so are you.'

The cab swung cautiously round.

'I do not believe the fog changed direction that time,' I said.

'Not in any navigationally helpful way,' he agreed, 'but there are forty-seven potholes and three unlevelled mounds along that stretch of road before Marchmont Street.'

'I shall count them on the way back,' I warned.

He slipped the flask, still corked and hardly sampled, into his satchel. 'Please do, though you will find there are only thirty-four potholes on that side, partly because the Tavistock Hotel paid for repairs outside their frontage last year. And this is Burton Crescent. There is a Jews' Deaf and Dumb Home over there... and a temperance hotel that way.' Sidney Grice waved a woollen glove vaguely. 'Number 45 is the headquarters of the Society for the Rescue of Young Women and Children, whilst 49 tends to deserted mothers. Goodness, where does it end?' He rubbed his shoulder. 'Midwives, pharmacies, clergymen, doctors. I know of at least two prominent social reformers who have established their lairs here. Left again.'

'I knows,' the driver said peevishly.

'What a concentration of good works,' I said.

'Indeed.' Mr G shuddered. 'It is possibly the most pernicious distillation of philanthropy in the world.'

A breeze was getting up now and the fog thinning slightly.

'You cannot object to all good works,' I protested.

'Can I not?' He pondered my statement. 'I believe I can.'

I looked sideways at his dripping face.

'You are exceptionally ill-humoured today,' I told him.

'I hate fog,' he admitted. 'It deadens the senses and without my senses I have only my superlative intelligence, inordinate wealth and fine breeding to elevate me from the snuffling masses.'

I could just make out a concave row of buildings to my left as we worked our way along.

'This house,' Sidney Grice returned his attention to our itinerary, 'once belonged to a Mr Harold Pin, who had the distinction of being the first – but one hopes not the last – Scottish bank manager to be digested by cannibals.' He banged with his stick again. 'And very shortly,' he told me, 'we shall—' his voice rose – 'stop.'

A hunched shadow hurried by – a man in a top hat, barking, doubled up in his efforts to breathe.

'The morgues will be busy tonight,' Mr G forecast grimly as he rose to pass his payment up through the hatch.

'Don't fink I can find my way back,' the cabby confessed.

'Not to worry,' Mr G reassured him. 'If you wait here an hour or two I shall guide your return.'

'Fanks for nuffink.'

'Nothing is a strange thing for which to express gratitude.' Mr G pinched the crown of his soft felt hat. The flaps clicked open and we clambered out. 'But it is always something I am happy to give.'

The driver spat but he must have decided to risk finding his own way back, for he flicked his reins and the horse edged reluctantly forward.

I turned round and the outlines of the houses rose before me, the brick façades almost grey in the sickly light. But, at the end of the curve, a massive edifice arose, set about three feet back from the building line and out of parallel with it, behind a street sign proclaiming *Gaslight Lane*, which was screwed to a stone post.

'But where is it?' I strained to see a road leading off.

'This is it.' Sidney Grice held out his arms expansively. 'The original road ran up the side of the house just to the left of that path. But James Burton built numbers 28 and 29 across it and other developers followed suit behind and obliterated it, though you might argue that Sawtree Mews, where it opens into Brigadier Road, was the end of it. Until the speculators set to work, this was a country lane with a dairy halfway down. The old Boulton Gasworks still operates sporadically. That is one of their meters.' Not for the first time I wondered if my guardian had a telescope built into his right eye, for I could only just make out a blob on the wall of the north wing. 'But this occupied part of the house is supplied by the London Gas Company now.'

The path that he had referred to ran between the house and its unwelcome neighbours to the left, and must have led into the back garden once. But now it was blocked just behind the coal-hole by a fixed grille across it, rising maybe thirty feet and topped, I could just make out, by vicious spikes.

'There was a privet hedge here once.' He dug at a bit of root that was trying to sprout greenery. 'Note,' his arm hinged up like a railway stop signal, 'if you can, the water mains repair along-side the neighbouring abodes.'

'Half of London seems to be dug up at the moment.' I glanced over.

'How can a city *seem* to be excavated?' Sidney Grice wandered towards a trench in the road. 'Like income tax, it either is or it is not. And,' his arm fell to the clear position, 'the proportion at any given time is unlikely to be greater than one-hundredth.'

I moved closer to the house and could not help but be struck by its grandeur, a huge old structure set beside and at odds with the late Georgian-style terrace adjoining it to the south, on the left-hand side. Nathan Mortlock's old home rose four lofty storeys and stretched the width of a good half dozen of its neigh-bours. The north and south wings of the house were separated by a towering block, jutting some ten feet or more forward of them and pierced on its front face by a Gothic arch in which was set a tall, broad oak door.

'Gethsemane,' I read from a brass plate on the wall. 'It looks like a prison.'

The dwelling itself had also been fortified with heavy iron-work guarding the long sash windows, most of which were bricked up and, judging by the soot deposits, not recently.

'Most of the residences here have bars on the lower floors,' Mr G informed me. 'There are rookeries round the back which a platoon of guards would be terrified to enter.'

'What are rookeries?'

'Slums,' Mr G said, 'over slums piled upon slums beneath slums under slums; derelict odious heaps of stinking wrecks; rubble and rubbish shored with worm-holed timber and awash with effluent; street urchins lying with pigs under rags for warmth; and the greatest concentration of vicious criminals outside of the Bank of England.'

'Such poverty beside such wealth,' I lamented. 'Something must be done.'

'I quite agree.' Mr G paced through the clouds. 'They must all be swept away.'

'The best way to be rid of the poor is to make them prosperous,' I said. But he was more interested in that front door and the metal straps running across it.

He dabbed a pyramidal stud as if it were hot. 'The servants must have to use the same entrance and egress as their master.' Mr G pulled his overcoat around his neck. 'A practice that reeks of communardism and will choke the life from our city more effectively than this foetid air.'

I tapped the guard over a narrow basement window. 'Nathan Mortlock must have been a very frightened man,' I commented.

'And with good grounds as it turned out.' Sidney Grice marched up the steps.

I looked behind us. 'Is that a central garden I can see?'

'Fenced and locked,' he concurred, 'against all but the grimly generous residents.'

'The straight side of Burton Crescent is failing already.' His voice was curiously thin through the fumes. 'An admiral once lived in number 6 and there were two professors further up, but some of the larger ones have been divided into apartments and many of the houses take in lodgers now.'

'As did Mrs Samuels at number 4,' I remembered as he yanked on the doorbell. I heard it clang.

'Indeed.' Sidney Grice chipped at the short path to the gate with his heel. 'The brickwork is uneven.'

'Could somebody lift them to get into the cellar?' I asked, but knew as I spoke that he would answer, 'No.'

The door opened.

'Mr Grice,' a footman declared. 'We have been expecting you, sir.'

*

I see him in the shadows of Gethsemane, looking up at the tower where once he saw the curtain flutter, steeling himself for what he must do. He hesitates, makes up his mind and runs four paces away, but something pulls him back. Love made bitter and the need, the biting need, and the fear that is greater than fear.

He is going into the house.

*

And the footman stood aside to admit us.

16

The Vertex of Vacuity and the Sleeping Journeyman

THE FOOTMAN WAS a fresh-faced man with sandy hair. He was dressed in livery with a splendid gold-buttoned and trimmed red coat, a sandy waistcoat and breeches. Only his black neckerchief and armband gave any indication that there had been a death in the household.

'And you must be Miss Middleton.' His eyes were blue and glittered in the dull light.

'Since when does a servant introduce callers to themselves?' Mr G demanded.

'Hi am sorry, sir.' The footman was chastened. 'But Hi am quite new to this job and forgot myself in all the hexcitement.'

'Is that all it is to you,' my guardian glowered, 'a vulgar titillation?'

'Hi meant no disrespect, sir.' The footman's face fell further.

'Then do not show any.' Mr G scowled. 'Why is your arm encased in gypsum?'

It was only then that I noticed the footman's left sleeve was bulging with a plaster cast from which only the ends of his fingers projected.

'Hi fell downstairs—' the footman blushed – 'after a few drinks on Christmas night and broke it.'

'Are you right- or left-handed?' I asked.

'Left, miss. Hi put it out to save myself.' He held up his right hand, bent back with hooked fingers. 'And this is not much use to me since Hi got it tangled in the spokes of a homnibus two years ago.'

'Do not imagine that being a bungling fool incapable of committing the murder relieves you of any suspicion,' Sidney Grice lectured him, though I rather thought it might. 'I shall interview your doctor later.'

'Where are you from?' I asked.

It was a long hallway, wider than ours in Gower Street, but thinned by a disproportionally broad ascending staircase to the left.

'Yorkshire, miss – Hilkley – like hin the song.' He was in his late twenties, I judged, though he wore no spectacles for me to apply Mr G's rule of thumb.

'Ilkley Moor baht 'at,' I quoted and my guardian looked aghast.

'And I thought my maid had scaled the vertex of vacuity.' He flicked through the coat rack with his cane. 'Tell me your name and age, if you know it.'

The footman straightened and stuck out his chest like a private on parade. 'Sou' Easterly Gale Nutter, aged thirty-two, sir.'

'I am sorry—' I stifled a laugh. 'Is that your real name?'

'Yes, miss,' he told me, 'though everybody calls me Easterly. Hi have two brothers, Westerly and Northerly, and ha sister called Southerly.'

The floor was laid with a maroon oilcloth embossed with the Garstangs' lamb and cross symbol.

'Was your father a seafarer?' I inquired.

'No, miss, but he wanted to be.'

Mr G rolled his eye. 'Discourse upon your previous employment. Details of what, when and where will suffice for now.'

'Hi was a coachman, sir, for Mr Garstang and Hi used to help in the house ha lot, but when Mr Mortlock came he did not keep his own horses and so Hi went to Dr Crispin Holland hov

Highgate West Hill, until five months ago when Hi applied for the position hov footman here.'

I quailed at the mention of Highgate – I had seen a man die horribly there, his head split by the axe in my hand – but Mr G's expression did not change.

'And was your last employer murdered?' Sidney Grice clipped on his pince-nez and leaned forward until his nose almost touched the footman's.

Easterly Nutter flinched. 'As far has Hi know, Dr Holland is still in good health for a man hov his advanced age.'

Mr G pulled away and let his pince-nez drop to hang on a blue string from his top buttonhole.

'Did you have to change jobs because of your hand?' I asked as my guardian worked his way through the umbrella stand, running a finger through the folds of a blue parasol.

'Hi did manage for a bit.' Easterly relaxed a little. 'But, truth be told, miss, Hi don't like horses and they don't care for me, and hi don't like the outside. Hi just wanted the uniform. Young ladies – present company hexcepted – like a man hin uniform.'

I did not tell him that I had once loved a man in uniform, though it was that of a cavalry officer who, unlike Easterly, adored horses almost as much – I used to tease him – as he cared for me.

Sidney Grice tilted an ornate brass wall mirror to check behind it.

'So you got yourself an indoor job where you could still dress smartly?' I concluded.

Easterly tipped forward. 'Hexactly, miss.' He scratched around the edge of his plaster.

Mr G turned his attention to the door, sliding the bolts across and rattling the handle. 'Two locks,' he commented. 'Who has the keys?'

'Mr Hesketh, the valet, is in charge hov them now, sir. There's only one other complete set and Mr Mortlock used to keep them in his room at night.'

'Explain,' Sidney Grice placed his cane on the hall table, 'exactly what you mean by *complete.*'

Easterly blinked rapidly. 'Hi mean *full*, sir.' And, seeing that his response was not satisfactory, he added, 'There was also a single key so that a servant might come and go during the day.'

'And where was that kept?' I ran a hand under the hall table just to prove that my guardian was not the only one searching for clues.

'On a hook in the housekeeper's room.' The footman polished the toe of his right boot on the back of his left trouser leg. 'It is no use in the night because both locks are on.'

Mr G snatched up an ebony swagger stick and looked along it at the footman like a member of a firing squad. 'According to the police, an item of Mr Mortlock's bloodstained clothing was found in your room.'

'Yes, sir.' Easterly swallowed. 'Hi was there when one of the constables found a shirt hin the back hov my wardrobe.'

My fingers came away slightly greasy.

'Explain its presence.' Mr G lowered the stick until it touched the flooring – raspberry oilcloth, the surface sheen worn away, but still decorated with hundreds of small shields emblazoned with white lambs bearing gold crosses.

Easterly blinked. 'Hi cannot, sir. Huntil the policeman brought the shirt out Hi had no idea it were – was,' he corrected himself, 'hin there.'

'When did you last look in that wardrobe?' Mr G shuffled sideways and the footman's hand went to the nape of his neck.

'Hi believe it was the Tuesday morning.'

'The day before Mr Mortlock died?' I clarified.

'Yes, miss.'

'So where do you hang your clothes?' Mr G bared his teeth in front of the mirror and tapped an upper incisor with his finger-plate.

Easterly tried to poke a little finger under his plaster, twisting his right hand awkwardly. 'Hi put them over the back of a chair, miss. The wardrobe is really just ha small cupboard. It has no rail nor hooks hin it. Often Hi put my wash things hin there to keep the room tidy, but Hi was hin a bit hov a rush that morning because Hi overslept.'

I wiped my hand but it was still sticky. 'Do you share with anyone else?'

My guardian examined a lower canine.

'No, miss, and nobody has any business going hin there. Hi clean the room myself.'

Mr G picked up a pair of white gloves and tried the left one on, his slender fingers lost inside its bulk. 'Summon the maid.' He shook his hand free and Easterly pulled a round white-enamelled handle in the wall. 'What happened to your predecessor?' He tossed the gloves back on to the table.

'Hi believe he was dismissed, sir, but Hi do not know the circumstances.'

There were footsteps and a maid appeared, smartly attired in a crisp white apron and starched hat. She was a pretty girl with discouragingly golden hair and she too wore an armband, though it was hardly noticeable on her black sleeve.

'Name?' Mr G rapped and she looked askance at the footman.

'This is Mr Grice, Veronique—' he began.

'Do not attempt to coach the witness on her appellation,' Mr G warned.

'Hi am sorry, sir. Hi did not hintend to.' He turned back to the maid. 'This is Mr Grice, the private—'

'Personal,' Mr G broke in. 'I am a *personal* detective.'

'Oh.' The maid went a light shade of pink. 'I am Veronique Bonnay, monsieur.'

'What is wrong with your accent?' He stuck his face close to hers and inhaled deeply.

Mademoiselle Bonnay blushed.

'I think Veronique is French,' I suggested and my guardian rounded on me.

'Is it not enough that he tells her what her name is without you telling her where she comes from?'

'I am from Normandy, monsieur.'

'The least ghastly part of France,' Mr G conceded, for he claimed to be descended from Charles Le Grice, who had arrived with William the Conqueror. 'But cease calling me *monsieur*. We are not in your unreliable country now.'

Veronique turned puce and seemed about to retaliate but only said, 'Can I 'elp you wizz anything, *sir*?'

'Fourteen things,' he told her. 'But for now, tea will suffice. Three cups.'

'Tree, sir?'

'Three,' he emphasized. 'What is the point of a nation whose inhabitants cannot voice their dental fricatives?'

'I am sure I do not know, sir.' The maid curtseyed gracefully and walked briskly away, and I could not help but notice how Easterly's eyes followed her trim form as she retreated.

There was a footman's chair to the right of the door as I faced it. It was not the grand arched structure of a stately home, but high-backed, and upholstered to match his livery in red satin with brass buttons and gold cording.

'Sit there and lift your left foot.' Sidney Grice produced a small metal rod and tapped the sole of Easterly's boot. 'Now the other.'

'Hi do not have any false compartments in my heels, sir,' the footman assured him.

Mr G straightened up. 'A peculiar confession to make.'

'Confession?' Easterly looked baffled. 'Hi only said it because Hi read how you found one in the *Adventure hov the Sleeping Journeyman*.'

'First—' my guardian stiffened – 'I do not have *adventures*: I have cases. And, second, those events oozed from the febrile imagination of a Fleet Street parasite rejoicing in the alias of John Tarantella, an ancient spinster from Barking.'

'Ho,' Easterly said uncertainly.

'Lower your feet to the floor.' Mr G brought a thin spool of coloured cotton out of his satchel. 'Hold that end.' He looped the thread round the back of the chair. 'Lean back.'

'What are you doing?' I asked as he wrapped it around Easterly's chest.

'Restraining this minion.'

The footman chuckled. 'With all due respect, sir, Hi could break that with the slightest hov movements.'

'Precisely,' my guardian agreed, 'but I shall know that you have strayed and you will never find a thread to match this one exactly.'

Sidney Grice went behind the chair and was hidden from view.

Easterly craned his neck. 'What colour his it?'

'Grice's Lilac,' Mr G declared, and re-emerged.

Easterly shifted apprehensively. 'Hi am to remain here then?'

'Until further instructions.' Mr G dropped the reel back into his satchel. 'This is a pleasant hallway.'

I thought so too. There was not much illumination through the fanlight over the door and the gas mantles had not been turned up, but even in the gloom I could see the Moresque wallpaper – a little old-fashioned perhaps, but I could easily picture how cheerful the bright greens, reds and blues of stylized flowers in geometric arrangements of swirling leaves would be in the sunshine, or when the five Turkish lamps suspended from the lofty ceiling were lit at night.

'Apart from the vulgar decorations on the oilcloth and the poorly aligned fourth banister rail.' My godfather qualified his statement.

A vase of peacock feathers stood on the long table.

'Shall we look about?' I asked, but Sidney Grice tilted his head sadly.

'A magnificent suggestion, Miss Middleton,' he said, 'but unfortunately we have an appointment.' There were footsteps in the hall again. 'With a pot of Darjeeling, to judge – as I feel compelled to – by the aromas.' And Veronique emerged more slowly this time, carrying a laden silver tray.

I smelled my fingertips surreptitiously. The stickiness was beeswax, so probably not a vital piece of evidence.

17

The Man Who was Not There

VERONIQUE LED THE way into a large drawing room that would have overlooked the streets had the shutters not been closed. This room too was decorated in an arabesque style, with rectangular Turkish rugs laid on the floor and a square one hanging from a wall that was topped with intricate cornices high above our heads. She placed the tray on an octagonal table, variegated woods inlaid with mother of pearl in curlicue patterns.

'Shall I serve, monsieur?'

Sidney Grice tutted at being so addressed, but did not trouble to correct her this time. 'You shall.'

The chairs were Chippendale style with ogee curves and finely carved Gothic tracery between the elegantly glazed bars.

'All tree cups?'

'Yes, and fill mine to within two-fifteenths of an imperial inch of the brim, and do not attempt to approximate that with your depraved centimetres. I shall not require space to contaminate it with milk or sugar.'

Veronique poured. 'Will zat be all, monsieur?'

'Not by any stretch of your limited Gallic imagination.' He indicated with a flick of the hand. 'Sit and take tea.'

She looked at him in confusion. 'You are very kind, monsieur, but it is not my place.'

'I shall tell you your place,' he insisted, 'and I am not in the least bit kind.'

'He is not,' I assured her. 'I think Mr Grice wants to ask you some questions.'

'Oh.' Veronique sat on the edge of her chair. 'What can I tell you, monsieur?'

'The truth.' Mr G rotated the pot to point the spout towards her. 'Where were you throughout the course of the night Mr Mortlock died?'

'Why, I am 'ere, monsieur.'

'In that chair?'

'In my bedroom, monsieur, on zuh top floor.'

'I will thank you to be more truthful and precise with your replies from now on,' he snapped and her cheeks flushed.

'Do you sleep alone?' I asked.

'Oui, mademoiselle. I share with another maid called Nelly when I come last May, but she leaves and Monsieur Mortlock does not replace 'er. 'E says zere is not enough work for two since Miss Charity is gone.'

Her light blue eyes were ringed darkly as were those of so many domestic servants, including Molly.

'I imagine you sleep soundly,' I sympathized and my guardian gazed at me balefully.

'If I had required your imaginary version of events we could have stayed at home where the tea is better, though not served by such a smart and efficient maid.'

Veronique smiled in embarrassment. 'Mademoiselle she is correct, though.' She thrust her tongue over her little white teeth to pronounce that last word precisely. 'I am very tired when I get to bed. Once I even fall asleep on zuh servants' staircase.'

'But not that night?' I asked and Mr G put a hand to his eye.

'Shall we dispense with this slavey altogether and let me interview you instead?'

'It was a question,' I pointed out.

'A leading question,' he retorted.

His eye went out of control.

'She is not in court.'

Veronique watched in disgust as my guardian struggled to get his lower eyelid over the coloured glass.

'If you wish to place a wager on it, the odds are that she shall be,' he advised and she put a hand to her mouth.

'Mr Grice only means that you will probably be called as a witness,' I reassured her.

My guardian rammed the eye back into place, exhaling hard as one might extinguish a candle. 'It is for me to know what I mean.' He lifted his satchel from the floor and laid it flat upon his lap.

'Oh, but I 'ave done nutting wrong.'

'Then how—' Mr G reached into his satchel and produced a silver box – 'do you explain this?'

He placed the box on the table, hinging the lid up to reveal the razor. Veronique shrank back and cried, 'She is Monsieur Mortlock's?'

'Answer your own question,' Sidney Grice invited her coldly.

'She looks like *la même raisor*,' she acknowledged. 'But she was covered in blood when zuh *gendarme* showed it to me.'

'Examine it,' he invited, but she drew back.

'I do not like to,' she whispered.

'I did not intend to give you pleasure.' Mr G picked the razor out. 'Or I would have offered you a slug sandwich.'

Veronique wrinkled her nose. 'Whatever the English think, zuh French eat snails not slugs, and not in a sandwich. I do not like zem myself.'

My godfather put his finger to the tang, hinging the blade out forty-five degrees.

'Oh.' Veronique made a soft moan. 'The blade he is 'orrible.'

'What damaged it?' he asked and she held her face.

'I do not like to think, monsieur.'

'Women rarely do.' The blade flipped fully out.

'Veronique,' I asked gently, 'do you know how it got into your room?'

The maid blew out between her lips. 'Per'aps zuh murderer put it in there; per'aps the *gendarmes*. I know only that I do not.'

'But it was found under your pillow,' I reminded her and she looked nonplussed.

'So zey telled me.'

'Have you ever used a cut-throat?' Sidney Grice touched the edge.

'Not to cut throat,' Veronique answered defensively. 'At 'ome I shave my father.' She fiddled with her collar. 'And now I 'elp Easterly.'

'Why?' He turned the razor this way and that.

'I like to do it and 'e say I am good.'

'Did you ever shave Mr Mortlock?' I asked.

Veronique was transfixed by that blade, her eyes following Mr G swishing it up and down, a careless barber shaving an invisible customer.

'No, miss.' She kept her gaze on it. 'Monsieur Mortlock 'e trusts no one but Monsieur 'Esketh to shave 'im.'

My guardian set to humming – almost the first four notes of Beethoven's fifth symphony, but flat and repeatedly, with increasing volume.

'Where did you work before?' I asked, if only to stop the noise.

'For Madame York,' she replied, 'in number 28. She die.'

'And what,' Mr G challenged, 'induced Mrs York to expire?'

The French maid struggled with his phrasing. 'Madame York she is an old lady. She go to sleep in 'er sleep. Madame Emmett, zuh 'ousekeeper, she know me a bit and she – 'ow you say? – recommend me. I thinked she is nice but she was not so nice when I come 'ere.'

'In what way?' I asked and she crossed her hands on her lap.

'She always find fault when zere is none. Why, even zuh morning before they find Monsieur Mortlock dead, she shout at me for burning zuh ironing when he is not burned.'

Sidney Grice jumped so suddenly that I thought he must have cut himself as he flicked the blade shut. 'Why would she do that? Six reasons will suffice.'

Veronique threw up her hands. 'I am not knowing.'

'Your ignorance interests me immoderately.' He replaced the razor in its box, leaving the lid open.

'Do you do all the ironing?' I asked.

'Only zuh beddings,' she answered. 'Monsieur Mortlock 'e send zuh *vêtements* – zuh clothings – to zuh laundry. 'E say zey put starch more nicely on 'is shirts.'

'You have not had your tea,' I reminded her and she took a sip uneasily.

The door opened and a tall, well-built man entered, also in sombre attire. He had on a swallowtail coat, buttoned up and topped by a neat cravat, and charcoal trousers. His boots were highly polished, though not new, for the toes were slightly scuffed. He was in his late fifties, I estimated. His heavily lined face was more creased by worry than by age, I decided, for the back of his hands were free of liver spots or wrinkles.

'Mr Grice?' His nose was long and Romanesque. 'I am Hesketh, the late Mr Mortlock's valet, and in charge of this house *pro tempore*.'

'Austin Hesketh,' my guardian mused. 'The man who was not here,' he raised his index finger, 'on both occasions.' His arm hinged down to point accusingly.

The valet's left hand twitched as if he were catching a tennis ball. 'I have borne a great burden of guilt for the last decade,' he admitted.

'If you are about to make a confession,' Mr G looked at him severely, 'you had better take a seat. Standing murderers who wish to unburden themselves invariably start to pace the room, which is most irritating. Also, they sometimes change their minds and decide to effect an escape, and I prefer not to pursue servants along thoroughfares and across the open spaces of Her Majesty's parks. It is *so* undignified.'

Hesketh lowered his grey head. 'My remorse lies not in my deeds but my neglect – in not being here on either occasion to protect the house I served.'

'Sit,' Sidney Grice commanded, and Hesketh pulled out a chair.

'I am sorry for the loss of your master,' I said.

'His naked lacerated body lies unattended on a slab,' Mr G reminded me. 'If any man is lost, it is not he.'

The valet winced and so did I.

'You went to see your sick mother in Nuneaton?' I asked, and my guardian slapped the table with both palms.

'It is a marvel that you are not a playwright.' He drummed loudly and arrhythmically with outstretched thumbs. 'You are so keen to write other people's scripts for them.'

'Yes, miss.' The valet looked at me, and his gaze was direct but deeply troubled.

'Have you often had to do that?' I enquired as Sidney Grice completed his recital with a flourish.

'I visit when I can,' he replied. 'I have only been called back urgently on those two occasions.' He fiddled with a button on his waistcoat. 'But she is an elderly woman now and I fear there may be more.'

'The other servants must fear it more than you,' Sidney Grice observed grimly, 'given past events.'

Hesketh's jaw tensed. 'The police looked very thoroughly into my movements after the massacre of the Garstang family *and* following recent events, sir. Several independent people attested to my presence in Nuneaton on both occasions.'

'What I believe the press would refer to as watertight alibis.' Mr G held up the razor and flipped the blade open, watching the newcomer intently as he did so. 'But a defence which does not leak bears the hallmark of something which is a whit too well constructed.'

'Or, in my case, is true.' The valet struggled to control his emotions.

'Do you have an identical twin?' Mr G scooped the blade through the air. 'Or a brother who could pass as you in an indifferent light? Be sure I shall find out if you are lying.'

'I have one brother,' Hesketh admitted. 'But he is short and thickset, and has a bushy beard.'

'How did you travel there?' I asked.

'On the quarter past seven train from Euston on the Tuesday night, and the seven o'clock train from Nuneaton the next morning. I still have the ticket.'

'Why?' Mr G demanded.

'The barrier was unmanned on my return, but the ticket was clipped by the guard on both journeys.'

'We shall want to see that,' I told him, 'and a list of your witnesses.'

'Written in two ways.' Sidney Grice folded the razor pensively. 'Chronological order and black ink. I am increasingly disinclined to read anything in blue these days.'

'Yes, sir.' Hesketh tapped his cheekbone. 'The ticket seller might remember Veronique buying it for me. She had an argument with him about the cost of the ticket,' Hesketh admitted ruefully. 'But that was my fault. It was so long since I went by train I did not realize the price had gone up.'

Sidney Grice blew his nose.

'Do you still need me, monsieur?' Veronique asked and Mr G looked at her long and hard. Veronique averted her gaze.

'I have only one more question for now and fourteen for another occasion,' he told her. 'Did you know any of the members of this household, other than the as yet elusive housekeeper, before you took employment here?'

'No, monsieur.'

'Not even by sight?' I clarified.

'I do not think so, mademoiselle.'

'Good.' Sidney replaced the razor and closed the lid. 'You shall stay where you are.' He looped a thread round her left wrist and the arm of her chair. 'And finish your tea. And you,' he pointed at the valet's chest with the silver box, 'shall conduct our tour.'

The maid looked about anxiously.

'Do not worry,' I told her. 'He has unusual ways.'

'*Mon Dieu, c'est vrai,*' she said to herself.

18

Noises in the Night

SIDNEY GRICE WENT to the window. An ornate copper vase stood as high as the sill. He lifted it to one side and opened the shutters. The bars, I saw, were set into a gate, designed to hinge open in the middle but secured by two hefty padlocks. He tugged at each of them experimentally before clicking them open with one of the keys he had taken from Quigley.

'Though the catches on the windows are self-locking, these,' he lifted the padlocks off, 'are not.'

'No, sir.'

'That was not a question.'

'No, sir.'

'Neither was that.' Sidney Grice swivelled back the brass catches and pushed up on the lower sash, then down on the upper. 'These slide easily enough and – as has become your wont – you may treat that as what it was not, *id est*, an invitation to make a comment.'

'Mr Mortlock always kept them in working order,' Hesketh told him. 'He was worried that he could be trapped in a fire if the windows jammed.'

'This,' Mr G tapped the lower pane, 'has been replaced within the last month.'

'Indeed, sir,' the valet acknowledged. 'We had a few things thrown at the window, mainly – excuse my language, miss – horse droppings, but a few stones, and one pane was smashed.'

'By whom?' I stood up.

'Street urchins,' Hesketh told me. 'The dirty devils. Excuse my language, miss.'

'Was it just this house?' I went over to peer out.

The day was clearing and I could make out the outline of a governess strolling between the copper beeches in the Burton Crescent gardens.

'Mainly us, I think, miss.'

I thought about what Inspector Pound had told us. 'Was this the room that Kate Webb, the maid, was found in – when the Garstangs were murdered?'

'I fear it was, miss.' The valet touched his Adam's apple.

In the pale light I tried to imagine it.

'There was so much blood,' George Pound struggled to whisper his next words and I could hardly hear them above Mr G's throat clearing. 'That her nightdress and hair were glued to the floor-boards.'

And I wondered what Angelina Innocenti, the deranged lady's maid, could have been thinking as she stood over the body, clutching the killing knife.

Hesketh came over and raised his hand to wave to the governess, I thought, but in reality to brush something away.

Sidney Grice grasped his wrist. 'I shall not permit you to interfere with evidence.'

'But surely it is just a cobweb, sir.'

I waited for my guardian to explain how crucial cobwebs had been in the Foskett case or in tracking down the Camberwell Witches, but he let go of the valet and said, 'Very well.'

'I am wary of touching it now.' Hesketh's hand fell away.

'Oh, for goodness' sake.' Mr G ripped the strands off. 'It is only a cobweb.'

Hesketh tapped his leg nervously.

'I have never seen a private home so heavily fortified,' I remarked and Hesketh touched his chin.

'Mr Mortlock was even more concerned about his safety than Mr Garstang,' he said, 'especially as it was never proved that the killer of the household was indeed Angelina Innocenti, since she was unfit for trial. If it was not her, Mr Mortlock wanted to be certain that the murderer could never regain access to his house. All the windows are secured in the same way.'

'Including the attic?' Mr G relocked the bars and went to the wall that separated us from the north wing of the house.

'Yes, sir,' Hesketh said.

'What about the basement?' I asked.

And the valet's eyes dropped as if he were looking straight into it. 'There was a back door leading up a flight of steps to the yard when the Garstangs lived here, but it has been bricked up. In addition to the usual spring-loaded bolt, the coal-hole lid has an extra bar welded on with one of those padlocks, and the coal cellar entrance is also padlocked.'

'Who has the means to open them?' Sidney Grice asked mournfully.

'Only me, sir.' Hesketh reached inside his coat and produced a ring. 'The police took the only other full set and I look after these.'

'What are they for?' I asked and he held them up.

'These two are for the front door and this one is for the windows and coal cellar.'

'Give them to me.' Sidney Grice took the ring and clipped on his pince-nez. He peered closely at each key through his magnifying glass. 'They have not been copied recently.'

'To the best of my knowledge, they never have been,' Hesketh informed him. 'Mr Mortlock kept them locked in a drawer in his bedroom and the key to that on his watch chain. I have not let them out of my sight ever since.'

'That is a lie,' Mr G declared, 'for though we are dissimilar in many ways and there is a chasm between us which you shall never traverse, we have fourteen defects in common, the one pertinent to my diatribe being an inconvenient requirement for sleep.'

Hesketh stiffened. 'And, when I do, they are on a string around my neck.'

'Could somebody have sneaked into your room and taken them from you?' I asked, not sure why it mattered after the murder, but Hesketh dissented.

'I have always been a light sleeper. A valet learns to be.' He fingered the fine gold thread on his coat lapels. 'Besides which we have all taken to using wedges under our bedroom doors when they are shut at night.'

'Whose idea was that?' I asked.

Sidney Grice gave him back the keys.

'Mine, miss.' Hesketh's eyes clouded. 'Only the murderer knows if he or she is still in our midst.'

'Assuming that the murderer is not suffering from one of the four major or nine minor known causes of episodic amnesia.' Mr G put his ear to the wall and rapped with his knuckles. 'There are two parallel vertical depressions under the wallpaper, approximately fifty-four and a quarter inches apart,' Sidney Grice said accusingly. 'I have six theories about that, one of which I find especially appealing since the underlying plaster has a different resonance to its surroundings.' He eyed the valet. 'Enlighten me.'

Hesketh leaned towards the faint lines. 'It used to be a passageway, but Mr Nathan had it bricked up when the house was divided, sir.'

'Thus it was so.' My guardian picked at a tiny tag of loose paper.

'Why did your master not simply move home?' I enquired as my godfather wandered away.

'Mr Mortlock did place Gethsemane on the market before he found out that the terms of his inheritance forbade him to sell the Garstangs' home.' Hesketh distractedly watched my guardian work his way along the wall. 'But its reputation attracted only ghoulish sensation hunters or ghost trackers.'

'Is the house haunted?' I dodged away as Mr G hauled a small bookcase from the wall and peered behind it.

'We have had a number of staff quit over the years after claiming to hear noises in the night, but most were excitable and some sold accounts of their imagined experiences to the newspapers,' Hesketh said wearily. 'But I have never heard anything that could not be put down to a creaking floorboard or the wind over the chimney tops.'

'Who else is infesting this garishly ornamented and biblically dubbed house upon this vaporous day?' Mr G pushed the bookcase back.

'Only Mrs Emmett, the housekeeper.' Hesketh stepped aside as my guardian ran five paces backwards. 'She is below stairs.'

'Are there no other servants?" I asked.

'There was a new young scullery maid, who took fright and ran away when she heard the news. I have not heard from her since, though she is owed a week's wages.' The valet pursed his lips. 'We have still not replaced Cook, who went elsewhere at the end of last year.'

'From whom did this fugitive, juvenile and anonymous maid receive the tidings?' Mr G sprang to the drinks cabinet.

'I am not sure, sir.' Hesketh rubbed the nape of his neck. 'I would guess from an onlooker. There was a large crowd outside.'

Mr G extracted the stopper from a broad-based port decanter. 'This is not the dingy parlour of Miss Middleton's childhood hovel, convenient for the arctic circle, where we might unhappily engage in guessing games while your lost last master lies at room temperature upon his nicely trimmed Edinburgh granite block.' He replaced the stopper and hurried to the hearth.

The servants looked at him, me, then each other blankly.

'Which of you live in?' I raised my voice to be heard above my guardian's stamping across the room towards the hearth.

'Myself, Easterly, Mrs Emmett and Veronique,' Hesketh listed as Mr G bent over the unlit fire to peer upwards. 'There are bars set into the chimneys, sir.'

'That footman must be getting lonely.' Mr G emerged, miraculously free of soot.

Easterly was still in his chair, the lilac thread intact, and he made to rise, but Sidney Grice halted him with a gesture and ambled down the hall. It was a rectangular space, about twelve feet by twenty, with a carpeted staircase to the left. Mr G walked past the stairs and disappeared round the back of them. A door opened and closed.

'I take it this leads to the servants' hall,' he called.

'Indeed, sir.'

Sidney Grice sneezed. 'Are there any other ways down there?'

'None, sir.'

'I doubt Her Majesty has better security,' I remarked.

'She has worse,' my guardian informed me. 'I have locked that door.'

Hesketh raised his eyebrows. 'Would you like to see round the house now, sir?'

And my guardian perked up. 'Do you know, Hesketh,' Sidney Grice said happily, 'I believe that I would.'

19

Flesh and Blood

THE HALLWAY WENT the length of the house. It had three doors coming off to the right side and the trace of a blocked doorway on the left, at the foot of the staircase beyond Easterly's chair.

Behind the front sitting room was a similarly sized dining room, the table surrounded by twelve chairs. Because of the way the house had been partitioned, this room had no natural light source apart from a fanlight above the door, but there were two gas mantles on each of the four walls.

'Mr Mortlock never used this after Mrs Mortlock left,' Hesketh told us. 'He ate from a tray in the study.'

This next room was entered from beside the staircase and extended to the back of the house. It had a rear window, also barred of course. The walls were lined with glass-fronted bookcases, packed with heavy brown-backed tomes. An ancient globe stood between the two leather armchairs.

'It must be like living in a prison.' I slid a book off a shelf, bound copies of *Punch or The London Charivari*.

'Your master had a sense of humour then?' I flicked through a couple of pages and came across a cartoon with a laboured pun on the words *here* and *hear*.

'Mr Mortlock was more interested in philosophy and the spirit world,' the valet told me. 'That was one of Mrs Mortlock's journals.'

'It was probably all she had to laugh about, living with him,' I conjectured and Hesketh did not demur.

'Most of the other books were inherited from Mr Garstang,' he said.

'I cannot see anything about art,' I remarked and, seeing that Hesketh did not catch my drift, asked, 'Did the drawing found in Mrs Emmett's room belong to Mr Mortlock?'

Hesketh gave the world a spin. 'Mrs Seagrove, the house-keeper, overheard Mr Nathan telling Easterly he had won it playing cards. She told Mr and Mrs Garstang, who were so shocked by the subject matter and the sinful way it was acquired that they instructed Mr Nathan to quit this house immediately.' India drifted behind his fingers. 'It was only when Mr Nathan swore that he had burned the picture and promised never to gamble again that they relented.' India re-emerged. 'I believe there were threats to disinherit Mr Nathan at the time.'

The world stopped turning.

Across the hall from the library were two doors I had not seen from the other end. One was in the back of the staircase and presumably led to the basement. The other door to the rear of it entered a music room, with a medium grand piano, its music rack holding something by Brahms.

'Mrs Mortlock is an accomplished violinist.' Hesketh touched a dusty harp. 'Miss Cherry played that piano but under suffer-ance, I fear.'

'And Mr Mortlock?' I asked, though I feared I knew the answer.

'Not very interested in music, miss.'

Mr G stamped on the floor and tapped at the green-friezed wallpaper.

'That once opened into the south wing of Gethsemane,' Hesketh volunteered and Sidney Grice shrugged.

'When did you first meet Mr Mortlock?' I played a one-fin-gered scale on the keyboard. It was badly out of tune.

'I knew Master Nathan as a boy, miss. His father, Mr

Garstang's brother-in-law, drowned at sea when Nathan was a baby and his mother's nerves collapsed. She spent most of her life in private hospitals. Mr and Mrs Garstang sent Nathan to school and he stayed here for most of the holidays.'

Sidney Grice bent lower than seemed possible without support, to look at something on the floor. He sighed loudly and straightened up.

In the corner furthest from the back window was a sewing area.

'I am surprised they could see their needles,' I commented.

'When the gas was on and the candles lit, this could be a lovely snug room in winter,' Hesketh said.

My guardian ran his fingers over the oval table and lifted the circular rug on which it stood, to peer beneath.

'The Garstangs certainly did their duty to their nephew.' I opened the split lid of a wicker box, still packed neatly with cotton reels, and a deeper sadness filled the valet's face.

'I believe it was more than a duty to them, miss. Master Nathan was their flesh and blood, the closest they ever had to a son, and for him they were the parents he never knew.'

'What about Lionel Engra?' I pricked my finger on a pin that had been used to hem a never-to-be-finished handkerchief.

'They were his godparents, but only because his father was a junior partner in the printing business.' Hesketh closed the lid and slipped the peg back through its loop.

'Were Mrs Mortlock and Cherry ever guests here?' I sucked off a drop of blood.

'Miss Charity came several times as a child.' Hesketh looked wistful. 'But Mrs Mortlock was a Roman Catholic and they would not have her under their roof.'

'It must have come very hard to Mr Mortlock when they were murdered,' I suggested.

'Cushioned by a considerable bequest,' Mr G murmured, but Hesketh did not appear to hear him.

'It broke his heart, Miss Middleton. He worshipped Mr and Mrs Garstang, and their money brought him nothing but misery.'

'Money *never* brings misery,' my guardian asserted, 'only the misuse of it.' He closed his eyes briefly. 'I have finished.'

The hallway felt light and airy after the desolation of the abandoned chambers. There are few things more melancholy than a house that has lost those who loved it.

Easterly perked up as we rejoined him.

'Stay,' Sidney Grice commanded, striding round the back of his chair to stand at the front door. He brought out the keys and tried the lower of the two locks. 'A little stiff.' He tested the door and it would not open, then repeated the process with the upper lock. 'Less stiff. Explain,' he commanded Hesketh, who had come to stand close by.

'I imagine—'

'Kindly do not do so.'

'The lower lock is older, sir.' Hesketh stood as erect as a soldier on parade. 'The upper was only fitted when Mr Mortlock came.'

'That is an interesting and possibly candid answer,' Mr G acknowledged.

'I think you will find that I always speak the truth, sir.'

'Then you belong to a highly exclusive club of which I am the only other member,' Sidney Grice told him, 'though, as founder, I have appointed myself lifetime president and chairman at any meetings.' He looked up at the valet sharply. 'Do I amuse you?'

Hesketh struggled to control a smile. 'Indeed not, sir.'

'Oh, Hesketh.' Mr G sighed. 'Though I scarcely know you, I am not convinced that you are so bizarre as to arrange your features in such a diverted fashion when you are not diverted. Austin Anthony Hesketh, you have just disbarred yourself from my club and now I shall be all alone at its annual dinners.'

'How disappointing,' I murmured, 'but at least you will get to choose the menu.'

If I ever thought I had ceased to be puzzled by my guardian's shenanigans, he had disillusioned me yet again.

'Might Hi ask a question, sir?' Easterly craned his neck in a futile attempt to see what was going on.

'I feel it only fair to advise you,' Mr G crouched to examine the front-door locks with his magnifying lens, 'that such a process may not merit a response or elicit that for which you were hoping.'

Easterly looked at me, baffled, and I said, 'That almost means *yes*.'

'Hi presume—'

'Stop.' My guardian clutched his left eye as if expecting it to fall out as easily as the right. 'People who do that always presume the wrong things and it unbalances my gentle disposition and, if I were not out of your line of vision, you would see that I have adopted an attitude of despair which I am about to discard.'

The footman flicked about in confusion.

'Go on,' Hesketh advised as my godfather made a little ball of cotton wool appear between his thumb and forefinger.

Easterly gave the matter some thought. 'Hi assume...' But Mr G groaned and Easterly continued rapidly. 'Hiv you tied me and Veronique up to stop us hinterfering with clues we have had all the time in the world to hinterfere with them already. Not that we have,' he added hastily.

'I shall not tell you the proportion of criminals who have almost every opportunity to dispose of evidence, but only try to do so as the police are breaking down their doors, for I am unsure of the exact figure.' Sidney Grice clipped the ball in a pair of locking tweezers and poked it into the upper keyhole. 'But it is approximately somewhere between eight- and nine- thirty-sevenths.'

'Hi am not sure Hi understand,' Easterly admitted and Sidney Grice jumped up behind him.

'The ways of a personal detective are recondite.' Mr G walked round to confront Easterly with the cotton wool. 'And I do not fully comprehend them myself. This small sample of wadding is faintly begrimed but dry.' He dropped it into a large white envelope, which he folded. 'Therefore the lock has not been oiled for many a year.' He slipped his the envelope into his satchel and sighed.

I took a look. 'You can easily see if the bolts are across or not, so you would risk it being noticed if you only locked one of them.'

'She speaks the truth,' Sidney Grice intoned, his hand raised in a papal blessing.

'Did the Garstangs sleep up there?' I touched the newel post.

'No, miss.' Hesketh indicated the general direction of the north wing. 'Mr and Mrs Garstang shared a room in the main body of the house.'

*

'Holford Garstang was lying on his side, turned towards his wife,' Inspector Pound told us. 'His neck had been cut in two places; the second wound was much deeper.'

'How do you know it was the second?' Sidney Grice had two halfpennies flat on the palm of his left hand.

'Because the other cut was only about an eighth of an inch deep and two or three inches long.' Pound brought out his meerschaum pipe. 'Why would you wound a man fatally and then nick him?'

'I can think of thirty-nine reasons.' Mr G closed his hand on the coins. 'But I do not wish to suffer your company long enough to declaim them.'

George Pound's lips moved.

'That would be most uncomfortable,' Sidney Grice told him.

I dabbed at a tea stain on my sleeve. 'So do you think the murderer had a tentative go and then steeled himself to deliver the fatal attack?'

'Something like that.' Pound blew down the stem. 'Augusta Garstang's death was even more violent. The killer had climbed over the bed.'

'Again, how do you know?' Mr G clicked the halfpennies.

'There were foot- and knee-prints on the cover.' The inspector unbuttoned his tobacco pouch. 'Clumps of her hair were torn out. Most likely she was woken by the attack on her husband and *the murderer leaped at her, wrenched her head back and killed her with one wild slash. The force of it broke the gold chain with crucifix that she always wore.' He gripped the pouch. 'The chain was buried in her throat.'*

*

Sidney Grice closed his eyes and lowered his head.

'Come, Hesketh,' he cried, so suddenly that the valet blinked. 'Escort me and my fledgling accomplice to a higher level of this reputedly accursed house.'

And up the wooden stairs we go.

*

Up the grand marble staircase I go. Step after step after step, on and on, ever higher, never higher, towards that red light but never any closer.

I wake up and thank God I never reached it.

'You reached it,' Holford insists fiercely, his rotting breath a stench in my nostrils.

Up I go again and sometimes I wake again, but sometimes I reach the top.

The house is very dark, not a ray of moonlight through the shutters and curtains, and the gas turned off for safety. I don't like it. I'll never let on to anyone but I'm frightened of the dark. That's why I keep a lamp hidden in my wardrobe.

But at least I know my way. I should do after all the times I have sneaked in and out at night, all the time I spent teaching Lionel to feel his way around.

The door swings open.

I had a dog that snored worse than them, Hesketh reminds me, until it got stabbed.

It upsets me to think of that. I hate cruelty.

Somebody opens the door.

A candle glares in the red-glass lamp in front of a statue of Jesus carrying a lamb, and I feel sick. What do they think a shepherd does with his sheep? At the end of the day he kills them. I've seen it.

'Sacrilege,' Augusta hisses.

Holford and Augusta are lying facing each other. His hand is on her arm. I always thought he was a big man, but he looks quite little in bed and his face has collapsed. He's taken his teeth out. That knocks me back – this man who always preaches to the women about vanity – I never knew he had ivories. They're in a glass on the table by his bed, grinning at me like a skeleton.

'You killed me the first,' Holford reminds me.

I had to so you couldn't protect her.

I see his skin part, a white line going dark, and his eyes pop open and he puts his hand to his neck and turns, and he says, 'Nutty! What are you doing?'

And he tries to sit up and Augusta is stirring, so I grab his whiskers and pull his head back and his throat parts, the air and the blood rushing out.

'It hurt, Nutty. It hurt so much.'

Augusta is up on one elbow.

'I did not know what was happening at first. I thought Holford was having a bad dream.'

She's trying to catch her breath for a scream and I jump over. He sort of grabs at me, but he's gone, and I get hold of her hair and she pulls away and leaves a clump of it in my hand, and she's scrambling out of the bed but I'm over it and grabbing hold of her nightgown and pulling her back, and she's gasping and saying, 'Nutty, no!'

'We always treated you well,' Holford says in my ear.

Too late for that. I push her down with the pillow over her face, but that gets in the way so I stab her in the breast. Five times.

'Like the five wounds of Christ,' Augusta says, sanctimonious to the last.

Five times, deliberately, and with each blow I tell her: 'Do... NOT... call... me... Nutty.'

They made a mockery of my name. They laughed at the way I talk, like saying Hi instead of I, as though not having all their advantages made me stupid.

I stop.

She's quiet, just the sound of her blood gushing on to the headboard.

It's then I think about how they used to be, and I wish I could put them back together. They were good to me in their way, as much as anyone is with an underling, and the saddest thing, I realize, is I loved them. And I think, Enough is enough, no more, *but then I stiffen my resolve.*

Be a man, *I tell myself.* You are doing this for Nathan.

20

The Staple and the Spikes

THE STAIRS WERE disproportionally wide and two men could have walked abreast, but we went in single file, with Sidney Grice in the lead and the valet to the rear.

'There were handprints on the walls, long wavy smears,' George Pound was seeing them still. 'They said Kate Webb must have made them as she tried to flee Angelina Innocenti.'

'But you are not sure?'

He pulled his right moustache. 'They were both covered in blood.'

'Who found Mr Mortlock's body?' My petticoats were fighting each other for the right to wrap around my legs.

'I did,' Hesketh told me.

I grabbed the banister rail to stop myself tumbling back. 'But I thought you were visiting your mother.'

'So I was, miss.' Hesketh had put up his hands, prepared to catch me, his eyes wide with alarm. 'But the train got in at nine twenty-five that morning and I was back here by ten o'clock.'

'Exactly?' Sidney Grice got to the top and stopped so abruptly that we almost collided. He skipped aside.

'Roughly.' Hesketh resumed his ascent. 'I know that it was ten after the hour when I passed through the hall with Mr Mortlock's shaving water because the grandmother clock chimed the hour, and it is ten minutes slow.'

'Nine.' Mr G tapped his way up with his stick.

'Did anybody see you return?' I raised my skirts a smidgen to avoid treading on them, but not enough to expose my repulsive ankles to the valet's gaze.

'Everyone, miss.'

'I most certainly did not,' my guardian retorted indig-nantly.

'I meant all the other servants,' Hesketh explained agitatedly. 'Easterly, Mrs—'

'When I require another list of their names, you may be the very man to compile it.' Sidney Grice pirouetted morosely but, by the time he had completed a revolution, his expression was almost amicable. 'Indeed,' he whispered to Hesketh's and my puzzlement.

'Did Mr Mortlock always rise so late?' I surreptitiously jiggled about to adjust my petticoats, which had risen and disarrayed during our ascent, but both men noticed and my guardian curled his upper lip. I had caught myself pulling that face a few times recently and I hoped it would not become a permanent part of my repertoire.

'He was never a good sleeper, miss.' Hesketh scrunched his brow. 'Midnight was an early turn-in for Mr Mortlock, and he would often rise and go down to his study in the night. Then he would take his laudanum and have trouble waking up.'

We stopped on the landing. Here a weak light oozed through a barred end window and I could make out a high wall a few yards away, topped in criss-crossing rows of spikes. Beyond that was still a sea of dun yellow.

'What inhabited these?' Mr G swept his cane to indicate the three brown-varnished doors either side of us.

'This room is... *was* Mr Mortlock's.' Hesketh pointed to the first door on the right. It was broken and had been secured with a padlock. It hung at eye level, passing through two big iron staples, one of which went through the vertical stile of the door, the other having been driven into the post. They could have been removed but not without marking the paintwork. The wood around the handle was cracked and splintered.

'How did the ingress to your dead master's private chamber come to be secured?' Sidney Grice marched jerkily ahead.

I refrained from pointing out that we already knew the answer to that one.

'Inspector Quigley insisted that we fit a padlock whilst the police investigations are under way.' Hesketh was as puzzled by the question as I.

'You are trying to make me ill and almost succeeding.' Sidney Grice clapped his hands briefly over his ears. 'I did not ask why. I know *why*. If I had wanted to know why I should have asked,' he rattled out. '*How* did it happen? Answer, man, before our corporeal functions disappoint us and we return to the dust from which we reportedly came.'

The valet shuffled perplexedly. 'Miss Charity agreed to his request,' he said hesitantly, 'and I arranged for it to be done the same day. Fisher and Son, a local carpentry firm, did the job. Until then we were not allowed upstairs.'

'Who used this room when the previous owners lived here?' I asked as my guardian took his hands cautiously away.

The carpet runner ran from the stairs straight along the corridor. It was edged by darkly varnished boards and, as far as I could see, neither it nor they had been disturbed.

'Only occasional guests,' Hesketh replied.

'This one?' Sidney Grice rapped with his knuckles on the next door along.

'That was Mrs Mortlock's.'

'Do they interconnect?' I asked.

'No, miss. All the rooms are separate.' Hesketh watched Mr G run a fingernail down a join in the wallpaper. 'The last door on this side leads to the attic and the servants' quarters.'

'Who had that back room?' I pointed towards the door opposite it.

'Miss Charity.' Hesketh's expression softened as he spoke her name.

'What about the one next to it?' I referred to the middle of the three doors on the left of the stairs.

'The bathroom, miss, and that,' Hesketh dipped his head

towards the door opposite Nathan Mortlock's, 'was where Master Lionel slept.' Hesketh closed his eyes and swallowed, and his next words came out huskily. 'And died. Nobody ever goes in there.'

Sidney Grice had been standing quietly for most of the conversation, but he perked up at the last announcement.

'Then we shall.'

Hesketh was nonplussed. 'I am sure you know your job, sir—'

My guardian moved close up, the top of his head only just above the valet's shoulder. 'It is not for you to be certain or uncertain about my professional competence.'

Hesketh coughed. 'I only meant that I understood you were to investigate Mr Nathan Mortlock's death, sir, but Mr and Mrs Garstang were murdered over eleven years ago.'

'What if the same person murdered the Garstangs and Mr Mortlock?' I proposed.

'But surely you know about Angelina Innocenti, miss?' Hesketh objected.

'Do you believe she killed those people?' I asked, and Mr G groaned.

'If what people believed was evidence, we should all be worshipping trees,' he reasoned, 'especially horse chestnuts.'

'She certainly went mad,' Hesketh said. 'I believe it took three men to restrain her and she was not an especially strong girl.'

'Show us the room,' my guardian commanded.

'There is nothing to see,' Hesketh warned, but did as he was bidden.

*

The boy was a sad case,' Inspector Pound had told us. 'Well, I call him a boy because I thought he was one at first. He had the face of one, but Lionel Engra was about twenty, I think. I've seen a lot of deaths, too many—'

'What would be the optimum number?' Sidney Grice interrupted with genuine interest.

'None,' I supposed on George Pound's behalf.

'Then the inspector is in the wrong job.'

'You expect that sort of thing down the East End,' Pound continued, 'and you get hardened to it.'

'I do not think I ever shall.' I forced myself to drink my tea.

'Women are made of kinder stuff,' Pound asserted.

'I could name a great many who were not,' Mr G argued, 'when I have nine days and six hours to waste.'

'What upset you about it?' I asked, for the memory obviously affected him still.

George Pound put his cup untasted back on the tray. 'Most of the household were attacked in their sleep. And even those who weren't tucked up in bed were dispatched as quickly as possible. But there was an element of cruelty in Lionel's murder.' The inspector hesitated to tell me. 'He had been tied up for some time before he was murdered.'

'How do you know?' my guardian asked.

'There was extensive bruising and rope-burn marks on his body,' Pound replied, and my guardian nodded in approval of his method.

'I read that you found him under the bed,' I stated as matter-of-factly as I could, for the memories were clearly distressing him.

'Strangled,' Pound said simply, 'with the curtain cord that was used to tie him up.' He parted his moustaches. 'Not a quick death, nor a painless one.'

'There is more to it than that.' Sidney Grice leaned forward like a panther about to pounce and our visitor edged a fraction away, and I could hardly hear his confession.

'He was not found until the next day.' The inspector ran a finger under his collar. 'And I could not help but wonder if...' he swallowed hard, 'when my constables first searched the house he could have been alive.'

And when I looked into George Pound's eyes, they were lost in a nightmare.

21

The Spare Room

A NOISE, A *sort of mewing.*
Oh God, is one of them still alive?
How strange to pray to God on this of all nights.
Has one of them come back from the dead?

*But a small man is standing just inside with his back to me,
and in front of him the Garstangs are not people any more. They
are monstrous.*

It's Lionel and he's hugging himself and whimpering.

*Oh, young lion. You aren't supposed to be here. You should
be with your mother.*

*I creep backwards but Lionel is turning. The demon steps
forward but I fight him off.*

Kill him.

*I drive the demon back into the spare room but Lionel comes
too. It doesn't occur to him that he could be following a murderer. He trusts everyone.*

Kill him. You can't risk it.

The demon is clever. He uses my voice in my head.

*I change the grip on the knife and stand behind the door as it
opens, and Lionel wanders in. He goes to the bed.*

Kill him.

'Who's there?' *Lionel asks and those two words could have
saved his life.*

I rush at him and get there just before the demon. Lionel

squeals and falls face down on the bed, and I get hold of the top blanket and pull it over his head to protect him. He wriggles about and squeaks, but he's a flimsy chap.

I cut the cord and tie him up. Not too tight. And he calls out something muffled.

'Nutty?'

Is that what he says?

22

The World Through Pale Glass

A S WITH THE other middle rooms, the only daylight to find its way in – and there was precious little of that – came through the door, but unlike the ground-floor rooms there was not even a window above it.

The room had been stripped – no furniture, bare boards and distempered walls.

'What was it like the day before Lionel died?' I asked.

Hesketh stood hesitantly on the threshold. 'The bed was over there on the right-hand wall. There was a chest of drawers on the wall facing me.' He scratched his jaw. 'A washstand to my left. That was all I think. I rarely came in here and never since that morning.'

'He was not related to the Garstangs?' I clarified.

'Not by blood,' he concurred. 'But they gave him a second home after his father died.' Hesketh fought to contain himself. 'He came to stay often, as did Nathan, but it was only by chance that he was here that night for he was supposed to go back to his mother, but we had a message that she was unwell and he stayed on.'

Mr G was attempting to twist the bars. 'How many other mothers were ill that night?'

'I could not say, sir.' Hesketh put on his servant's mask. 'I only know that mine made a partial recovery, but Master Lionel's mother had a seizure when she heard the news and died a week later.'

'I believe that he was found under his bed,' I said softly.

'That is correct, miss.' Hesketh's cheeks buckled.

'Did you see Lionel when he was dead?' Mr G paced the room, stamping on boards and rapping on walls with his cane.

Hesketh did not appear to have heard the question, but at last he said, 'Yes, sir.'

*

'His neck was clawed where he had tried to get his fingers under the rope.'

I remembered a maid hanging herself once. We had cut her down and the noose out of her flesh. It is not a gentle way to die.

'His eyes were so... they looked like they were ready to burst.'

I had seen the agony and the black froth of a choking death and so, I realized, had George Pound.

*

'I identified all the bodies when I came back from seeing my mother,' Hesketh announced flatly.

'When was that?' I asked.

'That afternoon,' he replied like a man in a dream. 'Mr Garstang had told me to stay on until my mother was well enough, but then a local policeman called.'

'What was his name?' Sidney Grice challenged, and Hesketh's eyes went up and to the left as he dredged his memory.

'Frank Hill. I knew him vaguely when we played a sort of cricket as children – just a bit of wood for a bat and a chalked wicket on a wall.'

'Do not trouble to explain the rules.' My guardian yawned. 'Show me your young mistress's boudoir.'

Hesketh hesitated. 'Perhaps I should seek Miss Mortlock's approval first.'

'Now,' Sidney Grice said firmly.

*

Cherry's bedroom was more prettily furnished with dusky-pink drapes, drooping lilac patterns on the wallpaper and a matching counterpane, and an Aubusson rug in pink and turquoise alongside the bed.

This room had a good-sized window of stained glass to hide it from the gaze of the rookeries and save the occupant from seeing them. The pattern of the glass was predominantly red and cast an eerie glow across my guardian's cheek as he went to inspect it.

I opened one of the four wardrobe doors and eyed Cherry's clothes enviously. She was better stocked than my favourite dress shop on Regent Street – vibrant colours and impossibly slender waists.

I could hardly recognize the slim young man in the photograph on her dressing table.

'Mr Nathan in happier times,' Hesketh confirmed.

'Happier for whom?' Sidney Grice was peering out through a small piece of clearer pale-yellow glass and he stepped aside to let me see.

I had seen the poor many times in England and India, but the square below was a different country. Children hobbled with swollen stomachs on bandy legs, clambering over what looked like a dung heap, women nearly naked, men clad in old sacking, oddly angular elbows hinging concave arms, all drifting across a muddy court or squatting unspeaking against bulging walls propped with bent timber.

'The barbarians are amongst us,' Sidney Grice declared in revulsion. 'Come, Miss Middleton. Hesketh shall lead us up.'

23

The Tyrant and the Mirror

THE SERVANTS' STAIRCASE was constructed from plain pine. 'Men on this floor, women on the top,' Hesketh recounted as we made our way up, my dresses brushing the whitewashed walls on either side.

This third level was much smaller than the first and second, and had only two doors facing each other.

'We are in the front of the tower now, miss,' Hesketh puffed. 'The rest has been closed off and is empty.'

'So much house going to waste.' I was slightly short of breath myself.

'Mr Nathan wanted the house as secure and easily searched as possible,' the valet explained. 'It was one of my duties to check the entire house every night.'

'Why do the women have to climb the furthest?' I objected.

'So that the male staff have no excuse to go past their chambers,' Hesketh replied. 'In the old days the men were accommodated at the other end of the house.'

'Brian Watts, the footman, put up a fight,' Inspector Pound said softly. 'He was a powerfully built man with a neck like a prize bull. It was hacked about and he had a gash on his cheek and on both hands.'

'And a struggle was indicated how else?' Mr G clacked his halfpennies together.

'*The room was all but destroyed. The washstand had been knocked over and the bowl thrown across the room and smashed.*' The inspector took a pinch of the Murray's Mix from his left hand and deposited it into the bulb of his meerschaum. '*The leg of a wooden stool was hanging loose and there was blood on all the walls.*'

'*All?*' Sidney Grice tossed the coins from hand to hand.

'*Every one plus the window.*' Pound lightly tamped the tobacco. '*And in several places on the floor.*'

'*How many is several?*' My guardian caught one coin in each hand.

Pound grimaced in irritation. '*I do not remember exactly. About twenty with a large pool where he fell.*'

'*Astonishing.*' Mr G made two fists. '*Because several is generally taken as being a number greater than three but less than eight.*' And when he opened his fists the halfpennies had vanished.

'*I found a broken penknife blade in the cellar.*' Inspector Pound put his pipe away. '*Much too small to be used as a weapon, though.*'

'*Some might say including eight,*' Sidney Grice ploughed on with his theme.

I beat some of the whitewash off my dress. 'The Garstangs must have been very proper.'

'Indeed they were, miss,' Hesketh concurred, 'as Mr Mortlock increasingly became, though he was less rigorous in his approach to alcohol. Mr and Mrs Garstang would not have it in the house.'

'No wonder the brewer's horse did not like it here,' I remarked and Hesketh raised his eyebrows.

'I would not pay too much attention to that story, miss.' Hesketh opened the door and stood aside.

The valet's room was comfortably appointed, with a narrow window too high for me to see out of, an immaculately made bed and a small pine wardrobe. On his chest of drawers stood a patchily silvered mirror, a varnished button box, a splayed hair-brush, a wooden wedge and a sepia photograph of an elderly lady resting on a garden seat with a studio backdrop of Venice behind her.

'My mother.' Hesketh smiled fondly.

'What a striking woman,' I said. Even the fixed pose that photography requires could not hide the way she sparkled. 'She must have been pretty in her youth.'

'Hah!' Mr G snorted and pounced upon it.

'My father swore she was the belle of the village.' Hesketh hovered anxiously. 'I only wish we were not so far apart.'

Sidney Grice had his pince-nez on and was scrutinizing the back of the frame.

'Did you never marry?' I picked up the wedge as the least personal item I could find. It did not feel right to pry with him at my side.

'A live-in servant can only marry another.' He gazed out of the window. It was too high for me to see anything through it. 'And a valet cannot consort with a scullery maid.' He straightened his neckerchief. 'The opportunities are few and far between.'

'Do you regret it?'

Hesketh turned towards me.

'Perhaps Miss Middleton could start a marriage agency.' Sidney Grice replaced the picture exactly where he had found it. 'She appears to have nothing better to talk about.'

'Whose is the next room?' I turned the wedge in the pretence of examining it, but it was just a wedge – no telltale stains or dents.

'Easterly's, miss.'

Mr G grasped the window grille, hauling himself up to peer out while I looked at the back of the door.

'Is this where the police found the curtain rope?' I touched the hook.

'So I believe, miss.' Hesketh tore his eyes away from my guardian's antics. 'I was not present while my room was searched.'

'Why is there no lock?' I asked, and Sidney Grice let go and landed on his feet with a crash that rattled the cheval mirror in the corner.

'That was to be my next question, though more intelligently structured,' he complained.

Hesketh scratched his neck. 'Mr Garstang was of the opinion that a servant had no business excluding him from any part of the house.'

Sidney Grice dropped on his haunches.

'He sounds like a tyrant.' I put the wedge back, though not with my guardian's precision.

'Which tyrant?' Mr G quizzed me. 'Nero Claudius Caesar Augustus Germanicus perhaps? Or that unusually resourceful Frenchman, the self-appointed Emperor Napoleone di Buonaparte?'

'I never knew him to enter our quarters.' Hesketh eyed my guardian as Mr G pulled open the bottom drawer of the dresser and checked around it with an outsized dental mirror. 'Though Mrs Garstang was known to enter the maids' chambers unexpectedly.'

'I have heard of many mistresses doing that.' I picked up a coiled iron holder with the stub of a candle in its base.

'Mr and Mrs Garstang were very strict in their religious views,' the valet conceded. 'There was a terrible fuss when they saw that drawing. Master Nathan was thrown out of the house and only allowed back when he swore he had destroyed it. But they were good people at heart. They were fair employers and kind to their poorer relatives, and when Masters Nathan and Lionel came to stay, Gethsemane rang out with laughter.'

Mr G put his mirror away.

'It is difficult to imagine merriment here.' I picked a waxen dribble off the stand.

'There has not been much in recent years,' the valet agreed sadly.

Sidney Grice rooted through the neatly folded clothes.

'According to *Bartwell's Guide to Occult Objects*, sixty per centum of things hidden in a triple-compartmented chest are to be found in the lower drawer, twenty-eight per centum in the middle and the remaining twelve in the upper.' He ran his long fingers through the pockets of a pair of trousers before lifting the garment to one side. 'And this,' he held up a small bunch of envelopes, 'would appear to fall into the first category.'

Mr G remained on his haunches as he opened the letters on the thin rectangular rug.

'Those are from my mother and brother, and a very old one from my father.' For the first time Hesketh flared. 'And, if I may say so, sir, they are personal.'

'In a murder investigation,' Sidney Grice flicked though the correspondence, 'the only thing personal is the detective.' He perused the handwriting. 'These, however,' he reassembled the pile, 'have depressed dullness into a tedium deeper than I had realized was possible.' He replaced the letters and the clothes, smoothing a shirt before sliding the drawer regretfully back into place.

24

Brian

'I TAUGHT YOU '*ow to blow smoke rings,*' Brian says. '*I covered up for you when Saint Augusta found your bottle of brandy inside the piano. I said it must 'ave been the tuner 'cause I 'ad smelled it on 'is breaf.*'

'*Yes, I know,*' I tell him, '*and I'm sorry about that.*'

'*Sorry? You don't know what sorry means.*'

Now Brian is a big man and he still looks it, lying on his back with the moonlight through his open window as I creep across the room. My clothes rustle but my tread is as quiet as a kitten's. Even I can't hear my bare feet fall on the bare boards.

I'm about a yard away now. And then I trip. The stupid ass has left his boots in the middle of the room. Who in their right mind does that?

'*A man who ain't expecting to be murdered by 'is friend,*' Brian says.

I go flying and it's all I can do not to land on top of him and, on a good night, I wake up, but there are so few good nights now.

I stop myself on the edge of the bed and the knife gets dropped, and of course Brian wakes and sits up and sees me, and says, "Ello, Nutty. 'Ad a foo, 'ave we? You're in the wrong room, friend.'

'*Remember that, do you?*' Brian asks indignantly. '*I called you "friend".*'

'*I saw the curtain move,*' I try to explain, but what's the use?

'Just looking for something,' I say, and pat the boards, feeling around.

Brian's eyes must be getting used to the dark. He says, 'Been in a fight, friend? You're covered in blood.'

That's when I find it, the sticky blade and then the handle, and Brian says, 'What you got there, Nutty?'

'A knife.' It must be the way I say it because he's swinging his legs over, and his knees are very hairy.

'What you been up to, Nutty?'

I can't move. I don't know why, but I'm crouching and watching Brian scratching a Lucifer and seeing it flare painfully bright, and he's lighting a candle and saying, 'That's not your blood, is it, Nutty?'

'No, it isn't my blood,' I admit because I don't like to lie.

And then Brian is angry. "Ave you 'urt Angelina, you dirty ____'

He uses a rude word and I HATE rude words.

"Course Hi haven't. Not yet,' I say, and, before I know it, Brian is on his feet and I get to mine.

'So it's like that?' he says. 'Come on then.'

I stick the knife at him but he's swung his fist into the side of my head. I kick him, forgetting I haven't got any boots on, and stub my toes on his shin and he sees that and grins and says, 'Want anovva one?' And he gets me on the arm as I put it up to defend myself.

Somehow I get the knife in his stomach but it doesn't seem to have much effect. I pull it out and he grabs me by the collar. I fall backwards and he falls on top of me, but when I wriggle out I see my knife is sticking in his chest this time. He pulls it out and throws it aside and knees me on my jaw. That really rattles my teeth but, for some reason, it never wakes me up. I scramble away and get to my feet by his old chair. Brian may be big but he's slow. I break it over his back and he grunts, and the language he uses is just unrepeatable, and he goes down on all fours and somehow I've got the knife in my hand and I'm on his back, and I get his chin and pull it back. He tries to bite me and he rears up, but it only bares his throat more and the blade goes through it like a wire through cheese, and he's splattering on the floor and coughing and putting his hand to his neck as if it will do any good. Nothing he can do will do any good now. He's down. Big Brian is down and out, and I feel sorry about that but also triumphant, and he shouldn't have called me those things.

'Manners maketh man,' Mrs Garstang says.

'You disgust me,' Brian says, and I think he means me.

It seems so real I could almost believe I was there.

25

The Lamp and the Lions

EASTERLY NUTTER'S ROOM opposite Hesketh's was just as I expected. I had gained the impression that he was a very particular person with his precise, if misguided, attempts to speak correctly, his neat uniform, his well-groomed hair and the careful way he carried himself – and all of these traits were reflected in his own domain. The few items on display were lined up with a precision that matched my guardian's, and his bedmaking would have satisfied a sergeant of the guards.

There was a wedge on the floor, a bit grubbier than the first, but I did not trouble to pick it up.

'Is that where the bloodstained shirt was found?' Sidney Grice opened the wardrobe. It had been emptied.

'The police took all the other clothes to check them for bloodstains,' Hesketh told us. 'Luckily, he has a spare uniform.'

Mr G pressed on one end of a plank in the floor of the wardrobe and it tipped up to reveal a secret compartment about nine inches deep. He glanced inside and wandered away. In the base of the cavity stood an oil lamp.

'He is not supposed to have that in his room,' the valet admitted, 'but Easterly is frightened of the dark. He has lots of nightmares.'

'What about?' I asked.

'Ghosts.' Hesketh replaced the plank.

Sidney Grice went through the chest of drawers. 'Aha.' He reached deep inside and came out with the husk of a bluebottle held by one wing in a pair of tweezers.

'Is that significant?' I asked.

'Only to the spider that desiccated it.' Mr G reached back in to replace it.

'So nothing surprising?' It seemed to me that we were finding next to nothing at all.

My guardian rose with no apparent muscular effort.

'The world will have to try harder than that to astonish me.'

There was a Bible on the pine bedside table, bookmarked with a ribbon, and I went to the page. There had been no passages marked about smiting thine enemies or any other exhortations to violence.

'And God sent an angel to shut the lions' mouths,' I read out.

'Too many mouths are closed,' my guardian complained. He whipped round with his cane jabbing the air an inch under the valet's chin. 'What are you not telling us, Hesketh?'

Hesketh's cheek tremored. 'If I knew of anything that would help catch Mr Nathan's murderer, if I knew of *any* way that I could assist, I would give my life to do so.'

There were tears in the valet's eyes and he wiped them hastily away, and I knew that nobody could feign such heartbreak.

'Pull yourself together,' my godfather said, and I imagined he meant it encouragingly because he made as if to pat Hesketh's back, but did not quite manage. Sidney Grice disliked physical contact with people, which made the time he had hugged me when I came home from hell all the more precious and – so far – unique. 'Come, Austin Anthony Hesketh, dignified and fastidious valet to two murdered masters. Come, Miss Middleton, whom I shall not essay to delineate at present. Let us climb another flight and emulate the matronly Mrs Augusta Garstang by bursting unannounced into Mademoiselle Veronique Bonnay's place of rest in the confident expectation of not encountering her there.'

26

The Hook

THE FOURTH FLOOR followed the plan of the men's quarters and we went into the right-hand room – Veronique's – first.

A double bed on an iron frame stood side on to us, the head of it against the right-hand wall. It had not been made.

'Maids rarely get time to look after their own rooms,' Hesketh excused Veronique. 'This used to be Kate's but I have never told Veronique that.'

'Is anything in here original?' I asked.

'It is difficult to be sure.' The valet surveyed the furniture. 'I know the mattress and bedding were burned and there was a rug, but I think the bedstead and the furniture are the same. I have only been in this room twice. Mr Garstang asked me to deal with a rat once and I was too occupied with that to notice much else.'

'When was the second time you were in here?' Sidney Grice browsed around.

'The fifteenth of May 1878,' Hesketh replied.

'A Wednesday, the feast of Achillius of Larissa and Hilary of Galatea, to name but two, also the start of the bullfighting season in that most Catholic of countries, Spain, which might have been of interest to Miss Angelina Innocenti, but –' Mr G strolled round Hesketh as he recited this information – 'I doubt that any of those occasions impinge much upon your servile existence.

How can you be so precise and does that indifferent repair to the ceiling have any bearing upon your anecdote?'

Hesketh recoiled. 'A maid at the time, Anne Smith, hung herself from a lamp hook.' He turned away. 'I helped to cut her down. Mr Mortlock had the hook taken out.'

I stared at the faint rhomboid patch of slightly rougher plasterwork overhead. 'Do you know why she did it?'

'I do not know the details but I believe she was unhappy in love.' Hesketh touched a pillow with the back of his fingers as one might a dead relative.

'Who is not?' Mr G said to himself and looked round, apparently surprised to find us with him. 'Your information is of severely truncated use to me,' Mr G grumbled, rather unfairly, I thought. 'Who identified the Garstang household's bodies?'

'I did, sir.' Hesketh closed his eyes, but he should have known that a memory can only be blotted out by keeping them open. Any child can tell you that horrors are the worst when there is nothing to see. 'The police took me round the house.'

'A terrible thing to put him through. I found it gruelling enough and they meant nothing to me personally. It was Hesketh who drew our attention to Lionel Engra being missing and took us to the room where we found him.'

We stood for a while as if in prayer – Sidney Grice, Hesketh and me – and, in the quiet of my heart, I did intercede for them, these people who had died so cruelly, and I waited for the valet to open his eyes again before asking, 'Is this the bed where the razor was found?'

Another wooden wedge lay on its side by the threshold, perhaps slightly dented, but I was bored with them now.

'So I am told.' Hesketh straightened a sheet automatically.

'Miss Middleton has a rare talent for eliciting hearsay information from people,' Mr G told him.

I trod on a creaking floorboard.

'The joist is sagging.' Sidney Grice tried his weight on it. 'But not alarmingly.' He searched the chest of drawers, humming to himself, before rising with his brow furrowed. 'Show me Senorita Angelina Innocenti's old dormitory.'

We did not even enter the last room, a mirror of Veronique's, the bed bars and the mattress thin. Sidney Grice glanced inside, clicked his tongue, and closed the door as if anxious not to disturb an occupant.

'Is there anything else you wish or do not wish to tell us concerning this domain of feminine slumber?' Mr G blew on his fingertips.

The valet hesitated. 'I do not think so.'

'Then accompany us to Nathan Roptine Mortlock's bedchamber, spurning any opportunity – real or imagined – for procrastination,' Sidney Grice flung his arm forward, urging his troops to battle, 'the very instant that you have absorbed this useful information.' My guardian paused. 'Pictures and coats may be hung: people – as many who have crossed my righteous path have borne witness – are not hung. They are hanged.'

'I am sure Anne Smith would be relieved to hear that,' I conjectured sarcastically as we went back into the corridor.

The loft hatch was, as Quigley had informed us, padlocked.

'Is anything stored in there?' I asked.

'Nothing you would want to bring down, miss.' Hesketh followed my gaze. 'Mr Mortlock was so afraid of somebody getting on the roof and removing tiles to gain entry that he had a dozen mantraps and all sorts of other contraptions installed.'

'How on earth did he live here?' And I tried not to picture Cherry, a child, in this house of horrors.

'In fear, miss.' Hesketh opened another door. 'In mortal terror.'

27

The Chasm and the Scar

HESKETH LED THE way down again, stooped now under the weight of Gethsemane's history.

Sidney Grice came last, bending his knees and jumping off the bottom step as a child might splash into a puddle.

'Who else used Miss Charity's room?' My godfather stuck his cane into a floorboard knothole and left it standing upright.

'Do you mean while she was here, sir?' Hesketh fiddled with his bow tie.

'Do not delude yourself – nor essay to delude me – that answering my question with a question answers my question.' Mr G fell rigidly to the floor, breaking his fall with his hands just before his nose did the job for him.

Hesketh put his left hand over his mouth. 'Nobody, sir.' His voice came muted.

'In fact, Mr...' Hesketh's words trailed away as he watched my guardian.

'Complete your sentence.' Sidney Grice scratched at a board like a dog burying a bone.

'I was only about to say that Mr Garstang did not care for visitors.' Hesketh stood mesmerized by Sidney Grice, who was snuffling along like a bloodhound searching for that bone.

I went to Nathan Mortlock's bedroom door. It was split and hung awkwardly, with the top outer edge a good inch or more below the lintel and extending past the post, so that it could not be fully shut. The paint was chipped and scraped through to the woodwork in places. The handle had been removed and a chain emerged from the hole and through a staple that had been driven into the jamb. The other end of the chain came from behind the door and a sturdy padlock had been passed through the links.

I wiggled the hasp. It felt secure.

'Why has the door been smashed?' I asked.

'I speculated rationally about that.' Mr G got on to his side. 'But I did not like to ask for three reasons, all of which must – and therefore shall – remain occult.'

Hesketh forced himself to concentrate on my question as my guardian rolled on to his back. 'After my master did not respond to my knocks, I raised the alarm.'

'How?' Mr G barked.

'I called down the stairs.'

'What did you call?' Sidney Grice crossed his arms over his chest and closed his eyes. 'And be sure to use the exact words.'

'It was something like—'

My guardian's eyelids flicked apart.

'Of all the things I did not ask for – and they are numberless – most especially I did not ask for *something like* your exact words.' Mr G sat up, arms still folded. 'Miss Middleton could have a guess at roughly what you said. Tell me now and tell me in a low voice.'

Hesketh frowned. 'I said *Easterly, come here at once.*'

Sidney Grice leaped to his feet. 'And where was the aforementioned footman whilst you were summoning him?'

'Where he is now, sir.'

Sidney Grice drifted towards the banisters and called in a barely raised voice, 'Are you still in your chair, Sou' Easterly Gale Nutter?'

And immediately the response rose from afar. 'Yes, sir. Shall Hi come up?'

'Only if you wish to arouse the wrath of Herr Sidney Grice, die wunderbare persönliche detektiv,' Sidney Grice cautioned.

No doubt Easterly thought my guardian's description of himself in German sounded menacing for, 'Hi think Hi shall stay here then, thank you, sir,' came back faintly.

Mr G jogged backwards to stand between me and the entrance, side-on to both of us. His left hand went out to stroke a panel but, for some reason, his gaze was fixed upon me. Did he wink or did I imagine it? He shuffled round to place his right hand over the left and whistled six notes between his teeth.

Hesketh's left hand was twitching afresh.

'Did you try the door?' I asked him.

The valet clutched his left wrist in his right. 'Certainly I did, miss, but it was bolted on the inside.'

'He must have been very frightened,' I said as he forced himself to release his grip on the ball.

'I have drafted a monograph on the reasons for locking bedroom doors.' My guardian yanked his cane out of its make-shift stand. 'And fear does indeed feature largely as a motive, though by no means exclusively.' He clipped on his pince-nez and scrutinized the valet through the left lens. 'What happened next, Austin Hesketh, and you may omit any dialogue. I do not care for the manner in which you deliver it.'

Hesketh caught another ball. 'I explained to Easterly that I could not rouse Mr Mortlock. He tried as well, to no avail, and so we decided to break the door down.'

'How?' Sidney Grice asked sternly.

'We put our shoulders to it but—'

'I can see how the door was broken,' my guardian butted in. 'How did you decide that you were going to do it?'

Hesketh patted his thick greying hair as if checking it was still there. 'I told Easterly that we would have to. He was nervous that Mr Mortlock might have taken a sleeping draught and be angry, but he saw the sense and—'

'One and a half moments.' Sidney Grice crouched, licked his left index finger and dabbed it on to a gouge. 'So, having realized that your efforts were painful and futile and that the only things likely to break were your bones, you used a hammer.' Mr G stood up, making a great display of effort to do so. 'Whence did you get it? And I shall regard any pretence that you had one to hand with extreme scepticism.'

'The cellar, sir.' The valet fiddled with his tie again. 'There was an old coal hammer there.'

'That was the correct answer,' Sidney Grice congratulated him and held out his finger. 'Regard the apex of this lightly moistened digit and describe what you observe in seven words.'

Hesketh leaned over. 'I can see a black particle, sir.'

'Full marks for numeracy.' Mr G opened his satchel. 'And I am relieved that you will not be needing my Grice Patent Folding Magnifying Glass. I dislike lending to anyone, especially murder suspects.'

Hesketh caught his breath. 'I fail to see how I can be suspected of a crime committed when I was many miles away.'

I waited for Sidney Grice to tell him about a man in Mexico who had been murdered by a woman in Chipping Norton, but he only smiled thinly and said, 'Your failure may yet prove to be my success.'

I came over and took a peek. 'May *I* borrow your glass?'

My guardian huffed. 'Very well.' And extracted a steel disc from his satchel, handing it to me as one entrusts a holy relic to a heretic. 'But please exercise extreme caution. I have hardly had a chance to play with it myself yet.'

I hinged the lens out and was struck by how clean his skin was and how regularly the rugae ran, but I learned nothing else from my experience. The tiny ragged black speck became a larger ragged black speck and I saw a long-healed demi-lunar scar that I had not noticed before, running down the side of his finger and disappearing into the first crease.

'Thank you.' I handed the glass back. 'That tells me all I need to know for the present.'

Mr G put a finger to his eye and took a closer look. 'Humph,' he humphed suspiciously and put his glass away.

'Shall we go in?' I suggested.

'How uncannily you have read my thoughts,' my godfather said without a hint of sarcasm, taking Quigley's key from his waistcoat pocket between his thumb and forefinger. 'For this...' the lock clicked and Mr G lifted it out to let the ends of the chain fall apart, 'I do not require absolute silence.'

And, with the flat of his hands, he pressed upon the door.

28

Beyond the Threshold

DARKNESS WAITED BEYOND the threshold, perforated by two small orange lights on the far wall.

'Amplify the illumination,' Mr G commanded and Hesketh hurried to turn up the gas.

The flames rose instantly and the mantles glowed yellow then white, flooding the room in their cold light.

'Dear God,' I said.

'One wonders where he was while this was going on.' Mr G stepped inside like a child on his first visit to the Crystal Palace. 'Taking tea with a vicar, I expect.'

Hesketh bristled at such profanity but held his peace.

I had seen a great deal of blood when I helped my father in his surgery and whilst I had accompanied my guardian on his investigations, but it never ceased to horrify me. Sidney Grice's face was alive, though, and I did not think it was just the flare of gaslight making it gleam.

The bed had been partially remade but left unchanged, and was heavy with stains. Great lakes of solidified blackness lay on the sheets, blankets and eiderdown, surrounded by smaller pools. The arched oak bedhead and the paisley papered wall behind it were smeared and bespattered with streaks and drops. The top of the two pillows was saturated in gore and still bore the imprint of the head that had lain upon it in those last agonized heartbeats.

'Who pulled the bedding back up?' Mr G probed.

Hesketh stood mesmerized by the scene. 'I did, sir. Inspector Quigley instructed me to reset the scene as closely as I could after Mr Garstang was removed.'

'How did your master's body present itself to you?'

'He was lying on his back, sir, with his arms under the sheets.'

'As I surmised.' Mr G shifted his weight. His right leg hurt him on prolonged standing, though he would never have admitted it. 'Proceed.'

Hesketh coughed. 'His throat had been cut. There was a gaping wound and a great deal of blood everywhere.'

'Did you touch anything?' I asked, unwilling to do so myself.

Hesketh interlocked his fingers. 'Nothing, miss. I shut the door and told Easterly to fetch the police.'

An empty picture frame lay face down on the dressing table, its back taken off and the contents removed.

'The Dürer?' I enquired and the valet raised his hands to chest height, perhaps in supplication, before confirming, 'The drawing of the lady.'

Sidney Grice was walking slowly round the bed, placing each foot carefully as if trying to step in another man's prints in the sand.

'Who lifted the pillow?'

'Inspector Quigley, sir.' Hesketh's voice was distant. 'He wanted to see if there was a knife underneath it.'

'And was there?'

'No, sir.' Hesketh blew out through his mouth. 'He put it back in exactly the same spot.'

'Oh, Hesketh.' Sidney Grice whipped out his spring-loaded knife and the blade flicked out. 'Untruths spray from your mouth like the venom of a spitting cobra. This pillow was replaced approximately fourteen degrees out of line as can be witnessed by the margins of gore around it.'

Hesketh flapped a hand. 'It was not a deliberate lie.'

My guardian levered a crusty plaque from the top sheet. 'A giraffe will be a giraffe whatever your intentions towards it.'

He popped his find into an envelope and pencilled a long series of numbers on it. 'Let us scrutinize the portal.'

There were two hefty brass bolts on the inside of the door but they hung loose now, the screws wrenched out of the battered woodwork, the brackets on the jamb into which they would have slotted torn out, the upper dangling by a bent screw, the lower lying on the floor. The white porcelain handles had been placed with their barrel in a change tray on the dressing table.

Mr G brought out his notebook and began to make sketches with his mechanical pencil. I crossed the room and opened the wardrobe. There was a strong smell of camphor and its hanging rail was crammed with coats and trousers and a long red dressing gown, all in pristine condition.

'Mrs Mortlock was always ordering clothes for Mr Mortlock from his tailors.' Hesketh came up behind me. 'But he wore few of them. He was a dapper man in his younger days and spent more than he could afford looking fashionable but, after the deaths of the Garstangs, he lost interest in such things.' He touched a smoking jacket hanging over the back of a chair. 'Most of the time he wore that.'

I searched the pockets – a tobacco pouch in one, a briar in the other, downy scraps of lint in both. Perhaps I should have been collecting samples of the fluff but I could think of no reason to do so.

'Take a look in Mrs Fortitude Mortlock's room.' Sidney Grice was scratching at the paintwork with his knife. I squeezed past and he tutted. 'Your skirts have removed at least four splinters and deposited two threads.'

And I saw that the cotton was plucked but not irreparably. There were actually five splinters. I picked them out. 'There you are. Have them back.' And I placed them in his hand.

'Thank you.' My godfather accepted them. 'I take it you do not want these returned.' He picked the threads off a ragged edge.

'I think I can manage without,' I assured Mr G. But he was already storing them away and all at once I felt like a suspect.

Hesketh followed me through and turned up the gas. The bed was still there, though covered in a dustsheet as were the dresser, chest of drawers and wardrobe. An enamelled mug stood on the washstand with a bar of soap in it and there was still a dusty puddle of water in the jug. There was a bar of partly dissolved soap in the jug and a brush behind it. A razor strop hung from a hook in the side.

'Not Mrs Mortlock's, I assume.' I ran a hand down the ragged edge and nicked myself.

'I kept it there to prepare Mr Mortlock's shaving things in the morning.' Hesketh offered me a handkerchief and I bound my finger. It was bleeding freely.

'How did it get damaged?' I asked and Hesketh shuddered violently as if doused with iced water.

'I can only assume the murderer did it trying to sharpen the razor.' He spoke the words as a schoolboy might recite a Latin verse which meant nothing to him.

The drawers were full of folded underclothes. I let the dust-sheet drop and something attracted my eye near the window drape: a man's green stocking. I held it up.

'Veronique often brings – brought – the laundry up at night.' Hesketh took it from me. 'And rather than disturb Mr Mortlock, she would leave it on the bed until the morning.' He rolled it into a tight tube. 'I suppose Miss Cherry will have it all cleared now.'

He helped me to lift a sheet and look inside the wardrobe. It was still packed with dresses, bright silks and flowery shawls.

'How pretty.' I picked out a cerise scarf.

'She had so few opportunities to wear them,' he said.

'Have you had any communication from her?' I picked up a pink slipper from the base. Fortitude must have had tiny feet.

'None, miss,' he answered ruefully.

I had a sudden thought. 'I wonder why the police did not take the strop.'

'It is not for me to say,' Hesketh said, though it was evident that he would, 'but how can I put it?' He lowered his voice.

'Inspector Quigley is a proud man, and I think when I suggested he might want to take the strop he decided to put me in my place by telling me he had no interest in such trifles.'

That sounded like the Quigley I knew and loathed. I tested the shutters. They were securely barred. 'What happened to this?' The left-hand curtain cord had been cut short. I wondered at how thick it was, but Quigley had been right about one thing – the length of material required for such a lofty room made the drapes exceptionally heavy.

'I had not noticed that before but we have always used the shutters rather than the curtains.' Hesketh checked the other one. 'This side looks all right.'

'Did you like Mr Mortlock, Hesketh?'

The valet crossed his hands at hip level. 'When he was a child and young man, very much. Master Nathan was a great favourite with the family and the staff.' A wistful smile appeared. 'He was such a mischievous child – never really naughty but full of pranks. Even as a young man he would get into scrapes, but he had such winning manners that he always talked his way out of trouble.'

'Except on the night of the murders,' I reminded him.

'I believe he was intoxicated on that occasion. Even so, he was too old for such behaviour, especially as he was a family man by then.' Hesketh's cheek started up again, but he kept his hands crossed and under control. 'His watch was stolen and he got into a fight with a man he thought had taken it. The man's accomplice joined in and Mr Nathan's friend, Danny Filbert, did likewise.'

'Filbert spelled with an F as with the nut?' I clarified.

'I believe so, miss.'

'What happened next?' I looked in a silver trinket box but it was empty.

'A lookout warned the pickpockets and when the police arrived they made themselves scarce,' the valet resumed his account, 'by which time Mr Nathan was so enraged that he fell into an argument with the policeman, then tried to push him

away, and both of them were arrested for being drunk and disorderly.' Hesketh smoothed out a crease in the carpet with his
foot. 'As things turned out, it almost certainly saved his life.'

I kneeled – no easy feat in a bustle – and opened the bottom
drawer. 'So he spent the night in a Marylebone Police Station
cell?'

'And was given a two-pound fine by the magistrate in the
morning,' Hesketh confirmed. 'Danny had no money and would
have had a short prison sentence, but Mr Nathan paid his fine
for him.'

'He was fortunate that his wallet was not taken as well then.'
I took out the neatly pressed white chemises and a pink petticoat.
There was nothing underneath.

'Indeed, miss.' Hesketh genuflected to help me replace the
clothes. He smelled freshly of coal-tar soap. 'And Mr Nathan was
even luckier than that. He got his watch back at the beginning of
this year, though in a rather ghoulish way.' Together we pulled
out the stiff second drawer. 'It was found on the body of a man
in the cellar of the North Wing.'

'The right hand side of Gethsemane as you face the house.'
I clarified.

'Indeed, miss.'

'How strange.' There was nothing under the camisoles. 'Who
found him?'

'A homeless family hoping to find shelter for the night, miss.
The mother told a constable.' Hesketh slid the drawer back.
'Might I ask what you are looking for?'

I was not going to admit that I did not have the slightest idea.
Sidney Grice could recognize a clue through a brick wall but, as
he was fond of reminding me, if the brick wall *was* the clue I
would not recognize it as such.

'Evidence,' I answered confidently and felt my way through
the next drawer. 'Did Mrs Mortlock take anything with her?'

'Only her jewellery and there was not a great deal of that.'
Hesketh stood up stiffly.

'Were you surprised when she left?' I made a half-hearted inspection of the top drawer and marvelled that anybody could need so many handkerchiefs. Perhaps Fortitude did a lot of crying, I speculated, taken aback at my own callousness.

Hesketh picked a dead moth out. Sidney Grice might have ranted at him for destroying evidence, but I made no comment as he let it fall.

'I was surprised that she left without Miss Charity.' Hesketh offered me his arm but I rose unaided. He would never have done the same to my guardian and I resented being treated as if I were helpless, though it would have made my ascent less of a struggle.

'This must be a miserable house to live in.' I steadied myself on the chest. 'And some of you must be frightened. Why has nobody left?'

'Where would we go, miss?' Hesketh looked at the shutters with no hope of seeing through them. 'We are all under investigation and who would admit a murder suspect into their homes, let alone employ one?'

Mr G was industriously measuring everything measurable when we rejoined him.

'I have found one piece of broken razor blade.' I held up the bloodied handkerchief.

'So I see.' He pencilled a few figures in his notebook. 'And so I heard. I shall take a look later.' He recorded the length of a diagonal scratch on a floorboard. 'But first I need to check all the locks and bars.' He opened his watch. 'The act will consume fourteen minutes and I trust no one else to do it. Go down and talk to those two servants again, Miss Middleton. They will be more relaxed with you. Pretend to be pleasant.'

'I shall try,' I promised.

'You,' Mr G told Hesketh, 'shall stand exactly where you are with your hands where I can see them.'

'Very good, sir.' Hesketh interlocked his fingers in front of himself.

'I heard your intercourse, Miss Middleton, and one of the

questions you asked was intelligent.' Sidney Grice leafed back though his book, at least four pages of hand-drawn columns crammed with tiny rows of numbers.

'Why would it not be? I am an intelligent woman,' I retorted, stung by his patronizing tone. 'Which one?'

He reeled his tape measure in. 'An intelligent woman would know the answer to that.'

'I am flattered that you trust me to walk downstairs,' I carped.

Sidney Grice dropped the measure into his satchel.

'Look upon it as a test of your initiative,' he challenged, unaware of how close I was to accidentally treading on his fingers.

And, on the way down, I heard an urgent message being passed.

'Hold your nerve, Veronique. They don't know anything.'

29

The Courtesan and the Mouse

EASTERLY LOOKED AT me expectantly as I returned.
'Am Hi to be untied, miss?' he enquired.
'Not yet, I am afraid,' I told him.

There was no point, I suspected, in asking about what I heard. He would only deny it and be put on guard. Better, I felt, to follow Sidney Grice's instructions and *pretend* to be pleasant.

'Only Hi don't feel right sitting while a lady stands.'

'Is that better?' I sat on the end of an ornate boot box.

'Thank you,' he said.

'Where did you get your accent from?' I asked. 'It is not like any Yorkshire I have heard.'

The box was very nodular.

'Hi taught myself.' Easterly lifted his chin proudly and I saw that it was dimpled, just like Edward's. 'By copying a toff. It is how Mr Grice and you speak, miss.'

'Is it indeed?' I murmured. 'How do you get your clothes on over that?'

Easterly tapped his plaster. 'Hi have cut the sleeve hoff my shirt and Veronique sews and hun-sews my coat sleeve every morning and night.'

'Did you hear or see anything different on the night Mr Mortlock was murdered?'

'Not ha sound or sight, miss.' He wriggled his neck.

'Did your employer act any differently?' A raised

ornamentation was digging in the back of my thigh – quite a trick through all my layers of cotton.

'He wasn't right the last week or so.' The footman twisted his neck in a circle. 'Not since the policeman came.'

'Did you like Mr Mortlock?' I struggled not to wriggle.

Easterly pulled his lips down. 'Not much. He was a quiet cove – surly, you might say – but lord, he had a temper.'

'Was he ever violent?'

'Not that Hi saw, miss, but he had such a tongue.' He wriggled his jaw. 'Though Hi never knew him shout at Mr Hesketh. Hi think Mr Mortlock had ha soft spot for him.'

I watched the footman as he answered me, and tried to think what I should be deducing. Mr G would have spotted a significant rip in a trouser leg or a nick in his fingerplate that would have solved everything, but all I could see was a pleasant man, discomfited and doing his best to cope with the situation.

'What sort of things did he get angry about?' I pressed.

'Anything and heverything and sometimes nothing.' Easterly shifted as much as he dared. 'His paper wasn't ironed properly. There was a cobweb that he must have crawled under the table to find. Whoever was around got it in the neck.'

I wondered if he would have found Sidney Grice any more amiable an employer, but I only said, 'Thank you, Easterly. If you can think of anything else, please let us know.'

I rose gratefully.

'How long am Hi to stay like this, miss?'

He looked so miserable that I would willingly have snapped the thread for him.

'Until Mr Grice decides otherwise.' I returned to the sitting room.

Veronique was still in her place.

'Have you had your tea?' I could see she had not.

'I do not like tea 'ow the English drink it with cow's milk.' She had little lively eyes that reminded me of a mouse.

'Then why did you add it?'

Her fingers were slender and pink.

'Mrs Emmett she say it is polite.'

'Mr Grice does not have milk,' I reminded her, and pulled out a chair on the opposite side of the table.

'Is Mr Grice polite?'

'Not very.' I stifled a laugh and sat to face her. 'What happened that night, Veronique?'

She puffed. 'I do not know, miss. I swear it. But I am foreign and so nobody like me and so everyone suspect me.'

'I think Easterly likes you,' I teased.

'I think so too.' Veronique went pink. 'But even 'e sometimes make fun and imitate 'ow I am speaking.'

'Your English is very good.'

She blinked rapidly. 'Not too good, I 'ope. Nobody want a French maid who speak like a – 'ow you say? – cockney.'

I laughed. 'I do not think you sound remotely like a Londoner. How long have you lived in England?'

'Five years,' she said. 'Five years too many. They are not nice people. Only last week 'Esketh unlock the garden so I can walk in it and, after 'e go, an old crone she shout and swear and 'it me wiz a 'orse dropping.'

'She was probably inebriated,' I suggested. 'Did you like Mr Mortlock?'

Veronique snorted. ''E is 'orrible. I 'ate 'im.'

'Enough to kill him?' I asked softly and she shrugged.

'Sometime but I do not do it.'

I felt the teapot. It was cold. 'Why did you hate him so much?'

''E try to – 'ow you say? – take advantage of 'is position.' Veronique's fingers closed round the arm of the chair.

'Did he force himself on you?'

She piffed dismissively. 'Not with blows. 'E start off being nice – too nice – telling me 'ow good I am at my job, how smart I look and then 'ow pretty. 'E give me an 'alf day then say I must spend it with 'im in the park. Then 'e keep ringing for me when 'e don't need me and find excuses for me to fetch things to 'is room.

'E put 'is 'and on my arm.' She patted her sleeve to demonstrate. 'And when I pull away, 'e tell me I must not be so stand-offish and remember my place. I tell 'im my place is to be a maid not a… courtesan. You know the word?'

'I know it,' I said. 'Did you never think of leaving? French maids are always much sought after.'

'And 'ow do I get a character?' Veronique weaved her right hand through the air. 'It is bad enough I do not know the story of this 'ouse when I come.'

'What will you do now?' I asked. 'Will you stay with Miss Charity?'

Veronique glanced nervously back towards the hallway and lowered her voice.

'I go 'ome,' she declared, 'never to brighten your shores again.'

'Not until I say you might,' Sidney Grice told her as he entered the room with Hesketh close behind. 'Come, Miss Middleton. If you have finished tittle-tattling, we have work to do.' He pointed at the valet. 'After Miss Middleton vacates that chair you shall occupy the one to the left of it.'

'Why not this chair?' I got up.

'Because it is an offence to decency,' my godfather informed me, feeling the quality of Veronique's sleeve. 'That seat is still warm.'

I went round the table. 'Did you find anything?'

'I always find something,' Sidney Grice told me as I followed him into the hall. 'The house is secure from ground to roof.'

'Hi could have told you that, sir,' Easterly volunteered from his chair.

Mr G pursed his lips. 'It is neither safe nor logical to assume that what you could have told me and what you would have told me, and what I might have believed, are one and the same thing,' he retorted without pausing in his stride. 'I never make assumptions and I am never illogical, though I am frequently unsafe. Why,' his cane whipped out like a rapier, 'have you burst your restraints?'

And I saw that Easterly was trying to hold the ends together.

'Sorry, sir,' he apologized ruefully, 'but Hi had to stand up to get this.' The tip of a peacock feather was sprouting from under his plaster. 'To scratch my wrist. It was driving me mad.'

'If only you could have been driven mad that easily,' Sidney Grice said to me drily. 'I shall not do something and you shall not do something else.' He marched jerkily down the corridor without pausing in his prophecy. 'I shall not waste further thread and you shall not quit your throne without my express permission again.'

I caught up with him as he stopped at the end stairs.

'Are we going down?' I asked.

'To an unspeakable place –' he unlocked the door – 'where servants rule and their masters fear them.'

30

Mutton and Mr Marwood

SIDNEY GRICE TURNED the key with great care not to rattle the lock, and inched the handle anti-clockwise to open the door, so slowly that I had difficulty seeing it move at all and found myself looking about me at nothing. When he had a three-inch gap Mr G brought the dental mirror, clipped it to the end of his cane and inspected the stairwell before flinging the door violently open.

'Do not be afraid,' he bawled down the opening, 'unless you murdered your master in which case you ought to be terrified.'

I listened but heard no response.

The steps were narrow and uncarpeted. They ran directly under the main staircase, into a whitewashed rectangular passage which must have been built directly beneath the hall but was much less wide. At the far end was a small, high-barred window through which I glimpsed a pair of clogs shuffling by.

The first doorway led into the servants' dining area with eight wooden chairs round a well-worn pine table. At the head sat a thin woman, verging upon being elderly, wearing a simple black dress and eating a slab of mutton. She looked up as we came in.

'Name?' Sidney Grice pounced towards her.

The servant half-rose with great difficulty. She was having trouble using her right arm and I remembered Cherry telling us about the head injury inflicted by Nathan.

'I am Mrs Amelia Emmett, the housekeeper,' she declared

proudly and toppled back into her seat. Her cheeks were grey and cross-hatched as if with a fine quill dipped in red ink.

A narrow opening led out of the room behind her right shoulder and she faced a closed door on the other side of the room.

Mr G tapped the quarry-stone floor with his cane. 'I shall do one thing and you shall do the other.' He put his ear to the whitewashed wall and rapped with his knuckles. 'I shall provisionally accept the truth of your statement and you shall stay exactly where you are with both of your unsightly proletarian hands resting on the superior surface of the table.'

Mrs Emmett clucked indignantly. 'I am in charge here and you cannot give me orders.'

My guardian's lips elevated at the corners.

'And I am the man whose investigations may entrust you to the tender care of Mr William Marwood, the staggeringly incompetent official hangman.' Mr G ambled behind her.

'I 'aven't done nothing.' Mrs Emmett's haughty manner and sham-refined accent temporarily collapsed into consternation.

'Your flimsy attempts at protestation will not rescue you from his attentions if I decide that you have indeed not done nothing.' Sidney Grice bowed until his head was alongside hers and whispered. 'Whilst there is breath in your clumsily constructed and poorly maintained body, you would be well advised to do as you are told.'

'Oh.' The housekeeper hugged her bosom as if it were a baby.

'What did Mr Mortlock ingest for his last meal?' Sidney Grice looked under an upturned bowl.

'Hagfish stew.'

'Sounds delicious,' I muttered.

'And so it was.' Mrs Emmett bridled. 'Mr Hesketh had a taste and said how sorry he was to be missing it, and that young police officer ate a whole bowl of it the next morning.'

'Are you the only one down here?' I asked.

'I was a minute ago.' Mrs Emmett eyed me coldly. 'And who might you be?'

'I might be anyone.' I helped myself to a chunk of meat from the carving board. 'But, fortunately for me, I am Mr Grice's assistant, Miss Middleton.'

I popped the mutton in my mouth. It was dry and not very fresh, but nonetheless a welcome change from the vegetarian fare of Gower Street.

'Oh yes – I've read about you – the downy one.' Mrs Emmett drew the joint away.

'Dowdy,' my guardian corrected.

'That as well,' she conceded.

The meat took a lot more chewing than I had anticipated and if I had been by myself I might have spat it out, but I covered my mouth and said, 'I think the word you are looking for is *doughty*.'

'Doubting what?' Mrs Emmett scratched her scalp with her fork and I began to think she might make a good companion for Molly.

I tucked the mutton into my cheek pouch and went to the door. 'Did this used to be the room of your predecessor, Amelia Seagrove?'

'What if it was?' Her jaw jutted indignantly. 'It's mine now.'

'Then it must also be the room she died in.'

Nancy Seagrove, the housekeeper, was killed with a single blow of a broad long-bladed knife, probably the same carver that was used on the other victims, George Pound told us. It went through her neck from right to left and ripped into her pillow, so she must have been lying on her left side. There was no sign of a struggle or even movement. She would have died instantly in her sleep. She was the lucky one.

31

The First Demon

IF MRS SEAGROVE *were to open her eyes she would see the shadow falling across her. But she is fast asleep, her hair undone, white and draped over her blanket like a mare's tail. And it's not until the knife rises in both hands high, like Abraham about to sacrifice his son, that I realize what is going to happen.*

'No!' But I can't scream and the knife is swooping down, and the only sound is the blade passing through her flesh like a spade being plunged into soil, then a thud.

Mrs Seagrove coughs and her eyelids flutter like the wings of a moth, and her mouth fills with life become death.

I pull the knife and her head lifts up with it. I put my hand on her head. It feels warm, like a living thing. And I pull again. I have to wiggle it a bit and the blood squirts into my eyes. It comes out suddenly and her head flops down.

I fall to my knees and bury my face in her sheet. It has the scent of soap. I never knew you could smell things in dreams. And, when I pull away, the image is preserved on the linen like that miraculous face of Jesus on St Veronica's cloth. But this is the face of Satan, not mine. MY face is in the water that I pour from the jug into the bowl, but it dives beneath the ripples as the murderer's fingers dip in and I hold my breath until he goes.

She could be alive now if not for that curtain.

32

The Psalms and the Bamboo Rat

I PUSHED THE door open and, uncomfortable at my own intrusion, tried but failed to swallow.

It was a small room with a bed, dressing table and chair, and a small armchair, but no natural light. 'Do you know how that drawing got under your bed?'

I closed the door, struggling not to choke.

'No.' Her face was lopsided. 'But if I had my way that filth would have gone in the fire.'

'Enough.' Sidney Grice slammed his cane on the table. 'Hands on top – now. Come, Miss Middleton.'

And both of us obeyed.

Directly off this area came the kitchen, the pans all polished, hanging from a row of hooks on a rack suspended from the ceiling, and a butcher's block at the end of a preparation table with nothing being prepared on it. The range was hot and it struck me as strange that Amelia Emmett did not sit beside it where she would be warm.

'It is beneath her menial dignity to eat in here.' My guardian must have added mindreading to his curriculum vitae. 'Upper below-stairs servants dine at table even when they are alone.' He took the lid off a red-enamelled caddy and sniffed. 'This tea is not fit to clean a carpet.' He pulled away. 'Small wonder somebody cut his throat.'

From the kitchen came the scullery, remarkably compact for

such a good-sized house, with its wooden draining boards and a barred and padlocked plain plank door. I managed to swallow the meat.

'I shall inspect the exits another time,' Mr G said, 'but let us build our premise for the time being on the possibly erroneous assumption that the doors and windows are all solid. What conclusions can we draw from that?'

'Perhaps the murderer was a servant,' I said, 'and did not have to force an entry. Or perhaps somebody managed to sneak into the house, hide, kill Nathan Garstang and hide again until he could sneak out.'

The meat was stuck halfway down my gullet.

'If somebody hid here I will find traces,' Mr G vowed. 'Where do you suppose that door leads?'

I ran a toe along the threshold. 'From the dust coming under it, I would say the coal cellar, which is why this room is so small. Our cellar goes under the pavement with the door in the moat, but there is no moat at the front here so the cellar has to extend into the house.'

I tried to punch my own back.

Sidney Grice produced a pair of dividers. 'But why secure the cellar so strongly if the only ingress from the street is through an iron lid which – or so we have been informed – is also locked?'

I had an uneasy suspicion that the mutton was trying to find its way back up.

'To stop anyone stealing?' I guessed, but my guardian tsked and remarked, 'The meat safe in the kitchen is not locked and servants are far more likely to help themselves to a joint of beef than a nugget of fossilized vegetation.' He made a quick series of measurements. 'This has been set four inches above the site of the original bolt.' He clicked his tongue like a disapproving schoolmistress. 'Yet Pound assured me that the old one was not damaged at the time of the massacre.'

'Perhaps it did not have a hasp to hold a padlock,' I suggested. 'But even without a padlock you would have had to break the door down to get in, for the weakest part is usually the fixing plate, but this goes straight into a slot in the brick wall.'

Sidney Grice made some more measurements. 'That is of little relevance to my puzzlement.' He reached into his inside coat pocket for his gold cigarette case and flipped it open. Where some kept Virginians, he had an array of keys and, instead of Turkish, lockpicks. He slipped out one resembling a darning needle, with a hooked point, and genuflected to insert it into one of the old screw holes. 'An empty hole.' He tutted and tried another. 'Ha.' He twisted his pick as if tackling a particularly complicated mechanism and slowly withdrew it. 'What do you make of that?'

Mr G passed me a tiny tube and I unrolled it, a torn-out scrap of paper.

'*In the name of the Lord I cut them down*,' I read in what feeble light seeped through the opening from the dining room. 'It is a psalm. Number 119, I believe.'

'Number 118,' Sidney Grice corrected me.

'Do you think it is a message?' I asked.

'Probably,' Mr G dropped the paper into a test tube where it promptly curled up again, 'not.' He opened the padlock with its key, slid the bolt back and pulled open the door. 'I do not feel tempted to enter in this remarkably fine attire,' he declared after a glance inside. 'Perhaps you would care to root about.'

'I would not.'

I just wished the food bolus would make its mind up one way or the other.

'When we return to 125 Gower Street –' Sidney Grice brought his oil safety lamp out of its asbestos pouch – 'consult a dictionary, preferably Johnson's. Webster's is American and therefore unreliable.' He lit the wick. 'I am convinced you will find that it defines an assistant as one who assists.'

'I wonder how it defines a guardian.'

It was a good-sized cellar, about twelve-foot square and brick-lined. A pile of coal lay on the floor about three feet high beneath the closed circular lid. Mr G extended his telescopic cane to almost twice its original length, hooked the lamp over the handle and held the light into the room at arm's length, illuminating even the furthest corners.

'The lid looks solid enough.' He raised the lamp to shine beneath it; the spring-loaded bolt was slotted into place. 'And even I, with my remarkable skills, could not have come through that hole on or after the fourth of January.' Sidney Grice raised the lantern to illuminate his point. 'That moss around the lid has not been disturbed in at least six weeks.'

'So not a means of entry for the murderer?' I raised my skirts but they were already dirty.

'Not unless he hid in the house for several weeks undetected – unlikely, but not impossible. Remember Sally Massie?'

'I will not forget *her* in a hurry.' I bobbed to pick up a stray chunk of coal and tossed it into the middle of the room. Several pieces rattled down. 'The whole pile would have collapsed if anyone had trodden on it.'

A few more lumps of coal clinked to the floor. I had started a mini avalanche, or was somebody trying to get out? A mangled hand broke through the surface on the nearest slope. For an instant I thought of a drowning man waving, and the priest who had been lost during a storm in the Bay of Biscay.

'Hurry.' I rushed into the cellar.

'I feel no compulsion to do so.' Mr G held back.

But I was scrabbling up the side – the pile collapsing around me – falling on to my knees to claw through the coal as once I had helped drag a worker from under the shale in Parbold Quarry. The hand came loose and I overcame my revulsion to whisk it up before it was buried again.

Sidney Grice lowered his lantern and, under its illumination, I saw that I was clutching the mummified corpse of a rat. I yelped and threw it back.

'Oh, I hate them.' I shuddered, remembering the night I had woken up in India with one running over my face.

'One day I shall tell you about the Case of the Large Bamboo Rat of Indonesia,' my guardian promised.

'Did it kill somebody?' I wiped my hand on my skirt.

'If only it had.' Sidney Grice was lost in thought. He dusted his hands with a white cloth.

The rat was rolling back down the incline towards me. I tried to boot it away and the pile collapsed around my ankles, throwing up another cloud of coal dust.

'Control yourself,' my godfather castigated me as I doubled up, catching his cane with my shoulder.

'I am trying.'

'Succeed.'

He was still in the doorway, his lamp swinging wildly to and fro, the face lit then hidden under a drape of dark which was just as quickly whisked away again. I put up my hand to steady it.

'Ouch.'

'Oil lamps get hot,' my guardian advised absently as I struggled but failed to fight down another coughing fit.

'Most likely.' Sidney Grice banged my back, more in irritation than sympathy and, at long last, the meat slithered down.

Mr G turned out his lamp. 'Congratulations on your find, Miss Middleton. Do you wish to take it home?'

'Do you think it is a clue?'

'Do you?' My guardian went back into the hall.

I took an old sack from a hook on the wall and found a short-handled shovel. 'I think we should let Inspector Quigley decide that,' I said and was rewarded with a snort.

33

The Eyes of Death

MRS EMMETT WAS still at the table, though, in defiance of my guardian's instructions, her left hand was no longer resting upon it. She was trying to harpoon the last pickled onion floating in a jar.

Sidney Grice rushed towards the housekeeper so violently that she yelped and slopped the vinegar.

'Oh, Mrs Emmett, Mrs Emmett.' He pushed his face almost into hers. 'When was the last coal delivery, Mrs Emmett?' He leaned forward and she tilted backwards and away. 'And do not attempt to distract me with your feminine wiles.'

'I couldn't say exactly, sir.'

'Then be silent, woman,' he snarled.

'Roughly,' I urged and Mr G snorted.

'At what juncture did we conclude that we would be satisfied with approximate evidence?'

'It is better than none,' I reasoned and, before he could respond, the housekeeper said, 'Just before Christmas.'

Sidney Grice shot up. 'You have an original, if somewhat bizarre, notion of what constitutes silence. I hope your concept is not universally adopted.'

Mrs Emmett stabbed her fork in again – she was holding it very oddly now – and the onion bobbed away. 'He was supposed to come the day Mr Mortlock died,' she recollected. 'Only his horse got spooked.'

'And now you are telling me when he did *not* come.' Sidney Grice snatched the fork from her hand.

'The coalman's horse?' I clarified. 'Not the drayman?'

'You're getting confused,' the housekeeper told me, her voice hollow and nasal. 'That wash when the Garshtangs were killed.' She cocked her head. 'Whash that ringing?'

'You are imagining it,' Sidney Grice said confidently for, if he could not hear a sound, there was none to be heard.

'And banging.' She covered her right ear with her left hand. 'Sho loud.'

'Are you all right?' I asked, concerned at her sudden deterioration in speech.

'Of course she is not.' Sidney Grice leaned over the housekeeper. 'This is highly interesting.' He clipped on his pince-nez. 'If I troubled to get out my mirror, I could show you that your right pupil is dilating whilst the left is not.'

'What?' I pushed in front of him.

'And, unlike mine, it is not vitreous,' he continued chattily.

'Whash?' Mrs Emmett slurred, the left side of her face collapsing.

'Can you lift your hands?' I asked her.

'Of cosh I can.' Her left arm rose but the right came up a few inches and flopped, and the housekeeper tried to rise.

'Sit back.' I pushed her firmly down. 'You are having a minor seizure but it is nothing to worry about.'

'On the contrary,' my guardian contradicted me, 'it is a great deal to worry about. From the speed of onset and severity of your symptoms I would wager – if I were a gambling man, which I am not – that your chances of making a recovery are exceedingly low as is your life expectancy.'

'Don't listen,' I protested, but Mr G was elbowing me aside.

'Listen very carefully,' he directed. 'You are almost certainly going to die very soon.'

'Whash?' The housekeeper tried to rise again but her strength was ebbing. 'Shwu.'

'If the Christian apologists are to be believed – and I am sceptical about some of their claims,' Sidney Grice carried on, 'you may be about to meet your creator and you would be well advised to do so with a good conscience.'

'Ish… Ish?' Mrs Emmett flailed, panic-stricken, but my guardian ploughed on regardless.

'Did you kill or help to kill Nathan Roptine Mortlock?'

Mrs Emmett's head went slowly side-to-side in desperate jerky denial.

I tried to silence him. 'For pity's sake.'

'Do you know who did, or anything about the crime that you have not revealed thus far?'

But a great calm fell upon Mrs Emmett. It entered her all at once. I forced my way between them and took her pulse.

'It was probably of great consolation to her primitive brain,' Sidney Grice commented in satisfaction, 'that she died whilst I was putting her in mind of her God.'

My guardian swept the remains of her last meal clattering and smashing away. He grasped the dead woman under her armpits, lifted her high and laid her on her back on the table. I tidied her clothes as best I could, crossed her arms and closed her eyes.

'God rest your soul.'

'Amen to that,' my godfather murmured, 'if he exists and unless she was the murderer or an accomplice.'

We went back upstairs.

'After he killed Nancy Seagrove, the murderer went upstairs,' George Pound told us, 'but then he came down again.'

'*How do you know?*' I asked.

'*There were bloody footprints on the servants' stairs, some very clear going up, but fading, and some very faint going down before they disappeared.*'

'*Do you mean that literally?*' Sidney Grice fiddled with the jackal ring on his watch chain. '*Footprints?*'

'Yes.' The inspector flicked off a stray spark that had jumped on to his trouser leg. 'The murderer had taken his boots off.'

'Hesketh, come,' my guardian called, as one might a dog, when we emerged, and the valet appeared.

Hesketh viewed us with concern. 'I am not sure if miss is aware that she has a few smudges...'

I did not trouble to check.

'I am sorry...' I tried, but Sidney Grice spoke over me.

'So am I,' he declared, 'for I intended to ask Mrs Emmett fourteen more questions and now she is a corpse.'

*

The fog had lifted a little more but I could still see no further than ten or fifteen yards. The roof at the end of the north wing looked in very poor condition, sagging in the middle with many tiles missing.

'Why did Nathan Mortlock not repair it?' I mused.

'A moot question.' Sidney Grice waved down a cab. 'Which we shall never be able to put to him.'

The hansom pulled over and the driver leaned out. 'I don't take blackamoors.' He cracked his whip and shot off.

34

The Axeman of Oxford Street

TWO MORE HANSOMS ignored us and only by virtually throwing myself at the horse of the fourth did I manage to get it to stop and persuade the driver to take us home for a triple fare in advance.

'Oh no,' Molly wailed as she opened the door. 'You aintn't not dead, are you?'

'Of course not.' I glanced at my reflection and understood her alarm. Streaky-faced, starry-eyed and seaweed-haired, I would not have liked to meet myself in a graveyard. My lip curled disapprovingly and, for a fraction of a second, my guardian's face looked through the glass back at me. *Good grief*, I thought. *I am turning into Sidney Grice.*

'You will take this overcoat to the laundry,' Mr G unbuttoned his Ulster, 'along with all the other items of my apparel, which I shall deposit in a brown paper parcel outside the bathroom door.'

'You could do with being sented to the laundry yourself, miss.'

I deposited my sack on the floor and Molly skittled back as if she knew what it contained

'Sent,' I corrected shortly, for I did not need anybody else to tell me what a mess I looked.

Molly wrinkled her nose. 'Don't smell like scent to me.' And I was not sure if she meant me or my find.

Sidney Grice started up the stairs.

'So you are bathing first?' I put my hands on my hips, but took them straight off again because I knew he would think the pose indecent.

'Of course,' he responded over his shoulder. 'There might only be enough hot water for one bath.'

'A true gentleman,' I muttered.

'Where?' he enquired without pausing in his ascent. 'You had better deal with him, March.'

I dropped my cloak and hat on to the doormat and followed him up, holding my skirts in to avoid touching the wallpaper.

'I am sorry,' I called back. 'I am getting dirt on your clean carpet.'

'Is it mine?' she crowed. 'You aintn't not died and I get a stairs carpet. What a dead lettuce day this is turning in to be.'

Forty minutes later I had a bath. The soap would not dissolve properly in cold water and I had to scrub very hard to get clean. My guardian was gleaming and finishing his tea when I went down.

'I have been waiting for twelve minutes,' he complained. 'Really, March. You are getting very selfish.' He put his cup down and sprang up just as the doorbell rang. 'Come along, God-daughter. We have work to do.'

Some girls were skipping outside, two of them turning a length of laundry line, while three of them jumped over it chanting.

> *'Lizzie Shepherd got the chop*
> *Right above the drinking shop.*
> *Janie Donnell got chopped too.*
> *Turn around. (They spun in the air) It could be you.'*

I shivered. Real murders did not strike me as something to be made a game of.

'Rivicenta,' Mr G mused.

Neither of us would forget that message in blood on the back-room wall of the hardware shop on Mangle Street.

A girl on crutches came by. 'Come and join us, Dotty,' one of the girls called out as we climbed into our cab.

She hobbled over and a smiling redhead held her crutches while two bigger ones held Dotty under the arms and jumped with her.

'How kind.' I reached into my purse for some pennies.

'They will get a shilling for the pair if they are lucky,' Sidney Grice predicted and I looked back to see the redhead running down the street, the crutches tucked under her arm.

'How desperate they must be to do such things,' I pondered.

'Indeed,' Mr G agreed. 'Desperately wicked.'

Marylebone Police Station was almost empty apart from a short stubbly man in a faded checked jacket with a ragged-edged sandwich board advertising:

THE

QUEEN

MUST

DIE

He stood forlornly by the desk, Constable Perkins keeping a tight hold on his collar.

'I keep trying to tell the officer,' the man objected to me. 'It said *The Queen must diet* and, when people asked me why, I direct them to the new gymnasium on Tott'nham Court Road, only some bleedin' likkle bleeders chopped the end bit orf when I was 'avin' an 'am san'wich.'

The bottom right corner of the board was certainly chewed away.

'Just get out,' Sergeant Horwich said wearily.

'But, Serg,' Perkins protested.

'Out,' Horwich pointed to the door and the man scuttled gratefully off.

'But, Serg,' Perkins said desperately. ''E nearly caused a riot on Oxford Street. 'Ave you seen the back board?'

The stubbly man had reached the main door now. At his back, scrawled in fake blood were the words:

I WILL KILL

HER MYSELF

WITH A

AXE

'Oy! Come back,' Horwich bellowed, but the man lifted his boards off and flung them at the pursuing constable, striking him hard on the right knee, and raced off down the street. Perkins howled.

'Wet bleedin' blanket,' the sergeant mocked. 'You run like a fropping girl – no offence, miss. Couldn't arrest my granny in a wool shop.'

'Can and did,' Perkins muttered as he rubbed himself better.

'Quigley,' Mr G rapped.

'Out on a case,' the sergeant fired back.

'Pound,' my guardian tried.

'Out on a case and may be some time.'

'How could he not be?' Mr G screwed up his face and his lip curled in *that* way. 'But, as there is nobody I wish to speak to, you will have to do.'

Horwich's massive military moustaches waggled. 'I am touched by your faith, Mr Grice.'

'You cannot be touched by what does not exist,' my guardian affirmed.

I placed the sack on the desk. It had leaked coal dust on to my once-blue dress and seemed to have no intention of stopping as it showered over the register.

'Fropping heck.' Horwich brushed the powder with the side of his hand, smudging it over the morning's entries.

'First, watch your language and, second, *remanded* usually contents itself with one *m*.' Sidney Grice blew a speck off his glove.

'Please tell Inspector Quigley that I found this in the coal cellar of Gethsemane,' I announced.

Perkins was hobbling dramatically around the lobby.

'Guess-so-many? That's the Garstang place,' Horwich realized.

'I know,' Mr G said. 'I was there when it was pronounced properly.'

'So I'm supposed to tell the inspector you found an old coal sack in an old coal cellar?' Horwich wiped his hand on a crumpled sheet of paper.

'Tell him to look inside it,' I advised. 'And, in case he is wondering, that is the part not on the outside. Tell him I would like his opinion as to whether or not it is a clue.'

Horwich received the command uneasily. 'Inspector Quigley don't apprecionate being told what to do.'

'I know.' I looked down and wondered if I could claim a dress allowance on expenses. 'I only wish that I could be here to watch you tell him.'

The door flew open and a man shouted, 'Gotcha, you bleedin' rascal.' There were sounds of a scuffle and then, 'Come 'ere, you bleedin' tyke.'

'Harris.' Horwich threw up his hands in despair as the door slammed.

'You were here when Nathan Mortlock was arrested for being drunk and disorderly, weren't you?' I asked and Horwich tapped his register, though it could not have been the one in question.

'Booked him in.' He mimed writing with an empty hand. 'Booked him out.'

'And you saw him during the night?' I stuffed my gloves in my pocket.

'You are nearly as good as Quigley at writing people's statements for them,' Mr G complained, but I ploughed on.

'Did you not?'

'Three times,' Horwich confirmed. 'I remember that

particularly because I don't usually go down, but Mortlock's friend was causing trouble.'

'What kind of trouble?' I ploughed on.

'At last, a non-leading question.' Sidney Grice leaned over to pick up a charge sheet, but Horwich slapped his hand away.

'Shouting and screaming, and he got his belt round the door bars and was threatening to hang himself.' Horwich chuckled. 'Some of the others was yelling to get on with it and let them get some kip.'

'He was not in the same cell as Mortlock?'

'They were kept separate after their fight.'

'I thought they were fighting the constable who arrested them,' I objected.

'We could stay comfortably at home while you write this out,' Mr G complained.

'According to Dutton, the arrestin' officer, they were fighting everyone and anyone.' Horwich pulled at his mutton-chop whiskers. 'The joke being that the real criminals, the pickpockets what stole his watch, got clean away.'

'If that is your idea of a joke,' Mr G turned his attention to a pencil shaving on the desktop, 'you would be wise not to bother pursuing a career on the stage.'

'You would probably be better at that than me,' Sergeant Horwich retorted. 'We often have a good laugh when you've been in.'

Mr G's expression was serene. 'Fools often laugh at the wise. That is why they are fools.' He put the shaving back where he had found it.

'Did you see Nathan Mortlock actually in his cell that night?' I asked.

Horwich chewed on his pen. 'I do remember Mortlock sticking his face to the bars and shouting out to his friend to have some sense.'

'At what time?' Mr G licked his finger and held it up as a man might check the direction of the wind.

'It was a long time ago and it didn't seem important 'til afterwards.' Horwich shrugged. 'But I think I said in my report, about four.'

'O'clock.' Mr G completed the sentence when it became obvious that the sergeant thought he had already done so.

'Is there any way he could have got out in the night?' I asked and Sergeant Horwich took a gulp from his enamelled mug of cold tea. 'You've spent a night there,' he reminded me. 'Those cell doors could withstand a battering ram.'

'What about the back door into the yard?' I persisted.

'Withstand two rams, that would, and I...' he tapped his right breast pocket, 'keep the key on me the whole time I'm on duty. I check 'em in and I check 'em out, and nobody goes strawberry-picking in the meantime.' The door opened. 'What the hell is it now?' he roared as Constable Harris struggled in with a small boy under his arm.

'Nabbed 'im stealing a gent's hankychief, Serg.'

'Name?' Horwich sighed.

The boy wriggled frantically. 'Oliver Frippin' Twist.'

'One P or two?' Sergeant Horwich picked up his pen.

'Home,' said Sidney Grice.

35

Crushed Flowers and Hearts

N ELDERLY WOMAN was sitting bent over on the top step when our cab deposited us outside our front door. She was clad in ragged mourning, her clothes unevenly dyed black and her veil so heavy that I doubted she could see through it. A bouquet rested on her lap, no more than a big bunch of wilted weeds.

'Clear off,' Sidney Grice poked at her stomach with his cane.

'She is not a piece of rubbish,' I objected.

'She smells like one,' my guardian retorted, with no attempt to lower his voice.

The woman started as from a deep sleep. She looked up but I could still see nothing of her. She grasped her bouquet in a gloved hand and struggled to rise.

'Let her rest,' I said. 'She is not doing any harm.'

The woman wheezed with the effort of getting to her feet.

'If I let her stay she will frighten off clients,' Mr G reasoned, 'and the next thing you know, she will have invited her family and friends to join her and be letting out the top step to lodgers.'

The woman was swaying now, though she did not appear to be intoxicated. The odour of sewage about her almost made me retch.

'Was that you under the tarpaulin the—' I began, but the woman stumbled and fell forward.

Sidney Grice stepped aside, but she snatched at his coat with her left hand and her right swung up, crushing the flowers against his breast. Sidney Grice grunted and pushed her away. The woman pulled at her bouquet but for some reason it stayed stuck to my guardian's coat. She let out a small cry and released her weeds, but still they stayed suspended.

Mr G put his hand to the greenery and it flew into the woman's face. She squealed and pushed him and he, taken off balance, toppled back against the railings that separated him from the moat.

'Stop her,' my guardian gasped, but I was transfixed by the sight of a carving knife sticking out of his coat.

The woman ran. She dodged behind a milk cart and round a furniture van.

'Mein Gott!' Sidney Grice surveyed the end of the blade projecting from his chest and the worn wooden handle. 'She has stabbed me through the heart –' he coughed three times in rapid succession – 'of my notebook.'

He jumped down the steps and looked about, just in time to see his attacker dropping under a brewer's dray twenty yards up Gower Street and disappearing from sight.

'What the hell—' I began.

'Language.' My guardian put a hand to his chest to hold his book and heaved the knife out. 'Though hell may very well be from where she came.'

And as he rang the bell I bent to pick something up – a tiny silver locket that she must have dropped. Perhaps it had a name inside.

'Stop dawdling,' Sidney Grice said as I stuffed it away.

36

The Prince and the Patella

MOLLY'S MOP CLATTERED in the hall and I refrained from speculating who could be at the door, having been subjected to my guardian's sarcastic responses in the past.

'Who on earth can that be,' he pondered, 'other than the entrancing Miss Mortlock?'

He whisked off his patch.

'How can you tell?'

Molly opened the door.

'At five thirty every evening Jarvis Thripple, the gentle beadle of University College, checks the windows of the lecture theatre in the anatomy building, which even you must have observed is opposite our happy home. Academics often fling them open in futile attempts to stop their students from falling asleep.'

Sidney Grice strained to insert his new eye, but I knew better than to offer assistance.

'But that was...' I checked the mantel clock, 'two hours and forty-two minutes ago. What of it?'

'He was six minutes late this evening as Dr Morrianty the gastrologist has a slight speech impediment.' Mr G frimped up his pink cravat. 'However, the end result was the same. Thripple lowers the roller blinds, thereby doing me the great service of converting the window into a serviceable mirror.'

The front door closed.

'So you saw her reflection?'

'Indeed.'

Molly trundled in, her cap secured at a rather precarious angle. 'That lady what aintn't not Goodsmell any more,' she announced.

'Mortlock,' Mr G snapped.

'But I dontn't know how to,' Molly stammered.

'Congratulations, Molly.' Her employer ran his fingers back through his thick black hair. 'You have redefined the zenith of ineptitude.'

Molly blushed and when Molly blushed she went a very deep puce indeed. 'Why, thank you, sir. I do my besterest.'

'Show... her... in,' he said.

'So I don't need to mort-clock?'

'Not today, thank you, Molly,' I said and she wandered confusedly away.

Sidney Grice leaned, his elbow on a filing cabinet in a rather theatrical study of casualness, and Molly returned, bellowing in fine parade-ground fashion, 'Miss Charitable Morgue Lock.' Her voice dropped to a stage whisper. 'That's a bit like what you was trying to get me to do, sir.'

'Tea,' Mr G barked and she scuttled away.

Cherry Mortlock marched in and refused my offer of a chair as I got out of it. 'I shall not be staying.'

'You will,' my guardian argued, 'though possibly not for long.'

Cherry's manner was brusque. 'I have had no communications from you, Mr Grice.'

'I am delighted to hear it,' Mr G breezed, 'for I have sent you none.'

Cherry lifted her veil back. 'Most private detectives send their clients daily progress reports.'

'So I believe.' Sidney Grice straightened up. 'Indeed, Charlatan Cochran has been known to send three or four in as many hours, but I imagine that you are labouring under many misapprehensions, Miss Charity Clair Caroline Mortlock, two of which are

of immediate significance, and I shall therefore enumerate them.'
He took a step towards his client. 'First, I am not, nor ever have
been, nor ever shall be, a private detective. My services are
without equal and they are personal.'

Cherry tugged at her gloves. 'You are playing with words.'

'I never play.' He touched his eye.

'He does not,' I confirmed.

'Second –' my guardian took another step, his feet in line like
a tightrope walker – 'I have no progress to report to you.'

Cherry ripped off her left glove. 'You have made no progress?'

'Have I not?' Mr G opened his hands in a gesture of surprise.

Cherry gaped. 'You have just admitted it.'

Sidney Grice looked at her pityingly. 'I merely remarked there
was none I ached to report.'

Cherry Mortlock looked askance at me and I shifted awkwardly. 'Mr Grice does not like to discuss his methods.'

'But I am paying him to keep me informed.'

'To be fair,' I reasoned gently, 'you are not paying Mr Grice
anything at present and, when you do, it will be for capturing
your father's murderer.'

She gripped her glove in her right hand. 'But I want to know
what you are doing to achieve that end.' She looked down at my
godfather, standing before her, the image of hurt innocence.
'What are you going to do tomorrow?'

Mr G toyed with the patella of Charlie Peace that he used as
a paperweight. 'We shall be doing something I detest doing and
quitting this splendorous, squalid metropolis.' He weighed the
patella in his hand. 'On a journey to Crowthorne in the expectation of interviewing Senorita Angelina Innocenti.'

This was as much news to me as it was to our visitor.

'I am not interested in the lies and fantasies of a raving lunatic
about a crime she committed eleven years ago,' she fumed, and,
if Cherry's glove had been a living thing, she would have squeezed
the life out of it in her blanched fist.

'And I am not especially interested in what interests you.'

Sidney Grice selected the jawbone of Captain Johns, the Droitwich Diabolist, as a counterweight and inched towards her, arms out wide for balance. 'Which is one of the fourteen reasons we shall never go shopping together. I am interested in the truth and that is what I shall discover.'

'Perhaps the same person who killed the Garstangs attacked Angelina and killed your father,' I tried to justify our plan.

'I do not necessarily subscribe to that theory.' My guardian swayed.

'Then why in heaven's name are you going?' Cherry demanded and Mr G frowned.

'I am not altogether sure,' he admitted.

Cherry banged on the round central table with the side of her fist.

'I knew I should have gone to Mr Cochran.' She banged again in frustration.

Sidney Grice stepped off his imaginary rope. 'That is a meritorious scheme,' he concurred with alacrity, 'if you wish to squander your inheritance and let your father's murderer roam free, and if you wish to dismiss all your servants or spend the rest of your life uncertain if one of them slaughtered him and will do the same to you. At least Cochran will supply you with plenty of reading material for those long, lonely and impoverished winter nights.'

Cherry raised her chin defiantly. 'You cannot frighten me, Mr Grice.'

'Oh my dear, young and not unattractive Miss Mortlock,' my guardian blinked slowly, 'I promise you that I can, but that is not my intention. I merely wish to keep you out of the clutches of an incompetent fraud. You would be better off giving your money to my maid.'

'Oh yes, please.' Molly struggled in with a tray. 'Is it a lot? Please say yes and I can buy a cottage in the sea.'

'What on earth is that?' I pointed to Molly's stomach, bulging and writhing as if she had swallowed a live python.

'It's a nice house,' Molly enlightened me. 'I thought you might have known that, but then you don't refine the zenits off neptitude like I do.'

The side of Molly's apron exploded in a streak of white as Spirit sprang free and on to our client's breast, almost knocking her over.

'What in the devil's name?' Cherry rocked the round table with the swing of her bustle. 'You have no need to go to Broadmoor, Mr Grice.' Cherry shook with rage as she disentangled Spirit's claws from her scarf. 'Shall I enumerate?' she mocked. 'First, you are in a madhouse already – home sweet home for you, Miss Middleton – and, second, I have taken you off the case. And you can whistle for your bills or expenses.'

My guardian pondered briefly. 'Even on a good patch I should have to do an awful lot of whistling to collect that amount of money.'

'Bahhhhh!' Cherry Mortlock flung Spirit away and barged past Molly, who up until then had done sterling work in keeping her tray horizontal.

'Oh no!' Molly wailed as our periwinkle tea service shattered on to the floor. 'That'll all come from my wages what I dontn't not never get.' She hurled the tray into the pile, smashing a previously undamaged sugar bowl, and rolled up her sleeves. 'I'll knock your crudding dong-faced face off your crudding head,' she roared.

'Molly!' I put out my arm but Molly was beyond reason. She charged into the hall as the front door slammed, but even that did not give Molly pause for thought. She flung the door open and leaned out.

'And dontn't not come back, you ugly old grotch, only you aintn't not really old.' Molly's voice suddenly sweetened. 'Oh, good evening, Pruffelia. How clement it is for this time of year.'

Molly stepped back into the house.

'Oh, Molly, what have you done?' I cried, and her knuckles went into her mouth.

'Oh lor', miss. Whatever *it* is, I've been and done it good and unproper this time.' Her face drained as her employer limped grimly into view.

'You had better go and pack your bag,' he said, with a quietness that chilled us both.

Molly crumpled and when the blood returned to her cheeks it was in flared vertical streaks.

'We have a long journey ahead of us tomorrow.'

'Oh...' I said.

'And you, Molly, had better get a brush and dustpan.'

'Oh...' Molly said.

'You did well tonight, but for future reference I believe the expression is *dung-faced*,' he told her.

'But—' I said and he waved his right arm high in fury.

'Nobody – not Alexandrina Victoria, Her bovine Majesty the Queen; not her son, Albert Edward, the corpulent Prince of Wales; not her Prime Minister, that vile egalitarian, William Ewart Gladstone; not the doubtless tedious man who disappears elephants, who, incidentally, you may have an afternoon off to see, not the meddlesome Miss Florence Nightingale with all her demon army of nurses – *nobody* is allowed to throw my cat around like that.'

I did not mention that Spirit was supposed to be *my* pet but when Molly had disappeared in a daze down the steps, I went up to my guardian as he stood surveying Spirit, none the worse for her experience and lapping at the milk and sugar, and, to his undisguised disgust, I gave Sidney Grice a kiss on the cheek.

*

I read my Bible as always that night. Mr G had been right about the number, of course. It *was* Psalm 118.

Give thanks to the Lord for he is good. His love endures forever.

I closed my eyes and prayed, *Let it be true. Please let it be true.*

37

Trails and Snails

S IDNEY GRICE WAS down to breakfast before me as usual the next morning, scribbling such copious notes in the margins of his dog-eared book that the printing was almost oblit- erated. He had cancelled his usual stack of newspapers that morning after an argument with the newsagent about the delivery coming five minutes early and disrupting his routine.

'Drabden's *Biochemical Analysis of the Mucoid Trails of Terrestrial Pulmonate Gastropod Mollusca*,' I read when he grudgingly showed me the cover.

'Snail slime,' he interpreted, though I could have worked that out myself.

'And snail slime to you, dear guardian.' I did not trouble to look under any of the three silver domes on the sideboard, but sat at my end with a rack of pale toast. 'Have you had any more thoughts about that woman who attacked you yesterday?'

'Yes.' Sidney Grice crumbled his charred toast into a bowl of prune juice.

'Do you think she might have been somebody, or connected to somebody, you helped convict of a crime?' I put the egg in a silver cup.

He stirred the mixture with his knife. 'Yes.'

'Or a dissatisfied client?' I cut the top off my egg.

'Did she look like a woman who could afford my outrageous fees?' He sipped from his soup spoon, creating a rather dashing thin pair of sepia moustaches.

The locket was still in my other handbag and I resolved to fetch it the next time I went to my room.

He turned back a page to underscore a word and broke some more toast into his prune juice.

'Did you write this book?' He jabbed at it with his pencil. 'You might as well have, for it is riddled with feminine illogicalities.'

'Are you angry because Cherry Mortlock has taken us off the investigation?' I spread the conserve.

Mr G gaped. 'When?'

'Last night.'

He ran a hand over his brow. 'I wish I had known that before I put my travelling stockings on.'

'But you were there.' I gaped back at him. 'In your study, just before Molly nearly gave her a right hook.'

'Molly's most favoured punch is actually her left jab,' he informed me, then tapped the table as a toastmaster might for silence. 'I think I know where your stupid misinterpretation of events was created.' My guardian dabbed his mouth with his napkin. 'You have created a silly fantasy that, when Miss Mortlock said she had taken us – to quote her peculiar turn of phrase – *off the case*, she was empowered to do so, whereas once I accept an investigation it is in my written terms that only I can decide whether to abandon it or not.'

'But if we carry on anyway,' I cut my toast in half, 'surely she will refuse to pay us.'

'Not necessarily –' he stood up – 'for I shall discover the identity of her father's murderer.' He checked his watch. 'Come, March, we leave in thirty-seven minutes.'

'But that gives us plenty of time.' I reached for another slice of toast.

'Not if you are to put on something presentable to wear.' Mr G wandered to the window.

It was a new indigo-blue dress with puffed sleeves and a tatted collar, and I thought I looked rather smart in it but, apparently, I was wrong.

38

The Menace in the Mist

OUR TRAIN SET off at eight o'clock, but it was almost noon by the time we reached our destination.

We began with a seemingly interminable cab ride to Waterloo, then there was a delay while a reported bomb in the waiting room was investigated. It turned out to be a wrapped dolls' house, forgotten by a harassed mother, but since the Fenian dynamite attacks at Paddington and Westminster Bridge stations the previous October, the authorities could not afford to take any chances.

We disembarked at Crowthorne and took a fly through the pretty village and out on to the country lanes, winding through the tightly packed pines of Bracknell Forest and up an incline to the hospital.

Broadmoor Hospital rose menacingly through the mist, a huge mass of red-bricks, every window barred and towers flanking a massive arched gateway.

My guardian watched me closely.

'I am afraid I do not recognize anything,' I told him as we disembarked. 'I was very confused at the time.'

'I have never seen the point in being confused.'

A jolly attendant checked our papers against his register and signed us in.

'She don't get many visitors,' he said and passed us on to the deputy director, Dr Whelkhorn, an equally jolly man with a drooping left eyebrow and an arched right, who told us, 'She doesn't get *any* visitors, not one, and I was here before her.'

Whelkhorn was a tall grey man with long arms hanging loose almost to his knees. His bony wrists projected at least an inch below his cuffs and there was something odd about his hand that I could not immediately identify when he took mine.

'Welcome back,' he greeted us both expansively.

We followed him down a long well-lit corridor, the tall windows on our right looking straight across the grounds towards the opposite wing. Most of the doors to our left were wide open, revealing the empty cells.

'Where are the occupants?' I asked.

'Most of them are in the recreation rooms around now,' our guide replied.

'Recreation?' My guardian puffed indignantly and the doctor chuckled. 'This is a hospital, not a gaol, Mr Grice. We have patients not prisoners.'

'Dear lord.' My guardian shook his head in disbelief. 'I have helped put three men and two women in here. I might as well have booked them tours with Thomas Cook.'

'But they are ill,' I protested.

'They are mad,' Mr G insisted.

Dr Whelkhorn's grizzled eyebrows separated.

'We have suspended the playing of croquet,' he admitted, 'since our Supervisor Mr Orange was attacked by the Reverend Dodwell with a mallet, in 1882.'

Sidney Grice tossed his hair. 'I have long ruminated on my Great-Aunt Drophsilla's hypothesis that insanity is contagious.'

Dr Whelkhorn frowned as he chewed the thought over.

'I have never met your Great-Aunt Drophsilla,' he declared at last, thereby dismissing her theory. 'But what a beautiful name. Was she pretty?'

'I have heard her compared,' my godfather tugged his waist-coat down as if preparing to meet his relative, 'unfavourably to a fruit bat.'

Somebody was whistling close by – 'Lily Bolero' – and I remembered a military band playing and a young man in uniform, the sun beating on his golden hair and catching his spurs, and his eyes flooded with love as he kneeled in the dust before me.

A rosy-cheeked young woman appeared through an open doorway as we approached. She smiled prettily.

'Then you shall die the rather for that,' she told me conversationally.

'Good old Blossomy.' Whelkhorn wiggled his strange fingers at her as we passed by. 'She's a laugh.'

For once I joined my guardian in failing to see the joke.

We stopped at a locked door where a muscular middle-aged attendant was leaning against a wall, humming 'Jimmy the Fish' and, on Dr Whelkhorn's instruction, he got out his keys.

'I should tell you that Angelina has not been herself lately,' Dr Whelkhorn warned as the warden put a key in the lock. 'She was always a gentle soul until about a week ago when she became subject to sudden tantrums.'

'Do you know what set her off?' I enquired.

Sidney Grice put his left eye to the spy hole.

'It was around the time that Miss Grebe from the next cell along –' Whelkhorn pointed to another open door – 'escaped. They used to be friends but they had a fight in this corridor on the last day, a real rough-and-tumble it was, and it unsettled Angelina a great deal.'

'How did she get out?' I tried to ignore the man with a broom who winked and leered as he passed by us.

'We do not know,' Whelkhorn confessed.

'Stupid man,' Mr G muttered, pausing to examine a pencilled message on the wall.

'Are you not worried that somebody else will use the same means?' I asked and his eyebrows lurched towards each other.

'But,' the doctor fiddled with his right eyebrow, 'if nobody else knows how she did it, then nobody else can.'

'I was overly kind with my last remark,' my godfather said.

'She has never attacked me or any of my colleagues, but I cannot vouch for how she will react to strangers,' the warden said and pulled open the door.

At first the cell appeared to be empty, the bed and chair unoccupied, but then I saw a pair of boots immediately to my right. The patient sat on the floor, her knees pulled up, her hands clasped round them and her head bowed so that we could only see her long, greying taupe hair. She did not react to our entry.

'Good afternoon, Angelina,' I said, but there was no response.

Sidney Grice marched four paces to the far wall, gazed up at the barred window and swivelled smartly round. He dropped to his haunches and peered under the bed.

'Interesting,' he said, jumping up and striding back towards the patient.

'She has been like this since the fight,' Dr Whelkhorn told us.

'Even at night?' I asked, for I knew from experience how cold a cell floor could get.

Dr Whelkhorn shook his head but said, 'Yes.'

There was still no reaction from the figure on the floor.

My guardian bent over her like a proud father inspecting his newborn heir and asked, 'To whom does that highly polished pair of brown boots under the bed belong?'

'Boots?' Dr Whelkhorn echoed.

'Highly polished,' Mr G reiterated.

'Why, they belong to Miss Angelina,' Dr Whelkhorn replied, as if he expected to be admitting Sidney Grice imminently.

'Then why,' my guardian demanded, 'is she wearing this pair?' He rested the tip of his cane on the toe of one boot.

'Well, she can hardly wear both pairs at once.' Dr Whelkhorn guffawed. 'Many of our patients have changes of clothing. They—'

'The fact that you are a halfwit does not entitle you to babble like one.' Sidney Grice raised his hand. 'Listen and learn.'

'Well, I...' Dr Whelkhorn blustered but nonetheless complied.

Sidney Grice pressed on his cane, his knuckles blanching as he ground it into the leather.

The patient jumped but stayed hunched over.

'You are hurting her,' Dr Whelkhorn protested.

'Am I indeed?' Mr G pursed his lips. 'Do you concur with the doctor's diagnosis, Miss Middleton?'

'Ouch,' the patient cried out.

'Yes.' I grasped his sleeve. 'Stop it.'

Sidney Grice gave the cane one final twist and pulled away. For a moment I thought he had used his spike stick with which he had pierced a man's foot for insulting me one afternoon in Kew. I was relieved, therefore, to see that the leather was dented by the outline of the ferule, but not pierced.

'That was pointlessly cruel even by your standards,' I scolded and Mr G shrugged.

'I am not a kind man,' he conceded, 'but my brutality is never gratuitous.' His voice rose. 'Is it, Miss Grebe?'

Dr Whelkhorn wagged his outraged fingers in my guardian's face. 'It is bad enough that you assault my patients, Mr Grice – and you need not imagine that you have heard the last of this – you might at least have the courtesy to get her name right.'

Sidney Grice's eye flickered as he withstood the flapping.

'When you have a spare fourteen seconds, take a look at that highly polished brown footwear, Dr Whelkhorn,' he said, 'and you may notice that they are a great deal smaller than the pair which this patient is wearing.'

'But her feet fill the larger pair or she would not have felt you squashing the toe of her boot,' I realized.

'Precisely.' My guardian smiled thinly. 'She would have had to have her feet bound at birth to fit into that pair beneath the bed.'

Dr Whelkhorn's left eyebrow drooped to almost obliterate his pupil. 'But I have seen her wearing them.'

I clicked my fingers – another habit my guardian abhorred in women.

'Perhaps you saw Angelina Innocenti wearing them,' I suggested, and the doctor rounded on me.

'Do you not understand either?' His shaggy right eyebrow

jiggled about. 'This *is* Angelina Innocenti. I should know my own patient.'

'Indeed you should,' Mr G agreed heartily. 'Which makes your failure to do so all the more culpable. She said *ouch*.'

'Of course she did,' Whelkhorn shouted, beside himself with frustration. 'What of it?'

'Many foreigners, including the attenuated and knock-kneed French, the Italians, Germans, Japanese and Bulgarians do not say *ouch*. Neither do the unfeasibly tall Swedes.' Mr G tugged at his earlobe. 'They ejaculate *aie, ahia, autsch,* 痛いで, *ox* and *aj* in that sequence, whereas –' he turned his attention to the other lobe – 'the Spanish are content to cry out *¡ay!* when expressing their appreciation of pain. Need I go on? I can.'

Sidney Grice prodded the figure with his toe and she balled up tighter, but a low, deep and quite musical sound emerged from within.

'Descuse meo, senior, but me do not know-ay key you mean-o.'

'That is Miss Angelina's voice,' the doctor declared triumphantly. 'I have heard it many times.'

'I can only suggest,' Sidney Grice told him, 'that you invest in an especially enormous and extraordinarily sensitive ear trumpet and use it at all times, though it will not compensate for the feeble and haphazard functionings of your primitive neural tube.'

'How dare you?' Dr Whelkhorn tore the air between them apart.

Mr G ignored his outburst. 'That was the worst attempt at an accent I have heard since Miss Middleton's derisive effort to counterfeit a dialect of the East End.'

'It fooled the mob,' I retorted indignantly, for I had saved his life by pretending to be a cockney when he was being attacked.

'There is scant skill in fooling fools.' My guardian grabbed a fistful of the patient's hair, wrenching her head up and back, and a face leaped out, distorted with rage, purple-rimmed indigo eyes straining to spring out at him, a tangled mess of green teeth jutting through fissured lips.

'Scut-nosed scrab,' she hissed and her clawed hand lashed out, her black and broken nails lashing at my guardian, but his cane whipped up and knocked her arm away. 'Frebbing grut,' she cursed, nursing her injured wrist.

'Good afternoon, Miss Grebe.' Sidney Grice greeted her more cordially than he did most clients.

The patient kicked out but Mr G stepped elegantly aside.

'But it is not possible,' Dr Whelkhorn whispered and Sidney Grice wiped his hand, a digit at a time.

'My dear doctor,' he said patiently, 'it is not possible that it is not possible because it has happened. This unhygienic representative of the female sex is none other than Hezzuba Punsella Chevita Grebe, the notorious pigeon poisoner of Primrose Hill.'

'But...' Dr Whelkhorn sagged inside his suit. His lips kept moving but nothing emerged except a tiny squeak eliding with a hiccup.

'So the woman who escaped was Angelina Innocenti,' I concluded for the doctor's benefit.

Hezzuba Grebe jumped into a crouching position, snapping the air rabidly. She reminded me of the faux mad women I had seen in India, eating grass to make themselves foam and get alms from people who were terrified of touching them, mainly British visitors.

'Precisely.' Sidney Grice prodded the prisoner in the stomach with his ferrule and she fell back into the corner. 'I feel obliged to commend you, so-called Dr Whelkhorn. Whilst detaining a dispenser of avian toxins, you have allowed the putative slaughterer of the Garstang household to decamp from what is supposed to be the most secure madhouse in the country, free to rampage unfettered through this wretched land, and you have not even noticed.'

'But...' Dr Whelkhorn rubbed his eyes yet, when he opened them, it was still the wrong patient. 'How?'

'That is a fourteen-guinea question.' Sidney Grice let his handkerchief fall and limped from the cell. 'Though I anticipate you will want it answering for free.'

39

The Last Straw and Wicked Wicked Women

'THE EXPLANATION IS certain to be simple,' Sidney Grice prophesied when we were in the doctor's office, a large room, freshly distempered and with two high windows overlooking the treetops.

Dr Whelkhorn steadied his left hand with his right as he poured himself a sherry. He gulped half of it down and topped up his drink before remembering to offer my guardian some.

'I never ingest alcohol,' Mr G told him. 'If I wanted to be befuddled I could beat myself unconscious with a plaster bust of Napoleon.'

'Steadies the nerves,' the doctor mumbled.

'Addles them,' my guardian corrected him.

'I will have one,' I put in.

'Are you old enough?' he asked over me to my guardian.

'I was old enough to be incarcerated here,' I reminded him.

The doctor looked embarrassed. 'Quite so.' And he dispensed a glassful. 'An amontillado,' he told me. 'There is a very good merchant in Duke's Ride.'

My guardian clucked. 'Shall I proceed or am I interrupting your festivities?'

Dr Whelkhorn drained his glass in a series of quick sips and joined us standing by a weakly gleaming coal fire. 'Are you quite cured now?'

'Mad as a parsnip.' Sidney Grice picked up a stack of unopened letters from the mantelpiece. 'Describe precisely and concisely the circumstances in which your Hispanic inmate absconded.' He leafed through the pile.

'Both women did voluntary work in the kitchens.' Dr Whelkhorn watched my guardian uneasily. 'Miss Grebe, being crippled from a failed escape bid nine years ago, would sit at a table and prepare vegetables. Senorita Innocenti often sat with her to help. On that occasion they were sorting through old sacks of vegetables for the slop wagon. We sell our waste to a local pig farmer.'

'By the name of?' Sidney Grice tossed two letters unopened into the bin.

Whelkhorn pulled his nose thoughtfully with his unusual hands. 'Jones Fred Jones.'

'Fred Jones,' I repeated.

'Jones Fred Jones,' Whelkhorn corrected me, and I realized that his thumbs were as long and slender as his fingers and had three joints each.

'And what was wrong with the pickled herrings?' Sidney Grice held a letter up to the light.

'But how on earth...?' The doctor stopped, baffled, but my guardian did not trouble to enlighten him and I was too proud to express my own surprise.

Whelkhorn pushed on his nose as if reattaching it. 'We had a rotten batch.'

'Supplied by whom?' Mr G rubbed his wounded shoulder.

'I do not remember details like that,' Whelkhorn protested. 'Tullbride's, I think.'

'If only you could.' Mr G slipped one letter into his pocket and quelled Whelkhorn's unspoken objection with a halt sign.

'So is it possible that Angelina Innocenti escaped with the rubbish?' I proposed.

'This foolish man will insist that it is not, but it is exceedingly likely.' My guardian leaned back against the wall.

'But the wagon is always carefully searched,' Whelkhorn protested.

'Is the rubbish put into any containers?' I asked and Mr G raised his left eyebrow in commendation.

'Barrels.' The doctor helped himself – but not me – to another sherry. 'But they are checked and filled in the presence of a warder. We are not as stupid as you suppose, Mr Grice.'

'You cannot begin to imagine how stupid I suppose you to be,' my godfather said amiably. 'If your men are doing their jobs properly, it would be almost impossible to quit this establishment in a slop barrel.'

'And they are packed so that nobody can hide behind one,' the doctor stated confidently.

'What about the herrings?' I asked.

'There was no point in repacking those.' Whelkhorn sucked his sherry out of the glass. 'The barrel was full of vinegar so, even if you managed to climb into it, apart from the mess you would create, you would drown in a fraction longer than the length of time you could avoid respiring.'

'You would be well advised – assuming you are literate and I have no evidence that you are – to read that educational tome, *The Art of the Cooper*, by a retired cooper conveniently named Mr Cooper. Though you may have as much trouble finding it as you do your escapees, for only twenty-five copies were ever printed and thirteen were destroyed in the great flood of Abingdon, and I shall not lend you mine.'

'What are you talking about?' Whelkhorn ran his strange thumbs over his temples.

'Barrels,' I told him, though that was as far as I understood the gist of my guardian's ramblings.

'The pickled-herring barrel, as supplied by Tullbride Brothers and eight other merchants of whom I am aware, has an unusual design and for good reason. Fantasize that you are trying to get the last few fish from the barrel. You would have to drain it and climb inside, a superlatively unpleasant prospect.' He rubbed his back up and down on the wall. 'To rescue you from this fate, the barrel is made tapered towards the base rather than with the conventional bulge in the middle. Bamboo hoops are affixed inside the receptacle on which trays some seven or eight inches deep can be rested, the smaller trays at the bottom, of course.'

'So, as you work your way down, you just have to lift out the next layer.' I tried the doctor's chair behind his desk.

'Even a woman can grasp the concept with greater rapidity than you,' Mr G told the doctor, to both our indignations.

'So Angelina climbs in, somebody puts the top tray or two back in so that if the lid is lifted to all appearances there is a barrel full of rotting fish, and nobody wants to root about too much in that,' I concluded.

'Oh.' Dr Whelkhorn poured another sherry.

'Did nobody see her?' I swivelled from side to side.

'Angelina attacked Warden Wilde as the wagon was being loaded – at least we thought it was her, but it must have been Miss Grebe, I suppose. She bit his hand as he passed her table and would not let go.' Dr Whelkhorn watched in disbelief as Mr G selected another letter. 'That envelope is marked *highly confidential*.'

'Fear not.' Sidney Grice opened it. 'I shall not divulge its contents to another living soul –' he perused the contents – 'unless I choose to do so.'

'I must insist.' Dr Whelkhorn snatched the missive from my guardian's hand and I glimpsed a coat of arms on the heading.

'So Angelina Innocenti and Hezzuba Grebe swapped places,' I calculated, 'and, behind all that hair, nobody noticed.'

'Oh my goodness.' The doctor put a fist to his mouth. 'Somebody must have helped Senorita Innocenti into the barrel and put the tray back over her. We are dealing with a mass conspiracy of bestial criminal lunatics.'

'I thought you said they were patients.' I spun on the chair but it jammed halfway, so I had to shuffle it back to face him.

'That was before all this.' Whelkhorn gnawed his fingerplates in what looked like a parody of anxiety. 'We had to carry the woman we thought was Angelina back to her cell face down because she kept twisting over.'

'And the reason she sat on the floor all that time was because she could not get up.' I was having trouble doing so myself with my bustle snagging on the back bars of the chair.

'This is all a dream.' Whelkhorn confided to himself, picking up a sealed envelope.

Mr G tossed a circular on the fire, scattering cinders on to the hearth.

I struggled free.

'If Hezzuba Grebe was a poisoner,' I remembered in surprise, 'why was she allowed to work in the kitchen?'

'It was a question of trust.' Whelkhorn laughed emptily, the envelope escaping from his hand as unnoticed as had the senorita.

'But why did she do it?' I asked, raising my glass in the hope that our host would notice it was empty.

'She claimed that she resented all birds for making her name ridiculous, and all people for making jokes about it.' Sidney Grice rooted through the open drawer, bringing out a discoloured ivory page-turner.

'I am surprised the court was so lenient after all those deaths.' I placed my glass upside down on the desk, just in case he thought I had not drained it dry.

Mr G inserted the blade of the turner into a thick blue book. 'She was fortunate to go before a sympathetic judge, Lord Swan.' He flicked open the volume and clipped on his pince-nez. '*Poldark's Diseases, Disorders and Dysfunctions of the Human Cerebrum,*' he remarked. 'His chapters on cranial measurements are highly original.'

'Quite so.' Whelkhorn forced himself to calm down. 'There is a lot to be said for the science of judging people's intelligence and personality by the shapes of their skulls.'

He pivoted awkwardly to pick up the letter.

'A great deal,' my guardian concurred, flipping through the pages, 'of tish-tosh.'

This, it appeared, was the last straw for Dr Whelkhorn. He

stamped his right foot and then his left, and then his right again, in an ungainly sort of war dance.

'Damn you, Angelina Innocenti; damn you, Hezzuba Grebe; damn you, unknown inmate or inmates who abetted her; damn you, Mr Sidney Grice.' He scrunched the letter into a ball and threw it at my guardian. 'Damn your eyes,' he yelled.

'Ladies,' my guardian reproved.

'Damn their eyes too,' Dr Whelkhorn raved, spraying white flecks around the corners of his mouth. 'Those wicked, wicked women, luring and taunting me with their pretty promises and fascinating bosoms, betraying me with their sweet deceptions.' He was vigorously spraying now.

Mr G extracted the page-turner. 'If it is of any interest,' he conducted something between a gavot and a waltz, 'I can tell you exactly where she was at twenty-six minutes past three yesterday post-meridiem.'

I wiped my sleeve. 'So that woman with the bouquet—'

'Surely, Miss Middleton,' my guardian closed the book, 'even your tobacco-damped senses must have appreciated the delicate perfumes of sour herring.'

'Quite so,' the doctor said because, of course, that had been his deduction all along.

Sidney Grice held the page-turner at an angle convenient for running our host through.

'Some might think that congratulations are in order, Dr William Walter Wilfred Wickery Warren Whelkhorn.' Mr G slapped the page-turner down so hard that I was surprised it did not shatter. 'You have set a homicidal lunatic upon the greatest personal detective in an empire upon which the sun is always setting.'

Dr Whelkhorn struggled to reconstruct his dignity. 'You may go now. I have work to do.'

'Yes indeed,' Sidney Grice agreed. 'You have a great deal of professional ignorance to dispel and knowledge to acquire.'

'And a fugitive patient to look for,' I reminded him as he hustled us out.

40

The Wages of Justice and the Burning of Bodies

A HOSPITAL VAN WAS about to set off to collect a prisoner from the station. Despite and because of Sidney Grice's peremptory manner, the driver agreed to give us a lift so long as my guardian sat in the back with the warders.

'That was productive,' he announced, rejoining me on the platform. 'After I tactfully exposited to my travelling companions how incompetent they were, they expressed the hope that one day they might be looking after me.'

'I am sure they meant it kindly,' I comforted him.

'I do not doubt it,' he agreed in all seriousness.

The train arrived on time and we settled into an otherwise empty compartment near the front.

'Why should Angelina Innocenti want to kill you?' I asked.

My guardian shook his insulated flask sadly. 'Probably because I refused to help her defence.'

'Did you believe her to be guilty?' I tried to ignore my craving for a cigarette.

'More importantly than that –' he pulled out the cork and upended his bottle, unwilling to admit to himself that it was empty – 'I believed her to be poor.'

'And you would not help her because she could not afford your outrageous fees?'

A drip fell on to the back of his hand just as it had that day in my cell.

'*You are hiding something from me,*' I said.

'*No,*' Sidney Grice told me very quietly. '*I am hiding a great many things.*' And then, '*If ever you get out of here, do you want to leave our home?*'

'*Where would I go?*' I was fascinated by an arc of blood vessels on the back of his hand. '*You are my protector and you called it our home.*'

My guardian patted my shoulder awkwardly and I looked down to see a drop of water falling for ever until it burst.

'Quite so.' Mr G slipped his flask away. 'I had another reason but, before you give vent to a bout of Middletonian self-righteousness, perhaps you would be so delightful as to satisfy my curiosity. How often do the police, the clergy, Members of Parliament or the admirals of our unparalleled fleet work for no remuneration?'

He spread out his copy of the *Bloomsbury Bugle*.

'I think you know the answer to that,' I replied grumpily, for it was difficult to live with a man who was always right, as my best friend Harriet often affirmed. I opened my Henry James novel.

'According to this, Dr William Price has been arrested for attempting to incinerate his dead son,' I was informed from behind the curtain of newsprint.

'I have no objection to cremation,' I chatted. 'It is common in India and shows every respect for the dead.'

'I care not a jot about what they do to cadavers three thousand, six hundred and fourteen miles away.' He lowered the screen. 'But to burn anyone here is an abomination.'

I resisted the temptation to hurl my book at him. 'You think an Englishman's body is worth more than that of an Indian?'

Mr G considered my question. 'A maharajah's corpse might be ransomed for more than that of one of the street vermin one stumbles over daily.' He forced his eyelids apart and dropped his glass eye into his palm. 'But I am more concerned with the criminological aspects. A body burned may be innumerable clues destroyed.' He shook out a lavender patch. 'How on earth could I have solved the Camden Vampire Mystery if those remains had been no more than eight bucketfuls of ashes?'

He raised the curtain and I reflected how Harriet had told me I was lucky. Her husband only thought he was infallible. My guardian very nearly was.

'What does that say on the back page of the *Bugle*?' I asked and he tsked.

'Even you might have observed that I have got no further than page three and am trying to read a report on the effects of vibrations from our underground railways on the habits of earthworms.' Nonetheless he folded his paper and turned it round. '*Horse Predicted the Murder of Reclusive Mr Nathan Mortlock*,' he narrated. 'I might have known. It was scribbled by the juvenile hand of your drinking companion, the Trumpeter.'

It was true that Traf Trumpington had bought me brandy once when I was upset by the murder of the Reverend Jackaman, but I had regarded him with nothing but suspicion since he wrote scurrilous innuendoes about my guardian and myself. I decided to let Sidney Grice's barb pass.

'What does it say?'

'See for yourself.' Mr G thrust the paper at me and I scanned the four columns.

'*Mr Gerald Feather, a Bloomsbury coal merchant, claims that his horse Megan has psychic powers because she was spooked—*'

My guardian pulled a sour face. 'How loathsome that last word is. I believe it is Dutch in origin but expropriated by those renegades who describe themselves revoltingly as,' he swallowed, '*Americans*.'

'Just as the day before the Garstang family was massacred, Boadicea – the horse belonging to Mr Nig, a purveyor of spirits – stampeded, when he was lifting a crate of sherry from his cart, the same thing happened to the coalseller's horse, Megan, the day after Nathan Mortlock met his end.' I précised and skimmed through the article. 'He says Megan has always been a placid animal and never pays any attention to shouts, the torments of street urchins or the noises of traffic, but she bolted in Burton Terrace on that one occasion.'

'Fascinating.' Sidney Grice brightened briefly.

'Surely you do not believe the story,' I protested. 'She is probably getting old and he wants to sell her to a travelling show – like that monkey who was supposed to be able to sing.'

'How cynical you are becoming.' My guardian observed me sorrowfully. 'I am delighted to note. Still, he may be worth interviewing.'

'You cannot be serious,' I objected.

'I am not in the habit of manufacturing comic entertainments whilst being propelled along the London and South Western Railway track.' He snatched his paper back. 'I am struck by the claims that the first horse predicted death but the second detected it.' He ripped out the article and stuffed it into his satchel. 'If the owner of the unfortunately named Megan were inventing the story, surely he would pretend his mare had foretold the murder too.'

We rattled over the points.

'So now you are a woman of means,' George Pound said, 'and therefore beyond my reach.'

I forced myself to concentrate.

'Do you think Easterly was telling the truth about having an itch?'

'Not entirely.' My guardian unhooked the leather window strap. 'He lied about staying in his chair. In the process of examining his shoes I dabbed the soles with a slow-setting ink.'

'The metal bar,' I recollected.

'The Grice Patent Marking Rod.' He pulled the strap up a notch to close the window.

'So he left marks on the floor.' I wished it had been a corridor train, then I could have gone up the corridor for a smoke.

'The process of deduction goes some way beyond repeating what you have been told, but in a slightly different way,' he expounded. 'And, to save your tongue from further unnecessary exercise, the exuberantly dubbed Sou' Easterly Gale Nutter left evidence that he had walked some distance along the hall away from the pot of peacock feathers. Unfortunately, the ink was exhausted after five paces but the marks were close enough together to suggest that he was creeping.'

My guardian folded the newspaper with great care.

'He may have been trying to walk off his cramp.' I suggested. 'There are several innocent explanations for his action.'

'But none for his lies,' Sidney Grice retorted. 'I shall interrogate him about it tomorrow after my appointment with one Joseph Penton, known to his customers as Bookie Joe.'

'What time are we setting out?' I enquired.

Sidney Grice clapped the back of his head and his eye shot into his other hand. The suddenness of it still unnerved me sometimes, with that dark cavity staring into my mind.

'We?' he cried in astonishment.

'But we always question witnesses together,' I protested and waited for him to list the many times when we had not.

My guardian polished his eye. 'My dear March Lillian Constance Middleton, I have a much more important task for you than that.' He glanced at my book. 'What are you reading?'

'*The Portrait of a Lady*,' I told him.

'Not a description of you then.' He sniffed and returned to his worms.

41

The Man in the Shrubbery

IT WAS NOT difficult to find where Gerald Feather lived – the *Bugle* had said he was from Francis Street Mews – but I hesitated to go along the narrow cobbled alley, ankle-deep in filthy straw mucked out from the stables either side and clogging the wide central gutter. The last time I had been there I was kidnapped and thought that I was about to be killed. At least this time there was no van waiting to rush me away.

A stocky man, even shorter than I but solidly constructed, leaned against a wall, hands in overcoat pockets. He was sucking on a long clay pipe but still managing to whistle – 'My Mother was a Mermaid in the Sea' – and he had just got to the part about *cockles* and *bokkles* when he looked up. A grey-green cloth drooped over the top of his head, but it was not this makeshift cap that obscured his face. His hair was so long and tousled and entangled with his whiskers, beard and moustaches that you might have thought a pitchfork of garden waste had been deposited over him.

The pipe wiggled in a figure of eight. 'There don't be no carriages for 'ire down 'ere,' emerged from the undergrowth.

'I am looking for Gerald Feather,' I told him.

If he had eyes they were well hidden and I marvelled that he could see me through the untamed shrubbery in front of them.

'Why?' It sounded like he spat but nothing broke to the surface.

'I am interested in his horse.'

I moved closer to the man to allow a handcart to pass. There was the shape of a small body under the sacking and the youth who pushed it was sobbing.

'Why?'

I noticed that the pipe was unlit and the bowl empty apart from a crust of tar.

'Would you like a cigarette?' I wanted one myself if only to fumigate the air between us.

'Ciggies is for girlies.'

'I wish you would tell my guardian that,' I said.

'And who might 'e be then?'

The cart passed and I stepped gratefully back but into something that squelched unpleasantly.

'Mr Sidney Grice,' I told him, pulling my foot out of whatever it was.

'Old Puddin'?' emerged from the undergrowth. 'Why's 'e so interested in my Meg?'

'I only know he is willing to pay...' I struggled to remember what Mr G had told me about the rates for extracting information, 'a shilling for your account now.'

A sickening guttural sound bubbled somewhere deep inside that wilderness. 'That geezer from the paper gave me ten bob and a quart of brandy for my story.'

I could not imagine Traf, with all his experience at extracting information, paying more than sixpence, though the brandy sounded more his style. I had my flask of gin on me but I could not bear the thought of it passing through that filthy mass into whatever existed as a mouth within it.

'What a pity,' I said. 'He only gave me a shilling. I am sorry to have wasted your time.'

I knew from experience that most hagglers will let you walk at least six paces before relenting, but I was still turning away when an arm shot out in front of me like a ship's boom in a storm.

'A shillin' it is then,' he said gruffly, 'but don't you be lettin' on I spoke for so cheap.'

I unclipped my handbag. 'Can I see Megan?'

'That's a two-shillin' job, that is.'

I clipped up my bag. 'What a shame.'

He gripped my cloak. 'But seein' as I feels sorry for you with your looks an' all, we'll throw 'er in for free.'

The man stepped aside and opened the top half of a stable door, and an elderly dappled horse poked her head out, blinking at another ashen London sky.

'When you said she was *spooked*, what exactly happened?'

Whatever I had trodden into was still trying to glue me to the cobbles.

'I never said *spooked*,' he complained.

I patted the mare's nose. 'So what happened?'

The coalman recited at a gallop, 'I'm deliverin' a load to 28 Burton Cressint next door, but they 'ave the road up so I 'ave to park up alongside the Gaslight Lane 'ouse, Geth-what's-it's-name.' He took a breath before cantering on. 'I'd just emptied my first sack and started back when Megan puts 'er ears back and bolts. She's round the Cressint and 'alfway up Flaxman Terrace to Bibberough Street wiv the baker's boys goadin' 'er on afore I catches up and calms her down. The end. Pay up.'

'And she has never done anything like that before?'

'Not never,' he asserted and stuck out his paw.

'What sort of accent is that?' I raised my arms.

'Where?' he looked about in expectation of an accent snuffling up the alley.

Feeling more than a little self-conscious, I flapped my cloak like a demented crow and jumped towards Megan, shouting, 'Boo!' at the top of my voice. Megan regarded me politely and I opened my bag again. A shilling for her master and a potato for his horse.

42

❖

Sarus Crane and the Caspian Sea

C HERRY MORTLOCK WROTE me a letter. She was sorry that she had thrown Spirit off her like that, but she was distracted by my guardian's and Molly's behaviour on top of all the grief and confusion that she was suffering already. She hoped that Spirit had not been injured or used up any of her lives.

Cherry had gone to see Charlemagne Cochran on Baker Street and found him to be a charming man, most reassuring and efficient. His fees were almost as high as Sidney Grice's but he promised to bring the matter to a speedy conclusion. She was meeting him at Gethsemane herself that afternoon and he was bringing a team of experts with him to search the house from top to bottom.

She hoped that she and I might remain on amicable terms but never to see my guardian again.

You should quit 125 Gower Street, March, for Mr Grice will bring nothing but misery and peril into your life, she wrote.

Cherry Mortlock was by no means the first person to give me that advice.

Dorna Berry had written: *I am afraid for you, March. You must leave that house. Leave it today or Sidney Grice will destroy you, just as he destroyed me and just as surely as he murdered your mother.*

But I did not want to leave. Where would I go? He was my protector and one of the only two men I had left to love.

'Nobody could love you like I do,' Edward had said as we sat by the lazy green river watching a Sarus Crane, so tall with its grey-blue plumage, its face and neck ruby red, foraging with its steely spike of a beak for freshwater crabs on the opposite bank. 'Only I know that it is your imperfections that make you perfect.'

And we kissed until I thought we would melt together, and walked hand in hand along the bank. That was before Edward tripped on the root of a jujube tree and fell into the river, dragging me in with him.

'Come, March.' Mr G bustled into the study. 'We must leave in four minutes.'

'But where are we going?'

'Euston Station,' he replied with exemplary forbearance, for there was nowhere else we could possibly be going.

'Oh, but where are we going to?' I was not really dressed for a long journey.

'Eus-ton Sta-tion,' he repeated loudly and slowly. 'Is that too complicated a concept for your feminine cranium to absorb? Dear lord!' Sidney Grice dashed to the mantelpiece. 'One and a half minutes slow.'

He hinged open the front of the clock.

I tried again. 'Where... are... we... going... to... from Eus-ton Sta-tion?'

'To 125 Gower Street.'

I swallowed a small scream. 'You will be happy to learn, beloved Godfather, that it has not escaped my notice that we are already at 125 Gower Street.' I spoke through clenched teeth. 'So why, in the name of Lucifer, are we go-ing to Eus-ton Sta-tion?'

He edged the hand forward.

'Because we have an appointment, though not with his satanic majesty.'

'You did not tell me that.' I folded Cherry's letter and Sidney Grice tutted.

'If you had had the foresight to force open the top middle

drawer of my desk, you would have seen it in my diary.' He closed the glass front. 'I must get that fool of a so-called clock repairer back. That is the second time in eight years it has gone wrong.'

He raced out of the room and I did not like to tell him that I had adjusted the time because I thought it was a fraction fast.

*

A hansom arrived almost immediately, but Sidney Grice sent it away as there was a plaque on the side advertising *Lilly's Ladies' Nervous Tonics*.

'But it's the top mustard,' the cabby protested.

'Then put it on your ham,' Mr G advised. 'I shall not be seen to endorse any product, least of all one for hysterical females. It is bad enough living with three of them.'

'Thank you very much.' I closed the door while we waited for the next knock.

'You do not thank me for insulting you.' He viewed himself approvingly in the mirror.

I did not respond, unsure if he was trying to outdo my sarcasm, in which case he was winning hands down.

The next cab was unadorned and therefore acceptable.

'I had a letter from Cherry Mortlock this morning,' I announced over the hubbub of traffic and the family at number 119 practising on their kettledrums.

'I know.' Mr G put his satchel on his lap.

'Did you see it?'

'No.'

We both tried to outwait the other.

'Then how did you know?' As almost always, I caved in first.

'I smelled it,' he recounted. 'Miss Mortlock wears an unusual combination of scents, which another man might find bewitching.'

'But not you?' We jolted into a poorly refilled trench where an electricity cable had been laid.

'As I'm sure you are aware,' Sidney Grice primped his necktie,

'I am not the kind of man to be seduced by intoxicating perfumes, nor enchanted by a sweet delicate face as pale as the waning moon, a trim waist, soft black hair or eyes reminiscent of the sun coruscating on the Caspian Sea at dawn.'

'No, indeed,' I concurred, seeing his face sparkling like the evening star over the slag heaps of Wigan.

'Nor dainty hands with long and slender fingers,' he added dreamily.

'She apologizes for treating Spirit so roughly,' I told him.

A mongrel darted at our horse's heels but a smart kick sent it rolling yelping away.

'I knew she would.' My guardian hugged his satchel.

'But she has engaged the services of Mr Cochran.'

I awaited the explosion but Sidney Grice only smiled serenely. 'She will come back to me.' A girl jumped on to the running board with a posy. 'They always do.'

'Flowers for the lie-dee.' She held them out enticingly.

'Not today, thank you very much,' he replied sweetly and poked her away with his cane.

43

The Stationmaster, Whisky and the Rabid Cur

EUSTON STATION HAD been my introduction to London when I came to stay with my godfather in May of 1882, and I had returned there a number of times to meet my best friend, Harriet Fitzpatrick, and whenever I travelled to and from Parbold. It had always impressed me with its grandeur, but there was something about it I did not like. Perhaps it was the absurdly grandiose entrance arch or the great hall dominated by a monolithic George Stephenson, grasping his frock coat in one hand and some important plans in the other. But I think it was the grand stairway that irritated me most. Partway up it split in two, fanned out and rejoined itself for the final ascent. It looked marvellous until you had to trudge all the unnecessary extra distance.

Our appointment was on the upper floor and Sidney Grice, who loved to sprint up stairs, grudgingly acceded to my request for an arm.

'I do not know why women dress so impractically,' he complained as a telegram boy pushed past us on his way down.

'Because men insist that we do,' I retorted. 'Would you allow me to wear trousers?'

My guardian looked nauseous. 'What a repulsive idea.' And he did not speak again until we reached the top.

The stationmaster's office was an imposing affair that might have been better suited to the ruler of a central European state than someone whose job it was to run the trains on time. But Mr Armstrong Bantam-Hoverly was definitely the person to occupy it. A man of majestic construction, he was enthroned behind a desk, the proportions of which could have housed a small family with livestock.

'Mr Grice.' His voice rang out like Hector's challenge to Achilles by the walls of Troy. 'This is indeed an honour.'

'For whom?' I wondered, unintentionally loudly.

The stationmaster rose massively, bewhiskered and mustachioed enough for a brigadier general, and bestrode the route round his desk to greet my godfather.

'For me,' he boomed, dwarfing Mr G as they shook hands. 'Why, this man is a giant.'

I stifled a laugh with great difficulty and he eyed me with concern.

'Do you need a glass of water, dear lady? I shall not insult you by tendering anything stronger.'

I rather wished he would but declined his kind offer.

'Mr Grice is the man who rescued the royal train,' Mr Armstrong Bantam-Hoverly informed me, but Sidney Grice held up a hand.

'Miss Middleton needs know nothing of that until she is twenty-nine.'

'Why, that will be at least a decade away.' I was not sure if the stationmaster was being gallant or insulting me, but decided to accept it as a compliment.

'If not more,' I said and he squinted through an embedded monocle.

'I doubt that,' he said gravely. 'Scotch and soda is your tipple, I believe, Mr Grice.'

'I shall not disabuse you,' my guardian said as Mr Armstrong Bantam-Hoverly trekked to a drinks cabinet just our side of the horizon, near a long high window overlooking the platforms, the mighty locomotives pulling in and out almost inaudibly through the glass except for the cheery farewells of their whistles. Busy people scurried by, some of them followed by porters struggling with cases or dragging trolleys, disappearing behind clouds of steam and smoke, the unmistakeable smell permeating everything.

The walls were of marble, lined with pillars and plinths bearing busts of Victoria and Albert, and many other men so important that I had no idea who they were. The stationmaster had his back to us, but I heard a clink or two and the syphon gurgling.

Sidney Grice leaned over and for a moment I thought he was going to blow in my ear. 'For five reasons which I shall not divulge, he cannot know that I do not take alcohol,' he whispered. 'You must find a way to drink surreptitiously.' He pulled away a fraction, embarrassed by our proximity. 'You have had plenty of practice at that over the years.'

'Practice?' The stationmaster returned with two capacious tumblers philanthropically filled.

'I am learning to play the bagpipes,' I lied and Mr Armstrong Bantam-Hoverly beamed with teeth big enough to carve epitaphs upon.

'As is my wife. You must come for dinner and bring your instrument.'

'It does not travel well,' I said. 'Shall I hold your drink, dear guardian?'

'There is a table over there,' the stationmaster pointed out.

'I like to hold it for him,' I insisted, snatching it off the tray and slopping some down my sleeve. 'Tell me, Mr Armstrong Bantam-Hoverly, who does that statue third from the left represent?'

'Sir Ian Coverly,' he told me, eyes fixed on my chest as if he had never seen one – or one quite like it – before.

'And is that your pet mouse hiding behind it?' I enquired.

'What?' He twisted his neck and I took a hasty quaff.

'I believe I spoke distinctly,' I said as he looked back

The stationmaster hurried over and I took another gulp. Whisky is not my tipple and he had hardly broken the surface with the squirt of soda but I struggled gamely on.

'There is nothing here.'

I swallowed. 'I must have meant the second one.' The whisky must have been at least half a dozen of my gin measures, and I am not stingy.

'Hurry up,' Mr G urged and I downed the rest in one.

Edward would have been proud of me, just as he was when I won the yard of ale contest at ladies' night in the officers' mess. He would have been less proud when I broke into a coughing fit.

'Dear me. I think you could do with something to settle your system.' Mr Armstrong Bantam-Hoverly spoke solicitously, dampening the base of a glass with water. 'And let me top you up, Mr Grice. I cannot see any mice.'

'A trick of the light,' I suggested.

'More likely your febrile girlish imagination.' He handed me my glass and took Mr G's empty one away. 'Come,' he barked in response to a knock, and the door swung open to reveal a tall, slim man with neatly trimmed moustaches and dressed in the dark blue uniform of a West Coast Main Line Railway guard.

The mighty Mr Armstrong Bantam-Hoverly put his and my guardian's tumblers down.

'Enter.'

And the guard came in, looking about himself like a child in a fairytale castle.

'Smith, this is Mr Grice.'

The newcomer took off his cap to reveal his short, light brown hair.

'And Miss Middleton,' I put in when it was obvious that nobody else thought it worthwhile. The whisky had gone straight from my empty stomach to my head, but I was pleased to note it had not affected my speech.

'Good day to you, sir, miss.' He was a quietly spoken man and I put his failure to make eye contact down to deference and diffidence rather than shiftiness.

'What is your full name?' Mr G asked sternly.

'Just John Smith, sir.'

'I do not like that name.' Sidney Grice hurred on his pince-nez. 'There are too many of you. A man might hide inside that name as a blade of grass might in a Shropshire meadow. Where were you born and what was your mother's maiden name, assuming that you were of woman respectably born.'

'Sedlescombe Road, sir, in Fulham. My mother was Mabel Lineker and my father was Alfred Smith.'

'I did not ask for that last piece of information,' my guardian said sternly, 'but it may be of greater use to me than you or I or my female companion can conceive at present.' He wrote the names in his notebook beside a symbol which looked like a child's drawing of a ship. 'Date of birth, if you know it?'

John Smith watched uneasily.

'Nineteenth of April eighteen fifty-one, sir. Am I in some kind of trouble?'

'It is not for you to ask me questions.' Sidney Grice added a mast to his drawing but it became something that looked like a daisy.

'You are not in trouble,' I reassured the guard to his undisguised relief.

There was another knock at the door and a man in a frock coat came in to announce, 'His Excellency's train is pulling in, sir.'

'But he was supposed to be on the quarter past.' For the first time the stationmaster looked flustered. 'You cannot bring him up here with all this going on.'

'Do you have somewhere else we could use?' I asked.

'Three along,' Mr Armstrong Bantam-Hoverly said hurriedly. 'Thurber will show you.'

'This way, please.' The frock-coated man opened the door.

I had a bit of a taste for the whisky now and had hatched a plan to borrow the decanter on the way, but, before I knew it, the frock-coated man had shut us in a small office with hardly any view at all.

'Do you mind if I ask what you are?' the guard asked uneasily.

'Yes.' Mr G perched on the desk while Smith and I sat down.

'We are investigating the murder of Mr Nathan Mortlock,' I said.

'Are you newspaper people?' Smith put his peaked cap on his lap, the badge facing me like a third eye.

'Why do you ask that?' Mr G swung his leg to and fro.

'Well, you ain't peelers 'cause they don't have women,' Smith reasoned, 'and the reporters 've already been sniffing about – no offence intended.'

'We are personal detectives,' I informed him and the guard perked up.

'What – like that Charlemagne Cochran?' he asked. ''E's the Pope's nose and no mistake.' He became quite chirpy. 'Work for him, do you? What a privilege. I'd love to meet him. What's he like?'

I watched my guardian's face go livid and then more livid.

'I will tell you what he is like. He is like a loathsome thing creeping out from under my shadow to bask in my glory. He is like a rabid cur clipped and dyed to vaguely resemble a pedigree. He is like an imbecile dressed in an academic mortar and gown. He is like...' He rustled his fingers though the air.

'A wolf in sheep's cloving?' Smith suggested.

'He is neither markedly lupine, nor is he specially ovine except in his intellectual qualities.'

'I take it you do not work for him then?' the guard asked ovinely.

'Mr Grice works for himself,' I explained and Smith looked deflated. 'I believe you saw Austin Hesketh on the train to Nuneaton on the night that Nathan Mortlock was murdered.'

Sidney Grice emitted a groan. 'Shall we just go home and conduct this interview between ourselves?'

John Smith looked at me in confusion.

'Is any of what I said not true?' I asked.

'No, miss.'

'How is it that you remembered seeing him?' I tried to pretend that my chair was not rocking.

Smith put out a hand to steady it, but thought better of his actions.

''E got the night train up, miss, the ten thirty-five. I asked for 'is ticket and 'e couldn't find it – went through all 'is pockets 'e did. I told 'im to look under 'is 'atband – lots of passengers tuck them in there – but it was no use. If it'd just been 'im I would've let it go. 'E was a nice quiet gent and 'e confided as 'ow 'is mother was bad but I'd already booked two men in the same carriage and they was cuttin' up nasty enough as it was.' Smith fiddled with his cap badge. 'So I took all 'is details and went back to my van. About five mile from Nuneaton 'e comes up and says 'e's really sorry but 'e just found it slipped into the side of 'is boot – an old 'abit from when 'e was a footman. 'E used to carry secret notes that way for his sweet'eart.'

The thought of Hesketh having a sweetheart was quite touching. I sniffed.

'Is that it?' Sidney Grice pouted in disappointment.

Smith polished his badge on his sleeve. 'Not quite, sir. I saw 'im again the next morning, just past Nuneaton, and for a minute 'e pretended 'e'd lost it again. We 'ad a good laugh about that. 'E was 'appy 'cause 'is mum was better than 'e'd thought and 'e would be back in time to do 'is duties.'

'What a pity,' Mr G said.

'Were there any other passengers in the compartment that time?' I asked.

My chair was getting most annoying now. The front left and back right legs must have both been too short.

Smith turned his cap upside down and looked into it like an old actor reading his lines. 'There was a well-to-do lady what was trying to smuggle her dog under the seat for free. I'd 'ave let that go too only she was so high and mighty, calling me 'er man.'

'I see.' Sidney Grice jumped off the desk. 'Goodbye.'

'Is that it?' Smith asked.

'Yes,' my guardian said.

Smith put on his cap.

'I don't suppose you could get me a signed photograph.' He paused in the doorway. 'Of Mr Cochran, I mean.'

'Go,' Mr G fumed. 'And you, Miss Middleton, will return to Gower Street. I have other railway employees to interrogate.'

And it was only when I stood up that I realized it was not my chair that was unsteady; it was me.

44

The Man Outside

OOK WAS TRYING a new recipe.

'I do not know what possessed her,' Sidney Grice grumbled. 'Food should be hot or cold and nothing else, but this...' he raised a piece on his fork, 'has got *ingredients*.'

It was a foul night. The rain battered the windowpanes and the wind yowled down the chimneys.

'It is an omelette.' I sprinkled some pepper on mine.

'I know what it is,' he rumbled.

'And you like eggs. You eat them every day.'

'Not when I had the fever,' he corrected me. 'Yes, of course I like eggs, but these have got *things* in them. I do not open my boiled egg and find vegetables inside, so why should I want them in my scrambled eggs?'

I cut mine open and tried a thin slice. It was a bit overdone and rubbery but otherwise quite tasty by Gower Street standards.

'It is just mushrooms and tomatoes and you like them too.' I tried a bit more. There was a fragment of shell but otherwise it was not bad.

'I like prune juice and I like tea, but I do not want them mixed together.'

'Try it,' I urged.

'And these things.' He raked through his dinner, looking for clues. 'What are they meant to be?'

'Herbs.' I washed mine down with some water. I had refrained from my usual pre-dinner gin and the effects of the whisky had long worn off. 'What did you make of John Smith's statement?'

'Oh, it was Smith's statement, was it?' He sowed salt in lines up and down his plate. 'I rather thought you had made it for him.'

'Perhaps you should not get me intoxicated while we are working,' I retaliated. 'And why could you not just tell him you do not drink alcohol?'

'It is too simple to explain.' My guardian cut his omelette into a square, and nibbled at a trimmed-off margin. 'But, in response to your previous question, the least and most we have discovered is that an allegedly independent, allegedly reliable employee of the West Coast Railway has corroborated Hesketh's claim to have been on that train and that he went at least as far as Nuneaton on both occasions.' He sampled some more. 'I shall consume this without further complaint,' he decided.

'Thank heavens for that.' I was quite enjoying mine. Mr G opened his book. 'More snails?'

'A little light reading this evening,' he confessed. 'A brief history of Joseph Hudson's quest to find the right sort of pea to put into police whistles. You might enjoy it.'

'I would prefer to see the dramatized version.' I had another mouthful. 'Do you think there is something odd about Hesketh's alibi?' I asked. 'It sounds as though he was going out of his way to be noticed on both occasions.'

'One certainly gained that impression,' he agreed, 'though it gives even greater credence to his claim to have been on those trains.'

'Could he possibly have come back to London and returned in time to catch the train back?' I proposed.

Sidney Grice took off his pince-nez and popped out his eye.

'It is difficult to see how. A coach would be too slow as would a cross-country journey on other lines. One would have to hire a special train but nobody took a special that night. I have checked.'

I had another thought. 'What if he smuggled the murderer into the house, went to Nuneaton and returned when the deed was done to sneak him out of the house again?'

'A solution which has an element of charm in its naivety and does not completely lack elegance,' my guardian conceded. 'But how would he let his accomplice out? The house was sealed and it was swarming with policemen almost immediately afterwards, and so I must reluctantly place it near the back of the pending file of possible explanations.'

'It might imply that Hesketh knew something was going to happen,' I reasoned and Sidney Grice closed his book.

'For once we are in complete agreement,' he said. 'Though whether he had any concept of what that *something* might be is another unresolved issue.'

There was something hard in my mouth and I removed it as surreptitiously as I could. 'I cannot think what motive Hesketh would have had – unless he benefited in Nathan Mortlock's will.' The hard piece was blue in my napkin.

'He did not.' My guardian cut a circular section out of the middle of his dinner and put it to one side. 'I have communicated with his solicitors, the incomparable Madder, Lynn, O'Shay and Head, of Suez Square.'

'In fact he could be putting himself out of a job,' I pondered. The blue bit was a glass bead, I decided, and placed it on my side plate. 'Cherry might not want a valet.'

'Indeed not.' He turned the disc upside down and reinserted it into his omelette.

'So what do we do now?' I scraped my plate clean.

'Perhaps we should defer our plans until we discover the identity of our caller.' He pushed his plate aside.

I did not admit that I had heard nothing but, a minute later, I heard footsteps.

'There's a man outside who wants to be inside.' Molly clutched her hands over her stomach. 'He's ever so handysome and wet. I like a wet man, dontn't not you not, miss?'

'What is his name?' I asked before her employer did so less politely.

Molly crossed her eyes and dealt with her itchy tooth. 'It's H... Hes... No, dontn't not tell me... Hesk-buth.'

'Close enough,' I said and we followed her downstairs.

45

The Conversion of Emergencies

IT WAS COMING down hard, that filthy used bathwater that passes for rain in London, and the wind was whipping Hesketh's umbrella up and the water under it. He came in gratefully.

'I am so sorry to disturb you both,' he panted, propping his umbrella in the stand.

'And Miss Middleton,' Molly prompted. 'You disterved her too.'

'It is a maid's job to be disturbed,' Mr G told her.

'And I certainly am.' Molly hung up Hesketh's overcoat and bowler hat, and he shook his trousers in an effort to dry them.

'Come through,' I invited and we settled in the study, me and my godfather in our armchairs, with Hesketh declining my offer and taking a wooden chair for himself.

Spirit was curled up on the hearth, her left whiskers crinkled from when she had lain too close to the grate.

'I would not dream of calling at such an hour if it were not important.'

'Has something ever so exciting happened?' Molly hovered in the doorway. 'Has a red-handed highwayman been terrorifying women in their beds?'

'Tea,' her employer rapped and she lumbered off.

'What has happened?' I asked.

'How unlike you not to have told him,' Mr G mumbled.

'Miss Cherry came back this morning.' Hesketh was still a

little out of breath. 'And she brought another detective with her. I believe you know of him.'

'Charlatan Cockerel,' my guardian breathed.

'He brought four men to search the house.'

'And did they discover anything?' I asked.

'They were very thorough,' he replied. 'They took everything out of all the drawers and cupboards and, to give them their due, they put it all neatly away again.'

'It never fails to astonish me how people insist on converting an emergency into an anecdote,' Sidney Grice grumbled.

'Please go on.' I reached down to stroke Spirit. Her fur was gritty with cold ashes.

'They even brought a ladder and went into the loft.' He wiped his face dry with a white handkerchief.

'And did they find anything up there?' I was trying hard not to take offence at his implication that Cochran was more meticulous than we had been.

'Only the mantraps,' Hesketh said.

'I do hope something dreadful befell him.' Sidney Grice brightened up.

'They measured it all,' Hesketh continued. 'And Mr Cochran calculated that there was a secret chamber over Mr Mortlock's bedroom.'

I sat up but Mr G leaned back, his eyes narrowed.

'They sent out for crowbars and sledgehammers and broke the wall down. It was hard going because it had been strengthened with iron bars and—'

'Oh, do let me guess,' Sidney Grice begged. 'They found they had broken into the loft of the North wing.'

'Quite so, sir.' Hesketh folded his handkerchief. 'Mr Mortlock was concerned when he divided Gethsemane because the loft space ran all the way along the house. He had reinforced partitions put in. I did inform Mr Cochran that this was the case, but he was adamant that his measurements were correct. Miss Cherry said he will have to pay to rectify it.'

'Rapture of raptures.' Sidney Grice clapped his hands. 'Did any other disasters befall them?

'I had never been in the loft before and I had not appreciated how fortified it was,' Hesketh told him. 'Long spikes have been fixed to the lathes – like a picture I saw of the defences against cavalry once.' Hesketh winced. 'One of the men trod on a spike and it went straight through his foot. They had great difficulty in getting him free and he had to be taken to the doctor's.'

'I do hope it was Spindoe,' Mr G said eagerly.

'I believe that was the gentleman's name.' Hesketh could not quite hide his distaste at my guardian's glee.

Sidney Grice brought his unusual display of exuberance under control. 'But you have not come out on such a foul night just to bring us tidings of comfort and joy.'

Hesketh mopped his face again, though more from distraction than to dry it, I thought. 'Mr Cochran then interviewed all the domestic staff, starting with me.'

'Clearly he has not demolished your well-constructed alibi or we should not be having this cosy fireside chat now,' Mr G surmised.

Hesketh's mouth tightened but he made no rejoinder.

'No, sir. They have arrested Veronique.'

'Well, they got the wrong one there,' Molly declared, backing in with the tray.

'Have you met my new assistant?' my guardian asked Hesketh.

'Lord bless you, sir, 'course I have,' Molly cackled. 'I met Miss Middleton a small number of years ago.'

'Mr Grice was not talking to you, Molly,' I tried to explain, and she put the tray down warily.

'Gawd, why not?' Molly knocked her hat sideways. 'Did he find that pillowcase what ripped itself when I was changering the beds and that I put at the bottom of the cupboard? Has he discoverered how I sneaked out the other day when you were at Miss Maud Lock's house?'

'He has now.' I shushed her before any more confessions came tumbling out. 'Why do you think the police had arrested the wrong person?'

Her employer leaned forwards, his jaw resting on his fist. 'Do share your wisdom,' he implored.

'Well,' Molly leaned her elbow on the back of the chair as if it were a public bar, 'Vernornic is such a lovely name and in all the things I've seen, wicked women have evil names like…' She twirled a lock of her hair around a finger. 'Hagabag or Little Nell or…' She noticed her employer's expression and whispered, more loudly than she had spoken, 'I'd better go now before you make him any grampier than he unusually is.'

'Why has Veronique been arrested?' I asked as I poured out three teas, on the assumption that Hesketh would like one but feel duty bound to refuse it if I offered.

'I am not sure of all the details, miss.'

'It would be pretty to hear at least one of them before the week is out,' Sidney Grice grunted.

I passed Hesketh the sugar bowl.

'I gather that Mr Cochran felt Veronique's explanation of the presence of the murder weapon in her bedroom was unsatisfactory.' He scattered sugar on the tray in his agitation.

'She offered me no explanation at all.' Mr G stirred his tea energetically in both directions.

'Nor to Mr Cochran,' Hesketh told him, 'which he found highly suspicious. Then there was the case of the razor being badly stropped.'

'So he can notice things occasionally,' Sidney Grice said acidly.

Hesketh added a splash of milk. 'Mr Cochran said that it must have been done by someone unused to doing it.'

'But Veronique used to shave her father,' I objected.

'That is what she tried to tell Mr Cochran,' Hesketh said, 'and so he put her to the test. He gave her an old razor and got her to shave one of his men.'

'Pitt?' Mr G asked hopefully.

'A Mr Cash, sir.' Hesketh dabbed the back of his hair, which was still dripping down his neck.

'Even better.' I had never seen my godfather enjoying himself so much.

'And unfortunately she cut him quite badly.'

Sidney Grice thrilled. 'On the neck?'

'Both cheeks, sir.'

'I suppose that will have to do.' Mr G leaned back and pulled the bell rope. 'Well.' He jumped up. 'I suppose we had better go and see her. Do you have a shaving kit, Miss Middleton?'

'Certainly not.' I gulped my tea.

'Then we shall have to use mine.'

'Run up the flag, Miss Middleton, then trot to the bathroom and fetch that ebony box which sits in splendid isolation on the window ledge.'

'Why cannot you get it?' I asked peevishly and he smiled.

'I would have thought you might have known by now that I *never* trot.' And, when Molly arrived with his insulated bottle, he told her, 'Get your overcoat, Molly, and we shall see if you still have faith in Mademoiselle Veronique Bonnay after you have met her.'

'Part of the team.' Molly skipped like a dancing bear.

'Your own solitary team,' he conceded.

'The bestest sort.' She clasped herself joyously. 'Shall I put on my going-out dress, sir?'

'The one that makes you look like a troglodyte?' he asked pleasantly.

'That's the one, sir, the one with brown sleeves and cuff, and brown collars and buttons, and a brown top and skirt, the only outside dress I've got.' Molly was more excited than when he had given her a nought per cent increase in pay.

'I think you look quite singular enough as it is.'

I had not realized what bad molars Molly had until she bared them when her master said that.

'Dontn't you worry, miss,' she reassured me. 'There'll always be a place for you in our solidary team – if you smarten yourself up.'

46

Feet, Elbows and Liver

HESKETH WAS SENT home with strict orders to report any further developments, and Molly squeezed herself with great difficulty and even greater pride between us into a hansom.

'We would be much more comfortable in two cabs,' I objected as she trampled on my skirts.

'But all the poorer for it,' my guardian replied as he breathed in.

I had never really appreciated how broad Molly was until that moment, nor what pointy and nomadic elbows she possessed.

'This is friendly,' she burbled, her overcoat flapping in my face.

'I never thought a scrap of a thing like you would take up so much space...' At first I thought she was addressing her employer, but she saved her job by adding 'miss'.

At least the wind had died down and the rain was no more than a cold drizzle.

'Or should I call you March now and—'

'Do not dare even to think it,' Mr G rumbled through whatever part of Molly was over his mouth.

It was just as well there was so little traffic for I was getting cramp in both legs by the time we arrived at Marylebone, not helped by Molly, because she was overlapping us both, scrambling out first and over me, though, from Mr G's protests, you might have thought it was over him.

Sergeant Horwich watched us approach with his usual world-weariness.

'Thought you might be coming,' he told us. 'But I wasn't expecting you to bring reinforcements.'

'I aintn't not been reinforced,' Molly objected.

'Where is she now?' Sidney Grice asked, never a man to waste pleasantries, especially with maids, and the sergeant jerked a thumb in the direction of the corridor.

'Interview room four with Inspector Quigley.'

'And who else?' I asked urgently.

'Perkins,' he said and I breathed a sigh of relief, for, unlike his superior officer, Perkins was a decent man. 'Only Perkins has gone for a cup of tea. Here, come back. You can't just barge in there.'

'How little you know me, Sergeant Horwich,' I called back.

There were footsteps behind me, the unmistakeable irregular rhythm of my guardian's gait and the thundering of a maid in full stampede.

'Stop,' my godfather commanded and I froze with my hand on the doorknob. He caught up with me. 'He's a tricky customer at the best of times. I think some finesse is required here.'

A degree at a time he turned the handle and opened the door a crack, just in time for Molly to hurtle through with an earsplitting, 'If you've hurted Veroncia I'll rip your liver out of your ears.'

'Not quite what I had in mind,' Sidney Grice murmured to me as we followed her in.

47

The Night of the Badger

A T FIRST I could hardly see Veronique Bonnay, just the top of her golden hair over Inspector Quigley's shoulder. He had her trapped in the far corner and was pressed against her. The only surprise was that he did not turn round to abuse us as we burst in, but only said urgently, 'All right, all right.'

Quigley was holding out both hands like a man being confronted with a gun and trying to back away, but Veronique was coming with him.

'Tell her to let go,' Quigley gulped and, as they came together to the middle of the room, I saw that the French maid had a tight grip on the detective's trousers.

''E think,' Veronique struggled with her *th*, ''e can do what 'e want wiz me – *sal bête*. If 'e try again 'e never try wiz anozzer woman.'

Her fingers tensed and Quigley yelped. 'All right, all right. Just a bitova misunderstanding. She don't get English very well.'

'You misunderstand again and I pull zem off,' Veronique vowed, and nobody in interview room four had any doubt that she meant every word.

'You had better let go now,' Sidney Grice instructed with some reluctance, 'if I am to get you out of here tonight.'

'You make 'im be'ave?'

Sidney Grice's mouth twitched. 'I think you have already done that.'

Veronique Bonnay's hand came away with a flourish that

would have done credit to Sarah Bernhardt. Quigley folded over, clutching himself.

'You'll pay for this,' he threatened through clenched teeth, but stepped back warily as Veronique put out her hand.

A heavy tread grew louder.

'A mug two-thirds full of hot water, Perkins, and be quick about it,' Mr G instructed without turning round. 'That means one-third empty.'

'Nobody orders my officers about.' Quigley snarled, but the footsteps were already fading.

'How does it feel to be in the same room with three women who have all beaten you in fights?' I asked.

'Bitch,' he breathed, I suspected at me, but he had his eyes fixed on the French maid, who was watching him like a swordsman en garde.

Sidney Grice strolled to the desk, put down his box and picked up a piece of paper.

'Leave that alone.' Quigley forced himself to straighten up but he could not mask his pain.

'Mademoiselle Bonnay's confession?' He flipped the page over. 'Unsigned.'

'And zat is 'ow she stays.' Veronique crossed her arms defiantly. 'Not one word of her is mine.'

'It is interesting, is it not, that she gives items their French sex when she speaks in English, for it is *la* confession not *le*.' Mr G clipped on his pince-nez. 'I have to give you credit for attempting the idiom but *really*, referring to the razor as *he* when any educated man would know it is *la raisor* not *le*... tut tut. Your tutor would have rapped your knuckles for that.'

My guardian knew full well that Quigley had left the ragged school when he was ten and was largely self-educated, and I thought it unpleasant of Mr G to rub his nose in it, but it was difficult to feel too sorry for the man who had threatened to beat a confession out of me in this very room and evidently Molly had similar feelings.

'You are an uncredit to your profission,' she told the inspector and Quigley emitted a snort of derision.

'Stupid mare.'

'Who you calling a pig?' She flexed her arms.

I put my hands up to halt her. 'Mares are horses, Molly.'

'No, they aintn't. *Horses* is horses. I see them every day.' Molly bunched her muscles. 'Do you want me to get a confessing out of him? Just give me five minutes.'

'Threatening a police officer,' Quigley told her lamely.

'I think he has suffered enough for one night,' her employer said, 'and we have a more important role for you presently.'

'With presents?' Molly skipped sideways.

Perkins arrived with a steaming enamelled mug and surveyed the room uncertainly.

'Sergeant Horwich was just about to 'ave a brew.' He put it down. 'So 'e'd be glad to get it back soon.'

'Observe, Inspector, whilst I demolish the central pillar of your fabricated case against this pleasant, albeit foreign young woman, which I have been given to believe is based on her alleged inexperience in the art of depilation.'

'That means *shaving*,' I told the inspector.

'Not alleged, proven.' Quigley's tone was more defiant now. 'Mr Cochran worked that out after neither of you two managed.' He gingerly stopped clutching himself. 'He worked out that the razor was all chipped because it had been stropped by someone who didn't know how to do it. This foreign bitch said she was good with a razor but when she had a go, she near chopped Cochran's man's ear off.'

''E gives me a blunt old *raisor* and I am nervous for they all shout and tell me I am going to the prison,' Veronique burst out.

'Then you shall have a chance to redeem yourself.' Mr G tapped the ebony box. An S and a G were embossed in gold upon it with something between, but I could not tell if they were other initials or ornamentation. 'My father gave me this on the occasion of my eighteenth birthday.' He hinged back the lid.

'Looks unused,' Quigley said suspiciously.

'It looks what it is,' my guardian agreed amiably. 'Facial hair is a primitive trait and when the rest of mankind has evolved as far as I, people shall be troubled by it no more.' He pushed the shaving set towards Veronique. 'Kindly demonstrate your skills, Miss Bonnay.'

Veronique approached the box and lifted out an ivory cut-throat. 'She is very sharp already.'

'Nevertheless I would appreciate it if you would use the strop.'

Veronique shook out the spiral of brown leather and, without hesitation, hung it by its metal ring over the door handle, pulling it into a long strap by the handle on the other end. Her hand flew as she worked the blade up and down it.

'Note how she twists the razor on to its spine when she changes direction,' Mr G pointed out, 'so as not to damage the cutting edge. You may stop now.' He peered over. 'A pristine strop and an edge honed to terrifying keenness, I think you will agree, Inspector.'

Quigley did not seem inclined to agree with anything. He rubbed his signet ring.

'What next?' Sidney Grice asked Veronique.

'The lather.' She pronounced the second word with great precision and proceeded to swirl a cylinder of soap in the water and work up a foam with the brush, holding the short wooden handle expertly with a thumb and middle finger.

'Silvertip badger hair,' my godfather announced, 'the most expensive on the market because it comes from the white hairs of the aforementioned carnivore and does not have to be bleached. It is reputed to have the least spiky feel of any brush.'

'Not that you would know,' Quigley sneered.

'Indeed not,' Mr G agreed cheerily.

'Like a woman,' Quigley scoffed, but, unlike my guardian, I was not going to let that pass.

'Your observational powers have deserted you, Inspector,'

I noted. 'I, and these two are like women because we are. Mr Grice is like a man because he is. I shall not tell you, in polite company, what you are.'

Perkins guffawed.

'Out,' his superior shouted and he shuffled away. 'Well, there ain't no point in shaving Grice then, and I ain't going to volunteer, nor any of my men.'

'Is Inspector Pound in the station?' I enquired, not sure that he would submit to such an experiment.

'No need for that.' Mr G waved airily. 'We have brought our own customer with us. Take a seat, Molly.'

Molly jumped in surprise and landed on Quigley's foot.

'Stupid sow.' He hopped back as she sat on the wooden chair.

Molly's employer took a white cloth from his satchel. 'Allow me.' And he tucked it around Molly's neck.

'Am I to have dinner, sir?' she enquired hopefully.

'Have you actually been in the room?' Quigley scorned.

'Oh yes, 'Spector Quickly. I'm surprised as how you didntn't not notice when I trodded on your toe,' she reminded him.

'It's Quigley,' he snapped.

'What is?' Molly asked innocently.

Veronique set to work, spreading a thick lather over Molly's face jowls and around her mouth.

'It is OK?' Veronique asked uncertainly.

Molly's tongue flicked out and in. 'Tastes soapy.'

'Like Cook's potato soup,' I said automatically, horrified at the indignity to which she was being subjected. And Veronique set to work, standing behind our maid and scraping the thick beard of foam away and wiping it on to the cloth. She moved on to the neck and Molly shifted uneasily.

'Keep still,' her employer scolded, but, even watching, I could not help but cringe as the blade whipped over her exposed throat.

Veronique finished on Molly's upper lip with a flick under the nose and Sidney Grice threw Molly a handkerchief to wipe the last few flecks of lather away.

Molly was shaken. This was one humiliation too many, I thought.

'Not a scratching,' Veronique proclaimed proudly, shaking the razor dry, and I held up the box so that Molly could see for herself. Molly took one look and burst into tears.

I rounded on my godfather. 'How can you treat her like that?'

'No, it's lovely,' Molly wailed. 'My moustache – it's gone. Now I wontn't not keep getting food in it and it wontn't get snangeled in the baker's boy's teeth. Thank you, so much, sir. This is the best birthday present ever and it aintn't even my birthday.'

'One tiny point,' Mr G concluded. 'As I am sure even you noticed, Inspector Norbot Stillith "Sly" Quigley, Miss Bonnay is left-handed whereas the murderer is or was—'

'Get out,' Quigley raged, 'the lot of you.'

Veronique smiled triumphantly and replaced the razor. 'You 'ave a bit of stubbles – shall I do you next, Inspector?'

48

The Eye of the Beholder

SERGEANT HORWICH WAS taking a very rare night off. He had been forced to do an eighteen-hour shift to cover for Sergeant Jonty, who had broken an arm in a game of five-card stud, Sergeant Whittington told us.

'How on earth can you break an arm playing cards?' I asked.

'You can if you try to chisel Hanratty,' Whittington promised me.

'Who?' I had not heard that name before.

'Hagop Hanratty,' Sidney Grice enlightened me, 'the product of an Irish father and Armenian mother. Hanratty owns three gin palaces, two theatres and most of the East End streets between them. Jonty was lucky to get away with his arm still attached to his body.'

'It's only just,' Whittington grimaced.

Twister, the station tabby, ran through with a young rat still wriggling in her mouth.

'A present for Inspector Quigley, I hope,' I commented.

'Run us through the process of booking a prisoner in, Whittington.' My guardian rested his cane on the desk.

'Gawd, I fought you'd 'ave seen enough of those, Mr Grice.'

'For the lady's benefit,' Sidney Grice urged.

Whittington looked about for another female in the room before realizing that my godfather meant me.

'Well, we takes their names and addresses – if they 'ave one.

A lot of 'em 'ere are no fixed abode, or they pretend to be so the missus don't find out what they've been at, 'specially if there's a dollymop involved.' Sergeant Whittington picked up his pen. 'We write them in this book with the time in this column.' He dotted it with the nib. 'Then they are taken down and when they come up again I sign them out with the time in this next column. Simple.'

'Indeed,' Sidney Grice concurred. 'Anyone on archives tonight?'

'Arbuckle,' the sergeant said, 'but he's been busy all day looking stuff up for Inspector Pound.'

'Then he will be grateful for something different to do,' I said, without conviction, but Mr G must have agreed, for he was marching up a corridor on the far side of the desk and down a short flight of steps, along a dark passage and down three more steps, and through the door into a sunken room without so much as a knock.

'Good afternoon, Arbuckle.' My guardian breezed in.

The constable was a tall adipose man, almost bald but for one strap of hair about an inch wide, running ear to ear and dyed boot-polish brown.

'Mr Grice.' He looked up from several stacks of beige envelopes and brown cardboard boxes. 'I'm rather busy today.'

'Excellent.' My guardian rubbed his hands. 'Then you will not wish to waste time looking for an old register.'

'I certainly would not,' Arbuckle agreed with alacrity.

'Then waste no further time and do it immediately,' Mr G urged. 'The latter part of 1872.'

Arbuckle waved a sheaf of papers. 'I really don't have the time. If you could come back in a day or two.'

Sidney Grice cocked his ear to one side like a thrush listening for a worm. 'Chatter,' he bade me. 'Irritate him until he gives way.'

'About what?' My mind went blank.

'Frippery and foolishness,' he said. 'The sort of nonsense over which you bore me into a stupor.'

I took a breath. 'I see that Dante Gabriel Rossetti's poems are coming out in a new collection.'

Arbuckle sighed. 'There is nothing new about Rossetti's verse. Most of it was filched from Swinburne and some of it reads like nursery rhymes. I mean to say, take 'is translation of François Villon's *Ballade des dames du temps jadis*. I know you sacrifice something of the rhythmical sense when you transcribe a poem, but he completely loses the flavour for me.'

'I saw a new dress today,' I began.

'Oh yes?' Arbuckle perked up. 'I can't decide between the *Ladies' Polonaise* number one or two myself, though I'm inclined to think the number two a bit fussy but that's just my personal opinion.'

I tried again. 'Verdi—'

'Now don't start me on Giuseppe.' Arbuckle chuckled. 'If—'

'Just find the register,' Sidney Grice burst out and Constable Arbuckle reached up to a high shelf to his left, and pulled out a dusty red volume with hardly a glance. 'There you are.' He sat on a pile of boxes. 'So what did you make of *Traviata*? Lord, the passion of that music and what a libretto. I wish I could see it. Me and the wife went through the score, but she can't hit the top notes and I'm shaky on the basso profundo.'

'I am almost grateful,' Mr G said and was back up the steps with the register under his arm. 'Oh, and when you have the time, Constable – by which I mean today – send me all the notes you have on the body from the North Wing of Gethsemane.'

'Bloomin' liberty,' Arbuckle boiled as my godfather disappeared.

'Yes,' I agreed. 'But that is your vocation, Constable – to keep our liberties blooming.'

He sat on the top step and I next to him, and he laid the book across our knees just as Maudy Glass and I used to do in the attic at The Grange when we had an exciting story to share.

'September the twenty-first.' My godfather ran his fingerplate down the fore-edge, slipped it in and flipped the register open at exactly the right page.

'How did you do that?' I asked.

'When I was a child I learned to count.' He stabbed at a line. 'There we are. Nathan Roptine Mortlock, booked in at two fifteen in the morning. I see he gave 1 Gaslight Lane as his address.'

'I cannot imagine Mr or Mrs Garstang would have been happy if they had seen that in the papers – a resident in their home on trial for affray,' I commented and leaned over. Our hair touched but Mr G did not recoil. 'Daniel Filbert – Nathan's friend. He gives an address in Butcher Street, number 121B.'

My guardian sniffed. 'If only the police had known their own district. Butcher Street ends at number 80.'

'So we do not even know if that was his real name.' He had still not pulled away and I sat squashed up against him, breathing in the fresh scent of his soap.

Sidney Grice's left eye took me in and flicked away.

'You are beautiful,' he murmured.

I caught my breath, unable to quite believe what I had heard. 'I am sorry?'

'Why are you sorry?' Sidney Grice asked softly. 'You are not hurting me.'

'I meant, what did you say?'

'You are beautiful,' he said simply and took my hand in his. 'You are covering his initials.'

He lifted my hand away and then I saw it – Uriah Roger Biewtiffle. Mr G let my hand fall.

'Perhaps his parents thought it was a joke,' I answered automatically and forced myself to concentrate on our task. 'I see they were both checked out at nine forty-four that morning.'

I edged away to create a small gap.

'In good time for the ten-thirty sessions.' He turned the page and the clouds broke briefly, and a white light fell across my guardian's profile – his thick black backswept hair, his straight thin nose and pale blue eye, his unblemished complexion, full red lips and dimpled chin.

'Dear God.' I jumped up.

'What is it?'

'Nothing,' I blustered. 'I just have a cramp.'

I brushed past him up to the corridor and paced about to pretend to improve the blood flow.

'Which leg?' he asked with something akin to sympathy.

'The left.'

'Try limping on that one then,' he advised and closed the book. 'Take this back to archives. The exercise will set you aright.'

If only it would.

'Not sure about the ring cycle,' Constable Arbuckle greeted me. 'I 'ave 'eard it can't be beaten for dramatic spectacle, but it doesn't have the melodic inventiveness of Verdi. Why, miss, whatever is wrong? You've gone all blotchy.'

'Nothing,' I lied for the second time. 'It is just that I cannot bear it when people speak ill of Wagner.'

49

The Mathematics of Murder

SIDNEY GRICE HAD gone back to the desk.
''Arris should be down there.' Sergeant Whittington was busy trying to balance a penny on its rim on top of his inkwell. 'And if 'e's dozing give 'im a kick. 'E's in enough trouble with Inspector Quigley for falling asleep when he was supposed to be guarding that place in Gaslight Lane.' He gestured to the deserted foyer. 'I never known it so quiet. Don't no one commit no crimes no more?'

'Only with the English language.' Mr G picked up his cane.

'I was lookin' at that,' Whittington told him. 'Is that the one what shoots poisoned arrows at people?'

'It is the one I use as a walking stick,' my guardian told him.

'What else does it do?' I hurried after him down another corridor.

Mr G stopped and wound the top of his cane several turns. He pressed a tiny screw, the handle went into reverse and the air was filled with the sound of a music box – 'Oh, for the Wings of a Dove'.

'But you hate music.' I listened for a while as the tiny tuned teeth pinged and the clockwork whirred. 'What on earth is it for?'

'It confuses people,' he expounded.

'I think you are quite good at that already.'

We walked on.

'Stop humming.' He switched his walking cane off, turning

ninety degrees on his heel, and leading the way down the long stone stairs that so many men and women had passed in shame and despair.

Constable Harris stirred as he heard our footfalls on the worn stone and tried, but failed, to look like he had not been dozing.

'Make your choice,' Harris invited as I joined them on the worn flagstone floor. ''Cept number five what Nettles is 'aving a kip in, and number two 'cause Mrs Vishnovski had had the pick of that.'

Harris had the most naturally red hair I had ever seen. In the rare London sunlight it looked like a burning bush – he was never able to flatten it – and, even in the gloom of the prisoners' block, it had a wispy halo around it. Children had been known to knock off his helmet just for the sake of a view.

I saw two hands closed round the bars in the observation hatch.

'How do you do?' the occupant inquired charmingly, an elderly woman with white hair piled busby fashion and sprouting bamboo sticks from it. 'I am Mrs Malgorzata Vishnovski. I am quite safe but very dangerous, and I not speak a word of English.'

Her accent sounded Edinburghian to me.

'Do you know why you are here?' I asked and Mrs Vishnovski clapped her hands in delight.

'At last somebody who speaks Polish,' she chortled. 'Tell these men that I am innocent, quite safe but very dangerous, and I not speak a word of English.'

I hesitated.

'You 'ad better tell us.' Harris winked. 'We'll get no peace until you do.'

'This lady,' I began.

'No! No! No!' Mrs Vishnovski howled. 'In English – Ennng-lish – understand?'

What the hell? I thought.

'Burbley burbley burble,' I said.

'And the rest,' Mrs Vishnovski urged.

'Burbley—'

'No, you've told them that already.' She kicked the inside of her door.

'Bibbley boppley boopy,' I told them and Harris responded wisely.

'I shall let my superiors know at once.'

'Perhaps you would like to translate that for the prisoner's benefit,' my guardian suggested blithely.

I refrained from the first response that came to mind and turned back to Mrs Vishnovski who, at three feet away, must have heard every word.

'Zippy zappy—'

'What are you doing?' she shrieked. 'You are talking gibberish.'

Sidney Grice strolled over. 'Would you like to hear my music box, Ethel?'

'Ethel?' Harris and I chorused.

'No.' She backed away, still grasping the bars. 'It confused me last time.'

'Then sit down and keep quiet,' he ordered.

'Ethel?' Harris performed a solo this time.

'Ethel Turp,' Mr G identified her. 'I am surprised you have not come across her before. She gives dancing lessons, spins the gentlemen so fast that they get dizzy and fall over, takes their wallets, watches and boots and – as I believe her colleagues might term it – scarpers.'

'Why their boots?' I wondered. 'They cannot be worth much compared to a good cravat, for example.' The men exchanged knowing, silly-little-girl looks. 'So they cannot chase after her,' I realized.

'Sergeant 'Orwich won't be 'appy when 'e gets back,' Harris forecast. ''E 'ates crossings out in his register.'

'It is not my mission, nor my ambition, to make Sergeant Horwich happy. In which cell were you accommodated, Miss Middleton?' Sidney Grice allowed his cane to play one note.

'I'm going,' Ethel Turp called hurriedly and disappeared from the hatch.

'Three.' I looked through the opening and it was much as I remembered, as far as I *could* remember – a single bed with a thin blanket that barely covered the boards and nothing else. 'It was dark and I was confused.'

'If only one could earn a living being that.'

'I do,' Harris quipped cheerily.

'Many a true word,' Mr G agreed.

'I thought the wall was a darker colour.' I struggled to remember.

It was white now.

'Repainted a couple of weeks ago,' Harris told me.

'Three to four, judging by the faintness of the smell,' Mr G surmised.

'Used to be brown,' Harris said.

'It was green when I first saw it, then blue,' Mr G recalled.

'Gawd,' came a complaint from number five. 'What is this – a decorayta's conference?'

'According to the book, Mortlock was in cell one.' Sidney Grice limped towards it.

'Pro'ly,' Harris agreed. 'But we do tend to move 'em abart if there's any trouble – separate people and so on.'

'But you only had four prisoners that night,' I pointed out, 'in cells five, one, six and ten. So they were all in the four corner cells, Nathan Mortlock in number one and his friend Daniel Filbert opposite in ten, either side of the back door.'

'They pro'ly let 'em be then,' Harris acknowledged, 'but it was all before my time.'

'I did not know you could even tell the time, never mind have one,' Sidney Grice said so amiably that I wondered if he were aware when he was insulting people.

'Shall we take a look at cell one?' I suggested, while the constable thought about that.

'Why were you in prison?' he asked my godfather.

'On one occasion to gain information about an assassination plot against the Crown Prince, who shall one day be known as

Kaiser Wilhelm the Peacemaker.' Sidney Grice examined the door. It had two sturdy iron locks. 'On the other occasions I was detained against my will.'

'Not against your Wilhelm then?' Harris joked.

And Mr G looked at him blankly. 'It must be inconvenient having a surname that you cannot even pronounce correctly.'

'What? 'Arris?' Harris quivered with mirth. 'It's an easy one.'

Cell one was on the left at the end. Inside it was identical to my cell, a basic bed, no windows, approximately ten feet long and eight wide.

'The back door leads to the courtyard, does it not?' I asked.

Harris was still chuckling as he agreed with me. 'Can be useful for getting troublesome prisoners in and out without going through the station, or sometimes to avoid the newspapers.'

'It would be a pity to lose the cash they have to slip you for information,' Mr G remarked tartly and the constable stuck out his chest.

'Now that is a dirty libel.'

'It would fall more into the category of slander were it proved to be untrue.' Mr G stepped smartly into the cell and closed the door behind him.

'Shall I lock him in?' Harris nudged me.

'Probably best not to,' I demurred, but my guardian said, 'Kindly do so.' Which Harris did with alacrity, admonishing him, 'Now you be'ave yourself, you gnaw'ee boy.'

Sidney Grice rolled his eye and sat on the bed. 'If you could enter cell ten, Miss Middleton.'

'You will not lock me in?' I sought assurance. The last experience had been enough for me.

'I won't double-lock it, miss,' the constable promised, 'but these are slam locks so you won't be able to let yourself out.'

'Very well.' I went in and shut the door – the bolt clicking into place behind me – and stood at the bars to peer across the passage to see Mr G in the opposite cell returning my gaze.

'Now where would you be if you were on so-called duty?' my godfather asked.

'No talking from prisoners.' Harris laughed uproariously before catching Sidney Grice's expression. 'Mainly upstairs, sir.'

'So there is no permanent guard?' I clarified.

'No need.' Harris paced up and down between us. 'This place is like the Tower of London.'

'I could – though you shall not seduce me to do so – tell you nine thousand and forty-six ways in which it is not,' Mr G asserted, 'but it would certainly be difficult to escape from, even with my picks.' He held up the gold cigarette case in which he stored them. 'There is no keyhole on this side and it would be impossible to reach the lock through this hatch without my special cane to which I can attach them.'

'We ain't goin' to allow you sticks in cells,' Harris guaranteed.

'I might possibly fashion something from the bed,' Mr G conjectured, 'but that would take a great deal of time, plus the lock is seven lever and would take a tremendous effort to pick even under ideal conditions, which these are not.'

'Release us now, Harris.'

'If only Inspector Quigley could see you both like this.' Harris made towards the steps.

'Please,' I begged.

'You're no fun.' Harris pouted as he opened my door, then my guardian's, and we went back into the hall.

'Never do that again – pleading with the lower orders,' Sidney Grice said coldly. 'Who has the key to the back door?'

'Only the desk sergeant,' Harris replied, miffed at his joke being scotched. 'So nobody can overpower the constable and let themselves out.'

'Could you pick those locks?' I asked my guardian.

'It would take a good half-hour each and then you would have to relock at least one to avoid raising the alarm.' He kneeled to peer through the keyholes. 'So let us say an hour to unlock the cell door from the outside; half an hour to relock it; one hour to unlock the back door; half an hour to relock it from the outside; then, on return, half an hour to reopen the back door; and an hour for both locks. Half—'

'Why bother with both when you come back?' Harris butted in.

'Because sooner or later somebody would find one unlocked and report it. You would be taking a risk that no one else would use that door by leaving one unlocked while you were out,' I reasoned.

'Half an hour to pick the cell door and another hour to relock it from the inside,' Mr G ended.

'That is at least five and a half hours for an expert locksman with all the tools of his trade, undisturbed, and three hours of that time in this room, hoping that no constables appear and that no other prisoners are watching and thinking to get their sentences reduced or charges dropped by reporting you.' Sidney Grice stood up. 'The yard has a gate to the street as I recall.'

'Two locks on that as well,' Harris confirmed. 'The same sort.'

'So a minimum of another three hours,' I calculated. 'That's eight and a half hours.'

'And, in all likelihood, your picks would have fractured long ago with so many heavy-duty locks.' Mr G looked about him.

'A minimum of fifteen minutes to Gaslight Lane, even if you had a cab waiting for you,' I estimated. 'So half an hour travelling time. Nine hours. Then you have to get into the house, murder seven people one by one and get out again, sealing the house after yourself.'

'Charlie Peace couldn't do all that,' Harris pondered. ''Ow long was Mortlock in 'ere for?'

'If the register is accurate, seven hours and fifteen minutes,' I told him.

'That don't add up then,' Harris said and I waited for my guardian to make some cutting remark about his mathematical skills, but he was walking away, his shoulder dipping badly.

'Have you still not realized the real reason why it cannot possibly *add up*?' he called back to me.

'Sergeant Horwich,' I remembered. 'He saw Nathan Mortlock at about six o'clock, roughly the time of the murders.'

Sidney Grice disappeared up the steps.

'Eh?' Harris contributed.

'So Nathan Mortlock cannot possibly have killed the Garstangs,' I summarized.

'Gawd, is that what all that racket has been about?' Nettles emerged from cell five, his hair tousled boyishly. 'I could 'ave told you – that loopy Spaniard biddy did it. Read the papers for cripes' sake.'

50

Tracking Tigers

I HAD TO run after Sidney Grice. He was already past the desk and stalking through the front door on to the street, and I lost sight of him in the crowds, but then his cane rose above the sea of umbrellas, so terrifying to him, as he hailed a passing hansom.

'What is the hurry?' I panted as I caught up with him.

'Thank heavens you are here,' he cried and closed his eyes. 'Now I do not have to look at them and, if I cannot see something, it cannot be seen to exist.'

I guided him to the platform and he climbed aboard.

'Number 125 Gower Street,' he called weakly to the driver and flopped back in his seat.

'What on earth is the matter?' I just had time to settle next to him when the cab set off.

'It is too bad!' my guardian cried, 'Too bad. I spend my life seeking the truth. I track it like a Bengal tiger. I hunt it mercilessly and eventually I kill it – stone-dead truth with me posing, foot on its neck, looking magnificent in my solar topi and puttees. I hang it on my wall and wait for people to admire it.'

We bumped the side of a roadside stall but the driver did not stop and my guardian gave no sign of noticing.

'I know you care about the truth,' I assured him.

'If only I only cared,' he moaned. 'It haunts me, March. It fills every waking second. When I think I am stalking it, it springs out on me. It prowls and howls in my dreams, this monster truth.

Sometimes I hate it and yet I have loved it longer than I loved—'
He stopped.

'Loved what?' I hardly dared add, 'Or who?'

'Rabbit skins,' he whispered. 'There were rabbit-skin gloves in that handcart.'

Sidney Grice fell into a brooding abstraction.

'But what has happened?' I pressed him.

'I have lost it, March.' My godfather flopped. 'I can neither see it nor smell it. I cannot find its spore. Where is it?' He brought out his notebook, olive-green backed with multicoloured ribbons, and opened it to show me the tiny hieroglyphics, the lines, circles and squares, some cubed, the arrows sweeping round the pages, the block capitals of *BLOOD POURED*, plans of 1 Gaslight Lane with dozens of measurements pencilled over every surface, the word *AMPHIBIAN* diagonally up a page and then nothing.

'But we have often had difficult cases,' I pointed out. 'You sometimes complain that they are not difficult enough.'

'But usually I have so many ideas that I reprimand myself for not reining them in,' he protested. 'Stop it,' he told the woman in the next hansom, who was drunkenly blowing him kisses. 'You have an unsavoury periodontal condition.'

He brought out a blue polka-dotted handkerchief and folded it into the shape of a flower.

'Perhaps you need to sleep on it,' I suggested.

'Rat traps, ratty-ratty rat traps,' a man bellowed from the pavement, holding out a clumsy wooden box.

We squeezed through the stationary traffic and round a corner and speeded up.

'I have a secret.' Sidney Grice let out a groan, an empty cry of pain, almost a death rattle, and was quiet for so long that I thought that he had decided not to tell me. 'I am suffering from...' he confessed at last, but I had no hope of hearing him above the rattling of wheels on cobbles and the clashing of hooves on stone.

'What?' I cupped my hand to my ear, something I have never found to be useful.

'*Mens—*' he began again, the muffin man's bell clanging like Big Ben beside us.

'I—'

'Get yer loverly muffins. Fill yerselfs to stuffin's.'

'*Mens impeditone inquisitor,*' he yelled.

'Loverly loverly muffins.'

'The blocked mind of an investigator,' I translated quietly.

'For goodness' sake,' my godfather cried. 'Why do you not scream it in the whispering gallery of St Paul's? Why not place an advertisement on the front page of *The Times*?'

'I—'

'No,' he shushed me. 'Do not say anything. It is bound to be foolish and will upset my normally placid temperament even further.'

We turned right up Howland Street.

'Buttons. Best bone buttons,' a woman sang out, her tones much too refined for somebody in her occupation. 'All shapes and sizes. Please buy my buttons.'

'Lady Camellia Fainwatsinthorne,' Mr G emerged briefly from his morass to inform me. 'The twenty-third wealthiest hostess in London and reputed to be the ninth prettiest and third wittiest before she fell in love.'

'With another man?' I asked.

'Worse than that,' he replied. 'Lady Camellia fell in love with her husband.'

'But that is—'

'Embarrassing.' He completed my sentence with a word I had not intended. 'The poor may marry whom they can, but nobody worth over twenty thousand a year marries for anything other than titles or possessions. Lord Fainwatsinthorne, who had become accustomed to his wife, had no choice but to divorce her and that was no easy task as she had the support of—'

If Sidney Grice had been clockwork, I would have wound him up. He had ground to a complete halt.

'Support of whom?'

'The Home Secretary,' he managed at last. 'I must make an appointment to see him.'

''Ere we are.' The hatch slid open. 'I suffer from men's problems too,' the cabby told my guardian, 'but don't bovver wiv no secritries. There's a noo clinic at the 'versity 'ospital. They fixed me up a treat.'

I could see the accumulation of mercury in the blue margins of his swollen gums.

'Pay him.' Mr G rammed the flap open and clambered out. 'I have things to do and a telegram to send.'

'Mind that puddle,' the cabby called after I had given him his fare. 'Oh, too late.'

Instead of going up to the front door, Sidney Grice was leaning over the railings.

'I hate going down there,' he grumbled, as if I had suggested such a thing.

51

Moses and the Ape

I HAD SEEN a caricature of Sir William Vernon Harcourt, his beard running under but not over his chin, by Carlo Pellegrini, the *Vanity Fair* artist better known as *Ape*. The Right Honourable gentleman looked rather pleased with himself, his pendulous lower lip curled superciliously above the peculiar low beard.

'Not as evil a man as you might think from his liberal convictions,' Sidney Grice informed me as we inched along Whitehall. It had been an agonizingly slow journey and my guardian was draining his flask of tea by the time we glimpsed the vast neo-Gothic King's Tower soaring over three hundred and twenty feet over the House of Parliament. The decisions made there decided not only the fates of the masses thronging the Westminster streets, but the lives of everyone from the incalculably wealthy Maharajas to the children of convicts in New South Wales on the other side of the globe.

'But did he not oppose the Cross Act to demolish slums?' I argued.

'To his great credit.' Mr G tapped his cork back into place regretfully. 'Where are the poor to live if you demolish slums?'

'In housing fit for human habitation,' I answered.

There was a heavy mist rising from the Thames nearby. It soaked through my clothes, making them cold and heavy and cling to my legs.

'It is attitudes like that which deprived young children of the right to work in factories.' Sidney Grice looked at his hunter watch. 'We shall be late.' He banged on the roof. 'Get a move on, man.'

'Where to?' the cabby asked, quite reasonably, for we were hemmed in on all sides by stationary carriages, omnibuses and goods wagons. 'You'd do better gettin' awt. It's an easy stroll from 'ere.'

But, even as he spoke, the lorry in front of us moved, a gap appeared and we muscled into it. Twenty feet down the road, we pulled over.

My guardian screwed a small copper bowl on to the ferrule of his cane.

'I would have thought you could have walked that, Miss Middleton.' Sidney Grice passed up the fare in his bowl with great ceremony, but then spent two minutes trying to get the bowl off again. 'The threads do not quite marry.' He wrenched it off in exasperation.

'Enjoy the wedding,' the driver called cheerily after us.

Most of the crowd that we now pushed our way through wore top hats or bowlers, depending upon their status, but Sidney Grice stuck to his soft felt hat, an odd choice for one who laid so much store by formality, but I had long expected my guardian to make odd choices.

A policeman was trying to redirect traffic further up the road, but so many people were ignoring him and pushing into whatever gaps they could find that he served no purpose other than as another obstruction at a chaotic crossroads.

I could not see the front of the Home Office for we were too close to it, but like all the other government departments there was an unnecessary profusion of stone pillars, no doubt intended to emphasize that the occupants of these buildings ruled an empire that dwarfed that of the Romans and was destined to last at least as long.

The interior was similarly grandiose with enough marble in there alone to have emptied a good-sized quarry, I estimated, while a doorman escorted us to a desk constructed with enough mahogany to fit out a frigate.

A young man with flowing sandy locks took our details, and wrote them in the register as carefully and floridly as a monk working on an illuminated Bible.

'You are thwee minutes late,' he scolded.

'And you have wathted thixth minutes whiting our namth,' I retorted unkindly. I did not like to be treated as a naughty child.

'Are you making fun of me?' He looked up through his golden lashes.

'Yeth,' I said, and he picked up another pen and inscribed in plain block capitals *TM*.

'What does that mean?' I asked, and he simpered but did not reply.

'It means Trouble Maker,' Mr G informed me as we were conducted by a tall, lean, older man down the echoing, arched central hallway, 'Your name will go on a list now and they will start a file on you. They will investigate your history and note whenever you go to another administrative office or engage in any political activity.'

'Such as wanting votes for women?' I suggested and the official glided to a halt.

'No *loquor hic talia*,' he counselled. 'Do—'

'Not speak such things in here,' I translated.

'There are men here who work tirelessly and selflessly to relieve women of the worries of state,' our guide told me with a tremor in his voice.

'And there are women all around you who dream of being treated as equals,' I retorted.

A Sikh came towards us, resplendent in his blue chola, the flared robe and baggy pyjama trousers, his beautifully wound cherry-coloured turban, his ceremonial short curved sword tucked into his belt. He bowed in acknowledgement.

'*Sat shri akal*,' I greeted him and he smiled, but I was ashamed that I could not understand his response. Had I forgotten so much in the time since I left India?

'The language of savages,' the official told my godfather in what he probably fantasized was a discrete manner, and I was about to retaliate when the Sikh said politely, '*Chitta bander.*' And moved on.

'That was an old Hindoo greeting,' our guide exposited, and I did not trouble to tell him I thought it meant *white monkey*. 'He was probably looking for the colonial office.'

'Ignoramus.' Sidney Grice rolled his eye towards our guide.

'Quite so,' the official agreed, then stopped at two enormous oak doors, parting them – like Moses at the Red Sea – to reveal an office whose area could probably be best measured in acres. No doubt the view would have been spectacular had the Thames mist not enveloped the windows by which the great man stood.

'Have a seat.' He ushered us into two chairs and sat in a third. 'Will you take refreshments? A gin.'

I perked up at that, hoping to find myself in a similar situation to the one at Euston Station, but Sidney Grice declined, telling the Home Secretary, 'I am far too busy for that nonsense.'

Sir William Vernon Harcourt's puffy eyes widened. 'If only I had so much to occupy me.'

'The minister was being ironic.' A young man appeared behind Sidney Grice with a notebook.

'I think not,' Mr G disagreed. 'You must supply me with an exhumation order, Sir William George Granville Venables Vernon Harcourt.'

'What a loss you are to the diplomatic service.' Vernon Harcourt raised his brow languorously. His hair was long, parted near the middle and sweeping out at the back of his head like a fan. *Ape* had not exaggerated in his depiction of the beard. It hung under but not over his chin like a disguise that had slipped. 'I take it this is in furtherance of an investigation?'

'Yes,' Sidney Grice replied and the Home Secretary frowned.

'The Garstang massacre,' I contributed and he leaned towards me.

'*The* massacre? The one in Gaslight Lane?'

'Yes,' I said.

'As opposed to all the other Garstang massacres,' my guardian mumbled.

'You wish to disinter the Garstangs?' Sir William's eyes widened.

'I did not say so.' Mr G rubbed his wounded shoulder.

'He did not, Minister,' the young man concurred from his notes.

'It is the body of a man that we think picked the pocket of Mr Nathan Mortlock, the man who was murdered recently,' I answered.

'Do we?' my guardian exclaimed, reaching for his pencil. 'This is a fresh development.'

I modified my statement. 'Mr Mortlock's watch was found on his body.'

'And what is the name of this man?' Sir William's eyes protruded.

'We do not know,' I admitted.

'Yet,' Sidney Grice qualified.

The Home Secretary's eyes drifted back as he assessed the situation.

'Four minutes to your next meeting, Sir William,' the young man reminded him.

'But you are convinced this is necessary?'

'Yes,' Sidney Grice said impatiently, 'or we should not be here wasting my time.'

The minister looked at his subordinate quizzically.

'This is most irregular,' the young man said. 'There are channels of procedure to be gone through.'

'And no doubt channels within those channels.' Vernon Harcourt patted some papers together and I wondered how many lives would be affected if he were to thrust them into the fire.

'I hear that you are destined for the Exchequer,' Sidney Grice stated. 'Which means I shall have to waste time training your successor.' My godfather turned to the secretary who was just about to announce that our time was up, and said, 'You may not record those remarks.'

'But how could you know about the chancellorship? I only found out myself an hour ago.' The Home Secretary dabbed at his beard, as if trying to stop it slipping any further, before answering his own question. 'Your charming mother.'

'I do not have a charming mother.' Mr G rested his right ankle on his left knee.

'Would you not like to quit office as the man who brought such a notorious murderer to justice?' I proposed.

Vernon Harcourt did not need to ponder that question very long.

'And you are convinced that this will provide the evidence you need to do that?'

'No.' Mr G returned to monosyllables. 'But you owe me four favours.'

Sir William's lips worked against each other. It seemed he did not like to be reminded of that. 'Very well,' he decided.

'We are one minute late,' the young man announced in despair.

'Make a note, Henry.' The Home Secretary rose majestically. 'Exhumation order on my desk as soon as Mr Grice supplies the details. And now I must deal with some trade unionists.'

'To have them imprisoned?' Sidney Grice enquired hopefully.

'Dear Mr Grice,' Vernon Harcourt said mournfully. 'How you must miss the like of Viscount Castlereagh.'

'At least he knew how to deal with insurrectionists.' Mr G referred wistfully to the Peterloo Massacre.

'Best not record that either, Henry.' The Home Secretary ushered us so skilfully that I was hardly aware we were being shown out.

'I am not sure I liked him,' I commented as we rejoined the crowds.

'He will not harm you.' Sidney Grice turned a cigar butt over with his toe before sending it into the gutter. 'It is the nice people who are the most dangerous.'

He waved his cane.

'Then you must be a perfect lamb.' I put my fingers in my mouth, but a cab pulled over before I had the chance to blow.

52

The Gates of Hell

I HAD BEEN to Highgate Cemetery once before. It was early morning and I was running away, unsure if I had killed a man or whether I would be killed. I had been drugged with alkaloids and did not really know where I was. This visit promised to be even less informative.

I could hardly see the massive gates, and I doubted that hell had any more sinister an entrance than that tunnel disappearing into the night between the towering turrets of the gatehouse. It was a cloudy, moonless night, not one star puncturing the sky.

Sidney Grice lit two lanterns and handed me one, the smell of paraffin seeping over me. A light appeared at the far end from inside the cemetery, swaying towards us.

'Miss Middleton.' The tall figure approached.

'Inspector Pound, I did not know you would be here,' I greeted him.

And I felt very reassured that he was. My guardian would protect me to the death, I was certain, but then so would the inspector and he would be a great deal less cross about it.

'Your good friend Quigley didn't want to come,' he announced, and I found myself slipping my arm naturally through his while Mr G hurried ahead, his light swinging wildly, like a man trying to stop a train. 'He says it is nothing to do with his case and, quite honestly, he wants to distance himself from that too. He does not want to be remembered as the man who couldn't catch the Mortlock murderer. And –' he steadied me as I slid on the wet cobbles of the turning circle inside the gates – 'since I am the most senior surviving officer from the Garstang case, I have some interest in this case. I believe they are all buried here. I think Mortlock paid for the servants' plot.'

We turned down a narrow path. Mr G's light was disappearing round a corner.

'A guilt payment?' I said.

'I heard about you checking on his night in the cells.' He lowered his lantern to help me see my feet. 'But I could have saved you the trouble. I saw him myself that morning and his clothes were not bloodstained.'

Sidney Grice appeared from behind a yew tree. 'And you are certain it was him?'

I jumped but George Pound was not so easily rattled.

'Saw him again at the inquest,' the inspector confirmed. 'He'd smartened himself up – lost a bit of weight around the middle and had a proper shave – but it was definitely the same man.'

'Plus Horwich checked on him a few times,' I added as my guardian sped into the darkness again.

'He's a good man,' Pound said and scratched his jaw. 'Perhaps the grave *was* guilt money.'

I looked up at his face glowing in our united pools, the shadows being chased wildly with every footstep.

'How could that be?'

'Perhaps he felt guilty about not being there to share their fate, or possibly save them,' he said carefully.

We both stumbled on a low kerb, but we kept a tight hold of each other.

'My father told me that men who survive battles sometimes kill themselves, often years later,' I agreed.

'I am sorry for the way Colonel Middleton died,' George Pound said. He had never mentioned it to me before. 'But at least you brought his killer to justice.'

'Some justice.' I still could not hide the rage in my voice.

'He will answer to God one day.'

'Then I hope God will not forgive him.'

We turned round a sleeping man, his top hat on his chest, his whiskers beautifully chiselled in marble, his prominent nose covered in pigeon droppings. There were a few lights ahead of us now.

'Don't become bitter, March.' I hardly heard his words at first.

I had killed the man I loved, my father had been murdered and the man I had come to love had rejected me for my money. I wanted to shake George Pound and scream it in his face.

You promised me, George Pound. You promised. You made me choose and when I chose you, you threw me aside.

But I only said, 'I try.'

I could hear low voices now and the unmistakeable slice of spades into clay.

Two men were in the grave, shovelling the soil out. They were bent over but if they had stood straight their heads would hardly have reached the surface. The gravestone had been laid on a piece of sacking. Cut into the still-white marble were four words:

GOD

SHALL

KNOW

YOU

Sidney Grice stood at the foot of the grave, with two men to either side holding lamps on sticks out over the workers. The ground was boggy underfoot after all the rain and they had all rested their coats on a nearby raised vault.

A blade hit something hard and one of the men grunted in satisfaction.

'Have a care,' one of the lamp holders advised. 'You don't want to split it.'

They held their spades nearer to horizontal now, scooping the wet clay out. One stopped and kneeled to wipe away the earth at his feet.

'Found the plate,' he announced.

The shadows thickened to the far side. A shape formed and grew, solidifying into a man, his great height exaggerated by a high top hat and a long black cloak.

'Show me.' He leaned over while they lowered a lamp. '*Unknown but not unloved*. That is the one.'

'How could he doubt it?' I kept my voice to a whisper.

'Sometimes unscrupulous undertakers will put two or more coffins into one grave,' Pound explained.

'Not in my cemetery,' the stranger declared.

'Indeed not, Sir Grigsby,' the inspector agreed, and I realized that this must be Sir Grigsby German, the director of Highgate Cemetery.

The lamp holders were throwing ropes and the diggers attaching them and climbing up short ladders to the surface. All four men took an end each.

'Will the handles hold?' I asked.

I did not suppose timber would take long to rot in such wet conditions.

'If I know my caskets, that is best English oak,' Sir Grigsby lectured me. 'It sails the seven seas for decades. I think it can last a few weeks in the ground.'

The men began to heave and the thin crust of earth broke as the coffin started to rise.

'Blimey,' one said. 'It's heavy.'

'Lead-lined,' my guardian spoke for the first time, 'if Crepolius or his fictional sons have not cut any corners.'

'Snushall's of Gordon Street?' Inspector Pound asked, but Sidney Grice did not trouble to reply.

The top of the coffin was at ground level now, the men grunting and heaving for all their worth, one of them wrapping the rope around his waist, and I dreaded to think what would happen to him if the others lost their grip.

'It would be a good idea to stand clear.' Pound led me two paces back and it was only then that I realized our arms were still interlinked.

'Right, men, on the count of three,' one of their number, a stocky man, ordered. 'One two three. Pull.'

Every man strained every sinew in that final effort as the coffin rose just over the edge.

'Over to me... sway... sway, darn it.'

And, with one collective groan and final wrench, they swung the coffin over the far side of the grave, dumping it on to the heap of freshly dug clay.

'Hold it,' the stocky man shouted urgently as the coffin began to slip. Two of the men dug their heels into the grass in a bizarre tug-of-war, while the other two rushed round to help, and between them they dragged it on to solid ground.

It was a splendid coffin. Even in the patchy illumination of the lanterns placed round it I could see the varnish still intact, apart from a few scratches and gouges from the spades. The sides had been carved into an apron of oak apples and leaves along the base and the top into a simple bevelled cross above the brass plate. The handles were brass too, solid, beaded and hinged into fleur-de-lis brackets.

'We'll need more men and a cart to carry this weight away,' the stocky man predicted.

'You can keep the coffin.' My guardian spoke for the first time. 'I am only interested in its contents.'

Sir Grigsby pondered the problem. 'It would be easier,' he conceded. 'We will never find a suitable vehicle at this time of night and there is an interment three plots away in the morning.'

Sidney Grice looked at his hunter. The stocky man brought out a screwdriver and set to work – sixteen screws shone gold in the flames, each one carefully placed in his waistcoat pocket.

'Best keep back,' he advised as he and the other three took hold of the lid and lifted.

From the splaying of their neck muscles, the lid alone was quite a weight. They shuffled to one side and bent their knees to put it down. Sidney Grice was first at the foot of the coffin, lantern raised to illuminate the interior.

'Good lord.' His right eye wriggled free and clinked unheeded into the casket.

'What is it?' I freed myself and hurried round with George Pound in close pursuit.

Sidney Grice said nothing. He was transfixed by the sight that greeted him. The unknown man was not lying peacefully back, arms crossed, as I had anticipated. His arms were lifted, palms up, fingers hooked with torn ends, and his head was raised from its silk pillow. But the worst of it was his face. I had never seen such a look of terror. His eyes bulged, white and staring madly. A bandage had been wrapped over and under his jaw to keep it closed and his lips had been sutured, but the stitches had been ripped out when the lips had pulled apart.

'Oh dear God above,' I gasped. 'He was buried alive.'

53

The Shadow of an Angel

INSPECTOR POUND WAS the first to break the silence. 'But that is not possible. This man was long dead when he was found.'

'Are you sure it is the same man?' I could not tear my eyes from the nightmare before me.

'I have never seen him before, but I can get my constable to confirm it.'

A breeze ruffled the hem of the white shroud.

I forced myself to look closer. 'His nails are broken,' I said in horror.

'But not in the coffin.' Sidney Grice pushed past a workman and stood at the feet. 'That Gothic fantasy so beloved of Mr Poe and the sewage sifters of Fleet Street is just that, a fantasy. Imagine you were to fill this occupied coffin with buckets of water. How many would it take?'

He spun round like a schoolmaster, but nobody seemed inclined to answer. I was not even convinced they had heard him, mesmerized as they were by that gruesome find, but I was used to him firing questions by then.

'Thirty,' I guessed wildly, but he accepted my calculation as if I had great experience in flooding caskets. 'So, sixty gallons.'

'According to Dr Harold Mitre, a man at rest requires two gallons of air per minute. This goes up fifteenfold with exercise and twenty in a panic. That would give him at best two minutes' air. It took this capable and experienced sexton approximately two minutes and nine seconds to unscrew the lid and the reverse action is similarly time-consuming. So, if this man were to wake in the coffin, it would have to be while the lid was being put down, giving him plenty of time to rap, kick or use whatever means he chose to draw attention to himself.'

'What are you saying, man?' Sir Grigsby was unmistakeably rattled.

'I do not care to be addressed as *man*,' Mr G told him pleasantly. 'It is only three inches away from *my man*.' He raised the wick on his lamp. 'A term which would be insupportable, even from a parvenu knight of the realm such as yourself.' He disregarded the poppings of pricked dignity behind him. 'If you were paying attention, Sir Grigsby, which you were not, I was explaining in quite simple terms that this man was not alive when placed in the coffin unless...' He directed the question to me.

I filled the space. 'Unless the undertakers were deaf or deliberately ignored him.'

'Precisely.' My godfather viewed me with paternal pride. 'Inspector Pound shall get his stolid constable to identify the body as being the same one with which he was presented, but in the meantime I would draw your attention to the fact that none of the beautiful and unnecessary silk lining has been plucked or ripped, even though the cadaver's fingerplates are, as the inelegant but occasionally useful Miss Middleton has already observed –' he stopped suddenly and clipped on his pince-nez – 'torn.'

'What is it?' Pound craned over me.

Sidney Grice's hand disappeared and reappeared with his knife, the steel flicking out. With his left hand he took the dead man's right, and it flashed through my mind that he was about to take a finger for his anatomical collection, perhaps to have it mounted on his desk next to the shrunken ear of Amelia Dyer. But my guardian looked more intent on performing a manicure. He was running the tip of the blade under the edge of the plate of the middle finger.

'What indeed?' he replied as something fell into his palm. He laid his knife down, took out his notebook and dropped his find on to an open page.

'A bit of dirt,' Sir Grigsby said dismissively. 'Interesting though that is, we need to get this resident removed, and his casket temporarily replaced in the grave and covered over. Visitors do not want to discover that we are disturbing their loved ones' rest.'

The men took the body and placed it, still twisted, on a sheet of canvas, taking a corner each to carry it up the gravelled path in Sir Grigsby's wake.

'*Resident.*' Sidney Grice closed his knife scornfully. 'And for that they gave him a knighthood.'

'You'll get yours one day, Mr Grice,' Inspector Pound forecast.

We set off after the sorry group.

'Not after I discovered what one of Her Majesty's progeny was up to in Whitechapel,' my guardian replied gloomily.

'Which one?' the inspector asked.

'What did he do?' I put in simultaneously.

But Sidney Grice was hurrying on. 'Believe me.' He paused to read an epitaph, the shadow of an angel's wings sprouting from his back. 'You would not thank me if I told you.'

There were lights in the windows of the gatehouse and I saw them dip as the men lowered their charge.

54

The Name of Pathology

THE DEAD MAN had been laid on boards on a bier in a chapel of rest. He was dressed in a shroud and still tilted disconcertingly upwards, his head a foot or so above the table, his nose flattened at the tip where it had pressed against the underside of the lid and his arms raised like a prizefighter about to attack his opponent. The gaslights had been turned up. They did nothing to alleviate the look of fright on his face, but I could make out several areas where the skin was sloughing away and his left eye had a discoloured half-moon under it.

'Is it possible he had a spinal deformity?' I suggested.

'That would not explain the position of his arms.' Sidney Grice dismissed the idea with a toss of his hat on to the altar.

'Have some respect,' Sir Grigsby protested.

'I sometimes respect that which respects me.' Mr G threw his overcoat after it. 'You and your men will leave us now.'

'I beg your pardon?' In the light the director did not look quite so impressive. His eyes were small and perfectly round like a cheap doll's, and his lower jaw receded so far behind his upper that it was difficult to imagine how he ate.

'There is no need to do so,' Mr G assured him breezily. 'Go now.'

'We have to examine the body now,' I told him. 'I do not imagine the public would like to think of you as an onlooker for such indignities.'

Sir Grigbsy tussled briefly, balancing the thought of being evicted from his own domain with the bad publicity he might be subjected to.

'Very well. I shall adjourn to my office.' He mustered his dignity. 'You men go back and tidy up.'

The four gravediggers were leaning wearily against the wall.

'Thirsty work, I imagine.' I gave them a florin each.

'Expecting a gratuity too?' Sidney Grice asked, as Sir Grigsby loitered, and was answered with a slam of the door.

'His body was found in the cellar, was it not?' I asked.

'In a disused cesspit, I believe,' Pound replied, 'buried in quicklime.'

'I thought quicklime burns bodies,' I objected.

'I've known a few murderers use it to dispose of their victims,' Pound agreed.

'Dry quicklime does,' my guardian conceded. 'Calcium oxide can be gratifyingly corrosive, but wet quicklime becomes calcium hydroxide and an unparalleled alkaline preservative.'

'So the body could have been in it for years,' I conjectured.

'A very long time.' Sidney Grice patted the dead man's chest.

'It sounds hollow,' I remarked.

'Probably because it is.' Mr G pulled the neck of the shroud down an inch. 'The outside has been conserved – cured, one might say – but the slaked quicklime would not penetrate the body more than half an inch or so.'

'So the inside has decomposed,' Pound concluded, 'and we are looking at a husk.'

'Where have you seen bodies adopt similar poses, Inspector?'

'Only after a fire,' Pound replied.

'The pugilistic pose,' I remembered too late. 'The muscles contract with the heat.'

'But he has not been in a fire,' Pound argued. 'Not a hair has been singed.'

'We are discussing the wrong crime,' Sidney Grice announced. 'How did he die?'

'Strangulation with a ligature round the neck.' I pointed to a sunken ring round the dead man's throat. 'Probably.'

'Possibly.' My guardian qualified my diagnosis. 'We shall pass him presently to those who aggrandize their anatomical desecrations in the name of pathology.'

He took off his pince-nez.

'His expression.' Pound shuddered. 'I shall never get used to rictus grins.'

'You will have one yourself soon enough,' Sidney Grice prophesied.

'Take more than death to make you smile,' the inspector retorted.

Sidney Grice tugged his scarred earlobe. 'Is there more than death, Inspector? It would be pretty to think so.'

55

The Elgin Marbles and the Size of a Teardrop

IT WAS AFTER three in the morning when we got home.

'Why do we not take a key?' I asked as Sidney Grice jangled the bell impatiently.

'Because I have another device for opening doors.' He rang again.

'Your lockpicks?' I could not see the point of breaking in to his own house.

'Molly,' he replied as the door swung open.

Our maid viewed us through thin slits between her puffy eyelids. She looked all wrong without her hat on. Her hair had expanded into a ginger tumbleweed and had clothes pegs poking out of it.

'I wasntn't not sleeping,' she defended herself against the anticipated attack, for her employer would never accept that she needed any rest at all.

'I think you were, Molly,' I said gently. 'But did you fall asleep in your uniform?'

'It saves time in the morning.' She yawned without covering her mouth and, if there had been a tonsil-growing competition, I felt sure she would have walked away with the cup. They sat like two lobular apricots either side of her throat, so close together I was amazed that she could swallow.

'I told you she slept in her clothes.' My guardian waited for Molly to take his hat.

I put my hat on the table. 'I thought you were joking.'

Mr G greeted that remark bleakly. 'Then you have seen a side of me I do not have.'

'The skittish playful side?' I hung my cloak on its hook.

'The very same,' he concurred, rearranging his sticks. 'How many times have I told you not to polish my canes, wretched skivvy? Do not answer that. It is four hundred and sixteen.'

'Sorry, sir.' Molly rubbed the handle of one absently with her sleeve. 'But I aintn't not skinny,' she mumbled, adding all too audibly, 'not like somebodyone I could mention.'

'What are you doing to your hair?' I asked.

The more I looked, the more tangled it seemed.

'I always wanted straight hair.' Molly patted it underneath with the ball of her thumb. 'Not like yours, miss, but nice.'

A tress dangled lackadaisically.

'But wrapping it round pegs will only make it wavier.' My boots were muddy and I genuflected to untie the laces.

'That's the clever bit.' She twisted the tress round and pegged it up again. 'Cook tolded me hair dontn't not never do what you tell it to – just like yours dontn't not, miss – so if I tell mine to curl…' Molly opened her arms to allow me to conclude her irrefutable logic.

'Tea.' Her employer pushed past her into his study and the peg fell out.

Sidney Grice had lit an oil lamp on his desk. Its base was moulded from the head of the sledgehammer which Prince Albert had used to smash the Elgin Marbles, necessitating their replacement with the clumsy forgeries that decorate the British Museum to this day.

He was bent over a sheet of white paper and appeared to be slicing his fingertip with a scalpel, but as I drew closer I saw that he was trying to cut into a dark flake, the shape of the wing of a housefly but about half the size.

'What are you doing?'

'Failing to separate the layers,' he mumbled. 'Hold my magnifying glass.'

'This brass-handled one that you never let me touch?' I picked it up.

'I have allowed you to touch it twice,' he argued, 'and you have used it nine times without my permission when I am not in the room.'

I did not tell him that Molly had used it once as well.

'Not counting the time you let Molly use it to insert a thorn into her finger,' he grunted. 'Hold it steady... and ten-elevenths of an inch higher. That is only nine-elevenths.' He picked at the flake again. 'Hold it steady.'

'What about holding your finger steady?' I suggested.

'It is not I who tremors.' He was probably right but I was disadvantaged by having to lean over the desk. 'This is hopeless.'

I walked round it to join him. 'Is that what you dug out from under that man's fingerplate?'

'If I were to trouble to answer that enquiry, it would be in the affirmative.'

He took a glass slide from his microscope box.

'What is it?'

'Possibly his calling card.' Mr G put a blob of glue, the size of a teardrop, into the shallow concave well on the top of his slide. 'What shall we talk about while we wait for that to get tacky? I do so hate these awkward conversational gaps and the more one thinks about them, the more difficult they become. My mother once sat with the Grand Admiral of Lichtenstein for twenty-nine minutes trying to exchange pleasantries with him, only to realize that he had died the day before. She had noticed that he was lying on a table, but then one expects eccentric behaviour from foreigners.'

'But not from Grices,' I put in.

'Quite so.' He prodded the glue with a needle. 'Ah, that is tacky now.'

With the tiny droplet on the end of his needle, Mr G lifted the flake and very carefully deposited it against the blob on the slide.

Molly plodded in.

'Deposit the tray and leave instantly,' her employer commanded, manoeuvring the flake minutely.

Molly opened her mouth.

'Perhaps you would like to go to bed, Molly,' I suggested.

'Aintn't no p'raps about it,' she said. 'Only—'

'Now would be a good time,' I said. And her mouth clamped shut and she was gone faster than the magician I had seen once at the Pier Pavilion in Southport, but without the alarming puff of yellow smoke.

Mr G straightened his back and I saw that he had fixed the flake so that it stood on its edge, glued at its base on one side. He placed the slide on his microscope platform and peered through the eyepiece.

'Push the lamp cautiously closer... three-eighths of an imperial inch more... stop.'

He rotated the slide about ten degrees and fiddled with the focus.

'*Wunderbar*,' he breathed and made a final fine adjustment. Sidney Grice was transfigured. He had seen the light and now he almost radiated it. '*Ausgezeichnet*.'

'*Was is est?*' I stretched my German vocabulary to its outer limit.

'Have a look for yourself,' he invited me, in English, I was happy to hear.

My father told me that you should keep both eyes open while looking down a microscope so that you could draw your specimen at the same time, but I could never manage, and now I screwed my left eye shut.

'You should keep one eye open so that you can make an accurate—'

'I know,' I snapped. 'All I can see is a thick black line.'

'You are very good at not doing what you are supposed to do,' my guardian complained.

'But not as good as I am at doing what I am not supposed to,' I responded, rubbing my eye. 'Oh, I can see three lines now.'

'Precisely.' Mr G clapped his hands like a sultan summoning his favourite wife. 'And what colours are they?'

'From left to right,' I squinted hard, 'brown, blue, green.'

Sidney Grice was virtually skipping by now. 'And what do those colours mean to you?'

'If they are the colours of another country's flag, I am hopeless at those,' I said, but did not add that my childhood friend Barney had known a hundred of them.

'Think,' my godfather urged.

'I am trying.'

My G started pacing behind me. 'There is no point in trying. Molly tries to think and Cook may well make an attempt herself one day. Just think.'

He slapped the desktop and the lamp wobbled.

'How can I think when you are behaving like Wackford Squeers?' I jumped up and nearly butted him under the chin, but Mr G whipped away.

'Who?'

'He was a cruel schoolmaster in *Nicholas Nickleby*.'

Mr G threw up his hands. 'Perhaps having pupils like you drove him to it. Perhaps he used to be a mild-mannered man, as I was before you entered my life.'

'The last time you were mild-mannered was one year and one day before your first birthday,' I retorted. 'And until you learn to moderate your behaviour, I am going to follow poor Molly's example and go to bed.'

'Perhaps you could shout up and ask her to look at this fleck of—' he began scornfully.

'Paint?' I interrupted his eloquence. 'You did not tell me it was paint.'

'Of course it is paint.' He checked his tongue, perhaps a tad guiltily.

'The cells at Marylebone Police Station,' I realized.

'*Hoera*,' he breathed sarcastically.

'And stop speaking German.'

'That was Dutch.'

'Why are you speaking Dutch?'

'There is little else that one can do with it. Dutch is not a language worth writing or reading.'

I retraced my thoughts. 'So the dead man was held in a police cell some time before I was.'

'A long time before.' Sidney Grice went to the window and looked out between the drapes. 'Tonight, Miss Middleton, you had the privilege of meeting the long-lost friend and drinking partner of the late Mr Nathan Roptine Mortlock, Daniel Filbert.' His arms rose and parted as if to acknowledge the applause of an audience, but there was only the dustman's cart creaking past the gas lamp. 'I have that tiger in my sights now, March.' Sidney Grice revolved a hundred and eighty degrees, arms still high as if to embrace me, his face aglow with the fire of his zealotry. 'See how steady my hand is. It shall not be long before I pull the trigger.'

'We could do with a new hearthrug,' I observed.

56

The Pendulum and the Pit

MR CREPOLIUS SNUSHALL rose obsequiously until our silhouettes solidified and he realized who we were.

'Miss Mortlock has given strict instructions that you are not to be given access to her father again.' His voice had a coolness in it today.

'We have not come to look at anyone's body,' I told him, perceiving the glimmer of hope that arose within his aged breast.

'You have changed your mind and wish to arrange your own funerals?'

'That is a damnable lie.' Mr G swept his hat off so flamboyantly that he almost smacked Mr Snushall in the face with it.

'It was a question.'

'Then kindly raise the pitch of your pre-penultimate syllable – *fune*rals,' he demonstrated, 'so as to provide an audible question mark in future.'

My guardian skimmed his hat through the air to settle over the top finial of an empty coat stand.

Mr Snushall uncoiled from his miserable servile stoop and I was surprised to find him looking down on us with a good four-inch height advantage.

'I think I should like you to leave,' he declared, his voice distinctly icy now.

Sidney Grice promenaded round me, his cane tucked under his arm.

'You think?' I clarified. 'So you are not sure?'

'I know I would,' he corrected himself.

'But you said *think*,' I reminded him.

'I meant *know*.'

'Do you really know or do you just think you know?'

'I *know*.' The ice became steely.

'They are very different verbs,' I pondered. 'Do you find you get your words muddled more as you get older? It can—'

'What are you doing?' Mr Snushall challenged.

'I am trying to ascertain how certain you are in your wishes,' I answered.

'I meant him.' He pointed accusingly at Sidney Grice, who had gone behind the desk and was leafing though a thick black-bound volume with black-margined pages.

'That is very rude of you,' I reprimanded.

'It is more than rude.' Mr Snushall tried to pass by me to get at his book, but I sidestepped.

'I was talking about *your* manners,' I informed the undertaker, 'interrupting me mid-sentence to try start a conversation with another person over my shoulder. Is this the way you treat all your customers?'

'I have clients, not customers,' Snushall corrected me.

'She does that to me sometimes.' Mr G turned another page. 'It is almost annoying.'

'And neither of you are customers *or* clients.' The undertaker barged me aside, rushed to where Mr G stood and snatched the book away. 'That is confidential.'

'Tell us about the man you buried in Highgate Cemetery with the headstone reading *God Shall Know You*,' I invited the undertaker.

'I shall not.'

'Not even for money?' I opened my handbag, hoping he did not spot my flask and cigarette case.

'Not for ten thousand pounds.' He threw back his head.

And I clipped my bag shut. 'I was not thinking of going that high.'

'You do a lot of work for charity,' Sidney Grice commented.

'I do my Christian duty.' Mr Snushall closed the book.

'But not for free.' My guardian frowned. 'The Methodist Women's Charity for the Decent Interment of the Unidentified Poor pays you a goodly sum to bury anonymous bodies found on the street.'

'The labourer is worthy of his hire,' Snushall quoted piously.

'Do they attend the funerals?' My right breast hurt from him elbowing me but I could not rub it in their presence.

'Their cases are poor people. I give them simple caskets and a marked plot, but it is not an area where gentlefolk would care to visit.' Mr Snushall put the book in a drawer and locked it.

'Saint Cecil's Cemetery in Limehouse,' Mr G stated. 'You are right about one thing, Mr Crepolius Jimmy Snushall, boxer and burier of human carcasses—'

'Boxer?' Mr Snushall shrieked.

'No lady *would* want to go to Saint Cecil's,' Sidney Grice agreed, 'nor could she – because it does not exist.'

Veins rose in cords on Mr Snushall's temples and up his balding dome. 'You will leave here immediately or I shall call the police.'

Whoever swept up did not get right into the corners, I noted. It was probably another of Dorolius's duties.

'We shall leave here, though not immediately, and we may call the police ourselves.' I gave him a playful nudge. 'This is your last chance to tell us about that funeral before we become unkind.'

The cords engorged and became varicose. 'You cannot threaten me.'

'It is strange, is it not, how people often tell me how I cannot do what I have already done,' Mr G chatted to me.

'I have found that of late too,' I agreed. 'Perhaps it is a London habit. I never noticed it in Parbold.'

Mr Snushall reached for a bell pull, but, before he got there, Sidney Grice's cane swished out and jabbed into the undertaker's chest, pushing him back against the wall.

'Explain to this sinister grovelling parasite what this cane can do.' My guardian swung his cane like a pendulum.

'Is it the one Molly dropped last week and made you angry?'

Mr G's eyes narrowed. 'It is.'

'That,' I announced, 'is the Grice Patent-pending Compressed Gas Gun. If Mr Grice presses a button on the handle it will fire a lead ball some half-inch in diameter through your coat, waistcoat, shirt, undershirt, skin, fat (though you do not have much of that), ribs, intercostal muscles – they are the ones between your ribs – pericardium and heart, reversing that sequence to exit by way of your back, passing through your nasty flock wallpaper—'

'That cost two guineas a roll,' he protested.

'To lodge, considerably flattened by its journey, in that wall,' I finished.

'Oh,' Mr Snushall's veins fluttered.

'Pull down the blind, Miss Middleton.'

'The one saying *closed*?'

'The very same.'

'You cannot do that,' Snushall said angrily.

'This is exactly what we were talking about,' I reminded him. 'I already have.'

'I saw him kill a mad dog once.' I wiggled my nose. 'It was very messy.' I felt the paper. 'You could have got this flock at half the price in Grinton's.'

The veins collapsed. 'But that's where I got it.'

'Perhaps they recognized a fellow swindler when they saw him,' I suggested.

'How dare you?' There was appreciably less conviction in the undertaker's indignation.

Sidney Grice adjusted his grip and Snushall squirmed.

'I will see you again soon.' I gave the undertaker a little wave as I pulled back the curtain.

'You cannot go in there,' he protested.

'There you go again,' I remarked lightly.

Dorolius Lacrissimus lay asleep in an elm coffin. He leaped up guiltily as I bid him a good morning.

'Mr Snushall says you are to show me the pit,' I told him, but Dorolius was not convinced. 'Five shillings says he did.' I took out my purse.

'Ten.'

'Four.'

'You've got a funny way of 'aggling.'

'It works,' I told him.

But he still hesitated. 'I 'ad betta check wiv Mr S,' he decided, clambering over the side.

'Perhaps I should come and explain how I discovered you.'

Dorolius jumped to the floor.

'Cor,' he said admiringly. 'First you tell me a lie; then you try to bribe me; then you 'aggle over the price; now you're resortin' to blackmail, and all in a minute. You're my kind of gal, you are.'

'Perhaps a bit old for you.' I smiled.

'Yeah,' he looked me up and down, 'and plain.' He patted down his trousers, which had a fine sawdust on them. 'Foller me.'

I *follered* Dorolius down the corridor and through a back door, across a yard stacked high with long box shapes covered in tarpaulin. I did not need my guardian to guess what they were.

''Ere we are.' Dorolius opened a door. 'Only don't go in.'

I could hardly see into the unlit interior, but I just made out a rectangular shape with a slabbed path all the way round it, similar to an ornamental garden pond. It was full almost to the top with a white powder. A draught ran over the surface and tossed it at me. I stepped back, covering my nose and closing my eyes.

'Is that what burned your fingers?' I spluttered when I was a couple of yards away.

''Orrible stuff, ain't it.' Dorolius closed the door. 'You won't get me in trouble?'

Those big innocent-wicked eyes regarded me.

'I shall not,' I promised.

''Ow about that four bob then?'

I patted him on the shoulder and gave him five.

57

Heaven and the Man in Black

SIDNEY GRICE STILL had the undertaker pinned to the wall when I re-emerged.

'Quicklime,' I announced.

'The b-builders left it there,' Mr Snushall stuttered. 'I use it for g-getting rid of rats.'

'You can lock away your diary but my memory is not so easily disposed of,' my godfather said. 'The last time that those well-meaning Methodist ladies arranged for a body to be delivered here was yesterday afternoon.' He prodded the cane in and Snushall squealed. 'Where is it now?'

'Already buried at Saint Cecil's.' Snushall was sweating now. 'I do not know exactly where that is because I never attend the charitable funerals myself.' An idea struck him. 'Perhaps the men steal the bodies.' He jerked his elbows about. 'There's a good market in the medical profession and second-hand coffins are easy to sell at the lower end of the—'

'Professor Duffy,' I broke in.

'Who?' Snushall's lower lip quivered.

'The anatomist. He told us that you approached him with an offer to sell him bodies for dissection.'

'The rotten snitchy swine.' Snushall clenched his teeth.

I coughed, partly to hide a laugh at his choice of words and partly because of the powder I had inhaled. It had been a lucky guess anyway.

'Do we really have to get men to rake through the lime?' Mr G sighed.

'That will not be necessary,' Crepolius Snushall decided. 'What is your price?'

'The truth, the whole truth and nothing but,' Sidney Grice replied.

'And you will not call the police?'

'Not if you cooperate fully,' Mr G promised. 'But, if you attempt to hide any information or tell even the tiniest of *porkies*, Miss Middleton will be straight out of that door summoning a constable at the top of her shrill and gratingly raucous voice.'

I held my tongue.

'Very well,' the undertaker agreed, 'but may I sit down first?'

'You may.' Sidney Grice lowered his cane. 'But we shall stand.'

I would quite like to have rested my legs but I decided not to squabble.

'Keep your arms on the inexpertly tooled top of your shoddily fashioned counterfeit Versailles escritoire where I can see them,' Mr G commanded. 'I have been attacked by five undertakers in the past and could not fail to be impressed by the range of armaments at their disposal – needles, scalpels, catheters and syringes. My left knee will take a good while to decay after being injected with embalming fluid during the Blankenberge Flower Festival.'

'Can we get on with this?' Crepolius Snushall asked agitatedly.

'Please do.' I looked at a picture of six angels carrying a soul to heaven. Their expressions were doubtless meant to be pious, but to me they looked rather bilious and their charge had his eyes rolled up as if the experience were the last word in tedium.

Snushall harrumphed, 'My name is Crepolius James Snushall of Greystones House, 23—'

'Oh, for goodness' sake.' Sidney Grice waved his stick and Snushall ducked. 'You are not making a statement in court. This is an informal chat, though admittedly it may end in you concluding your life in a disease-riddled gaol.'

'Or being shot,' I added.

'Ask him some leading questions, Miss Middleton,' my guardian urged, 'or we shall be here for the rest of the month.'

I rested my hands on the desk and tried to fix the undertaker's gaze but he looked shiftily away.

'So you admit that you accepted money from a charitable organization to give people proper funerals, but disposed of the bodies in that lime pit at the back of these premises?'

'If you put it like that,' Snushall mumbled.

'Yes or no?' Mr G rapped.

The *yes* was just about audible.

'So what happened to the man now in Highgate?' I asked.

'I do not know all the background.' Snushall interlinked his hands. 'I believe he was found in the basement of an old building. He could not be identified and so he was brought here at the request of the ladies. One had been to see if he was a lost nephew but he was not.'

'And her name was?' Mr G put his knuckles on the desk and stared at the undertaker too.

Crepolius closed his palms, thumbs on top as my friend Barney had taught me to imitate the hoot of an owl. 'Mrs Fitz-something...'

'You will have to do better than that,' Mr G warned.

'Williams, Fitzwilliams, I think. The society will know.'

'It is not for you to know what they will know,' Sidney Grice reprimanded him. 'Recommence but do try to be more entertaining. You have no concept of how tedious it can be dragging information out of a criminal. It is like pulling a ball of brown string through a puncture in the lid of a red box, and not knowing whether it will snag or when it will end.'

'Criminal?' Snushall whispered.

'A vulgar criminal,' I confirmed.

'It would appear that you have broken at least fourteen clauses of the 1872 Disposal of Human Remains Act, Great Britain,' Mr G said sternly. 'Shall I enumerate?'

'Perhaps later.' I hurriedly postponed his lecture. 'So you collected the body from the morgue?'

'My men did. I never go there – horrid place.' The undertaker quivered. '*The House of Death* they call it.'

'And...?' I urged, feeling we had hardly drawn the first inch of that imaginary string out yet.

Crepolius Snushall hinged his arms up and I waited for his avian imitation to begin, but he lowered his head and nestled the bridge of his nose between his thumbs.

'I instructed the men to put him in the disposal chamber.'

'The pit?' I clarified, and his head rose and fell. 'And...?'

'Something strange happened.' Snushall looked up in awe. 'His body did not dissolve.' He hinged his arms back down. 'I thought perhaps the lime was wet. It goes off when it is, but it was dry—'

'As a bone,' Mr G contributed.

'His skin started to burn,' Mr Snushall related, 'but then it stopped.' And so did he.

'And then?' I prodded.

'He sat up,' Crepolius said. 'I have seen it before. The reaction of a body with quicklime produces a lot of heat. I have even seen a corpse burst into flames. Sometimes the heat makes the muscles contract. We call it *horse riding*. It is not usually a problem because as the body is eaten away it collapses into the powder and is completely destroyed. This one was different, though. Something stopped him being burned up. The men were spooked—'

'Like horses,' I said to myself.

'One of them quit to join the Salvation Army,' the undertaker recounted sadly. 'He was a good man up until then.'

'The body had been preserved in wet quicklime for years,' I told him. 'I imagine that made the skin resistant.'

'I lost sleep over that one,' Snushall admitted miserably. 'I even considered actually doing what I was supposed to and burying him at my own expense.'

'How awful for you,' I mocked and Mr Snushall met my eyes fleetingly, grateful for my understanding.

'We have two inches of string and at least a yard to go.' Mr G straightened impatiently.

'Then my saviour came.'

'I hope you are not going to tell me you had a vision of Jesus.' Sidney Grice went to inspect the picture.

'My saviour was a man in black.' Snushall rolled his eyes up, but looked no more virtuous than the transported soul. 'He came and asked to see the body. I told him it was not ready for viewing, but he would not be deflected. He said he thought it might be his estranged brother-in-law. So we got the body out of the pit, hosed it down and laid it with extra pillows in a casket with a hinged top section in the lid for viewing. The man came in and I knew at once that he recognized the body – he gave that special small jump that they do – and he stood for a long time, and once he touched the departed's hair, just that special small stroke. Then we went back to my office and he gave me his instructions. He claimed not to know who the man was, but said he reminded him of somebody that he could not help and so he wanted the best for this one – solid oak, lead-lined, all the trimmings and a white marble stone with those words, *God Shall Know You.* I gave him a price and he hardly listened, said he would come back the next day and pay.'

'And did he?' Mr G looked behind the picture.

'Every penny.'

'Did he or anybody else attend the funeral?' I asked.

'Just him.' Snushall traced the course of a newly arisen blood vessel on his brow.

'Describe this ebony-clad benefactor in extraordinary detail.' Mr G rested his cane on the desk and the undertaker leaned sideways out of the line of fire.

'There is not much to describe,' he said.

Sidney Grice aligned his cane with Crepolius's heart.

I tried to help. 'Was he young or old, dark- or fair-haired?'

'It is difficult to say.' Beads popped up on his face again. 'I would say from his voice he was not very young and not very old. He stood quite straight. But, as I tried to tell you, he was completely covered in black, top to bottom, and a scarf wrapped around his face so all I could see was his eyes and not very much of them.'

I was halfway to sitting down when I remembered I did not have a chair behind me. I stood up.

'An ancient Chinese exercise,' I pretended. 'Did you see him after the funeral?'

'Never.'

'Were his clothes expensive or cheap, old or new?' Mr G took his hat off the stand with a scowl. 'And do not pretend you did not notice. You feed your greed by assessing people's fiscal worth and adjusting your accounts accordingly.'

'Middling,' the skilled assessor decided.

'What sort of accent did he have?' I asked.

'Foreign,' Mr Snushall reminisced. 'He said his words all like *I 'ear you 'aves zuh body off a man.*'

Sidney Grice's face was inscrutable.

'Exactly like that? And I mean *exactly*? You would stake a man's life on it?'

'I am a mimic without equal,' Mr Snushall avowed proudly. 'I often imitate clients behind their backs.'

'Imitate Mr Grice,' I challenged.

'Exactly like that? And I mean *exactly*? You would stake a man's life on it?' Mr Snushall recited and, though it was not uncanny, it was astonishingly true to life.

'That will be all for today.' Mr G swept his hat off the rack.

'That will be all for today.' Snushall's miming was spot on that time, including my godfather's toss of the head, and I could not help but laugh.

'We have finished that game.' Sidney Grice flopped his hat on and pulled down the brim frigidly. 'Shall I demonstrate how my cane operates?'

'No need for that.' The droplets sprang into pools, spreading and merging until the undertaker looked as if he had just rinsed his face.

'Yes, please,' I urged.

Sidney Grice put his cane to his shoulder and took careful aim.

'I meant no harm by my imitation, sir, only the young lady instructed me to.' Crepolius Snushall ducked and fell awkwardly behind his desk.

My guardian pressed a button in the handle and there was a distinct click.

'Mother!' the undertaker cried, almost drowning out the sound of 'Oh, for the Wings of a Dove'.

'I have died,' Mr Snushall sobbed.

Sidney Grice lowered his cane and twisted the handle, and the tune changed.

'I told you it confused people,' he said as he crossed the room and flicked up the blind.

It was raining heavily outside, but we stepped out smartly to the chimes of Mendelssohn's 'Wedding March'.

58

Monkeys, Cats and Dragons

GORDON STREET WAS blocked and, looking along it, the traffic on Euston Road was at a standstill too. The music box wound down.

'Why do we not walk?' I suggested. 'It will do us good to stretch our legs.'

Sidney Grice's mouth looked as if he had popped a rotten oyster in it.

'Men have legs,' he informed me. 'Ladies, when they are obliged to refer to them, have extremities.'

We skipped on to the road, the gutter swirling with brown water and clogged with droppings. The salt man's mare tried to chew my hat, but I tapped it on the nose with the pair of gloves I carried at my guardian's insistence but hated wearing.

'Why were you surprised when I told Sir William that Daniel Filbert was the pickpocket?' I shouted above the wail of a hurdy-gurdy.

An occupied hansom rolled back, crushing the tip of my left boot but just missing the extremity of my extremity.

'Watch where you are going,' Mr G castigated both the cabby and me, and he waited until we were on the other side before continuing the conversation. 'Because I have few reasons to suspect that he was.'

'But he was in possession of the stolen watch and we know he was short of money because Nathan paid his fine,' I reasoned with decreasing confidence.

'The policeman who returned the watch to Nathan Mortlock was in possession of it and ill-paid.' Sidney Grice sidestepped, snarling, 'Out of my way,' at a girl who held a tray of ribbons.

'I take your point,' I conceded.

'They ain't points, they's ribbons,' the girl explained. 'Nice yeller one to brighten up yer 'air, miss?' She held a pretty daffodil length out enticingly and I gave her a penny.

'What on earth are you going to do with...' Sidney Grice turned back. 'How much for that pink one?'

'Penny a yard.' The girl smiled appealingly. She had nice white teeth.

'How much for the reel?'

'There's eight yards.' She sucked her thumb briefly. 'So that's a shillin's wurf.'

'As even you, ragged, inarticulate and ill-educated as you are must know, there are twelve pennies in a shilling.' Mr G picked it up. 'And I doubt there are more than seven yards and four inches here.'

'It stritches longer,' she told him, 'and you're gettin' the reel for free.'

'If I had the rest of the day I could argue that out with you.' A shilling appeared between his fingers. 'My logic would be irrefutable but still I doubt that I should win.' He paid her the coin and pocketed his purchase.

'I would have thought blue was more your colour,' I teased.

'The colour of the material is immaterial.'

We shouldered our way past the barrel organist, churning out a barely recognizable rendition of 'Moonlight Mary the Girl from Tipperary' while his monkey bit a little boy in a sailor suit who had tried to stroke its tail.

''E's jest bein' friendly,' the grinder told a distraught mother as the child screamed and clutched at his bloodied fingers.

'Dangerous animals, children,' Sidney Grice commented, stepping over a beggar lying sprawled on the pavement and waving imperiously at an unoccupied cab.

'The Cat and Dragon,' he directed the driver as he climbed aboard.

*

'This is a public house,' Sidney Grice disclosed, though he had taken me in a few before. 'Keep a tight hold of your absurd handbag and a tight control of your behaviour, by which I mean no flirtatiousness with the customers.'

'I have never flirted with a stranger in my life,' I retorted, outraged and suppressing a few embarrassing memories.

'You bought one a drink in the Duke of Marlborough.' He pushed open the door.

'That was Sir Randolph Cosmo Napier.' I stepped smartly through the door as he let it swing after him. 'Who turned out to be an important witness,' I told his back.

Sidney Grice surveyed his surroundings, cane raised as if prepared to fight a duel but, apart from the publican, the saloon was empty. It was quite a small pub, only five tables and about three times as many chairs, but it was clean and had a welcoming air. The barman looked up, an oak tree of a man, tall and broad and solid.

'Good afternoon, miss,' he greeted me. 'A bit earlier today.' He put a great paw to the gin bottle. 'And Mr Grice, I wasn't expecting you in here, sir.'

Mr G's masseter muscles bunched. 'I was not aware that this was yet another of your haunts.'

'I'm terribly sorry, miss. I mistook you for a countess who frequents this establishment,' the barman retracted, but we both knew the damage was done.

'You might as well pour me one, Jim.' I rested my bustle on a stool.

'Why did you not tell me this when Pound mentioned Constable Dutton's name?' My guardian grasped the brass rail with his left hand.

'I only know Jim as *Jim*.'

'And for you, sir?'

'What do you have that is not poisoned with ethanol?'

'Sherry,' Jim replied. His hair was shaved in the Prussian way that became fashionable after Waterloo but was now more associated with an attempt to get rid of lice.

'I knew you were an ex-policeman.' I raised my glass. 'But I have never heard you called *Mutton*.'

'The first man that does will be straight out the door. I 'ate that name.' Jim recorked the bottle.

'Do you have any orange squash?'

'Three species of beer; gin, whisky, rum, sherry, port,' Jim Dutton listed. 'Oh, and we have lemonade for ladies what like a port and lemon.'

'I will have a lemonade.'

Jim polished a half-pint glass and filled it from a stone jar with a murky off-yellow liquid. 'Go easy, it's got an 'ell of a punch.'

'And one for yourself, Jim,' I offered when it became obvious that Mr G would not.

'Don't mind if I do.' Jim pulled himself a pint.

He and I raised our glasses but Sidney Grice left his on the counter.

'So what's George Pound been sayin' 'bout me?' Jim smacked his lips in enjoyment of his own bitter.

'That you arrested Mortlock and Filbert the night before the Garstang murders,' I said.

'Still not solved that?' Jim eyed Mr G over the rim of his pewter tankard.

'I have never been asked to,' my godfather replied starchily.

'I 'eard about Mortlock,' Jim commiserated, as if the loss were ours. 'Sounds like a rum affair.'

Mr G rotated his glass ninety degrees, though it looked the same from every angle to me. 'I cannot bring myself to thank you for your professional insight,' he muttered.

'Never made it to those politeness classes, did you?' Jim responded.

'Which ones were they?' Mr G asked with interest. 'I generally take every opportunity to improve myself.'

'I think Jim means—' I began.

'I know what ex-Police Constable James Mary Dutton means,' my guardian burst out. 'He means that I missed an opportunity for education about which I was never even notified. Give me the dates and I shall investigate this further.'

Dutton rolled his eyes.

'Mary?' I queried.

'It was meant to be Murray.' I swear that the constable blushed. 'But the registrar was deaf or daft or both, and my parents would have had to go to court to change it.' He quaffed his beer while Mr G sniffed his drink suspiciously.

'So what can I do for you, Mr Grice?'

'You could give me a cleaner glass.' He replaced it on the bar.

'Are you going to drink it if he does?' I asked.

'Certainly not.'

'Then there is no point in him doing so,' I pointed out.

'I shall not pay for—'

'My treat,' I said. 'Do you remember that night?'

'As if it was yesterday,' Jim replied, ignoring Mr G's mutterings of *were yesterday*, 'but only because of events the next day. Probably saved young Nathan's life taking him into custody, not that I got any thanks for it.'

'Where and why did you arrest him?' Mr G pushed his lemonade away.

'Outside the Blue Witch, drunk and disorderly.' Jim rubbed some froth from his mouth with the back of his hand.

'I know the charge.' My guardian produced a red striped handkerchief. 'But there must have been many an inebriate in that area at the time. What attracted you to this pair?'

'The Right Honourable Sir Nicholas Canning-White,' Jim Dutton answered simply. 'Minister for something important.'

'Almost every governmental department you could think of and a great many you could not,' Sidney Grice filled in. 'The man is such an ass, but with such powerful connections that they never sack him but move him on.'

''E and a friend were taking the air—'

'Nobody *takes the air* in Percy Street. There is not any to take,' my guardian declared.

'Where was I?' Jim had a drink to remind himself. 'Oh yeah, taking air – or whatever it was – when Mortlock attacked Sir Nicholas, grabbing 'im by the throat and swearing that Sir Nicholas had stolen his clock, and trying to search 'im. Needless to say the minister resisted; 'is friend tried to drag Mortlock away. Filbert came out of the White Lady a bit later, having mislaid 'is coat, saw two men laying into 'is pal and launched himself into them. I pulled 'em apart and I'd 'ave been 'appy to send 'em on their ways. There was no real 'arm, none, though Filbert got a nice shiner.'

'He still has,' I said.

Jim was taken aback. 'Must 'ave 'ealed in ten year. Same again?'

'Just a small one.' I slid my glass over, but Jim only ever poured one size and that was large – one of the attractions of the place for me.

Sidney Grice viewed my actions sourly but I decided that, if I was to be reprimanded, I would face it better with another drink inside me and it would take a good few to match that whisky he had made me drink.

'Daniel Filbert died very shortly after he was released,' I told Jim Dutton as he accepted my invitation to join me. 'He still had paint from his cell under his nails.'

'Your powers of observation knock mine into a cocked hat.' Mr G tucked his handkerchief away and left me puzzled as to why he had brought it out in the first place. 'For I only noted the presence of decorative pigments under the plate of one digit, his sinister forefinger.'

'Sinister?' Jim sloshed his beer down his arm but did not appear to notice.

'He means *left*,' I interpreted. 'So why did you not let them go?'

'I would've but Sir Nick was 'avin' none of that. He wanted them booked and cooked and 'e was the big smell, so booked and cooked they 'ad to be.'

'Did they put up a fight with you?' I asked.

Sidney Grice brought out his pince-nez and examined the grease marks on the brass pole.

'Quiet as cushions they was at first.' Jim moped his sleeve with a towel. 'Then we saw two blokes running off – nuffink unusual in that when you wear my uniform – but Mortlock swore blind they 'ad bumped into 'im in the pub, and 'e shouted they must 'ave been the lifters. But we'd never 'ave got them in those alleys with the locals all waitin' to accidently trip me up or block the way, and I didn't know if it was just a ruse to let 'im go, so I 'eld on to 'em both.'

Jim Dutton took a long draught.

'Who took them to Marylebone?' Mr G blew a dead fly along the bar top towards me.

'Me.' Jim was not the size of a man with whom you could easily argue. His hands made fists the size of footballs when he pulled on a pump handle or picked up a glass, and I would not want to make contact with them in an argument. 'They weren't no trouble after I'd banged their 'eads together a couple of times.'

I blew the fly back but it skidded off the bar into a slop bucket.

'And did you see them in court the next morning?' Sidney Grice pushed an ashtray away with his cane.

'I was called to give evidence,' Jim confirmed. 'My super didn't want Sir Nick on 'is back if they was let off but, in the end, they pleaded guilty anyway.'

'And they were definitely the same men? You would swear to it?' Mr G's eye drifted out as if he were signalling to somebody behind me.

'Not a crud of doubt abart it.'

'Ladies.' My guardian slid his eye inwards but it floated back again.

'It was this particular lady what taught me the word.' Jim finished his drink and I mine.

'Put it on my slate, Jim.' I gave up my half perch on the stool.

'Getting a bit big,' he warned.

'I shall settle next week,' I promised.

My godfather pulled his upper eyelid down. 'What depths you have sunk to.'

'You cannot sink to a level you have always been at.' I pulled my cloak around me and opened the door.

Mr G's cane clicked as he came towards me. He tried to turn it off but the clockwork whirred and the music plinked out – 'Oh, for the Wings' again.

'Oh, I like that one,' Jim said. 'Sumfink to do wiv pigeons, isn't it?'

59

Calvary Swords and Limbo

DINNER WAS INEDIBLE and I was glad I had a store of chocolate in my bedroom.

'How did you know that there was an elephant there if you could not see it?' I asked as Molly deposited a bowl in front of me.

Sidney Grice threw up his hands and returned to his drawings for a tunnel to transport *worthless people's* bodies far out to sea to be consumed by the fishes. He was occupied in designing sealed double doors and pumps to enable the corpses to be ejected without causing flooding. This would save hundreds of acres of valuable land for *worthwhile people* to build houses or business, he calculated.

'All these six or half a dozen men came along leading it with ropes.' She tipped a bowl, dribbling the dregs down her apron. 'You could see the collar bobbing up and down in the air like a tea cosy and the leg irons moving with the legs. Oh, it was marvelsome.'

'It was not possible that the ropes had wires through them?' I suggested.

Molly's mouth fell. 'Oh, I never even thought of that. You must be right, miss. It was *not* possible that the ropes had wires through them and after they marched it about and about, somebody stupid asked why the grass wasntn't not getting bent under it and the man with the big solid gold hat had to explainate that elephants is very light on their paws. Then some other peoples started being stupid and saying it was a swinzle, so the man with the big solid gold hat fed the elephant an apple, only it fell accidently down the man's sleeve and people started throwing things and they went straight through, but the man explainated that elephants is very good at ducking and the elephant was getting cross and might charge them at any minute, and it had horns – no I mean rusks – the size of calvary swords so he was going to take it away to save lives, so they turned it about and it made off through the undergrown and all the bushes was bending and shaking like Mrs O'Gonnery when she needs a brandy, and you could see that was real because there was men hiding in the undergrown with strings trying to hold the bushes still. Oh,' Molly clutched a dirty bowl to her stomach, 'it was marvelastical.' She panted for breath. 'Oh, who's that at the door?'

Her employer was sketching busily. 'Whose job is it to find out?'

And Molly laughed. 'Oh, sir, I thought as you'd have known that. It's my job.'

'Then do it.'

Molly looked puzzled. 'Shall I answer the door as well?'

'Yes please, Molly,' I said, 'but you had better take your apron off first.'

'Oh, miss,' she clattered the bowls together, 'Mr Grice would be very cross if I did that. It's part of my uninform.'

And off she trotted, calling back up the stairs. 'He's bringing a tiger next year, the biggerest and fiererest tiger in the whole wide world and Anfrica.'

'I wonder who that is?' I took a potato from the bowl.

'For once we are of one mind.' Sidney Grice mashed two of the potatoes with his fork. 'It is two people, one a female, but the other has not spoken yet. Here comes Molly doing her best visible elephant impression.'

Molly puffed her way back up. 'That Goodsmell lady and a footman,' she announced. 'Oh, he's ever so handysome. He's tall and handysome and a bit wet with lovely nose holes, and I would marry him tomorrow if only he would ask but he hasntn't not yet, even though I gave him my secret tickle.'

My guardian tossed his napkin on the floor. 'Am I never to enjoy my dinner?' He pushed his chair back.

'Not unless you employ a cook who can cook,' I muttered, glad to see the back of it.

I tried to check my hair in the mantel mirror but Mr G was in front of me, running a hand through his and primping up his orange cravat.

'Tell them to wait there.' He crammed his glass eye in and something about the way our reflections overlapped made me shiver. 'If you are cold you should try eating more,' he advised and whisked away.

Cherry Mortlock stood in the hall watching us come down. Behind her, with his head bowed, stood Easterly.

'Oh, Mr Grice, March,' she cried, before my godfather had reached the bottom step and I was halfway down. 'You must help me.'

I waited for Sidney Grice to tell her that he had no such duty now, but he went up to Cherry, took both her hands in his and said, 'Of course, dear Miss Mortlock. Do come through. How remiss of my maid to leave you standing like this and how thoughtful of you to bring your servant.'

Easterly had his outer coat over his shoulders, being unable to put his broken arm through the sleeve.

'The world is going mad.' Cherry paced about in great agitation. 'They have arrested Hesketh now.' She turned fiercely towards her footman. 'Tell them what you told me.'

Mr G bent backwards in a limbo dance and peered up into Easterly's face. Easterly tipped his head up and back and I saw that he was flushed.

'They cannot charge Mr 'Esketh,' he announced shakily in his native dialect. ''E's a good, decent bloke. I thought I were being clever but should 'ave known better and I cannot let 'im suffer for my sins.' Easterly looked at his mistress like a puppy caught chewing her slipper. 'I am so sorry, Miss Mortlock, for you have shown me nothing but kindness.' The tears welled in his eyes. 'But I shall tell the police exactly what I told you and, on my mother's grave, it is God's truth. 'Esketh did not do it.' He swallowed and had two attempts before he blurted out, 'God 'elp me, Mr Grice, but I did it. I am the guilty man.'

60

•◦•⊰•◦•

Ghosts in the Window

I DO NOT think I have been so taken aback by a confession before. I was well aware, as Sidney Grice never tired of telling me, that you cannot make judgements upon your impressions of people, but Easterly had struck me as such a gentle, even naive, man with his touchingly misjudged attempts to speak like a *toff*.

'Stand still.' The detective walked round the footman, inspecting him from every angle to end up in front of him again. 'And not a single superfluous glottal fricative, though six were struck down dead before they quit your lingual articulator.' He took another trip round the bewildered footman, in the other direction.

'Hi am sorry, sir,' Easterly sobbed, 'but Hi do not know what you mean.'

'When I wish you to know what I mean I shall inform you. Hold your tongue.'

Easterly folded in on himself and Mr G began to circumnavigate the servant again, but broke off for the window, wrenching the drapes as far apart as his reach allowed and standing holding on to them, arms horizontal, facing his street.

'My next three enquiries are destined exclusively for the sublime Miss Mortlock's attention.' Shadows swept by beyond his spectral image in the glass. 'First, who arrested your decorous valet, Austin Hesketh? I should prefer a one-word answer.'

'Inspector Quigley,' she replied.

'A gallant effort,' he commended her, 'though one hundred per cent over budget. Let us make another attempt. On whose instigation?'

'Cochran's. I have dispensed with his services.'

My guardian sighed, 'Sevenfold that time. I suspect, elegant Miss Charity Mortlock, that you are not really trying. However, I shall fall for your feminine wile and allow you to divert me from my third question by supplanting it temporarily with a supplement. Who are you hoping to employ now? You have dismissed the two most expensive detectives in London, though one of them does not merit that soubriquet – far be it from me to say which.'

'I should like to re-engage your services, Mr Grice,' Cherry said meekly, 'please.'

'We shall discuss that over a beverage presently,' my godfather promised, 'though I feel obliged to warn you that I find the prospect attractive. I do not like to leave cases unsolved. It makes my elbows itch. However, let us rejoin the flow of my interrogation: on what charge was Hesketh arrested? And you may be as profligate as you like in your response to that.'

'Murder,' Cherry said simply.

'A rather more urgent enquiry springs to mind,' Sidney Grice announced in the same leisurely tone. 'Does one or both of you intend to prevent Mr Nutter from concussing himself on my almost circular rosewood table?'

I had been so intent on the ghosts in the window that I did not notice how pallid Easterly had become. He swayed back and took two steps forward. Cherry and I rushed and just managed to take hold of him on either side before his legs buckled, by which time Sidney Grice was behind him, hands under Easterly's armpits and gently lowering the unconscious footman to lie upon the floor.

Easterly's skin was clammy. I brushed aside Cherry's suggestion that we sat him up and went to my handbag for my little blue bottle of sal volatile, taking off the stopper to waft the ammonia vapour under his nostrils, and could not imagine what Molly had found so irresistible about them.

'It is just a simple faint,' I diagnosed.

His pulse was slow and thready and his pupils dilated, though they responded to light when I opened them.

Easterly's eyelids flickered and he tried to pull away with an incoherent word, but I held on to him and the bottle.

'Murder?' He opened his eyes. 'I didn't know 'e was arrested for that.'

61

Brandy, Gin and Naval Slang

IT DID NOT take long for Easterly to regain consciousness, though he was still confused and shaky when we sat him in a chair. I opened the sideboard and poured him a brandy, something Sidney Grice only ever permitted as a recuperative measure.

'Are you feeling lightheaded?' I asked Cherry.

'I am a bit,' she admitted.

'So am I.' I poured two more glasses. 'Not my favourite tipple but better than nothing.'

We all had a restorative drink.

'What exactly were you confessing to?' I gave Easterly a large tot more.

'Well, the last Hi heard was Mr Cochran in the front sitting room accusing Hesketh hov stealing the gin because he caught him topping it up with water. Then he ordered me to wait downstairs and shut the door and we heard people coming and going and then Hi was called up and Mr Cochran said Hi had better tell my mistress what was happening, and Hinspector Quigley and two constables was taking Hesketh away hin handcuffs.'

'You silly fool, Easterly,' Cherry scolded in a futile attempt to hide her relief. 'Easterly sent me a telegram and I went straight to Gethsemane and told Cochran to sling his hook.'

'What hook?' my guardian asked.

'It is a naval expression,' I explained. 'It means to weigh anchor and go away.'

'I was not aware that Charlatan was a nautical man,' Mr G pondered.

Cherry shook her head in disbelief. 'I was about to rush straight to the police station when Easterly made his confession, so I thought there was only one man who could sort this out, the eccentric but ingenious Mr Sidney Grice.'

Mr G absorbed this information. 'My terms remain unaltered and inalterable.'

'And so do mine.'

Cherry held out her hand and Sidney Grice looked at it.

'You have well-proportioned fingers.'

'I meant one man and one woman,' Cherry added, much too late to make me feel that I was anything but an unornamental appendage.

'So *was* Hesketh stealing drinks?' I enquired from the outskirts of their lives.

'He was trying to cover up for me,' Easterly admitted. 'Hi am a bit too fond hov the liquid. Hesketh was beginning to notice and Hi tried to cut down, but it was too tempting with it sitting on display all the time. Hesketh had words with me and threatened to tell Mr Mortlock, but Hi knew he never would.' Easterly held out his glass hopefully, but I pretended to misunderstand and took it off him. We did not need an inebriated footman to add to our problems. 'Hi was feeling a bit nervy today with Mr Cochran snuffling about so Hi had a couple of stiff ones to steady my nerve. Hesketh was hiding the hevidence.' He poked a pen handle under his plaster.

'Green flag,' Sidney Grice instructed me. 'My client and I shall take the first cab. You and this pleasant but dull-witted servant will take the next.'

'I 'opes we 'as the brains a'tween us to do that, sir.' I mock-West-Countried.

'Indeed.' Sidney Grice hurried to the bell pull to order his tea.

62

The Price of Ink

I COULD HEAR raised voices as I raced up the corridor.

'This is scraping the scrapings of a scraped barrel even by your so-called standards,' Sidney Grice was raging at Inspector Quigley when I arrived with Easterly at my heels.

'Did your mother never teach you to knock?' Quigley asked calmly.

He was sitting astride a chair, his arms resting on the back, about six feet away from Hesketh, who sat bolt upright facing away from us. Quigley liked to place his prisoners so that they could not see who had entered or quit the room.

'At least I have a mother,' Mr G stormed. 'It is difficult to imagine that you even came from one.'

I paused to appreciate his quip, took in my surroundings, and said, 'I understood from Inspector Pound that Superintendent Loch had issued instructions for all interviews to be conducted in the presence of at least two officers.'

This regulation was introduced following a complaint from a Member of Parliament about his son's treatment at Inspector Quigley's hands.

'Section twenty-seven, subsection nine, paragraph eight, line three and a half,' Quigley sneered.

'We shall see how amused Loch is at your levity,' my guardian growled.

The inspector rocked back. I was hoping he would forget

that there was no support behind him but, disappointingly, he did not.

'For your information,' Quigley rocked forwards, 'the entire interview was conducted in the presence of two constables – Harris and Bannister. It was only after they left that the prisoner became violent and had to be restrained.'

'I have friends in high places,' Cherry blustered. This was news to me and probably to her. 'And I am telling you now, Inspector Quigley, this interview is at an end.'

'Not so.' Quigley picked at his inadequate beard. 'The interview finished over half an hour ago.'

'Good, then we can all go home and, if you wish to interview Mr Hesketh again, you can get a warrant and he can be questioned in the presence of my solicitor.'

'Too late for any of that nonsense,' Quigley jeered. 'He has already confessed.'

I walked round Quigley – who was leaning so far back on two legs of his chair that it took every fibre of my willpower not to kick it from under him – and round the back of the desk.

'Is that true, Hesketh?' I asked as I stopped in front of him. 'Bloody hell.'

Hesketh's left eye was swollen and bruised all around, his nose was bleeding and his upper lip was puffy and split. His right ear was gouged, presumably by Quigley's embossed ring from behind.

I rounded on the inspector. 'I wish to God Mr Grice had let Molly kill you. Not a jury in the land would have convicted her.'

'He's a big man.' Quigley forced an unconvincing smirk. 'He took some restraining.'

'I *did* confess, Miss Middleton,' Hesketh admitted indistinctly, 'but only to stealing the gin.'

'But we know it was Easterly,' I told him. 'He has admitted it.'

I did not like the look of Hesketh's eyeball. It was distorted and I was worried that, if it was haemorrhaging inside, he might lose his sight.

'Hit's true, Mr Hesketh,' Easterly said.

'Then this was all for nothing.' Hesketh felt an upper incisor gingerly. 'I am sorry, Miss Charity, I hoped that you would not dismiss me after so many years of service but, with Easterly having had warnings before, I was not sure his chances were as good.'

'Oh, Hesketh,' Cherry said, 'as you well know, I used to steal Papa's sherry myself. Did you really think I would be so harsh?'

Hesketh flopped his great hands. 'The staff are all worried you will be cutting down on our numbers.'

'You and I will speak to them all first thing in the morning,' Cherry promised.

'He ain't going nowhere except the magistrate's court in the morning,' Quigley vowed. 'You don't walk off with this one so easily.'

'Have I understood this correctly?' I asked. 'You are charging this man with murder on the grounds that he confessed to helping himself to his employer's gin?'

'That's about the size of it.' Quigley rocked forwards on his chair. 'Coupled with two witnesses Mr Cochran will produce, who heard Nathan Mortlock saying that he wanted to sack Hesketh for his thievery but was so frightened Hesketh meant him harm that he had taken to locking himself in his room.'

'That is a lie,' Hesketh asserted furiously. 'Mr Nathan would have trusted me with his life. He asked me to shave him every morning. He was like a son...' The valet's voice trailed away in emotion.

'Hesketh played with my father when my father was a boy,' Cherry protested. 'He gave him rides on his back, as he did with me.'

Hesketh lightly cradled his face and began to shake.

'How cosy.' Quigley rocked the chair back with a bang and jumped up. 'But evidence is evidence.'

'But, as Mr Cochran has demonstrated many a time, a witness is not necessarily a witness.' Sidney Grice clapped his hands. 'I am bored with this now. If you persist with this absurdness,

there are three people in this room who will swear that they saw
you make an unprovoked attack upon this prisoner. I never tell
lies but Miss Middleton is an accomplished prevaricator, Easterly
Nutter has the face and manner of a cherub and who could not
believe the enchanting, bereaved and beautiful Miss Mortlock in
the witness box. Some women cannot wear black but she carries
it off splendidly, do you not agree?'

Quigley kicked his chair aside. 'I can still get him for theft. He
made an unforced confession in the presence of two other officers.'

'That is true,' Hesketh conceded, wiggling the tooth experimentally.

'Is this the confession?' I asked and was about to pick it up
when the inspector slapped a hand over it. 'What colour ink is
that?'

'Predominantly sooty,' Sidney Grice decided, 'though I should
say there is more than a tint of Prussian blue in it.'

I picked up the inkwell and sniffed the contents. 'And quite
runny.' I upended it over the back of the inspector's hand. 'Oh,
silly, silly me.'

Quigley jumped back and the ink flowed over the confession.

'Damn it, you will pay for this, girl,' he swore, struggling to get
a handkerchief out of his right trouser pocket with his left hand.

'What does regulation ink cost these days?' I enquired and
placed two pennies carefully on a dry area of desk. 'I think that
should cover it.'

63

Gypsy James and the Gentle Fist

ON THE WAY out we saw Inspector Pound coming in.
'The forces are gathering against Quigley.' He stepped
over an old woman's bundle of bedding. 'And he knows
it but that only makes him the more dangerous. He will do anything for results now.'

The woman was attacking a wall with her fists, knees and
bare feet, while Perkins watched in amusement.

'A cornered rat,' Cherry said, and I saw the way Pound's eyes
dilated at the sight of her.

'Slam-bricking scrumble,' the woman cursed cryptically.

'You could have flattened that pipsqueak, Mr Hesketh,'
Easterly conjectured and Hesketh managed a crooked smile.

'Don't think it didn't occur to me when I heard my cheekbone
crack.'

'I am glad you did not,' Cherry said. 'A dozen constables
would have come to his aid and you would be facing very serious
charges then.'

'I suspect that many would have turned a deaf ear to his calls
for help.' Mr G put on his gloves.

'When I was a youngster I was quite handy with my fists,'
Hesketh admitted. 'I did a round with Gypsy James Mace at a
fair in Lambeth once and even knocked him down, but he got
right back up and put me straight to sleep.' Hesketh enjoyed the
memory before admitting, 'That was before he became famous.'

'I would never have put you down as a brawler,' I marvelled.

The woman butted the wall and sat down heavily on her bundle.

'Had enough?' Perkins chortled and dragged her back into the interview room.

Hesketh held open the door at the end of the corridor. I had never seen it closed before. 'Got into a scrap with an ironmonger once – can't even remember what it was about now – but I got arrested for that.' Hesketh paused, eyeing his mistress warily.

'Do not stop on my account,' Cherry urged.

'I went before the beak,' he continued, 'and for some reason he took against the ironmonger and a shine to me. *I should give you three months for what you did to this upstanding citizen,* he told me, but the way he said *upstanding* showed how he really felt. *I'm going to give you one day to teach you a lesson. But, if I ever see you in this court again, it's a year's hard labour for you, young man, on top of whatever else you've done.* The ironmonger made such a fuss he got three weeks for contempt.'

'I was speculating when you would mention your criminal record,' Mr G said as we reached the hall.

'But how did you know that?' I asked.

'He knows everything,' Cherry whispered.

'I know how to search rooms.' Sidney Grice put on his hat. 'And the release paper is still in Hesketh's shirt drawer.'

'I kept it to remind me.' Hesketh turned to his mistress. 'I am sorry, miss. I never told the Garstangs – they would not have forgiven me. But I told your father soon after he took over the house – I did not want it hanging over me – and I was going to tell you.'

'Oh, Hesketh.' Cherry sighed. 'What *will* people think?' She cracked into a grin. 'Gypsy James Mace, eh? I am so proud of you.'

Hesketh hesitated. 'I hope you will not think me too out of turn, Miss Middleton, but I should like to shake your hand for what you did tonight.'

My hand, which my guardian often told me was of similar proportions to a shovel, was lost inside that valet's gentle fist.

'Lower your head, Hesketh,' I enjoined him. 'A bit more.'

I stood on tiptoe and pecked his cheek.

'For heaven's sake,' Mr G expostulated. 'Osculating in a public place with pugilistic servants. Whatever next?'

'I dread to think,' I murmured. 'I hope I did not hurt your cheek, Hesketh.'

Hesketh put his fingertips to the site. 'Not at all, miss.' And I would have sworn there was a tear in his eye.

'Did your father keep a diary, Miss Mortlock?' Mr G enquired as he commandeered the first cab.

'I do not think so.'

'Endeavour to find out. He kept financial records?'

'Obsessively. He liked to account for every penny.' Cherry waved to another hansom.

'Very well. We shall arrive tomorrow promptly at ten twenty, when I shall scrutinize Mr Nathan Mortlock's fiscal chronicles, his last will and testament and any details you have of the terms of the Trust fund,' Sidney Grice announced. 'Have them in order. Goodbye.'

64

The Outrage and Arthritis

THE FOG LINGERED thinly the next morning, like the steam from a hot bath in a cold room, dripping down every surface and pooling on the ground. An ancient beggar stood across the road from number 2.

'Penny for a cuppa cha, gov?'

Much to my surprise, Sidney Grice went over to him and, even more to my surprise, instead of haranguing him about getting a job or going to the workhouse, reached into his pocket and gave him a coin. Perhaps, I thought, it was the fact that the man wore an eye patch that touched my godfather's heart. I was not even convinced he had much of one up until then.

'Gawd bless yer and yer loverly laydee,' the man croaked out.

'Get a job or go to the workhouse,' Mr G harangued him, 'and stop cluttering the streets pestering people.'

Sidney Grice rejoined me.

'You gave him money,' I accused, for he took some pride in his meanness.

'How razor-sharp your powers of observation have become,' he remarked.

I recoiled at my godfather's reference to razors, but he was busy yanking the bell pull.

'Good morning, sir and miss,' Easterly greeted us. 'Hi trust you are well.'

'It is not for you to investigate our medical conditions,' Mr G said severely, 'especially that of so poorly constructed a creature as Miss Middleton.' He flung his Ulster over the footman's arm. 'You have a lot to learn if you are not to betray the trust placed in you by your murdered master and your delightful not-yet-murdered mistress even further.'

'Hi am sorry, sir.' Easterly hung up Sidney Grice's overcoat and took my cloak. 'Miss Mortlock is awaiting you hin the drawing room.'

Cherry stood up to greet us.

'I tried to make Hesketh see a doctor,' she said, 'or at least stay in bed, but he would not hear of it.'

'Quite right.' Mr G sat down uninvited. 'There is too much shillyshallying with servants these days. Tell me about your father's estate whilst we are awaiting tea.'

Cherry kissed me. 'I have not ordered any yet.'

'Shall Hi tell Veronique to bring it now, miss?' Easterly enquired as he was about to shut the door.

'This is an outrage,' Sidney Grice fumed. 'Listening in to a private conversation.'

Easterly blushed. 'Hi am sorry, sir. Hi could not help but over-hear.'

'You hear a lot of things,' I explained, 'but you are supposed to pretend not to until you are spoken to.'

'Hoh.' Easterly blinked.

'We will have coffee,' Cherry said.

My guardian clucked and her valet hopped from foot to foot.

'Was that a private remark or haddressed to me, miss?'

'To you,' she assured him and he hurried away. 'Perhaps you could let me reprimand my own servants in future, Mr Grice.'

'I would be delighted if you would.' He looked at his watch. 'Your father's estate.'

Cherry settled me in a low-backed chair and the three of us faced each other across a round table with a lovely Ottoman vase in the centre, a flattened sphere swirling with flowers in vivid reds, blues and greens, with a high collar. My guardian tutted, took hold of the twin swan-neck handles and deposited it on the floor.

'Have a care,' Cherry protested. 'That is irreplaceable.'

'I have so many cares,' he told her, 'but we would be here for nine years and three months were I to recount them all accurately to you, by which time I would doubtless have acquired many more cares and so the recital might only end with one or both of our deaths.'

'Do you normally rearrange other people's ornaments?' she demanded.

'I am thinking of making it a habit,' he admitted, 'for they are often sources of irritation to me. This fine and doubtless expensive piece of Iznik ceramic craftsmanship was obstructing my pleasant view of your hands and, whilst people may lie with their voices, eyes and mouth, they rarely manage to do so with their fingers at the same time. But I weary apace when I am obliged to ask the same question in triplicate.' He leaned towards her. 'Kindly bestow upon me some information about your father's estate.'

Cherry watched anxiously as he rotated the vase by the side of his chair.

'He was a wealthy man,' she said, 'but the only person who stood to gain by that was me.'

'No generous bequests to servants or churches *exempli gratia*?' He patted the side of the vase loudly. 'Nothing for his estranged wife, your mother, that he had not troubled to cancel?'

'It is very simple,' she said. 'I get everything. Most of the Garstangs' assets were put into a Trust fund. The Garstangs were wary of leaving it all in one piece to my father, given his profligate past. And so he had an annual income and the use of Gethsemane on condition that he always lived here. Mr Burton had been very keen to demolish it and complete his crescent, but they were even more determined to preserve the house. They did not think to forbid dividing the house, though.'

Sidney Grice was rocking the vase and she stopped to glare at him.

'Did the Garstangs' will not provide for your mother?' I asked.

Cherry splayed her fingers. 'I suppose they assumed my father would do so himself, but he cut my mother out of his will within a few days of her leaving.'

'Did she know that?' I asked.

'You think she came back to kill him?' Cherry greeted my question incredulously. 'My mother is the most gentle soul you could hope to meet... but yes. He wrote and told her immediately, and she replied that she wanted nothing from him except to be left alone.'

'Not to see you?' I asked softly.

Cherry closed her eyes and inhaled. 'I reminded her of my father.' And when she opened those eyes they were somehow dulled.

'How much was he worth?' Sidney Grice reached into the vase.

'I do not have the exact figures but not a huge sum in capital assets, though the income is somewhere in the region of ten thousand pounds and the use of this house is worth a great deal.'

'I understand that your father closed off most of the house for security, but why did he never have the roof of the north wing repaired?' I listened uneasily as my godfather rapped on the inside of the vase.

'I think it was just to spite the Garstangs for trapping him here.' Cherry craned her neck. 'I shall not be happy if you break that,' she warned.

'Will you be a happy person if I do not?' Sidney Grice went in deeper.

'No, but—'

'Then it makes little difference whether I do or not,' my godfather reasoned, paddling his arm about like a child with a lucky dip. 'But fear not. I shall treat it as I would any vase.'

'You have a considerable inheritance,' I remarked. 'Forgive me for asking, but does your friend Fabian Le Bon know about it?'

'Neither of us did until the will was read.' Cherry did not appear to take offence this time. 'My father led me to believe that

I had been cut off without a penny and his fortune left to the Jews' Deaf and Dumb Home in the Crescent.'

'Why?' My guardian pulled his arm out so suddenly that the vase rocked and it seemed that Cherry's fears would be realized.

Cherry half-rose, prepared to leap out and save it, but the vase came to a standstill.

'I suppose he wanted to bring me to heel,' she conjectured.

Mr G flung out his arm, his sleeve catching the lip and setting the vase wobbling again.

'I am not interested in your suppositions,' he cried excitedly. 'I care nothing for your guesses or flights of feminine fancy.' He rested his hand on the vase.

'I cannot bear this,' Cherry muttered and, getting up, lifted his hand away, depositing it into his lap, picked up the vase and carried it to the octagonal table we had occupied when we first came what felt like a long time ago.

'Mind that you do not trip over the hem of your remarkably fine Anatolian Beylik carpet,' Mr G advised with his back to her.

Cherry placed her vase carefully and mimed strangling him.

'You do not have arthritic fingers, I trust.' He waved his stick towards the mantel mirror where he had a good view of her. 'My penultimate enquiry concerned your slaughtered father's choice of the institution which might benefit from his bequest.'

'You do not like Jews?' She came back to her chair.

Mr G patted where the vase was no longer, like a man in the dark searching for Lucifers. 'I dislike ninety-eight per centum of Semites,' he informed her. 'I also dislike ninety-eight per cent of Gentiles. Please answer my question, lovely Miss Charity Clair Caroline Mortlock.'

'Does he call all his female clients *lovely*?' Cherry's cheeks coloured.

'I have never known him to,' I admitted.

'That was not because none of the others merited such a description.' Sidney Grice clearly thought this was sufficient explanation of his behaviour.

Veronique entered with pink gold-rimmed cups, dominated by a splendid silver coffee pot.

'Have you recovered from your visit to the police station?' I asked.

'Better zan Mr 'Esketh, I am thinking,' she replied and departed.

'I think Mr Grice wants to know if there was any particular reason that your father chose that charity?' I asked.

'I think so too,' he agreed.

'My father was always concerned about deaf children after what happened to Lionel.'

'What *did* happen to Lionel?' I enquired.

Cherry picked up the pot, using a linen napkin against the heat. 'When Lionel was twelve he had a brain fever. The doctors thought he would die.' She poured three cups with steaming burnt-umber liquid. 'Perhaps it would have been kinder if he had. He recovered but, when he did, he was stone deaf. It affected his speech too. He spoke too loudly and he jumbled his words. The Garstangs thought he was a simpleton and put him in an institution. They believed it was for his own good, but he was miserable until my father persuaded them to bring him back into the world. He taught Lionel to play chess and tried to help him to lipread, but Lionel's sight was badly affected also. He was devoted to my father. If he had had a tail he would have wagged it off whenever they met. Lionel was so timid, but my father told him that he need never be afraid because his name meant *young lion* and everybody started to call him that.' Cherry smiled at the memory. 'Easterly was very fond of Lionel too. They would hiss and snarl playfully at each other whenever they met. He used to take Young Lion all over the house so that he could find his way around. After dusk Lionel could hardly see a thing.'

Sidney Grice sniffed his drink suspiciously. 'Coffee is number four in my list of comestibles that smell better than they taste. This has a pleasant aroma and I live in joyous expectation that it will not be too unpleasant to ingest.' He took a sip and put the cup down without passing judgement. 'Miss Mortlock, I regret imperilling the excellent relationship which we have thus far enjoyed, but I discover myself revolted by the manner in which you have hidden vital evidence from me.'

Cherry received this attack with almost as much astonishment as I did.

'I have absolutely no idea what you are talking about.' She scattered some sugar on its way to her coffee.

'Why did you withhold the information that Master Lionel Engra was impervious to sonic stimulation?' he demanded.

'I did not think it important,' she stammered.

Sidney Grice did not react to that last statement for so long that I was just about to ask if he had heard it when he said, 'I shall provisionally accept your explanation for the time being.'

'Thank you so much,' she said sarcastically.

'But, oh, Miss Mortlock, client and provider of acceptable beverages, if only you had thought in your feminine mind to grant me that knowledge from the outset, who knows what direction my investigations would have taken?'

'But what difference would it have made?' I poured my milk.

'Were you not listening?' Mr G watched himself in the back of his teaspoon. 'You do not suffer from Master Lionel's affliction. Who knows? Possibly none whatsoever.' He took another tentative sample of his coffee. 'I wish to see Mr Nathan Roptine Mortlock's accounts, if not now, then within the next three minutes.'

65

Double Entry and Blocked Drains

CHERRY MORTLOCK ADJUSTED her veil, which had fallen over her eyes.

'Hesketh had been helping me to sort through them,' she said distractedly.

'Why not your solicitor or accountant?' I asked.

'I neither trust nor like the members of either profession.' Suddenly Cherry sounded like my guardian.

'How wise beyond your years,' he mused fondly. 'I wish I could say the same about Miss Middleton.'

'I think we have put everything you need in the study.' She frowned sympathetically in my direction.

'Indeed?' Sidney Grice arose, leaning heavily on his cane. 'Then we must proceed there without undue delay.' He paused. 'That coffee – in case you are anxiously awaiting my verdict – was of a superior quality and pleasingly hot but, when all is said and done, it was coffee.'

'Your powers of observation knock mine into a cocked hat,' I quoted – with some satisfaction but to Cherry's puzzlement – and followed my godfather into the hallway.

Easterly rose but, at a signal from Sidney Grice, resumed his high seat. Hesketh was in the study, arranging stacks of documents. His left eye was almost closed now and his upper lip crusted in dried blood.

'You really should let a doctor examine you,' I advised, but the valet gestured in polite dismissal.

'Is there a cure now for cuts and bruises, miss?'

'There is not,' I admitted.

Hesketh gathered a few documents and patted them into a neat pile.

'Then my place is here, Miss Middleton. My mistress tells me that Mr Grice believes that Mr Nathan's accounts might help him to track the murderer.'

'Miss Mortlock told you nothing but the truth in that respect,' Mr G confirmed, 'though whether she has been mendacious in other respects I am unable to ascertain at present.'

'If I could have one wish,' Hesketh closed a drawer of the desk, 'it is, when you do find the son of a—' He choked back the word, though, of the three of us, only my guardian might have been shocked by it. 'That I might have ten minutes alone with him.'

'You may have as many wishes as you like, Austin Anthony Hesketh,' Sidney Grice assured him, 'but I cannot promise to grant them.' He flicked through a thin cardboard file, folded it up again and dropped it on the darkly varnished floor. 'I shall see what I can do.'

Hesketh's right hand twitched. 'Thank you, sir.'

'You may not thank me when that day arrives,' Mr G cautioned, but Hesketh was not so easily intimidated.

'Neither will he,' he vowed.

Sidney Grice scanned another file and placed it back on the desk with great precision.

'Describe the system by which you have arranged this information.'

'I have hardly any experience of these matters—' Hesketh began.

'Describe the system by which you have arranged this information,' my guardian repeated slowly and firmly.

'On my left are the documents which I believe relate to Mr Nathan's estate,' Hesketh recounted. 'Bank accounts, bonds, shares, and he had a few small properties and some farm land in

Shropshire rented out to tenants. On my left are Mr Nathan's account books. He was most scrupulous about recording all his outgoings and always prompt in checking and paying bills. These boxes are copies of invoices and receipts going back to shortly after he moved in to this house.'

'Goodness,' I said, 'are you sure you are not an accountant in disguise?'

Hesketh smiled and I wished he had not, for it opened up his cut lip again. 'Positive, miss. I can see what the papers are about but I cannot make head or tail of all those figures. This envelope holds a copy of the Trust-fund details.'

I looked in that one first, but it was all *first* and *second parties* and *furthermores* and *notwithstandings* and *estoppels*. It was too like my godfather when he had tried to explain a complex mort-gage fraud after midnight on Christmas Eve. I stuffed it back.

'You must do two things and then you must not do one,' Sidney Grice told Cherry and her valet. 'First, leave us as soon as I gesture in a peremptory manner. Second, you must arrange for us to be served tea and, third, you must on no account, other than an emergency, disturb us further until I activate this ugly brass bell pull.' My guardian waved imperiously. 'Which shall you examine, Miss Middleton, since the Trust fund was not diverting enough for you?'

Hesketh pulled the door to.

'The accounts.' I did not hesitate for I had helped my father with those for years, though I had known so little about his debts that the total of them had come as a dreadful shock to me when he died.

'Good.' Mr G settled comfortably in the captain's chair behind the desk. 'Needless to say I shall study his estate, a labour of love, for I am ever fascinated by the wealth of men.' He waved at Cherry in the doorway. 'Goodbye.'

I dragged a cardboard box over, and sat in a low armchair by an empty fireplace with an accounts book on my knees. It was dated January 1873 and pencilled in small but easily legible writing in five columns – the date, the payee, the item or service provided, the bill and the running total. I lifted a block of papers, tied with white strings through holes in the top right-hand corners, and a glance through them showed that they corresponded exactly with the entries in the book. I could not fault Nathan Mortlock's bookkeeping so far.

The first two pages were largely taken up with multiple payments to builders, iron merchants and locksmiths.

'He spent a small fortune fortifying this house,' I declared.

'If a fortune is small it is not a fortune.' Sidney Grice was writing in his notebook. 'Stop chattering.'

'What exactly am I looking for?' I asked and he growled impatiently.

'What are we always looking for? The truth.'

'Thank you for that clarification.'

'Shush.'

I ploughed on – butchers' bills, bakers, coal merchants, etc., etc., etc., page after precisely filled page of them; a blocked drain; wages for domestic staff and a governess; dressmakers' bills; five pounds cash on the first day of February to... I ran my finger across the columns. To nobody apparently; six pounds three shillings and fourpence as a *gift for* C. I wondered what it was. She must have been about twelve years old. Nothing improving, I hoped. After six pages I needed a smoke. After a dozen I needed a drink. Veronique arrived with tea – not the sort of drink I had in mind – and Mr G bustled her away.

'What are you doing?' I asked.

He was up and rifling through an oak cupboard. 'I never like being told what to look at.' The shelves were stacked with files and books. He whisked a few out. 'This could be interesting.' He tossed a fat red volume on the desk. 'And this.' A navy one followed.

'What are they?'

'Mrs Augusta Garstang's household accounts and Holford Garstang's petty cash book.'

'They sound like good night-time reading.'

'The truth is fascinating, whatever the time.'

'Some truths are tedious, ditto.' I poured our teas and battled on to March the seventeenth – Saint Patrick's day, I remembered idly, but no orders for shamrock or Guinness and I knew without a shadow of a doubt that I could not go through what was more than a decade of those figures without risking readmittance to a hospital for the insane.

I went straight to 1884. At least that would be a short year, I thought grimly. I had started admiring Nathan Mortlock's attention to detail, but now it had driven me past distraction to the place where distraction was a dot on the landscape behind me. He had purchased a new dressing gown from Hancock Brothers. That must have been the one we saw hanging in his bedroom, hardly worn. And preserve – four jars of plum jam. Five pounds cash again to nobody and again on the first day of the month. I flicked through to the third and the last entries. Nothing else unusual.

January 1884: the first entries were wages. Then there it was again. Five pounds cash, no payee. The same in February, and then another entry caught my eye – five guineas to Critchely on the fifteenth. I ploughed through the ledger and the pattern was consistent. Five pounds on the first of every month, five guineas to Critchely around the middle of the month.

And then in December the pattern changed. There was still the cash payment but – I totted them up – there were nine payments to Critchely, all for five guineas and all paid by cheque: forty-five guineas in one month.

Then 1883: nothing to Critchely until the fourteenth of April when the regular pattern began.

'Either you have found something or you are just trying to annoy me by making as much noise as possible,' my guardian grumbled.

'I am looking for his last cheque book.' I lifted a fistful of receipts out of the box. 'Got it.'

'Good. Will you be quiet now?'

I flicked through. The stubs confirmed the amounts, dates and payees.

'A few things stand out,' I announced.

'And they are?'

'I have found three payments so far of twenty pounds each for artwork.'

'Clearly that puzzles you.' Sidney Grice did not pause in his scribbling. 'Give me two meritorious reasons why.'

'Apart from the Dürer, I have not seen any works of art here. So where are they?' I began. 'And why would they cost exactly the same amount each time?'

'Relevant questions indeed.' My godfather glanced up. 'Let me know when you are able to answer them.'

'Also...'

Mr G put down his pencil. 'Go on.'

'Do you think Nathan Mortlock was being blackmailed?'

'Yes. Tell me why you do?'

'There are entries for five pounds cash on the first of every month since he came here. Everything else is very carefully item-ized, even when he bought a new pack of pen nibs,' I told him. 'What is your reason?'

'I hope to be able to tell you that this evening.' He took off his pince-nez and held it vertically to view me through one lens. 'The other item of interest is?'

I took the 1885 ledger to show him. 'Since April of 1883 there have been cheques for five guineas to somebody called Critchely around the middle of every month. At the end of the year he is making payments every two or three days.'

Sidney Grice clipped his pince-nez on his elegant nose and followed my finger jabs though the entries.

'Some of these are on Sundays,' he calculated.

'So not a shop.'

'I should think not,' he agreed. 'Look at the way it is spelled. I know of several people called Critchley with a T and L-E-Y, Crichley with no T and L-E-Y or Crichely with no T and E-L-Y, but only one C-R-I-T-C-H-E-L-Y.' He wrote the names in block capitals on a fresh page of his notebook. 'Open the door, March.'

I did as I was bid.

'Miss Mortlock,' he bellowed, so loudly and suddenly that I jumped. 'Come at once.'

I heard a low voice and then hurrying footfalls.

'What is so urgent?' Cherry asked anxiously.

'If I were to waste time chattering about things which are urgent,' Mr G informed her calmly, 'they would no longer be urgent. Who – and tell me truthfully if indeed you know the answer to my rapidly approaching enquiry – is or was Critchely?'

'My father's doctor,' she replied. 'He treated him for head-aches. Why do you ask?'

'You are paying me to ask questions.' Sidney Grice circled his last spelling. 'I do not pay you.'

'Your father wrote a cheque to Dr Critchely every month,' I remarked.

'My father saw him regularly for injections and pills, and to be galvanized across the temples, which gave some temporary relief.'

'Here or at the doctor's practice?' I asked.

'At Dr Critchely's usually because the electrical generator was too heavy to transport,' she said. 'But in the last few weeks of my father's life I believe the attacks were so prostrating that the doctor made house calls. Why is this so important?'

'What else are you hiding from us, Miss Mortlock?' Sidney Grice slapped his notebook shut.

'Well, nothing, and I was not keeping that a secret,' she replied. 'It did not seem relevant, I suppose.'

'In a few days' time I may present you with an outrageous account for deciding what is and is not relevant.' Mr G stood up.

'A few days?' Cherry's eyes sparkled. 'You really think you are that close?'

'Oh, Miss Mortlock, with what velocity you catch the subtle import of my words.' He packed his notebook and some of the sheets of figures into his satchel. 'Make a list of all the things which you believe to be trivial and bring it to my home in person at seven o'clock tonight. Stay to dinner.'

'Will you be there?' she asked me uncertainly.

'Of course,' I promised and, leaning forward to kiss her, whispered, 'Have something to eat first.'

'No need,' Sidney Grice assured her. His hearing was always much more acute than mine. 'I shall command Cook to put an extra turnip in the pot.'

'Yum yum,' Cherry said and sent Easterly to summon a cab.

66

The Storm of Stones

THE FOG FLED, pushed back towards the gardens by a gigantic tidal wave to our left, bricks hurtling through the ocean, crashing into the trees. And a door – I saw that quite distinctly – flying past. And then the most almighty bang I had ever experienced.

The ground jumped. Something punched me under the soles of my boots, banging me into the air and dropping me like a bun shaken loose in a tin. The paving stones went higgledy-piggledy, cracked, raised and sunken.

I grabbed my guardian's coat and we both staggered sideways. His hat blew off and down the street.

I put up my arm and my umbrella shot open and Sidney Grice, who was terrified of such things, put a hand up and shouted in a trough of noise, 'Cover your face.'

A storm of stones and grit hailed into my umbrella, rattling around my skirts. There was a pause and then a crash. I do not think that particular crash lifted the pavement. It was just that I jumped.

My guardian pointed down the road. 'Run, March.'

But he did not and so I did not either. He prised my fingers off his coat. A heavier missile had smashed a spoke on my umbrella and ripped the pretty powder-blue fabric. I lowered it and saw that the dust and rubble was coming from the northern end of Gethsemane. The windows had been blown out and a pair of shredded curtains fluttered through one of the apertures. On an upper floor the shattered glass hung from the frame like fangs.

People were running, some away from and some towards the scene.

'Stand back,' Mr G bellowed at two young clerks moving in for a closer look and, as we watched, the outer wall of the northern wing cracked and a line zigzagged between the bricks from top to bottom, as rapidly as ripping paper. The remaining roof tiles slipped, most into the gulley but some showering down. One hit a clerk on the leg and he yipped. The other took a piece to the head and he stumbled back, rubbing it but still standing.

'Fools' wages.' My godfather stooped to retrieve his hat and banged the dust out of it against his filthy trousers.

A soap man fought to calm his rearing horse.

'Do you think it will fall into the road?' I watched a hole appear in the roof, the lathes torn.

'I doubt it.' He reshaped the crown of his hat. 'But a damaged building can be as fickle as a woman.'

'Or a man,' I put in.

'We have not time for that nonsense.' Sidney Grice combed back through his debris-greyed hair with all his fingers.

'Gas?' I asked.

'Indubitably.'

I had seen the results of gas explosions before but never witnessed one happen.

'We are fortunate that the Boulton Gasworks are no longer fully operational.' Mr G patted his coat down in a hopeless attempt to spruce it up. 'If the supply had been under full pressure the whole Crescent would have gone up.' He shuddered. 'Imagine, March, if Sidney Grice had been killed in a domestic misadventure – how *infra dignitatum*.'

The fact that I would have shared my guardian's fate did not seem to trouble him unduly.

People were running out of their houses, maids curious to see what had happened, footmen gawking, an old man being helped down his steps, his wife hobbling behind clutching her jewellery box.

A policeman was racing across the Crescent, blowing his whistle with every outbreath.

Hesketh was at our side.

'Is Miss Mortlock all right?' I asked.

'She is unhurt and attending to Easterly, miss,' the valet told me. 'He is feeling lightheaded.' He blinked at a bit of grit in his eye. 'Do we need to evacuate the house, sir?'

'Go indoors and see to your mistress,' Sidney Grice instructed. He retrieved and replaced his hat at a vaguely jaunty angle. 'Come, Miss Middleton. You have been entertained enough for one day.' He straightened his Ulster. 'And close that damnable umbrella before you frighten me and the horses.'

The fire engines arrived, reeling out their hoses through the gathering onlookers, but we had seen enough. The fog was creeping back. We pushed our way through to Marchmont Street, where we persuaded a cabby to take us home for a triple fare in advance.

67

Ruffians and the Varnished Skull

THERE WAS A letter on Sidney Grice's desk and he handed it to me without comment. Inspector Quigley confirmed that the braid of the curtain cord almost exactly matched the marks on Nathan Mortlock's neck.

'A pity he did not check that while the marks were still fresh,' I commented.

'Quite so.' My guardian tapped the mantel clock as one might a barometer. 'It is four minutes past the magic hour of six,' he complained and, as if responding to his cue, Molly entered with our tea.

'Oh, miss.' Her face was blotchy. 'Cook has been telling me how the invisual elephant is a trick.'

She had been forbidden to discuss that with her employer since trying to make herself disappear by closing her eyes and walking into a wall with his breakfast on a tray.

'Surely not.' I suppressed my urge to have a nice quiet scream.

'Answer the door,' her employer sighed and the bell rang. 'And if it is a blind beggar, admit him.'

Molly lingered uncertainly. 'Does *admit* mean *lock up*?'

'It means *let in*,' I told her.

Molly greeted my explanation sceptically. 'Only whenever my cousin who aintn't not really my cousin admits things, they lock her up.'

'Go.' Mr G threw out his arm and Molly returned a minute

later with the man to whom he had given money on Burton Crescent.

'Well?' Sidney Grice demanded.

The beggar came in; his odour preceded him. Even in an age when many people had no means of bathing, it was so staggeringly noisome I was astonished that my guardian had allowed him in the house.

'Twenty-one Thimble Street,' he said.

'You are sure?'

Our visitor went to the window, his long, ragged overcoat flowing behind him. 'We're a solid team, Mr Grice. You know that.'

'Description.' Sidney Grice picked up a pencil.

'Male, speckled light brown hair, well trimmed, thin excuse for moustaches, otherwise clean shaven, five foot eight or nine, fifty to sixty years old, dressed like a clerk – grey suit coat and bowler hat, horn-rimmed spectacles – pipe smoker. Keeps a wife, a skivvy and tabby cat. Goes by the name of Sam Wells.'

'You are sure of that?' my godfather pressed him.

'A neighbour called good evening to him but my man, Tredge, was not close enough to catch what else they said.'

'You are very well spoken,' I observed. 'And how did you manage to walk round that table?'

'Show her, Prabberly.' Sidney Grice leaned back in his chair, hands linked behind his head.

The beggar took off his eye patch and raised it to the light and I saw that it was nothing like so opaque as I had imagined. I could see the room in outline through it. He put his fingers to his left eye and the glass fell into his palm. I had seen that trick many times but this was a thin disc and, when Mr Prabberly looked up, I saw that he still had an eye.

'Smoked-glass pupil.' He held it out in his hand for my inspection. 'I can see most things through that.'

'But it must be very painful.' I cringed at the sight of his bloodshot eye and swollen, purple lids.

'It certainly is,' he told me with great satisfaction. 'When it starts to weep, my takings go up exponentially.'

'Clip Prabberly and his colleagues are PRAMs, the Professional Ruffians Association Members,' Mr G informed me. 'When they are not begging, they put their skills to more disreputable purposes, such as loitering outside houses to discourage purchasers and drive the price down, but they can turn their hands to other things. Three of them went to Eton College.'

'A pretentious parvenu of a school.' Clip swatted the name to the ceiling. 'I'm an old Wykehamist myself.'

'You look very convincing,' I remarked.

'And smell it.' Sidney Grice fanned the air with a few sheets of paper.

'It is an irrevocable condition of membership that we never bathe,' our visitor said merrily. 'One of our band, Chisel Smith, fell into a laundry tub once and was suspended from active duty until he had slept in kennels for a month.'

My guardian's arm swung out, a misshaped scarlet ball flew over me and Clip caught a bag clinking heavily of coins.

He pulled the drawstring loose. 'Gawd bless yer, guv.' He put his patch back on and manoeuvred his eye cover back into place.

'You have done well. Now get out.' Mr G pulled the bell rope once and, after Molly had shown Clip Prabberly out, instructed her to bring candles and go out for some rosewater.

I took out my scent bottle and sprayed a few puffs of my precious Fougère.

'Cor, what a stink.' Molly wafted my perfume away.

She brought a box of *cangles* and set out on her errand.

'Why could we not meet Mr Prabberly in a public place,' I suggested, 'preferably upwind of him.'

'He took enough risk coming here.' Sidney Grice dipped a taper. He did not trust Molly to roam the room with a naked flame.

And, when the candles were lit and I had wasted still more of my perfume, I tackled him. 'Have you been paying people to spy on Cherry?'

'I have not.' He toyed with the idea. 'Do you think I should?'

Sidney Grice scrambled the coals into flames with the long poker to try to burn off the odour but, as so often is the case, pleasing smells are ephemeral but vile stinks are the unwanted guests who will not take the hint and leave. They linger and settle into your favourite armchair and are all but impossible to shift.

'Her servants?' I persisted.

'No.' He replaced the poker and dusted his hands off on each other.

'Her callers?'

'Indeed not.' He nipped out a candle and waited for the smoke to permeate before relighting it. 'Or not in the sense that you mean it.'

I changed tack. 'Who is Mr Sam Wells?'

'In this matter, and how my spirit shrivels in torment as I disclose this –' my guardian worked his way along the other candles on the mantelpiece – 'I am as distressingly ignorant as you. However,' he moved to the central table where four candles flickered, 'I am prepared to consider the painful possibility that I have just paid for faulty information. By Prabberly's own admission, his man could not hear very well.'

'So, if he misheard,' I toyed with the name in my mind before it came to me. 'Sam Wells could be—'

'I want to say it first,' Mr G broke in. 'Samuels.'

Molly returned, proudly bearing a bottle like a sporting trophy.

'Oh, it's ever so romantical,' she gushed.

'The candlelight?' I asked.

'No.' She put some of her employer's change in the bowl on his desk. 'The smell what you're trying to get ridded of – just like my gentleman friend Tarragint when he worked in the cats' meat factory drains.'

The bowl was made from a varnished skull-vault, all that remained of the Paddington Prowler after Sidney Grice had cornered him in Ramsay's Circulating Library.

'Do you have a clean apron to put on tonight, Molly?' I asked and she wrinkled her nose.

'This *is* my clean apron, miss.'

'But it has stains down it.'

'Lord love you, miss.' Molly laughed. 'It aintn't got no stains down it at all. It's got stains up it and up-stains dontn't not count for nothing.'

'Put—' her employer began but our maid was in full flow.

'And it was my clean apron when I put it on this morning, and I aintn't changed it so it must still be my clean apron. My other—'

'Put a clean one on,' he bellowed and Molly blanched.

'With no up-stains, sir?'

'No stains in any direction of any size, shape or colour and,' his voice sank to a menacing hiss, 'quit my study. *Now*.'

Molly left us with a bobbing backward curtsey.

Sidney Grice spoke. 'I shall change for dinner.'

'Oh.' Molly held up her spread palms either side of her face as she had seen a girl do on the cover of *The Cunning Cut-throats of Clapham Common* – not the finest volume on my bookshelf. 'What into? Not an umpire what sucks out people's blood.'

'Some people might say I am that already,' her employer said drily. 'Go and tell Cook we do not want our dinner incinerated tonight.'

'In where, sir?'

'Burned,' I said.

'I'll try.' Molly scratched her tooth. 'But she dontn't like her nap disturbed while she's cooking.'

'I think I shall get changed too,' I told my godfather.

'What on earth for?' He went back behind his desk. 'Nobody will be looking at you.'

I changed nonetheless. I would look at me even if nobody else would.

Edward loved to look at me. He would watch me until I felt silly, which did not take long, then angry, which did not take long either. One afternoon as he polished his sabre in our dining room, he told me I was the most beautiful thing he had ever seen without hooves and I struck him playfully on the head with the scabbard. He needed four stitches after that.

68

The Pipe of Dreams

CHERRY MORTLOCK ARRIVED at seven promptly.
'I have never liked people who are fashionably late,'
she apologized as I scuttled down the stairs to greet her.
'Oh, March, you look pretty.'

She had on an ebony gown, trimmed to emphasize her tiny waist and quite daringly décolleté in a way that was bound to shock my godfather – especially as she was still in mourning – and was hardly disguised by her silk shawl.

'No, Cherry,' I disagreed. 'I look plain in a poor light. You look lovely.'

'She most certainly does not,' Sidney Grice corrected me, coming out of his study. 'She looks breathtakingly beautiful, according to my calculations.'

Cherry's face reddened briefly. '*Calculations?*'

'I have no concept of or interest in beauty,' he informed her, 'but I observe what stimulates other men and I have worked out a mathematical formula for it, based largely on the symmetry and proportions of twenty-eight facial and fourteen bodily measurements, and you achieve a score of four point two seven six six seven.'

'That does not sound very high.' Cherry smiled uneasily and tried to ignore Molly's dropping of her cloak on the floor for the third time.

Mr G looked splendid in his cerise tails, starched collar and extravagantly generous white bow tie.

'It is scored out of four point two seven six six eight,' he told her and she laughed.

'I have forgotten what the first number was.'

'You are close to perfection,' I assured her.

We went to the upstairs drawing room. Occasionally I sat in there to get away from my guardian, but I had not been in that chamber with him since he had shown me around his home, the moment I had arrived.

'Before I forget,' Cherry reached into her velvet purse, 'I have brought a peace offering for Spirit.' She brought out a slightly flattened white mouse. 'It is made of cotton stuffed with catnip.' She fluffed up its ears. 'The man I bought it from swore that cats cannot resist the smell.'

'She is sleeping upstairs.' I popped it into my bulky sack of a handbag. 'But, if she makes an appearance, you can give it to her yourself.'

'She is getting a bit old for toys,' Sidney Grice opined ungraciously.

'What a pretty room,' Cherry said and, though I would not have gone that far, this was easily the most feminine room of the house, three chintz chaises longues in a semicircle round an Indian rug before a lit fire. The matching calico drapes were drawn across the front window.

'I often come here at night to watch over my city.' Mr G propelled Cherry backwards with a little more force than was necessary, on to one of the sofas, and settled on the one between us. 'Often for three hours and nine minutes, but occasionally for only one-seventh of that.'

'Twenty-seven minutes,' I calculated, to a stop-showing-off look from my guardian.

'You will consume a sherry shortly,' he told her. 'It is not quite dark enough to be a true amontillado, I believe, but I have been informed by what I would regard as a reliable source that it is from the Montilla region and perfectly acceptable to ladies of taste.'

Apart from when I was ill and he was acting on doctor's advice, I had never been served alcohol by Sidney Grice, but he poured and passed two schooners as if it were a regular ritual.

'You do not drink?' Cherry asked.

'The keenest of minds blunt the most easily,' he informed her, 'and what an even more unhappy world this would be were my genius not to be honed to perfection.'

'Quite,' she murmured.

'Quite what?' he asked, resting his left arm over the back of his chaise longue.

'Cheerio.' I raised my glass to fill the puzzled space.

'Your good health,' she toasted in return.

Mr G leaned towards me until he was almost lying sideways.

'How do you think it is going thus far?' he whispered, though Cherry would have had to be very deaf indeed not to have heard him.

'Very well,' she said kindly and Mr G shot upright.

'How discomfited you will be when I explain that my inter-rogation was dispatched towards Miss Middleton.'

'Cherry spoke for both of us,' I assured him.

'Had you authorized her to do so?' He pulled his lower eyelid up just in time to foil an escape bid by his eye.

'In writing,' I joked and, before he could ask to see the exact terms of that letter, Cherry weighed in with, 'Do you really have no interest in beauty, Mr Grice?'

'I have a titanic curiosity about how it affects the behaviour of others.' He rose to pour himself a tumbler of water from a crystal carafe.

'Inspector Quigley once told me that an ugly woman could quote the Bible and not be believed, but that a pretty one could tell a jury almost anything she liked,' I put in – irrelevantly it seemed.

'So all those compliments you paid me...' Cherry began hesitantly.

'Were statements of fact.' He glugged his water.

'Oh.' Cherry wilted.

'Would you rather I had lied to you?'

'I think Cherry would rather that you meant them,' I suggested.

'I mean everything I say,' Sidney Grice said indignantly.

'Felt them,' I rephrased.

'Oh, that.' He sprinkled invisible herbs. 'I have no time for feelings.'

He drained his glass, threw back his head and gargled noisily but did not, I was relieved to see, spit it out again.

Cherry emptied her schooner. 'I do not wish to be rude,' she began.

'It has only occurred to me nine times in the course of this evening that you might be,' he reassured her.

'But why did you invite me here?'

I brought the decanter and refilled both our glasses.

My guardian eyed his glass sadly and I topped it up.

'Before I answer that, might I ask – also with no intent to be rude – why you came?'

'I suppose I was intrigued,' she admitted.

'The hope of stimulating that reaction was the third reason I did so.' Mr G blew on his water as if to cool it. 'My first reason was because I wished to apprise you of our startlingly slight progress on the conundrum with which you have presented us and the sixth was my wish that you observe my demonstration of a childish trick. We need not concern ourselves with the other reasons at present.' If the table had been made of gossamer he could not have placed his glass upon it with greater delicacy.

The door burst open so violently that it crashed against the wall and Molly wobbled in, trying to bow and curtsey at the same time.

'Cook said to tell you dinner is served, only it aintn't yet 'cause I've just come up two frights of stairs to serve it for you, and she said to tell you it aintn't in-sin-whatever-you-said-burned.'

She toppled sideways but recovered like a roly poly doll.

'Well,' Sidney Grice rose with that knack he had of appearing to exert no muscular activity whatsoever. 'If you are not too intoxicated to walk, Miss Mortlock, perhaps you would care to join us.'

'I shall try my utmost.'

'I tried my outmost once but it was broken,' Molly announced cryptically just before her employer pushed her to one side to let us through.

I had never seen the table set for three before and I had certainly never seen it so loaded with knives, forks and spoons.

'What on earth is all this?' Mr G grasped a fistful. 'And do not tell me it is cutlery – I know it is cutlery, but why in the name of Grace Horsley Darling and her twenty-one-foot Northumberland coble rowing boat is twenty-eight per centum of my canteen weighting this table to the point of collapse?'

Molly shuffled her feet and looked to the ceiling for inspiration.

'I got fluttered after you called me *darling*,' she admitted bashfully. 'If that was a proposal I must ask you to do it better, like you did to Miss Middleton when she was a lunantic.'

Cherry tried to mediate. 'I think Mr Grice just wants to know why we have so many knives and forks and spoons.'

Molly looked at her as one might an especially simple simpleton. 'Because Miss Middleton sedded to make sure there were three sets of cuttery.'

'That was three sets of cutlery between us, Molly,' I told her, 'not each.'

Molly's teeth sprang forwards as she brayed in hilarity. '*Between* and *each* – why, miss, there aintn't not no difference.'

'Get the first course,' Mr G instructed, settling Cherry in my place at one end of the table and himself at his end, with me in the middle like a child between parents.

Molly stuck her head into the dumb waiter shaft and roared, 'Cook, you know that turnip what went runny and you added more water to make a soup? They're ready for it now.'

337

The ropes creaked and the lift rose and Molly brought out three bowls, one at a time.

'Where is the tureen?' her employer challenged and, to save breath, added, 'The big blue bowl.'

'Oh, we was hoping you wouldntn't not notice that,' Molly answered, 'only Cook had an accident with it... or I should say *in* it.'

Mr G shot a finger to his eye.

'That will be all for now, thank you, Molly.' I shooed her away as he inflated his lungs.

Our maid's description of the first course was unusually accurate – mashed turnip in a greasy puddle. Cherry tried hard not to show her feelings but her lips defeated her. She dipped a spoon in experimentally.

Sidney Grice stood with his hands clasped and such a pious expression that I thought he had remembered to say grace, but he was marching to the end of the table with a decanter of red wine to serve Cherry and, less generously, me.

'Some muck called Château Lafite Rothschild that the baron keeps sending me crates of. I throw most of it away.'

'But it is probably one of the finest Bordeaux wines that money can buy,' Cherry protested.

'Quite so.' Mr G limped back to his place. 'But you cannot escape the fact that it is *French*.'

'Why did you not get a German wine?' I enquired, knowing how he admired all things from that country.

He tipped a steady stream of salt into his hand. 'Because that would cost Miss Mortlock money.'

'Me?' Cherry raised her eyebrows.

'I assume you are aware that, being a business dinner, this evening will be charged to expenses.' He scattered the salt. 'Well, that is enough idle chitter-chat to fulfil my duty as the host.'

'I shall pay for dinner,' I promised.

Cherry snorted. 'If you do the job, I shall not quibble over the cost of a turnip.'

'Three turnips.' Mr G created clouds of pepper over his bowl.

Cherry sampled her wine. 'This is most palatable.'

'Yes.' My guardian tucked in with relish. 'I am fortunate to have a cook who knows how to extract the majority of flavour from most dishes. Food should taste of nothing but salt and pepper.'

'May I ask if you really proposed to your ward?' Cherry put off the moment of sampling hers.

'Yes.' He chewed another scoop of it.

Cherry sniffed her food.

'He wanted to stop somebody else getting control of my inheritance,' I explained.

'The idea was repugnant to me,' he added.

'Almost as repugnant as this effluent posing as food,' I said. 'Do not feel obliged to try to eat it, Cherry.'

'Indeed not,' Sidney Grice agreed. 'We can have it reheated tomorrow. Boadicea.'

'The horse that fled the day before the Garstangs died?' I clarified.

'What of it?' Cherry pushed her bowl away untasted. 'Thousands of horses bolt in London every day.'

'The most accurate estimate I have been able to arrive at is an average of forty,' Mr G informed her. 'By which I mean steeds that have run out of control for at least one-eighty-eighth of a mile.'

Twenty yards, I calculated, but only repeated Cherry's enquiry. 'What of it?'

'Let us imagine that the Garstang household was not murdered by Angelina Innocenti,' Sidney Grice proposed.

'She was seen covered in blood and standing over a body,' Cherry objected.

'I have been like that more than once.' I shook off the images. 'But that does not make me a murderess.'

Oh, Edward, I could not tell her that that I killed the man I loved, how I drove him away, how he risked and lost his life trying to get back to me, how I left him to die because I did not know him. Nothing I can do will ever wash that guilt away.

'But she was the only person left alive in an impregnable house.' Cherry wrapped her shawl around her. 'Besides which I am not concerned with their deaths, unless you believe the same man killed my father.'

'I think that unlikely.' Mr G put his spoon down. 'Though so many unlikely things have occurred in the course of my investigations that the unlikely may be the most likely explanation. However, let us return to my original thesis.'

'If the Spanish maid did not do it, who did?' Cherry challenged. 'And what has this to do with the drayman's horse? The Garstangs would not allow alcohol through their front door.'

The shawl slipped down Cherry's left shoulder.

'I have yet to come across a troop of servants who embrace teetotalism as enthusiastically as their betters.' Sidney Grice rang the bell.

If I had revealed myself as Cherry was doing, my guardian would have rushed to throw a blanket over me, but he did not seem to mind in the least.

'So they smuggled drink in through the coal cellar,' I realized.

And my guardian scowled. 'You might have let our guest surmise that.'

'So when the horse bolted, the murderer climbed in through the coal-hole,' Cherry deduced.

'In broad daylight on a busy road?' I objected. 'And how could he be sure that he would not be found if he hid in the cellar all day and half the night?'

'What if the killer used the opportunity to wedge the lid open a fraction so that he could come back later to climb though it?' Cherry proposed.

'It would still be very risky.' I reached for the wine and refilled our glasses. 'There are always homeless people roaming the streets who might see him.'

Cherry clicked her fingers without eliciting any signs of disapproval and I began to think that, if she had danced on the table singing *'ave you ever seen plums like these? Come and give them both a squeeze*, Sidney Grice would have applauded warmly and asked why I never did that.

'There used to be a privet hedge at the front of the house which could shelter an intruder from view,' she recollected. 'I remember my father having it torn down.' She turned over her thoughts. 'But the door into the coal cellar would have been bolted from inside the house,' Cherry realized, 'even though it was not padlocked in those days.'

'Love knows no locksmith,' Edward said, or I thought he did.

'Excellent,' Sidney Grice rubbed his hands. 'At this rate we will have this case solved in good time to invoice dear Miss Mortlock for a considerable portion of her estate.'

The dumb waiter began to rise.

'You think you have made progress by establishing that nobody broke into the house via the coal-hole?' Cherry Mortlock recapitulated in disbelief. 'All of which points straight back to Angelina Innocenti as being the only possible suspect.'

'Oh.' Sidney Grice rubbed his left eye sleepily. 'I had not realized that we had reached that conclusion.'

The dumb waiter juddered to a halt.

'You go round in circles, Mr Grice,' Cherry accused him.

'I prefer to think of my mind moving through a tangle of helixes, ever spiralling towards the central truth.' He interlocked his fingers.

'Well, that must be very stimulating for you, I am sure.' Cherry's patience was fraying. 'But what about my father's death? The lid was padlocked as was the coal-cellar door. And, apart from the impossibility of entering or exiting Gethsemane, I would like to know how somebody could have killed my father and got out of his bedroom, leaving it securely bolted from the inside.

The murderer could not have climbed out of the window or up the chimney.'

Molly's boots clacked up the stairs.

'Indeed not,' Sidney Grice agreed heartily, 'and I anticipate demonstrating exactly how it can be done before this marvellous evening is concluded.'

Molly trudged in and put out the plates, each piled with something that looked and smelled like the so-called soup, converted into a dried lump.

'Where is the rest of it?' her employer demanded and Molly wiggled her right thumb about in her left ear.

'I think there's more in the pan. Shall I call down and check, sir?'

'Are there no potatoes or carrots or anything else?' I asked and Molly planted her hands on her considerable hips.

'For once I aintn't wrong,' she asserted. 'The master said to tell Cook we were to have turnips, and that's what I told her and that's what it is.'

'I did not say turnips, more turnips and nothing but turnips,' her employer raged. 'What are we to have for pudding? Turnip pie?'

'Oh, you are a laugh, sir.' Molly rocked in a figure of eight. 'Quite the Jolly Gentleman Joe what sings those songs about the Zeololical Gardens.'

I was as nonplussed as my guardian, but Cherry giggled and sang, '*Oh, the lions in the zoo they ate the kangaroo. Now I ain't got no pouch to 'ide me money.*'

I laughed; my guardian could not have looked more stunned had she just decapitated herself. But Molly tucked her hair under her hat and said quite severely, 'No. That's all out of tune.'

'Go and tell Cook to make something else,' Mr G said icily. He rose and beckoned. 'Come, Miss Mortlock. There is just time to show you my bedroom.'

'Is March coming too?"

'Of course.' He tossed his napkin into his chair. 'We shall need to lock her in there – unless you would rather we used you.'

69

Snakes

I HAD ONLY ever been in Sidney Grice's bedroom once and that was when he had collapsed with a recurrence of a fever caught when he was in Africa.

'I do not allow any women to see in here as a rule.' My guardian put a hand to the door.

'Such a privilege,' Cherry said uncertainly.

'Indeed,' he agreed.

'What about Molly?' I objected. 'She must go in to clean.'

'Molly is not a woman, though we refer to her as *she* out of kindness. Molly is a servant.' Mr G opened the door. 'Enter.'

His room was much as I remembered with its red Regency striped wallpaper, the thick Turkish rug by his bed, the pyramid of books on the bedside table. There were two frames on the wall to either side of a chest of drawers, but the pictures had been removed, leaving white oblongs in their place.

The reel of pink ribbon lay on the top of his three plump pillows.

'Knife.' He held up his hand – a surgeon waiting for a scalpel – but the knife miraculously materialized in it and the blade flicked up nastily.

Sidney Grice cut off two lengths of ribbon, each about six foot long.

'Like your slaughtered father, I have bolts on my door, though twice as many as he did.' He tied the ends together into simple

343

knots. 'For the purposes of this demonstration, I shall only use the top and bottom devices.' He looped the ribbons round the handles of each bolt. 'You shall stay here, Miss Middleton, to readmit us upon demand. Come, Miss Mortlock.'

With that he closed the door, taking the knotted ends with him.

'Observe – if you can manage to pay attention long enough – me pulling these tapes,' I heard, muffled through the woodwork.

The ribbons tensed and the bolts slid across into place.

'Watch – if this is not too tedious for you – whilst I untie the knots... and pull.'

A moment later the ribbons snaked away and I was left behind the locked door.

The handle rattled. 'Quite secure.' A brief quietness. 'You may readmit us at your earliest convenience, Miss Middleton,' came through the barrier.

I had a childish urge to pretend not to hear, but it hardly seemed appropriate given the reason he was performing the demonstration.

'I learned that trick as a child,' I said.

'It is a pity you unlearned it then.' Mr G wrapped the lengths of ribbon around the middle fingers of his left hand. 'You might have saved Miss Mortlock the price of a reel. Good heavens.'

'What is it?' I asked.

Sidney Grice help up his hand. 'The girth of my second and third digits has been increased almost twofold.'

'Well, they would be.' Cherry looked at him sideways.

'A percipient and intelligent remark.' Mr G began to unwrap his fingers. 'If only Miss Middleton were capable of such incisive perceptiveness, my referrals to her as my assistant might be more than the overly generous courtesy title they are at present.'

Cherry's eyes widened. 'Do you ever feel like striking him, March?'

'She launches glassware and books at me sometimes,' he told her, 'but she is an atrocious shot.'

'Perhaps she does not really want to hit you,' Cherry suggested.

'No, I am a bad shot,' I confirmed.

'Come and get it,' Molly bawled up. 'Cook has squashed some carrots and a butato and sort of fried them.'

'My mouth is watering,' Cherry murmured as we set off.

'I am sorry to hear that.' Sidney Grice handed her a clean white handkerchief.

70

The Dead File

T HE FOG LAY patchily, here a damp haze, there an almost suffocating wall of wet smoke suddenly all around us. I covered my nose to no avail. If there is not enough air to breathe, you cannot breathe whatever you do.

'What do you know about Dr Critchely?' I asked before he asked me the same.

A riderless horse hurtled in the opposite direction, saddle askew and stirrups flapping. It mounted the pavement, scattering pedestrians, and was lost to sight.

'He claims to specialize in nervous diseases.' My godfather leaned back. 'Turn right after that pothole.'

'What pothole?' came through the hatch as the left wheel dropped into a rut.

'I think it was that one,' I contributed helpfully.

Dr Critchely occupied a narrow three-storey end-of-terrace house – not one of the more prestigious addresses of Bloomsbury, but a respectable area. The brass plate on the house next door advertised the services of an architect.

'Obviously not a very good one either,' Mr G remarked, 'or he would have a bigger house.'

'Is that how you evaluate people – by their earnings?' I knocked on the door.

'It is a reasonable rule of thumb.' He tapped the single step with his cane. 'The Duke of Westminster is of more value to our nation than the mudlark. One creates wealth. The other sifts effluent in search of a scrap of it.'

I was about to argue that the duke, splendid fellow though he might be, did not actually earn the vast wealth that had been passed to him, when the green paintwork swung back and a large angular head poked through the opening, crowned with a tangle of grizzled hair which looked as if it might have been plopped on when his maker was distracted by plans for a hyena.

'Surgery hours are nine until twelve and—'

'I am perfectly capable of deducing that for myself from your copper-and-zinc alloy plaque,' my guardian butted in. 'I, to save you the trouble of enquiring, am Mr Sidney Grice.'

In many places mentioning that name might have opened the door; in other places it would have been smartly shut. But here his introduction only resulted in: 'Do you have an appointment with me?'

'Are you practising under the name of Dr Ottorley Critchely?'

'I am.' The doctor scowled.

'Do *you* have an appointment with *me*?' Mr G enquired amicably.

'No.' The doctor's face was dreadfully pockmarked. I had seen no worse in smallpox survivors.

'Then I cannot possibly have one with you.'

Dr Critchely bared his worn-down teeth. 'Do you wish to make one?'

'Certainly not.' My guardian recoiled. 'I have taken an almost instant and equally almost intense dislike to you.'

The head withdrew and, rapier fast, Sidney Grice's cane extended, telescoping to three times its original length and shooting out into the gap, wedging the door open.

'Take that out.' The doctor kicked at the stick but it ended far behind him. He slammed the door and dented his woodwork. 'I shall call the police.'

'How?' Mr G raised a quizzical eyebrow. 'The nearest constable is in Brian's Café, eating a bowl of jellied eels, some one hundred and four yards away if the Ordinance Survey 1 in 500 scale map is to be trusted, which I am inclined to do with ninety-six reservations.' Sidney Grice began to walk to his right, holding his stick like an oar high on his chest, as he forced the door further open. 'He will not hear you unless you manage first to muffle the traffic and second to acquire a functional megaphone.' He stopped walking. 'My assistant, Miss Middleton, is of slight, some might say *scrawny* fabrication. I believe she could squeeze past you and, once behind you, belabour you with her parasol or spray perfume in your eyes – she is quite fond of doing that – with a view to inflaming them.'

'This is an outrage.' The doctor's neck muscles fanned out with the effort of restraining my guardian.

'There we have found common ground,' Sidney Grice assured him. 'Even I find my behaviour atrocious at present, but do not concern yourself on that account. I am currently granting myself absolution.' My guardian jerked his thumb towards the entrance. 'After you, Miss Middleton.'

I gawped at him. 'I cannot force my way into this man's home.'

'You think you need more space?' My godfather braced himself. 'I am never quite sure how compressible your bustle is.'

'No, I mean it is not right.'

Sidney Grice took another step and Dr Critchely grunted with his exertions.

'You have chosen an inconvenient time to commence acquiring scruples.' Mr G's face was unusually flushed. 'Duck.'

'What?' I ducked just in time for my bonnet to be whacked off and sent flying into the road as Sidney Grice raised the cane over his head and let go, sending it scything back, the door slamming on to it and Dr Critchely sprawling on to the floor.

'Had enough?' my guardian called through the opening.

'Yes,' came the strangled reply and the door swung open.

Dr Critchely got to his knees.

'What on earth are you playing at?' I yelled.

Mr G tidied his cravat breathlessly. 'Do you imagine for

one-sixteenth of a moment that I enjoyed that?' He swept back his hair.

'Yes.' I looked in concern at the doctor. 'I believe you did.'

'You are always telling me I should have more fun.' Sidney Grice stepped over the threshold and offered his hand.

'That was rather good sport.' Dr Critchely took the hand and struggled to his feet. 'You are the private detective, I take it.'

'Personal,' Mr G corrected mildly.

'You have unorthodox methods, Mr Grice.' The doctor held on to the detective's hand. 'As one might expect from a man with idiopathic atypical neurasthenia.'

'And how did you diagnose that?' I asked.

My guardian pulled his hand away and made a great display of wiping it on a cloth from his satchel.

'The signs are there, if you know where to look.' Critchely shut the door. 'He has a certain irritability, which you have probably not noticed. This is caused by overstretched neurons in the cerebral cortex – and a hint, perhaps, of erratic behaviour typical of synaptical occlusion – and the keen diagnostician might also observe an underactive optical nerve resulting in a vacant, glassy look in the eyes.'

'Both eyes?' I tested him.

'Of course.'

I waited for Mr G to explode with wounded pride, but he only said calmly, 'You exceed my truncated expectations. And what is your opinion of this unfortunate woman?'

Dr Critchely looked me up and down. 'Undoubtedly an hysteric. Does she ever have temper tantrums?'

'No, I do not.' I stamped my foot.

'Yes.' Mr G pressed the ferrule of his cane into the rose-patterned wallpaper to recompress it.

'An hysterical liar then,' Critchely concluded. 'Shall we go to my consulting room?'

Sidney Grice gave me a silencing look and we went through to a small back room, equipped with a helmet sprouting wires over the headrest of a dental chair, with restraining bands on both arms.

'Is this where you electrolyse people?' I asked.

'I prefer to think of it as galvanically revitalizing the nervous system,' he replied. 'How many hours a night do you sleep?'

'Seven.'

'Girls need ten or eleven.' He motioned me towards the chair, but I rooted myself to the spot. 'The connections in the brain are looser and less organized in the female sex, which is why forty-five times more women than men require treatment in mental institutions.'

'It is the men who drive us there,' I asserted, 'and the men who build such places and decide whether or not we are put in them.'

'A deluded hysterical liar,' the doctor decided.

'Because, when men are mad, they still have a number of career choices available to them.' I warmed to my theme. 'The army, the Church or the medical profession, to name but three.'

'Deluded hysterical lying shrew,' he completed his diagnosis.

'Or accountancy,' my guardian contributed, a little late, I thought.

I considered landing a right hook under the doctor's rectangular chin like Molly had taught me, but it suddenly occurred to me that this man might be able to get me recertified.

'Nathan Mortlock,' I waited for the name to sink in, 'was a patient of yours.'

Critchely reeled back, as if I had landed that punch after all and followed it with a jab to the solar plexus.

'Who told you that?'

'He did.' I shadowed him. 'In his ledgers.'

'What of it?' Dr Critchely adopted a hunted expression. 'What are you doing?'

'Looking through your confidential patients' records,' Sidney Grice told him from across the room. 'And please do not be so ridiculous as to tell me I cannot.'

'You are wasting your time,' the doctor told him. 'He is no longer in those files.'

'Goodness, I had no idea that the minister of war was a

patient of yours,' my godfather exclaimed. 'Is his mother aware that he harbours such feelings for her?'

'Put that back.' Ottorley Critchely rushed towards him.

'Gracious, he is of the opinion that his mother reciprocates and, if I know—'

Critchely leaped across and rammed the drawer shut just as Mr G whipped his fingers away.

'Get out.' Critchley screwed himself up and grabbed the nearest thing to hand.

'I fear we have made an unfavourable impression upon you, Dr Critchely,' I said, so sweetly that he lowered the ebony rule he had in his fist and replied, 'I fear you are correct, Miss Middleton.'

'What if we start again?' I suggested.

'With that tussle at the door?' Critchely's face lit up at the prospect.

'Perhaps not this time,' I demurred.

'With me saying I have taken an intense dislike to him?' my godfather suggested hopefully.

'Just for once, why do we not try doing it my way?' I proposed. 'Politely.'

'What a ridiculous idea,' Sidney Grice declared. 'But – ever the gallant gentleman – I shall, as oft, accede to your wish.'

'Good afternoon, Mr Grice.' Dr Critchely put the rule down to shake his hand and guide us into a small sitting room which also served as a study, and which managed to be grey without actually being grey.

'What can you tell us about Mr Nathan Mortlock?' I settled into the larger of the two leather armchairs. No woman would have arranged them so that they were not round anything – a table or a fireplace, for instance.

'Nothing.' The gaslight on Dr Critchely's face cast it into a gibbous moon, cratered and jaundiced in complexion. 'For I am constrained by the Hippocratic oath from revealing any details of his consultations with me.' He took the other armchair.

Sidney Grice's glass eye glinted with malicious intent.

'If you think you can shelter—'

'You promised,' I reminded him sternly.

'The fog must have seeped into my brain.'

'I am sure you do not need me, Doctor,' I continued pleasantly, 'to remind you that the duty of confidentiality dies with the patient, especially when his records are required as part of a criminal investigation.'

Critchely pulled on the fingers of his left hand one by one as he spoke. 'And I am sure you do not require me to refresh your weak, girlish memory with the fact that you are not policemen.' Apparently satisfied that the fingers were firmly attached, he gave his attention to the other hand.

'If you think…' Mr G began again, but silenced himself this time and settled for pacing up and down, inspecting certificates and testimonials on the walls.

'Miss Mortlock is most anxious that we proceed with this matter,' I urged gently.

'If she were to instruct me in writing, perhaps I might be of more assistance,' Dr Critchely reflected.

'We have no time for that twaddle.' My guardian fumed and glared at me. 'I did not promise to be mute.'

'Are you familiar with the journalist, Mr Trafalgar Trumpington?' I shifted in my seat and the leather cracked like the boards of a ship.

'That awful scoundrel who exposed Mrs Eagleby-Wisedom's past as a harpoonist?'

I did not tell him that Traf, as he liked to be known, also tried to besmirch my reputation.

'The correct term is harpooneress,' Mr G asserted, standing back to check if he had straightened the portrait of a military man to his satisfaction, and I remembered Mrs Emmett trying to spear an onion just before she died.

'I should hate Mr Trumpington to get the idea that you were withholding information that would help Miss Mortlock to apprehend her father's murderer.' I creaked noisily.

Sidney Grice lifted the portrait off the wall.

'But where would he get that idea?' the doctor asked blankly.

My guardian untied the cord.

'He has proved disconcertingly ingenious in extracting information from me in the past,' I confessed.

Critchely chewed that information over.

'And if the murderer were to strike again,' I drove the point home, 'especially if his victim were the sweet and innocent Miss Charity Mortlock herself, I would not put it past that wretch to depict you as having harboured him or even been an accomplice.'

Sidney Grice shortened and retied the cord.

The doctor made his mind up. 'I shall tell you what I can.' He got up and went to a small filing cabinet beside his desk.

'Miss Mortlock *is* sweet,' Mr G concurred after much consideration, 'but whether she is innocent remains to be established.'

Mr G rehung the picture and surveyed his work with satisfaction.

'Here we are.' Critchely lifted something out.

'Where else could we be?' My guardian nipped to the doctor's chair but only to look cursorily under the cushion, letting it drop like an unclean thing.

Dr Critchely returned with a cardboard box the size of a beer crate and sat back with it on his knees. 'These are the records of my deceased patients.'

'You have disappointingly few of them,' Sidney Grice commented.

'Forty-eight.' The doctor lifted a number of brown envelopes before withdrawing the one he wanted. 'Nathan Mortlock.' He pulled out a thick sheaf of papers. 'I can tell you the dates I saw him.'

'We already know them, fool,' my guardian snarled. 'If that is all you are willing to divulge, you might as well put those notes away.'

'Very well.' Critchely huffed and stuffed them back.

'Come, Miss Middleton,' Mr G rapped. He swung his cane;

there was a click and the end shot out again, this time punching into the box and sending it flying off the doctor's lap, scattering its contents over the floor.

'You maniac,' Dr Critchely yelled. 'You could have killed me.'

'That thought did occur to me,' Sidney Grice said regretfully and, laying his cane down, went round the chair to pick the records up.

'Leave them alone,' Critchely shouted. 'You have done enough damage already.'

'Some men might say *too much*,' my guardian chatted, then sprang up and backwards, knocking into an ornamental pedestal. The column wobbled and almost recovered, but somehow Mr G caught it with his arm and a blue vase flew off, shattering on the hearth.

'That was certainly too much,' I said as the doctor leaped up to see if it were salvageable.

Sidney Grice's foot twitched and I saw a shape skid under the chair, emerging the other side as an envelope. I did not need to read the name printed on it.

'Can *I* help?' I wandered over.

'No, you cannot.' Critchely was trying to fit two pieces together and, from the way he was setting about it, I guessed that he had never been much good at jigsaw puzzles.

I fell to my knees. 'Your floor is very slippery,' I complained. 'Small wonder you have had forty-eight patients die in this very room.'

'They did *not* die in here,' Dr Critchely bawled. 'Well, only two of them and they were twins.'

'Well, that is all right then,' I riposted.

'Miss Mortlock will reimburse you for the cost of replacing that garish miscreation,' Mr G promised as I tried to cram the notes into my handbag, but the envelope was jutting out of the top. I took it out but it was too thick to fold.

'Your satchel,' I mouthed.

'Is full,' he replied loudly.

'That was an irreplaceable Ming vase,' Critchely wailed.

'Made in Staffordshire,' my godfather corrected him, 'by Turner and Bantam. The glaze is hopeless; it is completely the wrong blue and, now that I have divided it for you, you may see the poor quality of pottery, fired at much too high a temperature. I am relieved that it did not explode under the weight of its own shoddiness and kill yet another of your patients.'

'Just get out, the pair of you,' Dr Critchely shrieked. 'What are you doing, girl?'

I was stuffing my handbag under my cape.

'Nothing.' I started guiltily and something repulsive slithered over the doctor's lips. I think it was a smile.

'You are imagining yourself bearing my child, aren't you?' he leered.

'Not until this moment.' A clammy finger crawled down my mind.

'Lots of my female patients do that and some of them are even uglier than you.' The loathsome thing migrated into his eyes as they flickered over me. 'Why not come back without this man and we can discus it more... comfortably?'

And for the first time, when it came to intimate matters, I felt as nauseated as Sidney Grice looked.

And, had I not hustled him away, I believe that the personal detective might have broken something else – the neurological doctor's jaw.

71

The First State

SIDNEY GRICE SKIMMED through the notes.

'We have committed a criminal offence,' I declared.

In the excitement of the moment it had felt like a prank, but in calmer reflection, I realized that what we had done was theft.

'Not so.' Mr G flattened the sugar with the back of his spoon. Any untidiness was inclined to distract him. 'The act of gathering illegal material for the purposes of an investigation constitutes the upholding rather than a flouting of the law.'

He separated the top half dozen sheets.

'In what way illegal?'

'Judge for yourself.' He held them out and I tipped forward to take them, flopping back into my chair.

The first page had Dr Critchely's heading printed along the top with his claim to be a *Specialist in Diseases of the Nervous System and Disorders of the Brain.*

Beneath was written in commendably neat handwriting that looked like small block capitals but was just about joined-up:

Patient: Nathan Roptine Mortlock
Address: Gethsemane, 1 Gaslight Lane, Bloomsbury
Date of birth: 25/08/1837
Profession: Gentleman
Date of first appointment: 15/02/1874

The patient complains of: severe headaches / prolonged and prostrating / constant feeling of intracranial pressure building to a climax where he feels he has to clutch his head to stop it bursting / shooting pains between the temples / ocular problems especially blurring of vision and bright flashing white lights / Occasional loss of consciousness twice witnessed by manservant with no convulsive episodes reported.

I had to give the doctor full marks for diagnostic note-taking.

On examination the only abnormalities detected were: a cardiac rate of one hundred and sixty and a pressure of two hundred and forty.

I resolved to look the latter figure up. Manometers had not been in use when I assisted my father.

The patient's hearing was exceedingly acute and his response to epidermal needle and feather applications sensitive in the extreme.

Provisional diagnosis: neuralgic neurasthenia with chronic inflammation of the cerebral cortex.

Recommended Dr Lestrade's Nerve Tonic, Gregson's Cocaine tablets and to double his dose of Mycroft's Extra Strength Laudanum.

Paid five guineas.

I slipped the sheet to the bottom and started on page two.

29/02/1874
On his second appointment the patient reported a worsening of his symptoms. He complains of recurrent nightmares but is unable or unwilling to recount them.

My tests with lodestones indicate a very sluggish movement of his cerebrospinal fluids and I have recommended galvanization to remagnetize his cerebellum and improve the flow. The patient felt disinclined to be subjected to that treatment on this occasion.

Paid five guineas.

I perused page three. 'Apart from his eccentric methods and excessive bills I cannot see anything illicit so far,' I commented, and turned to page four – more of the same.

An entry on page five attracted my attention.

The patient permitted me to inject him with 5 ml of opiate solution. This relaxed him enough to submit to mesmerization, under the influence of which he began to recall some of his nightmares. They were of such a distressing nature to him that I was forced to curtail the session and instructed him to cast all memory of it from his mind before bringing him out of his trance.

And on page six, where he described another visit from Nathan Mortlock, ending with:

I shall attempt to organize these dreams into a journal wherein his feelings about the deaths of each member of the Garstang household may be expressed more coherently.

'Dr Critchley is something of a Mr William Wilkie Collins,' Sidney Grice said. 'He likes to set the scene before he reveals the plot.'

I yawned. 'I do not think he would have made much money writing like this.'

'If you are looking for something to suit your taste for the sensational, try this.' My guardian passed me an ultramarine journal.

'His log of Nathan Mortlock's dreams?' I guessed.

In the same small handwriting but less tidily, scattered with crossings out and underlinings, the physician had recorded his patient's words.

I no longer know if I am dreaming or awake. The first state seems so real and the second so unreal that they are indistinguishable.

I read on.

'Bloody hell!' I blurted and waited for my guardian to berate me for my unladylike language.

'That sums it up quite accurately,' Sidney Grice concurred.

72

The Lanes of Logic

I READ A few more pages before I burst out, 'We cannot tell Cherry that her father was a murderer.'

Sidney Grice tilted the top rim of his pince-nez down and looked over it.

'Unless we are incapacitated, we can, but we may not have to. As Miss Mortlock is fond of reminding us, she is not paying us to investigate those deaths.'

'But I still do not understand how he could have done it. Nathan Mortlock was locked in a cell all that night.' I clicked my fingers, to my guardian's chagrin. 'It was not Nathan in that cell but somebody that looked very similar – a twin or close relative.'

'And what impels you to hurtle unchecked towards that conclusion?' He tipped his eyeglasses back again.

'My reasons are twofold.' I imitated my guardian so badly that it is unlikely he realized I was doing so. 'First, there is no other possible explanation. He could not be in two places at once. Second, Inspector Pound commented that Nathan Mortlock was a tubby little man when he saw him in the police station but the photograph showed that the real Nathan was quite an athletic-looking man, and he was not corpulent when we saw his body.'

Sidney Grice shuddered. 'You have a special gift for finding and taking wrong turnings on your journey from premise to conclusion.' He hugged himself with crossed arms. 'And with your usual generosity of spirit you cannot resist sharing that gift with all and sundry at every opportunity.'

I wandered round the back alleys and lanes of logic for a while before coming up with, 'What is your explanation?'

He pulled his mouth down in his way of demonstrating assent.

'We know where the rope that was used to tie and strangle Lionel Engra came from,' my guardian said. 'But I have my suspicions about where the rest of it went.'

He closed his eyes.

'And are you going to share that idea with me?'

'Consider those two simple facts.' Mr G brought out his half-pennies. 'A coil of rope goes missing and a thin man looks tubby.'

He clacked the coins.

'Of course!' I realized. 'Nathan wrapped it round his waist.' I remembered Sidney Grice's trick with the bolts on his bedroom door. 'Which is why you were so excited about your fingers being fat with the ribbons.'

'Indeed.' Mr G threw the coins into the air where they disappeared.

I forced myself not to ask how he did that. 'But...' I tried to clear my thoughts. 'But you have already proved that Nathan Mortlock could not possibly have got in and out in the time available.'

'If that is the case I must be going prematurely senile,' Mr G put his fingertips together, 'for I have no recollection whatsoever of doing so.'

'But you went through all those timings.'

'I remember that as clearly as if it were recently.' He separated his hands to support a large invisible bowl. 'Which it was. Come, March, let us make a sentimental journey to the scene of our former triumphs and resolve that matter for once and for all.'

Sidney Grice snapped his fingers and the coins fell into his hands.

73

The Empty Harness and the Black Maria

THE LOBBY OF Marylebone Police Station was quiet, the only signs of life being a greyhound sprawled snoring over one of the benches, with no sign of its owner, and, at his usual post, Sergeant Horwich, who looked almost ready to fall asleep himself.

'Which one of you has arrested which one of you today?' he joked. 'Plenty of room in the cells for you both.'

'Mr Gladstone's moral crusade must be paying dividends,' I observed. 'The police may have to start committing crimes to keep themselves in work if business stays this slack.'

'Just wait for Saturday night.' Horwich primped his moustaches with the back of his crooked first finger. 'It'll be standing room only with space for one more on top.'

'Are any of the cells occupied at present?' Sidney Grice peeped at the register but the sergeant slapped it shut.

'Not even Nettles having his afternoon nap,' Horwich assured him.

'Good.' Mr G twirled his cane. 'Then you can show us round.'

'I'm not a bleedin' tour guide,' Sergeant Horwich objected.

'Indeed, you show no visible signs of haemorrhage,' my guardian agreed.

Horwich rolled his eyes. 'Anyway, I thought Harris did that the other week.'

'But not as nicely as you can,' I told him and he preened a

little more. 'I cannot imagine anyone is so knowledgeable about it as you.'

It is a myth put about by men that only women are dupes for flattery. Everybody is. Tell any man how dashing he looks in his uniform, or how you love a man with a few extra chins and no teeth, and he will be fresh clay in your hands. I have never met a man yet who did not believe that he was handsome if you told him so. I know a great many beautiful women who are knotted with self-doubt because their hair is not straight or curly or dark or blonde enough, no matter how ardently a beau may seek to give reassurance.

'You must have had some fascinating experiences here.' I poured some honey on the flattery and Horwich almost visibly lapped it up.

'I suppose I could spare a couple of minutes,' he conceded, and bellowed over to the back office, 'Nettles. Come and look after the desk.'

Constable Nettles appeared, fumbling with the top button of his collar.

'Arrested each other, 'ave you?' he greeted us.

'Steal my joke once more and I'll have you patrolling Berkeley Square for the rest of your short career.' Horwich pushed back his chair. I was so used to seeing him sitting that I had almost forgotten what a massive man he was, keg-chested and a good eight inches taller than my godfather or me.

'But that is a lovely area,' I objected.

'Too lovely,' Nettles complained. 'I'd spend my days telling sweet old ladies the time and helping them across the road. Not much chance of promotion for me there.'

'Or anywhere else,' Sidney Grice put in unkindly. 'Do not forget your keys, Sergeant Ezekiel Trueblood Horwich.'

Few men dared address the sergeant by his full name but Mr G was not easily intimidated. Horwich took a key out of his outer breast pocket to unlock a wall cupboard behind him, snatched the ring off a hook and clipped it on to his belt, then marched out from behind his desk, along the corridor to the stairs.

Despite it being empty, the lights were turned up. I supposed that one would not want to be fiddling with gas mantles when there was a troublesome prisoner. All the doors were opened outwards.

The sergeant pouted. 'What do you want to see?'

'I am especially interested in cell one.' Sidney Grice ambled towards it. 'You cannot imagine how ungrateful I would be if you could show me how you lock it.'

Horwich chuckled and not for the first time I marvelled at the façades we all construct. Nobody – not even my godfather – could have known, from his manner, the distress the sergeant must have been suffering.

'Ungrateful?' He unclipped the bunch of keys. 'Got your words a bit muddled there.'

'Why so many keys?' I asked.

'One for each door.' He rattled them. 'And, in case they get taken off an officer by somebody wanting to let all his pals out, they are in a jumblificified order.'

'So how do you know which is which?' I asked, restraining myself from saying that he must be very clever, in case he thought I was mocking him.

'The biggest one is for the outside door.' Horwich held it up. 'The next is cell two, then one, then four, then three and so on.'

'So you finish with nine and ten?' I forced myself to say, and the sergeant smiled benevolently.

'You nearly got it.' His hand reached out and I resolved, if he tried to ruffle my hair, to do the same to him, but Horwich's fingers came to a halt just an inch above my bonnet. 'Ten and nine. I bet Mr Grice could have worked that out.'

'It would have taken me an inconsiderable time,' Sidney Grice said drily.

'Tricky, isn't it?' the sergeant commiserated.

'You must be very clever,' skipped shamelessly off my tongue.

'All the men think so.' Sergeant Horwich preened his moustaches. 'But that's not for me to say.' He put the second key in the lock.

'Kindly execute your half-witted stratagem, Miss Middleton,' my guardian directed, 'before my cerebro-spinal fluid needs remagnetizing.'

'Ooh, nasty,' Horwich sympathized. 'My missus gets a touch of that in this cold weather. It's the damp what gets deep into you.'

'Strange how the dark plays tricks,' I mused. 'I imagined the cell was quite small but that must be at least eight paces long even for a big man.'

I went in to demonstrate, in baby steps, eight in and eight out again, and Horwich chortled.

'Why, bless you, miss. A grown man could do that in half as many.'

I decided that asking him what half of eight was might be going a bit too far, but only dissented dogmatically. 'I think not.'

The sergeant bristled. 'Right then.' And he strode into the cell. 'Three,' he declared triumphantly. 'What the—?'

Sidney Grice slammed the door and I turned the key.

'Very funny, I don't think,' Horwich fumed. 'Which of the men put you up to this? If any one of them dares come down to look he'll be digesting his truncheon for a week.' He put his face to the observation hatch. 'I'm very surprised at you, Mr Grice, indulgifying in pranks like this.'

He hammered on the door.

'It puzzles me when people do that,' Mr G pondered. 'He must know that we know he is in there and wanting to be let out.'

'I think he is venting his frustration,' I conjectured as Horwich grasped the bars and wrenched at them.

'If I call for help, you could both be arrested for illegally holding me prisoner and obstructifying a police officer in the course of his duty,' the sergeant threatened. 'Both those charges carry stiff sentences.'

'And you would live it down in a matter of moments,' I forecast. 'Shall I call the men down for you?'

Horwich fought down his mounting anger. 'Right then. What's your game?'

'I would have thought you'd know by now that I do not play games, Sergeant.' Mr G removed the key as Horwich made a hopeless attempt to squeeze his hefty arm through to grab it.

Sergeant Horwich extricated himself. 'What then?'

'I wish to consult you, as an experienced detention officer, to learn how you intend to get out of that cell.' My godfather stepped sideways and unlocked the back door.

'I do not imagine that even you could break that door down, even if you used the bed as a battering ram,' I debated.

Sidney Grice opened the back door on to a large high-walled courtyard.

'Of course I bleedin' can't,' Horwich retorted.

A Black Maria stood, its harness empty. I liked to think the horse was having a rest.

'Do you know how to pick locks?' I asked.

'No, I do bleedin' not.'

'It would take a long time to tunnel out,' I remarked.

'With what?' he demanded. 'My granny's arse?'

'I have not witnessed what a coarse man you are before this moment.' Mr G closed the door and relocked it. 'I am rapidly reaching the conclusion that the only way out is with these.' He held up the ring.

'You've had your fun,' Horwich wheedled. 'Just hand them over and we'll say no more about it.'

'But how will you persuade me to do that?' Sidney Grice rattled the bunch. 'Shall we go for tea, Miss Middleton?'

'That would be jolly,' I agreed readily.

'I'm warning you,' Horwich stormed.

'He does not say what he is warning us about,' my guardian noted.

'Probably to take care crossing the road,' I speculated. 'Goodbye, Sergeant.'

If Sergeant Horwich could, he would have ripped that door

out of its frame and battered us to death with it at that moment, but the door held firm no matter how hard he kicked at it with his scuttle-sized boots. He walked back and launched a fling kick with both feet, landing heavily on his shoulder.

'Bloody damn and piss it,' he raged. 'Open the fropping door, you soddened gits.'

Sidney Grice leaned back on his stick like a holidaymaker admiring a mountain view. 'You cannot appreciate yet – though you shall shortly – how encouraged I am to hear you say that. It confirms my belief that I am steering a steady course towards the truth and that our incarceration of you was fully justified.'

'You might have to get used to it,' I warned and Horwich scowled.

'You won't get me to fall for that trick again.'

'Probably not,' I agreed.

'For some time I have been vexed by the problem of Nathan Mortlock's alibi on the night of the Garstang massacre.' Mr G leaned sideways to take some pressure off his right leg. 'It puzzled me that the man who had everything to gain by their deaths went out of his way to get himself arrested for the first and only time in his life on that particular occasion.'

'How the hell would I know?' Horwich gave the door another kick. 'All I know is that he turned up D and D. I booked him and unbooked him on his way to court.'

'The problem is,' I explained, 'that he could not possibly have got out of here, committed the atrocity and returned in the time available to him.'

'Of course he couldn't,' Horwich rumbled. 'I've told you that until I'm blue in the face.'

I refrained from remarking that he was actually puce and said, 'Unless.'

'Unless what?' the sergeant shouted.

'Unless he was let out by the man with the key,' I concluded.

Horwich closed his eyes, inhaled and opened them. 'For the last time – *I* was the only one with the keys and I don't let anybody else lay a finger on them while I'm on duty. They stay locked in that cupboard – and I keep the only key for that – or on my belt. Nobody could have let him out without me knowing.'

'*My* knowing,' Mr G corrected and unbuckled the flap of his satchel.

'Oh, Sergeant Horwich,' I sighed, 'that is exactly what I was afraid you would say.'

74

·───✦───·

Dead Men's Dreams

ORWICH BLINKED.

'For once you're speaking more riddles than your guardian,' he complained.

Sidney Grice brought out the ultramarine book, opened it on the page he wanted without a glance, held it out in front of him and read out:

The military man comes. His face is framed in the window, divided by bars, big with bristling moustaches. He—

'What the hell are you talking about?'

'It is a diary of Nathan Mortlock's dreams,' I informed him.

'So you have falsely imprisoned an officer of the law with twenty-five years of service on the strength of a dead man's dreams?' Horwich threw back his head in disgust.

Mr G read on:

He puts a finger to his lips. I cannot hear the key go in or the lock turn or the well-oiled door open. He does it all so slowly. Twice he stops to check behind him. I hear my friend. He is sobbing. He is saying, 'Please. It's all closing in. Please. I can't breathe.' He is panting and I want to go and comfort him. But I know I can't and he can never know the reason why. The big man signals for me to stop. He walks silently like a dead man, this, this—

'*This, this* what?' Horwich interrupted. 'This is just rubbish. If you are trying to make some accusation of derelictionment of duty, you will be laughed out of court.'

This sergeant major.

'Well, there you are,' Horwich cried. '*Military man – sergeant major.* I've never been neither of those.'

'One can quite understand why somebody would describe you in that way,' I reasoned.

'I won't even start on how the men describe you,' Horwich mocked, 'but it doesn't make you guilty of anything.'

My guardian read on.

He opens the back door. I hesitate but he motions me to hurry. 'Get a fropping move on,' he whispers and half pushes me out. It is windy and wet and, when I remember what I am out there for, I turn to go back but he has shut the door. I can feel the cold even in my dream. It chills my bowels and sets a block of ice in my heart.

'Is that it?' Horwich struck his temple with the ball of his hand. 'A dead man's dreams about a sergeant major? You must have been infected with Miss Middleton's madness, Mr Grice, or maybe you gave yours to her.'

'Fropping,' I quoted to the shock of both men. 'I have only ever heard three men use that word – you, and Constables Nettles and Harris, who must have picked it up from you.'

'You move in much more gentile circles than what I do,' Horwich said.

In happier times I would have found his Mollyism amusing, but there was precious little to laugh about now.

'Dear Sergeant Horwich,' I said. 'Nathan Mortlock goes on to give accounts of the murders with details that were never made known to the public or even the family.'

'Perhaps he had a vivid imagianation,' Horwich proposed, 'or met the real murderer.'

'It goes on.' Mr G leafed back. 'The dreams were not in chron-ological order and I would have been highly sceptical if they were.'

I run. I run all the way along the street, miles and miles of them. My legs are heavy and the air syrup. I can hardly make any prog-ress. Sometimes I am drifting backwards.

'This is all very interesting,' Horwich broke in, but my godfather read on without a pause.

At last I reach the door. I scratch on it four times. That is our signal. But there is no answer. I wait a lifetime and try again but still nobody comes. A wave of panic crashes over me for I know, if I can't get back in, I am as good as dead. I scratch again and I whisper as loud as I dare, 'Sergeant Horwich, let me in.'

That bit knocked Horwich backwards. 'You're making that up.'
    'I have read it too,' I told him.

Horwich opens the door. 'Shut your stupid fropping mouth,' he hisses. 'Your friend has been making a fuss again and I've only just got him settled.'

The sergeant paled. 'It was just a dream. Maybe he had it but it doesn't mean anything. I dreamed I stole the Crown Jewels last night but my missus wasn't wearing a crown this morning.' He looked about him. 'Maybe he made it all up to spite me for writing down his real name. He asked me not to. I remember that now.'

'After eleven years?' I watched a bead of sweat roll down the side of his nose.

'My Old Mum,' Sidney Grice declared loudly.

'What?' Horwich looked genuinely confused. 'What about her?'

'Surely you have not forgotten My Old Mum?' Mr G flipped his stick to point a foot away from our prisoner's face. 'My Old Mum changed your life, Ezekiel Trueblood Horwich. You had ten shillings on the first three places in the two thirty at Newmarket, and it was all going wrong for you until the final furlong when Brian Boru stumbled and My Old Mum came in by half a nose ahead.'

'I remember hearing about that race.' I frowned. 'Brian Boru was such a hot favourite and My Old Mum so unfancied that there was a stewards' enquiry. Boru's jockey was exonerated, but he was never given a good ride again.'

'But lucky old Ezekiel made one hundred and eighty-two pounds out of that race,' my guardian marvelled. 'An absolute fortune for a young sergeant who had only just sewed the stripes on his sleeve.'

'Many men would have been tempted to buy a cosy pub by the seaside.' I saw the sweat snowball and, by the time it reached Sergeant Horwich's splendid moustache, a dozen more had sprung up to replace it.

'Coincidentally, it was exactly the amount he was in debt,' Mr G revealed.

'Goodness,' I expostulated, 'that must have been an intolerable burden for a young sergeant who had only just sewed the stripes on his sleeve.'

'All right.' Horwich held up his hand. 'You've had your fun. Yes, I did used to be a gambler and I did get myself heavily in hock. I expect Gerry told you that, though I told him in confidence over a drink once. But I had a lucky break and I learned my lesson and I've never bet a penny since.'

'You must be very proud of yourself,' I told him. 'Most people would have taken that as the start of a lucky streak and got themselves back into debt.'

'It wasn't easy,' Horwich admitted, 'but I'd been living in fear of my life at that time.'

'Bookie Joe,' Sidney Grice said. 'He bought up all your debts.'

'Lucky for you he took that last bet then,' I remarked.

'Only Bookie Joe does not remember it that way.' My guardian held his cane out steadily. 'He remembers being very surprised and disappointed that you managed to pay him off. Hagop Hanratty was offering him two hundred and fifty to take over your debt. An obliging police sergeant, especially one in charge of the station book and keys, would have been worth his weight in aluminium to a man in his position.'

'I never done anything to help scum like that,' Horwich declared with a passion that could only have come from the heart. 'It was me who arrested his brother, Aram.'

'You will not have heard of Drake, Frick, Garrard and Leaf.' Mr G lowered his stick until it was a foot above the stone slabs. 'But, to summarize, they are a company of auditors, that is, accountants who scrutinize company and personal finances, especially if there is a suspicion of irregularities. Miss Charity Clair Caroline Mortlock does not know it yet, but she will be paying them a considerable number of guineas – the exact number of which is none of your concern – to draw up a detailed analysis of her father's affairs.' He tapped the floor three times like a magician performing a trick. 'Nathan's record-keeping was exemplary and Mr Harold Tewkesbury of the aforementioned Drake, Frick, Garrard and Leaf was able to account for almost every penny of Mortlock's expenditure since the day he inherited the Garstang estate, excepting two things: first, a payment of ten pounds, increasing to thirty pounds in cash on the first day of every month; second, in October 1872, when there was an unlisted withdrawal of—'

'One hundred and eighty-two pounds.' Horwich filled the pause. 'I just wanted to clear my debt, not a penny more,' he burst out.

'And for that you released a man to murder an entire household.' I shook with disgust.

All at once the sergeant aged. 'I didn't know. I swear to God. He told me he was getting married – I didn't know he already

373

was – and that he was staying with his future in-laws who didn't approve of him, and the engagement would be broken off if they found his bed had not been slept in.' He wiped his nose with his sleeve. 'He made it sound romantical and a bit of a joke. Then when I found out – what could I do? I couldn't say I had released him. That would make me an accomplice. Even if they didn't hang me, how long do you think a peeler would last in Pentonville with the animals he helped put in there?'

'I believe six and a half days is an average.' Mr G clapped the book shut. 'You will not attack us or try to make an escape.'

Horwich nodded dumbly. I unlocked the door and swung it open, and there was a clatter on the steps.

'Two duffers and a roller to book in, Serg,' Nettles called down.

'Card cheats and a professional woman,' Mr G interpreted, though I probably knew more slang than he.

'Just deal with it,' Horwich ordered.

'What, by myself?'

'Yes,' I said, as Horwich fought to catch his breath.

'Fropping liberty,' Nettles muttered as he climbed back up.

75

Blood in the Gaslight

Sergeant Horwich came out of the cell and, though he still towered over us, he was physically diminished.

'What now?' he mumbled.

'You shall sit on this bench.' Sidney Grice tapped it with his cane. 'And we shall sit on that one.'

We faced him across the hall, perhaps ten feet away.

'I meant no harm by it,' Horwich burst out. 'I swear it.'

'But you still took the money even when you knew what he had done,' I pointed out.

'He had no more right to it than me.' Horwich's voice broke. 'And I only took what I needed to make a fresh start.'

'As an accessory to murder,' I reminded him.

'I didn't know,' he vowed.

'You may have been an unwitting dupe before the act,' Mr G granted him. 'But afterwards you sheltered him for four thousand, one hundred and fifty-nine days and nights, one of the most notorious murderers of this century, and he was not short of competition for that title. That makes you an accessory after the fact.'

'Do you think it hasn't haunted me?' Horwich looked over his shoulder as if he had heard a noise. 'You can't imagine how many nights I've lain in bed thinking about those poor people, and if handing myself in would have undone what I did, I would have done it like a shot, I swear it, Mr Grice.' His breath was short and fast now and he jumped again. 'Somebody is coming.'

'Nettles and his prisoners,' my guardian said. 'Delay them.'

Horwich's eyes shot side to side. 'Take those suspects to interview rooms one, two and four, Constable Nettles, and make sure they are kept there. And do *not* interrupt us again.'

I could not catch exactly what Nettles muttered to that, but I think I got the gist.

'Mortlock led a respectable life after that,' Horwich pleaded.

'Tell that to Mrs Rachel Samuels, the widow who lived and died at number 4 Burton Crescent,' I challenged and Horwich's jaw clacked shut.

Sidney Grice went back to the journal. 'In the latter pages, Mortlock does not even pretend he is dreaming.'

She saw me climbing out, the nosey prying bitch. She was walking the dog. Who in God's name does that at three in the morning? She kept walking but she hesitated, just enough for me to know. I tried to tell myself that she couldn't have recognized me in that light and, after a few weeks of sweating every time the doorbell rang, I almost convinced myself that I was right. But she was biding her time.

Two months later she came to me. Her son was having money problems. I said I was sorry to hear that but so are thousands of others.

'You WILL help him,' she said. 'There is a loose brick on the path outside your front door. You will put five pounds there in ten-shilling notes on the first day of every month.'

She had thought it through. She must have been prodding about outside my house. For two pins I would have strangled her there and then, but she must have seen what I was thinking because she said, 'And if anything happens to me I have written it all down.'

For six years I paid that bitch. Then one day she calls me round and says her son needs more money. Ten a month should do it. What choice did I have? Somebody comes to the door. He is delivering a chair. I can't be seen there, so I hide in the parlour, but I watch through a crack in the door. The furniture man wants a signature. People have been claiming things never arrive. He hands her a docket and she goes to rest it on the table. I can see it there. She takes his pencil and makes her mark – an X. The old bitch lied to me. She can't even write her name, let alone an account of what she saw, and what exactly did she see anyway? A shape on a dark night. My alibi would hold against that. The help comes and I turn my back. Mrs Samuels tells her I am looking for lodgings and sends her out to get a bloater. There is a rolling pin on the draining board. I hold it behind my back. Mrs Samuels is trying out her chair. I go behind as casually as I can and bring it down on her head as hard as I can. I hear a crack but it's the rolling pin. She must have a skull of stone. She jumps up and rubs it and I can see blood on her hand. It gleams in the gaslight. And she says, 'You'll pay for that. Fifty pounds a month.' And that was the last she ever said apart from moans and groans and a 'no' right near the end, and when I had finished her head was caved in and her ugly leering face was raw meat. I rinsed the pin in the sink and myself as best I could. I think about the help, but she didn't get a proper look at me so I will let her be. I don't want to hang around anyway, in case one of her lodgers turns up. I cannot kill all the Crescent, though I sometimes think I would dearly love to.

Horwich was a man in shock. He stood up.

'Sit down,' Sidney Grice commanded, but the sergeant did not hear him. He started to walk. 'We are not finished yet.'

'What else can there be?' he asked dully.

'The truth,' I answered simply. 'Did you murder Nathan Mortlock?'

76

The Wounded Tiger

SERGEANT HORWICH SWAYED and if he fell I was not confident of being able to catch him. He clawed at the wall to steady himself and slumped on to the next bench with us standing over him.

'How can you even considerate that, Miss Middleton?' he appealed. 'I've knocked a good few heads together in my time but to cut a man's throat? You know me better than that.'

'I thought I did,' I agreed.

'You made fools of us both, Sergeant,' Sidney Grice said forlornly. 'It is not difficult to deceive my assistant, but the only reason I did not refute Nathan Mortlock's alibi immediately was because I did something I am always warning Miss Middleton not to do – I took a man at his word and that man, as you are probably becoming dimly aware, was you.' My guardian's eyes darkened. 'I trusted you, Ezekiel Trueblood Horwich. I placed some of my most interesting murderers in your care, falsely secure in my misplaced belief that you would not be letting them out of the back door the moment I went off for a well-earned pot of lapsang souchong.'

Horwich's eyes twitched alternately. 'I would never have done anything like that, but I know you will not believe me now.'

For some reason I *did* believe him, but Sidney Grice was a wounded tiger and his voice soared with the emotions he always claimed to despise. 'For heaven's sake, man, I would have trusted you with a little of my very money.'

Sergeant Horwich sagged back, a boxer on the ropes taking blows when he no longer had the strength to raise his arms.

'I did not kill Nathan Mortlock,' he whispered.

'You had a motive,' I pointed out. 'If he was ever arrested or decided to make a clean breast of it, you would be implicated in his crimes.'

'I didn't. I just didn't.'

'Then tell me this.' Sidney Grice brought his cane under the sergeant's chin and I saw he had a spike extended from the tip. It was only three or four inches long, but I had seen what it could do. 'Why did you go to Gaslight Lane ten days before he died?'

———◆———

77

The Fallen Woman

S ERGEANT HORWICH CHEWED at the insides of his cheeks.
'You have seen the report, I assumptionize.'
'That did not, does not and never will even begin to
launch the ship of truth,' Sidney Grice said coldly.

I sat down.

'It wasn't a secret.' Horwich tugged at his mutton-chop whiskers. 'I wrote it in my report that I returned Mortlock's watch.'

'You have not even broken a jeroboam on the bows yet.' Mr
G extended his metaphor testily. 'I did not ask *what* you did.
I want to know why.'

'I wanted to see him, I suppose.' The sergeant wiggled his
whiskers side to side. 'I had not set eyes on Nathan Mortlock
since the day he went to court and I had never been in that house.
I don't know what I expectorated. I wanted to know… if he had
repented – I think – but I never got the chance to ask him. He was
very nervous but his butler said he was always like that.'

'Did you tell him about the body?' I shifted about.

Horwich brought out his old briar pipe. 'He said he knew
nothing about it and that part of the house had been empty since
the Garstangs' time. Before he bricked it up, they had a few
vagrants try to set up home there. It must have been one of them
fell into the old cesspit. Some of the roof tiles were pinched and
it got wet rot before anyone noticed.' He found a box of Lucifers.
'The servants confirmed all that.'

'I think we know the real reason why he could not let workmen into that part of the house.' I wished I could stretch my legs comfortably apart like men are always doing.

The sergeant struck a match, but Sidney Grice leaped up, dashed over and blew it out. 'You may poison yourself but you may not poison me.'

The bench was hard and, with my bustle jutting into the wall behind me, I could only just perch on the edge of it.

'Was he pleased to get his watch back?' I turned to sit at an angle.

'Not really.' The sergeant broke the matchstick and dropped it on the floor. 'He just took the watch, stuffed it away and said, *So you have found him.*'

'And what did you make of that?' I asked.

Mr G tsked. 'Apparently we need suspects to interpret evidence for us now.'

But I nodded at Horwich and he released his whiskers. 'That we had found the pickpocket, I supposed. I don't know.'

'But why would he think the pickpocket would still be in possession of the watch a decade later?' I queried.

The sergeant rubbed his throat. 'Maybe he thought the pickpocket had liked the watch and kept it. I don't know, miss.'

'One of the few things I cannot do is to enjoy sterile speculation.' Mr G retracted the spike and sat beside me.

'Perhaps he knew that the man with the watch was dead,' I suggested. 'Perhaps he knew that the man was not a pickpocket but his professed friend, Daniel Filbert.'

Sergeant Horwich chewed that over. 'I did sort of wonder if he knew more than he was letting on, but I suppose I didn't want to believe it.'

I slipped off the bench, grabbing at the slats behind me, but ending up sprawled inelegantly on the floor.

'Good grief,' my guardian groaned, but the sergeant was on his feet.

'Are you all right?' He offered me his hand in genuine concern and I took it.

'Oh, Horwich,' I cried out. 'Why did it have to be you? I liked you. I respected you. I bought you a drink in the Cat and Dragon.'

The sergeant answered automatically. 'Don't look like I'll be buying you one back now.'

Sidney Grice stood up, regarding my struggles with disgust.

'I have done all I wish to do today.'

Horwich heaved me up.

'Might I ask one favour, sir? I know I have no right.' He let go of my hand. 'But could the arresting officer be Inspector Quigley?'

'But he is so brutal,' I protested.

Sergeant Horwich drew himself to attention. 'I know, miss. But Inspector Pound would be kind to me and I could not bear that.'

I looked at this man, so strong and decent at heart, and he met my eye and we both burst into tears.

78

The Price of a Life

I FOUND A handkerchief and gave it to Horwich and he took
it and gave me his and I took it and used it, though it was
quite grubby. My guardian, I knew, would berate me severely
for such unprofessional behaviour, but Sidney Grice had his
back to us and was inhaling heavily.

He walked slowly to the end door, rested his cane against it,
and took hold of the posts to either side.

'I have not made my mind up yet,' he said slowly.

'I will run up and tell Quigley and that will decide it,' I threatened.

My godfather made no attempt to stop me, but rested his
forehead on the woodwork as if trying to cool his brow. I brought
my tears under control.

'Thank you, miss,' Horwich managed.

'But I have not made my mind up yet,' Mr G objected.

'Then I will make it up for you,' I insisted.

'Whether to have him arrested at all.' Sidney Grice spun round.
His face was drained. 'I will sleep on it but on one condition.'

'And that is?' I asked.

'That Sergeant Horwich gives me his word that he will not try
to flee.'

Horwich gaped. 'You have it, Mr Grice. On my daughter's life.'

Mr G caught his eye mid-fall. 'Her life is of no use to me but
I live in hope – against all reason and experience – that your

word still is.' He put on his left glove, a startling shade of Grice's Lilac. 'Do *not* attempt to make a fool of me again, Ezekiel.'

Horwich chewed his moustaches. 'No, sir.'

'You will come to my house at precisely ten o'clock tomorrow morning for my decision.'

'Yes, sir.'

The sergeant and I swapped handkerchiefs back.

'You will not do anything silly, will you?' I asked.

'The sergeant has already done something very silly, four years ago.' Sidney Grice paced smartly to the end of the corridor. 'He voted for a liberal candidate in the last election.'

'I was talking about suicide,' I clarified reluctantly.

'So was I.' Mr G put on his other glove. 'The political suicide of the foolishly enfranchised.' He put a foot upon the first step. 'Come, Miss Middleton, if you have quite finished snivelling, we have work to do.'

79

The Lilac Finger

WE HARDLY SPOKE in the hansom.
'Are—' I began, but my godfather put a lilac finger to his lips.

Molly came to the door.

'I require two things,' he told her. 'Tea and as near close an approximation to silence as is mortally possible.'

Molly threw me a warning glance, certain that the remark was aimed at me, pinched her nose to hold her breath and slid along the chessboard tiles, a proud nail in the sole of her left boot making a faint screeching noise and, to judge by her employer's flinch as he went to his study, I was not the only one to be suffering physical pain. Molly gurgled like a drowning man as she reached the stairs to the basement.

'I hope I dontn't not have to do that all the time,' she meditated at the top of her voice.

Sidney Grice was already in his chair, eyes closed, the right lid sunken into his empty concavity, the glass prosthesis watching me from between his thumb and forefinger, a thick bloodstained drop hanging from the inner corner.

I went to his desk.

'What are you doing?'

'I am going to clean your socket.' I opened the bottom drawer and found the small pine box.

'I am quite capable of doing that myself.'

I pulled a wooden chair over and hinged back the lid. 'Open.'

Not for the first time I envied him those long curling lashes.

The lids parted obediently and I dabbed as gently as I could at the socket with a ball of cotton wool. Sidney Grice willed himself not to pull away. The foramen where the optic nerve would have passed never completely closed and I often worried that the infection would track back up it, but my guardian was of the opinion that his brain was more than a match for the craftiest bacterium. I threw the stained cotton wool into the low fire and swabbed three times more until it came out almost clear.

'This will sting.'

'For reasons which may have escaped you, I am fully aware of that.'

I unstoppered and upended the tincture of iodine bottle into a fresh ball.

My guardian flinched involuntarily. 'How pleasant it is to find you have spoken the truth for once.'

For once he could not hide the pain and I had a sudden powerful urge to kiss him better, but I only prised open his now-clenched fist and said, 'You should soak them in alcohol every night.' I took the eye, wiped it and wrapped it in a clean square of gauze before he was permitted to put it into a new felt pouch.

'You are a good-hearted person,' he said as I wiped the violet tears from his cheek, 'but I live in hope that time and experience will sour you.'

'Inspector Pound hopes that it will not.' I slapped Mr G's hand away as it went to his socket.

'I should like to say something important on the subject of you and that adequate officer,' Sidney Grice spoke softly, 'but I shall not.'

I was never quite sure exactly what my guardian knew, but I could not imagine George Pound confiding in him. Molly sidled in and deposited the tray so carefully that, had she not caught a saucer with her thumb and toppled a teacup over, I would hardly have heard it being put down.

'Dannit,' she swore beneath her breath and slunk away.

'What will you do about Sergeant Horwich?' I asked anxiously.

'Exactly what I promised,' he said. 'Sleep on it.'

I knew all too well that when Mr G was determined not to discuss a subject, no amount of probing from me would induce him to change his mind.

'We know how Nathan Mortlock got in and out of his cell,' I pondered, 'but how did he get into or out of the house? It does not sound from the diaries as if he was let in by anybody.'

'Nor was he,' my guardian concurred. 'Or he would not have gone to such lengths. We have considered,' he pressed on, 'how the coal-hole lid could have been wedged open after Mr Nig's horse, Boadicea, stampeded the day before the Garstangs were so unkindly dispatched.'

'But the door from the cellar to the house would have been bolted,' I objected.

'Psalm 118,' he said simply.

'So it *was* a message?' I realigned the milk jug and considered with a shock how many of Sidney Grice's traits I was adopting.

'Who,' Mr G demanded, 'except a man with my exceptional powers – and I have yet to meet him – would discover it? No, Miss Middleton,' he turned the jug five degrees back, 'the new lock was not fitted in the same position as the old because the original holes had been enlarged.'

'And the screws were wedged into place with paper so that Nathan could easily push the bolt out from the coal-cellar side,' I concluded. 'Then all he had to do was replace the bolt and re-wedge the screws and the door would look unscathed.' I forced myself not to line up my spoon. 'But then he could not have got out the same way.'

'Much as I loathe speculating,' Mr G put the key into the back of his watch, 'if I were to kill my last victim near an open window, I might be tempted to avail myself of that egress.'

'And the windows were self-locking with no padlocks in those days.'

I poured our teas. The handle of the silver strainer was still bent from when Cook had tried to pick the lock for the kitchen door. She had retrieved the swallowed key and I did not want to know how.

'I am curious,' Mr G stirred his beverage thoughtfully, 'as to whether or not Daniel Filbert has been reinterred yet. It would be a nuisance to have to dig him up again.'

*

I had been to the morgue on my first day in London to see the mutilated body of Sarah Ashby. On that occasion I had pretended to be a building inspector to gain admission, but Parker, the attendant, knew me by now and greeted us both mournfully.

'Daniel Filbert,' I informed him.

Parker was a small, unsavoury man. He had lost all his hair through ringworm and replaced it with a crusty scabies, through which spiky white hair regrew in tufts reminiscent of Sidney Grice's shaving brush in miniature.

'Gone.' Parker's breath had never been fresh, but it had worsened over the years until it was almost as putrid as the worst of his charges.

'Has he been reinterred?' I enquired.

'No.' His left nostril had been packed with so much clot-soaked wadding that his whole nose was distorted and that eye partially closed.

'Then where is he?' I asked impatiently.

Parker was not fond of answering questions without at least one coin changing ownership.

'Not here.' He pushed a wick back inside with his thumb.

'Who took him?' I tried again as he inspected his wet thumb sullenly.

'I suppose the Garstang estate can spare another shilling.' Sidney Grice tossed a shiny coin.

Parker fudged the catch as it bounced off his chest. 'Duffy,' he said.

'The anatomist?' I stepped back, covering my mouth as Parker coughed spasmodically.

'From across the road to number 125,' Sidney Grice grumbled. 'A good job I told the cab to wait.'

But our cab must have been washed away in the sudden downpour that greeted us when we went outside again, for it was nowhere to be seen.

80

The Mary Murders

P ROFESSOR DUFFY WAS already in the dissecting room. His cloak had been draped over the shoulders of a skeleton on a stand. I had met him a few times before and always thought that, if he were wanted by the police, he would be a very difficult man for them to describe. He was of average height and build with the normal light complexion of an inhabitant of London who rarely sees anything resembling the sun. His nose was not overly large or small and his chin not protrusive or regressive, as far as I could see, for his face was heavily bewhiskered as was common in those days. I could see no distinguishing moles or scars. Apart from being completely bald there was nothing to note, and a hat would have disguised that feature. If I were called upon to assist, I would tell them to look for a man who was extraordinarily ordinary.

'Had him brought here.' He extracted his hand with a squelch from an old woman's abdomen to shake ours, but we determinedly ignored it. 'Much more convenient, better light, more equipment and that man Parker worries me. I autopsy healthier corpses than him every day.'

Mr G was happily pottering about, looking at a heart in a jar and a bottle of pickled toes.

'You have Daniel Filbert's body?' I looked about but all the bodies were lying flat under their formalin-soaked sheets.

'Most unusual.' Professor Duffy went in again up to his elbow.

'The state of preservation is remarkable.' He delved about. 'And I have never seen such a splendid pugilistic posture. I may keep him to put in my museum.'

Sidney Grice ambled over to a long crate in the corner, slipped his cane under the cotton cover and lifted it aside. Daniel Filbert lay in his coffin, still trying to claw his way out, his face still frozen in a silent howl.

My guardian sorted through a tray of surgical instruments and selected a broad serrated-edged retractor to slip under the upper lip. It took some effort, for the tissues were stiff, and there was a distinct ripping noise as he hauled the lip up.

'I thought I glimpsed it at Highgate,' he said in satisfaction and I had a look.

The upper-left central incisor was the best part of a quarter inch longer than its companion tooth.

'On to something?' There were more sounds like a boot being pulled out of a bog and Duffy joined us. 'Oh, a sticking-out tooth, how exciting.'

'But is that not very unusual?' I reasoned. 'A longer tooth that is not proclined or over-erupted? It is actually longer.'

'I suppose so,' Professor Duffy granted me. 'Anyway –' he grinned broadly revealing a picket fence of enamel – 'that's nothing. Look what I found.' He opened his hand. 'Tucked away behind her ascending colon.'

At first I thought it was a bullet but as the professor rinsed it under the tap I saw that it was a porcelain statuette, no more than an inch long, a lady in a long blue gown with her hands together in supplication.

'The Mary Murderer,' Sidney Grice exclaimed delightedly. A wistfulness fell over him. 'I wish he or she would kill a Mary with family rich enough to employ me.'

*

I read my Bible as always, but I did not look at Edward's letters in the secret compartment of the writing box I had bought him, and I did not slip his ring upon my finger. I lay in bed with the drapes open and waited for my eyes to capture the illuminations of London, for the city is never truly dark. A million lights cannot be extinguished.

I wished I could talk to George Pound about it. He was a good man and wise; kind, but with a strong sense of justice.

I reached out and cradled the image of his face, my fingers clutching the night air and my body aching so much that I thought it would break.

81

Walking in the Sky, Black Snow

I HARDLY SLEPT that night and rose early but, as almost always, Sidney Grice was at the table before me. Unusually, he was not reading the stack of papers at his side but wagging a finger at Spirit, who sat in unrequited hope of a titbit.

'Roll over.' He twirled his hand to demonstrate but Spirit merely dabbed his shirt cuff.

'She will not do it,' I predicted, helping myself to two boiled eggs from the bowl on the sideboard.

'Of course she will.' My guardian clucked. 'I could train you or Cook to do it, and even Molly with a little cruelty, and this is far and away the most intelligent female in my house. So why can she not learn to do it?'

'She does not want to.' I buttered a slice of toast.

'We shall see about that,' he mumbled, returning to his prune juice and snapping a *London Times* open wide.

I lowered my fingers with a morsel of egg white and Spirit sauntered over to investigate it.

'Have you come to a decision about Sergeant Horwich?' I asked.

He evaded my question. 'What would you do?'

Spirit rejected my offering and maundered off under the table.

'I would let him go.'

Sidney Grice peeped over his paper. 'Present me with a logical catalogue of reasoned arguments to support your proposal, and

393

please do not say that he is a nice man. You have an unfortunate addiction to being affectionate to criminals.'

'He *is* a nice man,' I declared. 'He was tricked into an action, not having any idea where it would lead, and has regretted it ever since. He will never do anything like that again and he has suffered considerably for all this time with his terrible burden of guilt.'

Sidney Grice tore a column out of his paper and weighed it down with a fork.

'So – to take the last of your impassioned pleas – if a guilty man feels guilty he should be exonerated?'

'Perhaps he should be treated more leniently,' I suggested.

'To the extent that he suffers no consequences whatsoever for his crime? Seven people died in Gethsemane because of his dereliction of duty and at least two more as a result of his concealing his misdemeanour, not to mention the young woman condemned to be incarcerated in a mad prison, subject to the whims of that maniac Whelkhorn.'

'He did not know.'

Mr G ripped up his *Times*.

'He knew the next morning and he has known every waking minute since, and still he flouted the law he is sworn and gainfully employed to uphold.' He crumpled the paper into three tight balls. 'Damn it all, March.'

My godfather clawed around his eye.

'If you felt like that, why have you played cat and mouse with him?' I flared up. 'He was resigned to being arrested and you gave him false hope.'

'*Felt?*' he echoed in disgust. 'It is not a question of how I *felt*. I was considering the best interests of my client.' He hurled a ball on to the floor and Spirit leaped joyously upon it. 'How am I to tell her that her father was a murderer? It was bad enough when I was told that *my* father was.'

It was bad enough, I reflected, when I was told that my guardian was one too.

It was still only eight o'clock and so I went out. The fog was swirling like the first drops of milk in a stirred tea. My childhood friend Barney once told me that fog was fallen clouds and so, when we broke through them and into the sunlight, at the top of Parbold Hill, we were walking in the sky. In London it felt more like Dante's Inferno, with its sulphurous fumes of a million coal fires and the soot in flakes of black snow.

The crossing sweeper made a great display of brushing a path across the road for two young ladies who made a greater display of ignoring him. A shaven-headed child raked through the gutter with a short stick, hoping for dropped coins or the holy grail of his trade, a lost ring. He was one of the Gower Street regulars.

'You missed this one, Nippy.' I pretended to stoop and threw him a penny.

'I fink I prob'ly missed sixpence,' Nippy said cheekily and I tossed him a thrupenny bit.

I lit a cigarette – ignoring the scandalized glare of a cigar-smoking top-hatted gentleman – and walked the length of Gower Street, long, straight and grey, then crossed over and walked back. On the corner of Torrington Place, in her regular spot, a little girl was selling dried lavender. Her name, I knew from previous questioning, was Betty and she had the most iridescent green eyes I have ever seen. Her legs were badly bowed from lack of calcium, too weak to support her bird-like frame. I bought a sprig and pressed it in my notebook, and remembered pressing another flower in another world.

You risked your life for it, scaling the old fort wall, with rusty rows of spikes in the dry moat forty feet below you, to pluck a wild rose. I was furious. How could a flower be worth one moment of my anxiety for you? But I took it from your mouth when you triumphantly descended and replaced it with a kiss. And now it lies, crushed and dried in my journal. How foolish, I upbraided you, to risk death for a flower. But you only kissed me again and said no, love was worth more than life. I hope you were right.

I tossed my cigarette into an overflowing drain and went home to find Sidney Grice contentedly engaged in filing a series of reports about fresh sightings of Springheel Jack. He had stolen a magistrate's wife's petticoats in Kensington by jumping over her garden wall, and sprang from the top of the abbey tower in Barking to kiss three girls until their lips were sore. To me, most of his acts were no worse than those of the medical students I had seen tumbling out of the Duke of Wellington into University Street at all hours of the day.

It was nine thirty.

I tried to read *Immaturity* by George Bernard Shaw, but I could not get interested and did not think he was likely to be heard of again.

The mantel clock chimed the third quarter.

'Nathan Mortlock and Holford Garstang had at least one trait in common – a tendency to make mysterious payments.' My guardian held up Mr Garstang's pocket book. 'In 1855, Holford paid five hundred pounds in cash to an undisclosed recipient.'

'I wonder why.' But I was not really in the frame of mind to pay attention.

'I anticipated that you would.' He made a note.

I went restlessly to the window.

'This might interest even you.' He opened Fortitude Garstang's household records at a page he had marked with a frayed boot-lace, the one used by George Gurney, the Grimsby Garrotter. 'On the seventh of September 1872, two weeks to the day before the Garstangs were murdered and the sixtieth anniversary of the battle of Borodino...'

A man was pacing the pavement. Hunched and bowed, he looked very different from the man I knew.

'Just get on with it,' I snapped.

'Mrs Garstang paid for a new livery for her coachman.'

I had never seen him out of uniform before and he cut a much less impressive figure, with his slightly baggy grey trousers showing beneath a buttoned-up grey oil-cotton overcoat.

'She describes it as being for *our dearest coz, Easterly.*'

'Sergeant Horwich is outside.'

'He is early.'

'Yes, but it is cruel to keep him waiting.'

'Not quite as cruel as the acts that he permitted Nathan Mortlock to commit.'

'Shall I invite him in then?'

'If you must.' My guardian shut his scrapbook.

Molly was coming up the hallway with Spirit's tail poking out of her apron pocket.

'We've been playing Bind Men's Boff,' she announced, 'but she keeps cheatering by taking her bindfold off.'

'Cats do not like to have their eyes covered,' I told her.

'Well, she shouldn't play then.'

Spirit struggled out and climbed down Molly's dress.

'There is a man walking up and down outside,' I told her and Molly guffawed.

'Not there aintn't not, miss. There's thousands of them.'

'This one is just outside the front door.' I buttoned her collar. 'Please call him in.'

I returned to the study.

'Oy, you... yes, you, pacey man with the big nustache. Bring your coat in with you inside it,' Molly roared.

'She gets worse,' Sidney Grice groaned.

He still had his patch on but made no attempt to remove it or insert his eye.

'That man what was walking up and down outside and Miss Middleton made me bring in,' Molly announced disapprovingly before something lit up in her brain. 'Oh, it's you Sergeant Porridge.' She beamed. 'I didntn't not recognize you without your clothes on.' She clamped her mouth. 'Your uninform, I mean.'

'Go away.' Her employer shooed her off with his rule.

'Have a seat, Sergeant.' I offered my chair but Horwich stood to attention, hands clasped behind him.

'I would rather stand, thank you, miss.'

And so we all stood, two of us dwarfed by our caller. Sergeant Horwich nibbled his lips.

'Do you have anything to say for yourself?' Mr G walked round the back of him.

'I have no excuses, if that's what you mean, sir.' The sergeant fixed his gaze straight ahead. 'All these years I have tried to tell myself it was not my fault, but I always knew that it was, and then you told me about the other murders... I knew full well what kind of man he was and I left him free to commit more crimes.' Horwich swallowed. 'I appreciate your kindness in giving me one more night with my family but I know now that I have to face the music.'

'Music?' My guardian raised his voice bitterly. 'This is not a tea dance, man.' He whisked round to face the sergeant. 'Have you any idea how many of your victims are still alive?'

Horwich's face went blank. 'I am sorry, Mr Grice, I don't know to what you are referaling.'

'Angelina Innocenti,' I suggested.

But Sidney Grice took three steps back, his eyes fixed on the policeman, and Spirit, who had been about to rub herself against his leg, shot out of the way.

'Who is to tell Miss Mortlock that her father was a savage and habitual murderer?' he demanded. 'Who is to tell your recently bereaved wife or your recently bereaved and crippled daughter that their husband and father was an accomplice to these grotesqueries? And what will happen to them with no master of the house, no income, no pension and heaped with opprobrium because of your deeds? Have you any idea what poverty and abuse they will face?'

'You cannot imagine how I felt when they kissed me goodbye this morning.' Horwich's voice came thick and broken. 'They thought I was just going to work.' He coughed. 'I changed in the Cat and Dragon – told the regulars I was sneaking off to go fishing. Jim's keeping the uniform behind the bar for me.'

'Did your family not sense that anything was the matter?' I asked.

And Horwich hung his head. 'I told them I was upset about some nasty murders – which was true in a way.'

'And what about your constables?' Sidney Grice clutched at something invisible just in front of his shoulder and tore it down. 'They look up to you as their exemplar, Nettles and Harris and all the other fools.'

'They are good men at heart,' Horwich defended them.

'And Miss Middleton?' Mr G ranted. 'She has been like a bereaved hag since you were exposed. Am I expected to live with that?' My godfather brought his right hand to his left shoulder and hurled his nothing away. 'Get out of my sight, Ezekiel Trueblood Horwich.' His foot lashed out, bringing one of the central wooden chairs crashing to the floor, and a second kick sent it skittering away. 'Out.' He pointed towards the hallway, arm rigid with rage. 'And the next time I see you, make sure you are wearing your uniform.'

Horwich covered his face. 'I don't understand.'

I reached up to touch his hand. 'He is letting you go,' I said, scarcely able to believe my own words.

'On two conditions,' Sidney Grice said, instantly under control.

'Anything, sir. Anything.'

'First, you do not say another word to me until we meet at Marylebone Police Station,' Mr G commanded, and the sergeant nodded dumbly. 'Second,' Sidney Grice went back to his desk, 'you will never, under *any* circumstances, accuse me of having acted out of kindness. Go.'

My guardian shook himself like a wet dog, went to his desk and busied himself with his scrapbook.

I saw Sergeant Horwich out.

'God bless you, miss,' he whispered. 'I will never let you down.'

And I wanted to hug him, but I only said, 'You still owe me that drink.'

I was still shutting the door when Sidney Grice came out of his study and limped upstairs.

'The greatest point in Horwich's favour,' he announced, 'is that he never once mentioned that I owe him my life.'

'But how? When?' I called after his disappearing back.

82

The Bloodhound and the Beast

CHERRY MORTLOCK CAME.

'Can I not even devour my luncheon in peace?' Sidney Grice tossed his napkin on the floor in a dudgeon and for once I shared his disappointment. Cook had actually managed – probably by luck – to produce quite an agreeable approximation to a vegetable fricassee.

'Perhaps she will not be very long,' I speculated. 'I shall ask Molly not to clear yet.'

Cherry kissed me. 'I shall not keep you long,' she promised.

'Good.' Sidney Grice clapped his hands together.

'Let Molly take your cloak,' I prompted.

'Miss Mortlock may not even be staying long enough for that,' Mr G said hopefully.

'Nonsense.' I motioned to Molly, who tried to wrench the garment from Cherry's shoulders before she had unhooked it.

Cherry coughed and unclipped the neck clasp just in time to stop herself being throttled. I took her arm and led her into the study.

'It is really Miss Middleton I came to see,' our visitor said.

'Excellent.' And from halfway up the stairs my guardian called, 'But do not consume any more of my ostensibly superlative brandy.'

'I have gin if you do not mind that.' I showed Cherry my father's flask and she said she did not mind at all, so I fetched two tumblers from the sideboard. 'Cheerio.'

'I want to ask a favour of you, March, and I will quite understand if you say no.' Cherry sipped her drink.

'I will do what I can.'

Cherry took another nip. 'I am going to sleep in my family home tonight,' she announced suddenly and then, more hesitantly, 'and I was hoping that you would come to spend the night with me.' Cherry's lips quivered. 'I am afraid to sleep there alone, March.'

We went to the window. The drapes were drawn together but I separated them a foot or so. I liked to see London at night. We had gaslights on Gower Street, but they were too dim and far apart to illuminate everything and it fascinated me to watch people and horses emerge from the night and melt back into it.

'Do you think your father's murderer is still in the house?' I asked.

Cherry shook her head. 'Can you really imagine Hesketh or Easterly or Veronique as a deranged killer?'

'No.' I gave us both a drop more.

I could not tell her that I had never imagined Sergeant Horwich as aiding and abetting the crimes either.

'I have always been frightened in Gethsemane,' she confessed. 'Can you imagine going to live there as a child after all that had happened? Every noise and shadow terrified me.' The drink rippled. 'Oh, March, the nightmares I had in that place.'

An advertising van hurried by, presumably on its way home since the boards were almost unreadable – something about restoring your hair. I would have preferred to replace mine.

'Do you have to stay?'

'It is that or poverty,' she replied unhappily as Sidney Grice reappeared.

'That stupid wench has cleared away,' he groused. 'If I had wanted her to, she would still be dithering in the hallway.' Mr G sniffed like a bloodhound. 'Gin,' he suspired, only slightly less disapprovingly than he might if he had surprised us indulging in human sacrifice.

'Yes, I brought some with me,' Cherry said.

'What a poor liar you are, Miss Mortlock,' my guardian told her amiably. 'An unusual trait in the weaker sex.'

'And in women,' I put in, adding immediately, 'Cherry is going to spend tonight in Gaslight Lane.'

Mr G's eyes narrowed. 'Might I ask why?'

'Because Veronique and Easterly are threatening to leave.' Cherry put her glass on the sideboard. 'They are convinced that the house is haunted. So I am going to prove otherwise – to them and myself.'

'It is impossible to prove that a place is not haunted.' Sidney Grice looked at his watch. 'One can only say that one has not detected any supernatural presences at a particular time.'

'Do you believe in ghosts?' Cherry asked and the detective sniffed.

'I have seen a great deal of evidence for their existence but none of it compelling.' He clicked his watch shut. 'I have thus far found the supernatural to be anything but super.'

I divided the residue of the gin, ignoring his censorious looks. 'Cherry has asked me to keep her company.'

'I am going to sleep in Veronique's room.' Cherry picked up her glass. 'She is convinced that my father stalks her room.'

'It is not Easterly then?' I had not forgotten how his gaze caressed the French maid's figure.

Cherry half-smiled. 'She keeps the door wedged.'

'And where shall Mademoiselle Bonnay slumber?' Mr G enquired.

'There are plenty of rooms to choose from,' Cherry flopped her shoulders, 'though I cannot imagine she will want to be too close to my father's room.'

'Good,' my godfather said. 'It does not do to sleep with servants. I make it an almost invariable rule not to.'

Cherry's mouth twitched but straightened immediately. 'I only hope that I can persuade her to stay another night. She is not at all happy about being alone.'

Sidney Grice held my tumbler up towards a mantle. 'It is fascinating how precisely the pattern of finger ridges can be recorded on a vitreous surface.' He dragged himself out of his reverie. 'An animal might help.' He clipped on his pince-nez and rotated the tumbler, light bouncing off its lead crystal walls. 'If your pretty Gallic servant had a substantial beast to protect her, one that she was confident would not harm her but would savage any intruders, would that make her feel more confident?'

'Do you know of such a creature?' Cherry asked uncertainly.

'I possess one.' He thrust my tumbler back at me. 'A female by the name of Molly. She is intensely loyal and can be quite terrifying. I was happier doing battle with the Uxbridge Urologist than I would be against Molly in full tilt.'

'I have not forgotten how she reacted when I broke the tea service,' Cherry admitted ruefully.

And Mr G rubbed his hands. 'So that is you and Miss Middleton, Mademoiselle Bonnay and Molly organized, and I shall take your father's room.'

'But Cherry did not invite—' I began.

'Indeed she did not.' Mr G took the glass from Cherry's hand to compare it with mine. 'There are at least nineteen differences in the patterns.'

My guardian thrust my tumbler at me, as if he resented my making him hold it, and gently returned Cherry's.

'But you cannot sleep in there,' Cherry protested. 'It has not been cleaned.'

'Dear, lovely Miss Mortlock,' Sidney Grice replied. 'Do not concern yourself on my behalf. I once braved a railway hotel in foulest Surbiton. I am sure I shall be quite comfortable there. We shall set off directly after dinner.' He rubbed his hands. 'Parsnips tonight, I believe.'

And Cherry Mortlock hurried away before he could issue another invitation.

83

Ghosts, Ghouls and Demons

MOLLY WAS VERY excited about coming with us.

'The last time I slept out was on a train, but you'll never know about that because you were mad as a clock, and Mr Grice was chasing monks in some foreign country.'

'I did have a wisp of suspicion when I got a bill from the Great Western Railway.' Her employer selected a cane. 'But, with Miss Middleton facing either execution or a lifetime in the madhouse, your misdemeanour was relatively trivial and I deducted the expense from your wages.' He changed his mind and selected another. 'You may anticipate your next payment in June twenty thousand and sixteen.'

'Oh, thank gourd.' Molly clutched her pelvis where she imagined her heart to be. 'I thought I wasntn't not never going to get any money again.'

The doorbell rang and she opened it to Gerry.

'Take our bags to the hansom,' Sidney Grice ordered. 'That poor cabby cannot manage them all himself.'

I had packed my Gladstone and lent Molly an old carpet bag but she had also filled a canvas sack tied with string round its neck. Sidney Grice required a steamer trunk.

'We are only staying for one night,' I reminded him.

'I only need nine per centum of the contents,' he admitted. 'The rest I choose to take. I dislike going far without my two photograph frames, for example.'

'But they are empty,' I objected.

My guardian checked his collar in the mirror. 'And were I to have packed the teapot I should take that empty too.' He made some tiny adjustment to his neckerchief.

Molly's sack clunked metallically on the floor. 'Oh.' She felt the side of her carpet bag anxiously. 'You didntn't not say nothing about emptying it.'

The fog had not shifted and it was dark well before we inched into the murk.

'That date he said.' Molly chewed on a loose lock of hair. 'Is that next Thursday? Only I like Thursdays.'

'No,' I said, 'and stop sucking my hair.'

Easterly admitted us into a hallway lit only by two candles in glass chimneys on the long table.

'Hi ham sorry but we have no gas hat the moment,' he apologized, taking my bag from me.

'Do you have any oil lamps?' I could hardly see as far as the bottom step.

'Mr Garstang did not like them.' Easterly helped Molly with the trunk over the threshold. 'There was the risk of fire, hespecially with hevrything being so barred hand bolted.'

I could sympathize with that, having witnessed the speed and violence with which flames could spread from spilled paraffin.

Hesketh materialized into the glow, his eyeball bloody, with the pupil dilated, and his ear mulberry-coloured and scabbing over.

'Good evening, sir, miss.' He took us to the sitting room, his movement stiffened by the beating he had suffered.

Cherry sprang up to greet us. 'It is so kind of you to come.'

There were more candles here, four naked on the table and the same number enclosed on the mantelpiece but, when you have been spoiled by gas mantles, these were feeble indeed.

'Mr Grice is never kind.' I kissed her cheek.

'I am sure that cannot be true.' She leaned forward to my guardian.

'For once, Miss Middleton speaks nothing but the truth.' He dodged back and proffered his hand stiffly.

'I expect Hesketh has explained,' she said.

'Then I must dash your assumption on the infrangible rocks of truth.' Mr G dabbed his shaken hand with the tip of his tongue. 'You are using a different soap. I preferred your Castille.'

'The gas company thinks that the explosion might have cracked the main gas pipe.' Cherry struggled to steer the conversation back on course.

'It has not,' he pontificated.

'Well, they have cut us off whilst they check.'

Veronique brought us tea wearily; her eyes were dusky-rimmed.

'Are you all right?' I asked and she opened her mouth.

'Of course she is all right.' Mr G tugged a crease out of the tray cloth. 'She is a servant.'

'I am afraid,' Veronique replied, her face mirroring the truth of her words. 'I do not like to spend another night 'ere.'

'Dontn't not be scared,' Molly's voice shrieked out from nowhere. 'I'll look after you.'

'Thank you,' Veronique said dubiously.

Molly winked with both eyes. She could never manage one at a time. 'And I brought something to frighten any ghosts.'

'Your very presence should do that.' Mr G turned an inverted spoon over.

'And, when we are tuckened up, I'll tell you the tale of the Ghoul of Gruelsome Green,' Molly promised.

'I'm not sure that's a good idea, Molly,' I cautioned, and she snuffled in amusement.

'Dontn't not worry, miss. I'll blow the cangle out first.'

'You will keep the candle lit,' I said firmly.

'Why do you not take Molly down for some refreshment,' Cherry suggested to her maid and, when they had left, enquired, 'Have you both dined?'

'I said that we would.' Mr G dusted his chair before he sat. 'So we did. Wait here, Hesketh. Now, what is all this about a ghost?'

Hesketh's hand caught a ball. 'There has been a lot of talk about this house being haunted over the years,' he replied, 'and I have never paid too much attention to it. The boards creak and the wind sometimes catches on the chimney tops. It can unnerve imaginative people.' He squeezed the ball. 'But this is different.'

The valet faltered.

'In what way?' I urged.

'I heard something myself, the night I came back from Marylebone.' He sucked his cheeks. 'I always check the whole house before I retire to bed. Mr Nathan insisted upon it – though I could not think how anyone might break in – and old habits die hard. It was an odd shuffling noise, like a giant rat under the floorboards, and then...' he hesitated, 'a voice – a sort of husky rasp.'

'Could you hear what it said?' I asked.

'*Murderer*,' Hesketh whispered, seemingly afraid to even hear the word again. 'Or *murderess*, I could not be sure.'

'Where were you?' Sidney Grice rearranged the crockery.

'On the top landing, sir. I called out *Who's there?* But there was no reply, just another shuffling. All the doors were shut but I forced myself to open them. I'll admit it. I was scared.' Hesketh cleared his throat. 'Easterly and Veronique were in the basement.' He touched his cheekbone. 'There was nobody there.'

'Did you tell anybody else?' Mr G stirred the black tea that Cherry had poured for him.

'Nobody.' Hesketh's hand was pumping now. 'I tried to tell myself that my hearing was damaged by Mr Quigley's blows and I was imagining things.'

'Do you believe that?' I took two sugars.

My guardian frowned and rotated the teapot and milk jug.

'No, miss.' Hesketh opened his hand. 'I hear ringing noises now but I don't hear voices. Then Easterly told me he heard something, but perhaps he should tell you about that himself.'

'Out of the mouths of babes, sucklings and valets comes forth much wisdom.' Sidney Grice pulled a corner of the tray to align it with something.

'Thank you, Hesketh.' Cherry pushed the tray back and shifted all its contents into a random pattern, with evident satisfaction and heedless of Mr G's unsuccessfully suppressed tiny yelp of pain. 'Send Easterly in now, please.'

My godfather reached out to the tray. 'No,' Cherry said firmly and his hand retracted.

Easterly was not his usual chipper self.

'It was just footsteps,' he told us, 'in Veronique's room when Hi went to get ready for bed. Hi knew she was below stairs folding linen and Mr Hesketh was downstairs locking up, so Hi called out, *Who's there? Come out! Hi am armed and dangerous.* Hi got the Bible from my room—'

'To what end?' Sidney Grice leaned back aggrievedly.

'It was all Hi could think hov for a shield.' The footman got a quill from his pocket and scratched under the plaster. 'And Hi thought a ghost could not hattack a man holding the scriptures.'

'Why,' Mr G's finger swung towards him as a compass needle to the north, 'when you heard footsteps, was your first suspicion that it might be a supernatural presence?'

'Because Hi knew no living soul could be up there.' Easterly clutched at his own neck.

'Did you go up?' I asked, and a draught crooked the flames until they licked the wax.

'Yes, miss.' The footman's voice dropped. 'Hi crept up and flung open the door and jumped in.' Easterly mimed a little leap. 'But there was nobody there. Hi searched under the bed and in the wardrobe and looked out hov the window.'

The flames struggled up.

'Did you open it?' Sidney Grice's finger sank back.

'No, sir. It is barred and screwed shut.'

Mr G bent his knees as if preparing to jump. 'There is more.'

Easterly puffed up his cheeks and blew out. 'Hi was just about to go when Hi heard something h'else.' He steeled himself to tell us. 'Laughing.'

My guardian's finger tracked towards the footman. 'What

kind of laughing? Male, female, young, old, soft, loud, high- or low-pitched, brief, prolonged? Enlighten us.'

Easterly pinched his lower lip and tugged upon it.

'Satanic.' He stared into the shadows. 'Ha demon from hell.'

And, with perfect timing, the candles blew out.

84

Catching the Scream

D EAR SWEET KATE, *chestnut hair, long and wavy, a pretty doll's face with big brown eyes emptying of sleep and filling with alarm.*

Mouth opens, breast heaves and I catch a scream in the palm of my hand.

'Oh, sweet Kate, if you make a sound, Hi will run you through. Understand? Understand?'

Kate nods and I take my hand away and she only whispers, 'Please.'

'You don't have to say please. Hi am going to do it anyway.'

I pull down the sheet and Kate shivers, deliciously.

Her nightdress has four buttons but I soon rip those off and Kate makes a sound like a kitten when I get on top of her.

'You dirty beast.'

I twist my head, and it's Angelina, and I see she has an old banister spindle. She's got it raised and I've got my arms sort of under me, and all I can do is say, 'Wait your turn.'

And she's swinging it down and I try to twist away and it comes smashing into the back of my head, and I struggle up, but I feel a bit woozy and she's got it raised again, and I charge straight into her and knock her on the floor with me on top, and get hold of her head and bang it on the boards and shout, 'See! That hurts.'

And she doesn't answer, but she's still struggling, and I bang it again and again, maybe ten times, until there's blood leaking out of the back of it and she goes limp and quiet, and I've seen enough death tonight to recognize it. And when I look back sweet Kate has gone.

85

The Sound of the Devil

EASTERLY SQUEALED.

'Was that an imitation of the laughter?' Sidney Grice sighed. 'If so, it was not outstandingly Beelzebubic. Stay where you are.'

The candles on the mantelpiece were still burning and Easterly had started towards them, but he froze obediently mid-turn.

'No, sir. It was just me being nervous.'

'Re-create the sound accurately,' my guardian instructed and the valet baaed like a lost lamb.

'It was not really like that,' he confessed.

I stifled a laugh. 'What happened next?'

Easterly flapped his arms. 'Hi ran out and downstairs, and pretended Hi wanted a cup of water, and waited until Mr Hesketh was going up and went with him. Mr Hesketh is not afraid hov hanything.'

'You may see to the candles now, Easterly,' Cherry instructed and he went to the fire to light a spill, wedging the unlit end under his plaster and sheltering the flame with his injured right hand as he returned, his lower face disconcertingly vivid and the upper melted away.

I saw a man with no face once. He spoke my name in blood.

The candles briefly dazzled as they ate into the gloom.

'I wish to converse with your maidservant now,' Mr G announced, and Cherry signalled her assent to her footman.

'You seem very interested in this haunting,' Cherry remarked when there were only three of us.

'The subject of ghosts falls within the top eight thousand categories of things about which I am curious.' My godfather's hand crept spiderlike towards his tea. 'Only fourteen points ahead of panpipe recitals.'

He reached his saucer and withdrew in a reverse scuttle.

'Do you believe any of it?' I asked sceptically, but Sidney Grice had a hand cupped to his ear.

'Oh hark, I sense the approach of the slender Gallic target of the bizarrely christened Sou' Easterly Gale Nutter's ill-concealed aspirations.'

The footfalls came closer, bringing another light with them.

'Hi shall wait in the hall,' Easterly comforted Veronique.

The spill still projected from his plaster, no doubt to deal with his endless itches.

'You shall wait below stairs,' Mr G informed the footman and he dissolved away.

Veronique looked towards the fire.

'Sit.' Sidney Grice directed her to the empty chair between him and Cherry. 'I may develop a fear of interviewing perpendicular French maids, which could prove deleterious to the execution of my professional duties but convenient for the criminal classes.'

The maid looked for guidance to her mistress, who patted the chair.

'Why are you so frightened, Veronique?' I asked.

Veronique knitted her fingers. 'She is a 'orrible 'ouse,' she burst out. 'I am sorry, Miss Mortlock, for you are a kind lady, but she is a 'ouse possessed by the devil.'

My godfather rested his hands on the table as though conducting a séance. 'Justify that remark with factual evidence.'

'I 'ear 'im in my room,' she affirmed vehemently. 'I 'ear 'im drag dead bodies and 'e – 'ow you say? – cackle. 'E speaks to me – *murder, murder.*'

I put a hand on Veronique's sleeve, moving within her line of vision and slowly so as not to startle her. '*Murder*, not *murderer* or *murderess?*'

Veronique sucked the tip of her left thumb. 'It is 'ard. 'E speaks in whispers.'

Her thumb slipped into her mouth.

'But you are sure it is a male voice?' I stroked the back of her wrist.

'I imagine a man devil,' she said. 'But I never see 'im.'

'Where does the voice come from, Veronique?' Cherry questioned, and the maid touched her hat to check it was still clipped on straight.

She weaved her fingers in the air. 'All around my 'ead,' adding defiantly, 'but not inside 'er like 'Esketh tell me.'

'Goodbye,' Sidney Grice said brightly.

Veronique rose in a panic.

'I will see you along the corridor,' Cherry promised.

She took a candle from the mantelpiece and, a minute later, I heard her call for Easterly to come up.

'Where on earth is all this leading?' My tea was cold but I drained it.

'I have absolutely no idea.' Sidney Grice stood and hurriedly straightened the tea tray and its contents. 'But I know it is leading somewhere.'

Cherry returned. There was a hesitancy in her manner.

'Has something else happened?' I asked in concern.

Cherry went to an escritoire in the corner and returned with a bundle of perhaps half a dozen envelopes.

'I received this today... from my mother.'

She passed the top letter to me.

The stamp was Swiss but the postmark was smudged.

I read aloud for my guardian's benefit:

My Darling Cherry,

Please excuse the brief nature of this letter but I am anxious to catch the post as the service is very irregular here.

Thank you for informing me of your father's death.

I shall not be such a hypocrite as to feign grief, though I am sorry for any you feel.

Please do not think of delaying the funeral, as I shall not be attending.

Agostino and I are tired of Lake Geneva and are moving on. I shall send you our new address as soon as we are settled.

Forgive me,

Your ever loving

Mama

Cherry Mortlock's eyes were darkly underscored and reddened at the inner corners.

'I am so sorry.' I made to hand the letter back, but Sidney Grice abstracted it en route.

'Present me with all the other maternal epistles you have conserved.' He clicked his fingers, as if at an inattentive waiter, and Cherry passed him the rest of the pile resentfully.

'The earliest is from Bognor where she went on a rest cure,' she said bitterly, 'and, it transpired, met Montanari.'

'How remarkable.' My guardian laid the missives side by side and upside down. 'They are written in exactly the same handwriting.' He laid one copy on top of another and held them so close to the candlelight that I feared they would burst into flames.

'What else did you expect?' Cherry took the letters firmly from him, knocking the tea tray slightly askew.

'Why, nothing else at all.' He put his pince-nez away.

Cherry watched, her expression unreadable, as Mr G hastened to rectify her clumsiness, and only when he was satisfied with his rearrangement of the crockery did he turn his attention back to announce, 'Bedtime for you, young ladies.'

'You have asked for this,' Cherry warned and Sidney Grice

shrank back in horror as she set about disarranging his work. 'And, if you should get murdered in the night,' he cringed as she tilted a saucer, 'please do so as noisily as possible. I should hate not to be there for the kill.'

86

The Roar of the Demon

'NO ONE WILL *save you.*' *The roar of the demon shakes the house.* '*They are all dead-dead-dead,*' *it shrieks.*

Down the stairs, I go, two at a time into the darkness, following the pound of her feet. If she'd had the sense to creep I might never have found her in a house this size, not in the time I have left.

She's along the corridor. Her footsteps are more padded now by the carpet, but I can still hear them.

And then they stop. In the pitch-dark of that hellhole, Kate Webb starts to creep.

I stand in the corridor and listen. Nothing except me panting and my heart banging, and a voice in my head saying: Think. Where will she have gone?

Maybe to the Garstangs. The candle still shines through their open door and they are still dead, and exactly where I left them.

Where would I go? Not to Brian because I don't suppose she even knows exactly where his room is. I would try to get out. The doors are locked and she doesn't have a key. Her only chance is a downstairs window, but there are so many of them.

I go to the top of the marble stairs and I'm about to go down when I hear a creak. The fifth step on the wooden stairs in the tower.

I creep down them and stand in the hall, listening. If I go to the wrong room it will give her time to open the shutters and get out, and then I will be caught and people will know what I did and why, and what will happen to poor Nathan then?

I am just about to start searching the rooms one by one when I hear it. A definite click. There's a bar being lifted, and then another, and I think: Where would I try to climb out? Not into the garden where I could be trapped, but at the front, the first front window, the main drawing room. I'm so sure I'm right, I don't even worry about the noise. Speed is what matters now. I rush to the door and throw it open, and there she is, sweet little Kate, one slender leg over the sill, the wind in her chestnut hair, an inch away from freedom and life, but I'm on her. I throw her to the ground and slam the shutters closed, and I can't even dream about what happened next. The demon had taken over by then.

Merciful Jesus, I think, as I kneel beside her body, she looks like a saint.

*

George Pound put a thumb and forefinger in his philtrum. 'From the disarray of her nightdress and the bruising – quite apart from the knife wounds – I thought she had been... interfered with.'

87

The Mattress Murder

CHERRY AND I did not change into our nightwear. If anything happened we wanted to be ready to deal with it.

'We shall sleep with our door open a fraction,' Hesketh promised, 'so that we can hear if you need us. I am a very light sleeper.'

'Shut and secure your door,' I told him. 'You will have no trouble hearing my scream. I frightened a Bengal tiger off with it once.'

Cherry smiled. 'I cannot compete with that. The last time I screamed at a mouse, it ignored me.'

It had been arranged that the male servants would sleep in Angelina Innocenti's old quarters across the corridor.

We closed and wedged our door, looked under the bed and in the wardrobe, pulling it out a few degrees to make sure nobody had tunnelled through the wall. There were no side tables, so we put our two enclosed candles on the mantelpiece.

'I am sure Mr Grice would have noticed if anybody had,' Cherry commented.

'Not much escapes him.' I patted the mattress and felt round the sides.

Cherry watched me. 'Why are you doing that?'

'It is not a pretty story.'

'Tell me,' she urged.

'A man called Edgely Kinforth desired his best friend's wife. He waited until she told him she was visiting her mother and decided to murder the friend by cutting a slit in the bottom of the mattress, taking out some of the stuffing and hiding inside it.' I paused, wishing I had not begun. 'When he felt somebody climb into bed he stabbed upwards nine times until the body fell still and the blood soak through the casing. He wriggled out just in time to see his friend come into the room, and discovered that the wife had changed her mind and stayed at home.'

Cherry was aghast. 'I have never heard about that.'

'The friend was part of an international conference.' I sat on the edge of the bed. 'And it transpired that the woman he had lived with was not his wife at all but a woman from whose earnings he had been living. Her body was dumped in the Thames and in no fit state to be autopsied by the time a mudlark found it washed up in the estuary. That was barely reported. Who is interested in yet another woman who should have known better?'

She sat on the other side.

'And what of Edgely Kinforth?'

I rested my boots on a cloth at the bottom of the bed.

'It turned out that was not his real name. He escaped police custody and it is believed that he stabbed another prostitute to death outside St Pancras Station. There were some reports of a man answering his description in the King's Cross area, but they have never been confirmed.'

'Were you involved in that case?' Cherry asked in horrified fascination.

'Mr Grice was asked for advice.' I plumped up my pillow. It was quite well filled. 'And he told them to look in the Whitechapel area.' I propped the pillow vertically against the wall.

Cherry pulled a blanket over herself. 'Do you think he will murder again?'

'There have been no reports of similar cases, but often a prostitute's death will hardly be noted.' I leaned back. 'With any luck he killed himself in a fit of remorse.'

Cherry shivered. 'What a sheltered life I lead in my cotton-wool world.'

'I am sorry.' I looked at her face, so pale and anxious. 'I should not have told you.'

'I asked you to.'

A floorboard creaked and we sat up straight.

'Is that you, Easterly?' I called.

'Hesketh, miss,' came the reply. 'I have secured the house and am going to my room now. May I wish you both a good night.'

Two more boards creaked and a door closed.

Cherry lay on her back. 'Actually, this bed is more comfortable than mine. Maybe I will make Veronique swap. My bed is narrower and hard,' she paused, 'as... a... rock,' she finished slowly. 'Can you hear that?'

I listened and was just about to say that I could not hear anything except the sounds of a house settling when I heard it – something scraping. I put a finger to my lips. There it was again – a faint shuffling.

I put Cherry's raven hair back and murmured close to her ear, 'Do you have rats?'

Her breath was cool on my cheek. 'I do not think so. Perhaps mice.'

'Too big to be a mouse. Where is it coming from?'

'I am not sure.'

And then something else. A whisper. *Murderer.*

Cherry's lips had not moved but they parted numbly now.

Murderer. A loud suspiration close by, and then louder still and, hoarsely, *You WILL die.*

The candles danced wildly, casting us on to the walls in writhing tortured shadows.

'Who is there?' I called.

And there was a laugh, low and mocking. 'Die.'

There were footfalls somewhere in that room.

'Where are you?' I shouted uselessly.

There were footfalls in the corridor coming to our door now, and I am ashamed to say that we clutched at each other. Something struck the woodwork and Cherry let out a sob.

'Are you all right, ladies?'

'Is that you, Hesketh?' Cherry called weakly.

'Never!' the voice shrieked. 'Never-never-never-never all right.' And then, in a long rasping breath, 'Murderer.'

'Is anybody out there with you, Hesketh?'

'Only Easterly, miss. Shall we come in?'

'The door is wedged.' I realized that I was already sitting upright. 'I am coming.'

I swung my legs over the side of the bed and a cackle flew about like a trapped bird of prey. My skin prickled.

'No.' Cherry clutched at my skirt. 'I do not think that is Hesketh. It does not sound right. The thing is using his voice.'

There was a crash that shook the room.

'The ceiling!' Cherry cried. 'It is on the ceiling.'

I looked up and a fissure had appeared. And whatever she said next was lost, drowned by a piercing howl, and the fissure widened and webbed out into a maze of cracks, and the cracks opened.

I jumped off the bed, dragging Cherry over on to her side as she clung to me.

'They are everywhere,' she gasped. 'Do not let them take me to hell, March.'

Whatever or whoever was out there was hammering on the door.

'Get off the bed,' I shouted, grasping her wrist to haul her after me.

And Cherry Mortlock's face burst into blood.

88

The Deluge

I STOOD TRANSFIXED as Cherry's grip fell away. Her eyes trickled gore and another gout splattered on her breast.

'Come on,' I exhorted and heaved her half off.

'My face!'

'It is not your blood.' I yanked her towards me.

A chunk of plaster broke away, slamming into Cherry's pillow, and an eruption of dust rained over us.

'We are coming in.' The door juddered.

A loud splintering crack was followed by an arm that broke through above us, thrashing through broken lathes, the hand searching for something that was not there. We cowered from it. And then a head, long greying taupe hair, white with powder, hanging upside down, and the head turned round further than was humanly possible, blood showering. And I saw the face, the mouth opening and closing like a broken puppet, an oranged tongue flicking snakelike in and out, spitting goblets of crimson. The arm rose jerkily. There was a snap and the ceiling sagged, and the creature with it.

The door squealed inwards an inch.

'Put your hand through,' Hesketh's voice commanded.

'But I might never gerrit back,' Easterly objected in broadest Yorkshire.

'Just do it, man. Your mistress is in danger, and Miss Middleton.'

I tried to go to help, but Cherry clung on in terror of the obscenity that hung twitching over us. Something moved behind it, an umbra creeping through the hole.

'Oh God, there are more of them.' Cherry's fingers dug into my arm.

'I can't gerrit.' Easterly's voice. ''Ang on.'

The arm thrashed and the mouth stretched in an endless wheezing exhalation, and the eyes rolled, and a foul crimsoned tar vomited out of that mouth in three violent expulsions.

'Are you all right, Miss Mortlock?' Sidney Grice appeared in the crater.

The door burst open.

'Oh, thank the stars you're safe, Miss Mortlock,' Easterly gasped breathlessly.

Hesketh stumbled in. He breathed in relief when he saw us standing there, but then he looked up.

'Oh my sweet Lord Jesus.' Hesketh staggered two steps back and one small step forward. 'It can't be.'

And it seemed to me that the eyes drifted towards Hesketh and fixed upon him, and the arm reached out in supplication, with a final sigh, before it juddered down and the creature fell limp.

89

The Cobweb and Cold Ashes

SIDNEY GRICE SURVEYED the body and the occupants of the room.

'Why can it not be, Hesketh?' he called down from the loft.

'She is in Broadmoor,' Hesketh answered automatically.

I went to check Easterly, who was crumpled on the floor.

'Do not say any more.' Mr G took the cover off his portable safety lamp, illuminating himself like the portrait of a saint. 'All of you await my presence in the sitting room. On the way down, Miss Middleton will collect Molly and Mademoiselle Bonnay, assuming that neither one nor both of them is dead.'

My guardian moved sideways, watching his feet carefully, until he was just a tiny sea of light, the tide going out and leaving only the woman suspended in death through the wreckage.

'What is happening?' Cherry spoke like a woman in the dream she doubtless hoped this was.

Easterly got up groggily.

'Mr Grice will explain.' I forced myself to sound confident as I guided her towards the door with a gentle pressure on her back. And, once I had herded them on to the lower flight of stairs, I went to where the two maids had been lodged.

'Look after your mistress,' I instructed the men.

The door was open a fraction and I knew at once that something was amiss, for the room was in darkness. I pushed the door

426

cautiously open and stopped in my tracks. Molly lay sprawled face down off the bed, her head resting on a rug, and Veronique lay over the other side, also face down and her lower half over the side.

'Oh, it's you, miss.' Molly looked up. 'I was just teaching Vernornical to play Tip and Toe, where she touches my foot and I reach under the bed to touch hers, only we cantn't not quite reach. If you lied under we could all—'

'Why is the candle out?' I asked.

'I knock it over playing 'er Jump Backwards game.' Veronique rolled over. 'And she 'as been teaching me 'ow to speak better, aintn't you not, Molly?'

'Betterer,' Molly tutored patiently.

'You are both to come into the corridor at once,' I instructed, and left them to untangle themselves.

Cherry, Hesketh and Easterly were lost in their own thoughts when I rejoined them. I took Cherry into the bathroom, where she stood like a helpless child as I rinsed her off as best I could.

'Now we shall go down,' I told the assembly. 'You first, Hesketh, then Miss Mortlock and me.'

Cherry took my hand again.

I cannot have been the only one desperate to run out of Gethsemane and get as far away as possible, but I was determined to keep things orderly as we trooped into the sitting room.

There was a rattle in the hall and the sound of the front door opening. We all looked at each other.

'Shall I go?' Molly offered. 'I'm good at answerering doors. I even do it sometimes.'

'You will both sit at the table,' I directed.

'Allow me, miss.' Easterly peeked out. 'Ho, it's you.'

'I am fully aware of that.' The door shut and Sidney Grice came in, wearing his eye patch.

His clothes were crumpled and heavy with plaster. A cobweb heavy with dust formed an epaulette over his coat. His hair was peppered grey and his face as grubby as a mischievous schoolboy's.

'To whom were you referring?' He went directly to the valet.

'Angelina Innocenti,' Hesketh replied. 'I would know her anywhere.'

'But Hi thought she was hin that mad prison,' Easterly objected.

'She escaped,' I said.

Cherry shot round. 'And when did you know this?'

'Nine thousand, three hundred and fourteen minutes ago,' my guardian calculated.

'When we went to Broadmoor Hospital,' I clarified.

'And you did not see fit to inform me?' Her voice was diamond hard. 'The madwoman who killed all the household here came back to repeat her acts, and nobody even told me she was on the loose?'

'I did not think she meant to harm you,' I responded feebly.

'It occurred to me that she might,' my guardian admitted nonchalantly, 'but I dismissed the idea as fanciful.'

'But...' Cherry gawped incredulously, 'she has just tried to—'

'Frighten your father,' Mr G interrupted her.

Cherry quivered with emotion. 'How can you say that?' She brushed her sleeve distractedly. 'You must be as mad as she.'

'I do not think the alleged Angelina Innocenti kept up with the news during her incarceration.' Sidney Grice patted his own sleeve, creating a mini dust storm. 'For, as I followed her along the loft spaces, weaving with greater caution between the spikes than she was eventually to do, I heard her muttering to herself, *I'll get you, Nathan Mortlock.*'

'But how did you get up there?' I asked. 'The hatch is still secure. I looked when we went up before.'

'The same way that she did,' my godfather replied. 'There is scaffolding inside the end of the north wing now to stop it collapsing inwards. That part of the house has no floors and the basement was flooded by a burst water main during the explosion, so it is not occupied by the parasitic poor. They have already stolen some of the struts but it was an easy climb, even for a woman. What remains of the loft runs the length of the wing and – since Charlatan Cochran obligingly removed the wall – from thence into what proved to be Senorita Innocenti's deathtrap. She slipped on a rafter and impaled herself through the abdomen.'

Cherry gasped. 'What a horrible way to die.'

'Why did you say the *alleged* Angelina Innocenti?' I back-tracked before my godfather told her he could think of fourteen worse.

'The woman's lack of money was not the only reason that I refused to help her.' Mr G touched his dimple. 'She was no more Spanish than the Kaiser is Chinese – which, incidentally, he is not – but she would not admit it. I could not represent the interests of a client who was so patently and clumsily lying to me.'

'So who was she really?' I asked.

'Does that actually matter at the moment?' Cherry burst out. 'She is hanging dead through my ceiling.'

Molly glanced up, rubbed her eyes and chuckled. 'No, she aintn't, miss. That's just a spider.'

'Since you are so sensitive about the matter, we shall deal with that first.' Sidney Grice surveyed his soiled features in the mantel mirror and straightened his eye patch, which had slipped upwards. 'With your gracious permission, dear Miss Mortlock, I shall send the ostensibly youthful Mr Sou' Easterly Gale Nutter on a mission of great import but little personal peril.' The patch rose again. 'You are to go immediately and directly to Marylebone Police Station and draw the attention of one Inspector Pound to the extraordinary turn of events in Mademoiselle Bonnay's boudoir this very night. Impress upon him that I sent you. Goodbye and Godspeed.'

'Here.' Hesketh gave Easterly a few coins from a brown leather wallet, and the footman set out.

'Why not Inspector Quigley?' Cherry asked. 'I do not like him, but surely this is his case.'

Mr G held up his hands with the left thumb tucked away. 'I have nine pressing reasons for my action, only two of which need concern you, and the first you have partially answered yourself. Quigley distresses you and it distresses me to see you distressed.'

'I did not think you cared,' Cherry remarked acidly.

'Of course I do,' Sidney Grice assured her. 'When you are distressed you become very annoying.' He fanned out his fingers. 'Second, this death relates more directly to the case of the Garstang murders, which is more rightly in Pound's province.' He curled up his fingers one by one. 'And now I am going to say something embarrassing to Miss Middleton. There is a sliver of cedar lath in your rodential hair.'

'Talk about the pot calling the kettle,' I retorted and my god-father chewed the matter over.

'I choose not to,' he decided at last.

Cherry sat in an armchair by the cold ashes.

'Perhaps Veronique and Molly could make us some tea,' I suggested, to my guardian's approval. And, after we had con-sumed that tea speechlessly, he announced, 'I shall adjourn to scrutinize the cooling cadaver so inelegantly and inconveniently lolling upstairs.'

Cherry tried the pot but it was empty.

'Stay with me.' She held out her hand and, as I took it, I heard the door open and George Pound's voice. 'In the attic, you say?'

'Hi shall show you the way, Hinspector.'

And I heard footsteps go by, Easterly's first and then those of the man I had thought to walk beside.

90

The Ocean of Fears

I DREW THE drapes back a few inches. The night was turning grey outside and the trees were taking shape across the way.

Hesketh reported that the body was being removed and Inspector Pound had advised us to stay where we were with the door closed. We heard other men being admitted, at least three to judge by the voices and heavy boots.

'We need a ladder,' somebody said, and a low voice made a comment and there was raucous laughter.

'Show some respect,' Pound reprimanded. 'Go and find a ladder, Perkins. See if they have one where they're rebuilding that house next door where the trench is. If not, knock on a few doors. You go with him, Green. You two come up with me.'

The noises became more distant and the sounds of the city awaking from its troubled slumbers – for London never truly sleeps – grew louder: a wagon rumbled past, carrying a covered mound, with three children running after it, trying to steal some of whatever was under the tarpaulin. And Cherry Mortlock stirred as if she too had been dreaming.

'I must leave here, March,' she said. 'Even if I am unable to sell this house, I cannot live in it. I have always hated this place and what it did to the Garstangs and their poor servants, as well as what it did to my father in life *and* death.' She pulled her hand away. 'And now that awful mad woman.' She squeezed the bridge of her nose between both hands in prayer. 'Even if it is all over, how could I possibly be happy here?'

Cherry took my hand again to save herself from drowning in the ocean of her fears.

'And you are prepared to give up your Trust-fund income by leaving the house?' I queried.

'I can get by on very little.'

'What will you do?' I asked, for it is usually the people with money who think they do not need it.

Her fingers were long and fine and beautifully manicured, with marble-white crescent moons.

'I cannot rely upon Maria Feltner to put me up for ever. I shall sleep in Fabian Le Bon's studio.' And then she added defensively, 'He stays with friends when I am there.'

I smiled. 'I am not Mr Grice.'

'Nobody is Mr Grice.' Cherry tossed her head. 'Is he really like that all the time?'

'Sometimes he is better,' I assured her. 'Sometimes worse. What will happen to your servants?'

Cherry closed her eyes. 'I have not been able to pay them properly since Daddy... my father died, and I cannot until I am granted probate. They can stay here if they wish.'

'I cannot imagine that Veronique will,' I said.

'Then I will see if Fabian can find or borrow another couch for his studio. He is very resourceful.' Cherry's grip relaxed.

An omnibus loomed, the passengers blurred by the wet air.

'Will you marry him?' I asked.

'This may shock you.' Cherry watched a stray dog darting around the wheels. 'But Fabian does not hold with marriage. He says it turns women into possessions, stamped with their owners' names.'

I was getting cramp from leaning towards her and eased gently away.

'I have a friend called Harriet Fitzpatrick who describes her marriage as lawful slavery,' I told her, 'but I do believe it can be different with the right man.'

Hesketh entered and announced the once-right man. 'Inspector Pound, miss.'

I wondered if it were possible that Pound had heard my views, but I thought it unlikely through the solid door.

'Good morning, Miss Mortlock, Miss Middleton.' His voice was flattened with weariness. 'We have removed the body, though obviously the room is still in a... mess.' His troubled blue eyes settled on me. 'I shall need to speak to you both soon, but I do not suppose there is much you can tell me that I have not heard from Mr Grice already.' Was there something of the old way in how he looked at me? 'Now, if you will excuse me, I am in the middle of another murder investigation and I must get back to that.'

His gaze broke away.

'I suppose it is more important than this case,' Cherry challenged him. 'What is it – a member of the royal family?'

'A street child,' the inspector told her calmly, 'and I cannot bring myself to tell you how he met his end.'

'Was he a local boy?' I asked.

'You might have come across him on Gower Street.' George Pound's face disguised his feelings quite well but his voice could not. 'Lively chap, went by the name of Nippy.'

'You missed this one, Nippy.' I pretended to stoop.

'Oh please, God rest his little soul.' I crossed myself.

'I fink I prob'ly missed sixpence,' Nippy said cheekily.

'Amen to that.' The inspector bowed and walked smartly away.

'I am sorry,' Cherry called after him. 'I did not think.'

'No,' he replied as he went into the hall. 'Nobody ever does.'

We sat again.

'Did you know him well?' Cherry asked tentatively.

'Not really,' I replied, the boy's face jumping up at me. 'Nippy used to sift through the gutters for dropped coins, but he had a charm about him and some wit. Had he been born to better-off parents he might have gone far.'

'Nonsense.' Sidney Grice appeared, even more dishevelled than before. 'An urchin is an urchin. They are not like us.'

'Thank God,' I railed and wished I could storm off to my room to drink and smoke and cry my heart out.

*

Veronique readily agreed to go with Cherry, and Molly went up to pack a bag, the French maid being too terrified to go back into her bedroom. Hesketh was determined to stay and look after the house. They'd had sensation seekers try to break in after Nathan's death when they thought the house was empty and – after much vacillation – Easterly decided that he would stay too, but only if he could sleep in the same room as the valet and on the first floor. Hesketh accompanied Easterly to check for ghosts and help carry his things down.

'The dead cannot hurt you,' I reassured the footman, relieved that Molly was not present to contradict me with one of the stories I had made up for her, which she was adamant must be true.

Sidney Grice and I saw Cherry and her maid off.

'You go home with Molly,' he said, 'and have a bath. You look even more of a disaster than usual.'

'And you look like a chimney sweep,' I told him.

'Oh, really?' He perked up inquisitively. 'Which one? I do not think Joe Brindley exhibits much similarity to me. He is stout and has a broken nose.'

'I only meant...' I tried, but he was lost in considering his own question.

'I suppose Fred Woggle from behind at a great distance might bear a fleeting resemblance, but it would not be striking.'

A cab was approaching. I put my fingers between my teeth and blew.

91

Pan Troglodytes

EASTERLY ADMITTED US the next morning. He was still smartly attired in his uniform, so presumably Hesketh had sewn up his sleeve for him.

'Did you sleep well?' I asked.

'Hardly a decent topic for a young lady to introduce to a man,' Mr G scolded.

'Not very, miss,' Easterly admitted. 'Hesketh snores, but every time Hi fell asleep he woke me hup to tell me Hi did.' He stifled a yawn. 'And Hi kept thinking about what was hup there.' His eyes rose fearfully as if he were expecting to see Angelina Innocenti's body come through the ceiling imminently.

Hesketh appeared, looking just as exhausted.

'We have prepared tea in the sitting room,' he greeted us.

'We?' The footman drew himself up indignantly. 'Mr Hesketh rinsed the pot.'

'A valuable contribution,' my guardian declared. 'If Rory McMack's wife had done the same, he might not have choked to death on a live cockroach.'

'Why did he not see it in the strainer?' I gave my cloak to Easterly.

'He is one of those appalling people who do not essay to filter their tea.' Sidney Grice's cheek ticked in revulsion. 'The ear-eaters of Potziland have better manners.'

'Where on earth is Potziland?' I took off my scarf.

'Where is it not?' he answered enigmatically. 'But you were right to assume that it is on this ridiculous planet.'

We went through and, even though I knew she was not there, I almost expected to see Cherry rise from her chair to greet us.

'We will gather round the octagonal table.' Mr G sat to face the door and I to his right, facing the window, with Easterly to my right and Hesketh between him and my guardian.

'Shall I serve, miss?' Easterly offered and I gratefully accepted. Normally the task fell to me, for my godfather would never pour tea for anyone other than himself.

'But can you manage?'

'Ho yes, miss.' He wedged his clawed hand into the pot handle with a napkin.

Mr G took a deep breath. 'How many people could have killed Nathan Roptine Mortlock?' he bellowed, and Easterly spilled tea in my saucer.

'Hi am so sorry, miss. Shall Hi get ha cloth?'

'What?' Sidney Grice rumbled. 'And have us risk you sawing through the bars, and clambering up the side of the house like a liveried Pan Troglodytes, the common chimpanzee?'

'Hindeed not, sir.' Easterly slopped more tea on the tray.

'Do you seriously expect Miss Middleton to shimmy up drainpipes after you in her ridiculous and unattractive clothes?' Mr G fulminated.

'It is all right, Easterly,' I put a hand on his arm as he was about to try again. 'I shall do it.'

'Touching servants.' My guardian looked nauseous. 'Whatever next? No wonder we are on the brink of revolution. But your ingenious subterfuge will not deflect the arrow of my interrogation in its unerring flight towards exactitude. Answer the question, Sou' Easterly Gale Nutter, and answer it now.'

'No one,' Easterly replied in confusion.

Mr G brought out a small pair of binoculars. 'Was that a good or a bad answer?'

'I fear you are confusing him, sir,' Hesketh put in.

'Your fears are achingly tedious to me at present.' Sidney Grice adjusted the focus to scrutinize him. 'Unless you are terrified of being exposed as a dominicide.'

'If that means killing one's master, I have nothing to be afraid of.' Hesketh looked back at the lenses unblinkingly.

'Then keep quiet until I address you,' Mr G commanded. 'Miss Middleton is no longer in the first flush of youth and does not wish to fritter her years of fading plainness listening to irrelevancies.' He swung the binoculars towards the footman. 'How could nobody have killed your master?'

Easterly breathed deeply. 'I only mean nobody that I can think of, sir.'

'That was a better answer.' Sidney Grice kept the binoculars trained on him. 'Though not necessarily true. Let us all consider who, apart from your mistress, stood to gain by Nathan Mortlock's death.'

'I do not think he had any other relatives,' Hesketh answered, and it was my turn to splosh tea.

'*Our dearest coz, Easterly,*' I remembered my godfather telling me when I was too distracted by watching Horwich pacing the pavement to listen. 'Mrs Garstang referred to you as a cousin.'

A spoon clattered into Easterly's half-filled cup. 'Only a very distant cousin.' He mopped the tray distractedly with a napkin.

'With so few family members that distance may not be unbridgeable by an inheritance.' Mr G dipped his binoculars towards the footman's chest. 'Miss Mortlock has yet to be afflicted with progeny.'

'Hi did not do it.' Easterly swayed, on the brink of collapse.

'If you did not, and do not fantasize for more than an instant that I accept your protestation –' Sidney Grice cricked his neck back to examine the ceiling – 'we must concentrate our enquiries upon who else was in the house at the time.'

'Mrs Emmett could not have done it,' I postulated. 'She was already too disabled by her brain injury.'

'Which is unlikely to be feigned since it killed her,' Mr G conceded. 'What about Mademoiselle Veronique Bonnay? You have an eye for the ladies, Easterly. Is she not pretty?'

'Very,' the footman agreed blushingly, 'but that does not make her guilty.'

'What if she went to Mr Mortlock's room in the night and seduced him into opening the door?' My guardian lowered his spyglasses.

'Veronique is not that kind of a girl!' Easterly raised his voice for the first time since I had met him.

'Not for you, perhaps.' Mr G put the glasses down. 'But what a catch rich elderly Nathan Mortlock would have been for a girl of low breeding from the not very far-off shores of Normandy.'

Easterly sprang to his feet. 'You will take that back.'

'Back where?' Sidney Grice asked coolly. 'Back to Inspector Norbot Stillith "Sly" Quigley? Perhaps I would not interrupt his interview next time.'

Easterly pushed his chair away.

'But you established that Veronique knew how to handle a razor properly,' I reminded my guardian hurriedly.

'But not that she chose to do so when she murdered her employer.'

'Mr Grice, I really think—' Hesketh put out an arm to restrain the footman.

'Do you?' My godfather raised his voice. 'I want your thoughts no more than I wanted your fears, not four minutes ago. Send a telegram, Miss Middleton, to Marylebone Police Station, informing Quigley where Mademoiselle Bonnay can be run to ground.'

And I was about to join the two men's outrage when I felt a pressure on my left foot.

'Certainly.' I opened my handbag. 'I have the address Cherry gave me here.'

'You cannot hand her over to that... foul monster,' Easterly raged, trying to push past Hesketh, who rose to fend him off.

'Why not?' Mr G leaned back casually. 'There is only one

other suspect and Mr Mortlock was unlikely to admit you to his room in the middle of the night.'

'He did!' Easterly cried out. 'I admit it, Mr Grice.' Easterly burst into tears. 'I am so sorry, Mr Hesketh, but I killed Mr Mortlock.'

92

The Unexploded Bomb

SIDNEY GRICE PICKED up his cup and drew back his arm.
'Did you indeed?' He hurled the cup at the footman and
Easterly just managed to bat it away from his face, shattering it on his plaster cast. 'Then why did you fend it off with your
left hand?'

'The murderer was right-handed.' I lifted a cup handle out of
the sugar.

'So am Hi,' Easterly vowed. 'It was just my left hand was
nearer my face.'

'It was the other way round,' I corrected him. 'Your right
hand was above the table and your left below it. Besides which,
who would use their broken arm from preference unless it was a
lifelong habit?'

'Hi can use my right hand for a lot more than Hi let on,'
Easterly asserted desperately. 'And Mr Grice is right, Hi am next
in line for the hinheritance.'

'Oh, Sou' Easterly Gale Nutter,' my guardian sighed. 'Would
you really have faced the hangman to save a woman's honour?'

All the thoughts in Easterly's brain struggled with each other
to show themselves. His face was in a turmoil.

'I cannot put this more delicately,' I said carefully. 'Are you
and Veronique lovers?'

'No.' He took a step back until his legs touched his chair again.

'You will not shock me,' I assured him. 'And Mr Grice and

Hesketh are men of the world.' I considered briefly if they were. 'And I have seen the way you look at her, Easterly.'

'And she at you,' my guardian added. 'Miss Middleton might not have noticed that, for she does not understand women as I do.'

Nobody I have ever met understood women in the way Sidney Grice did, but I resisted the temptation to point that out.

'If she loves you too, she will not let you die for her reputation,' I reasoned. 'She will not even want to see you in Inspector Quigley's hands. We will think none the worse of you.'

'Why should we?' Sidney Grice asked expansively, with a tolerance I had not witnessed in him before.

'That is why you were able to hear what you thought was a ghost,' I realized. 'You could not possibly have heard scraping in the loft from the floor below.' I hesitated. 'Did you spend that night with Veronique, Easterly?' I pressed gently.

And the footman licked his lips. 'Yes,' he whispered.

'And you will both swear to that in court if needs be?' I asked, hardly able to hear his reply as he looked down.

'Yes.'

I toyed with the cup handle.

'Now I shall explain why I think none the worse of them,' my guardian told me, 'for the woman we know as Mademoiselle Bonnay is in fact the unfortunate bearer of the title of Mrs Sou' Easterly Gale Nutter.'

'The proud holder of that name,' a wounded Easterly asserted. 'But how did you guess, sir?'

Easterly might have spat in Sidney Grice's tea for the outrage that his question aroused.

'I *never* guess,' Mr G retorted. 'I deduced it from a series of careful observations. My suspicions were aroused by the lingering and emetic ways that you surveyed each other, reinforced by detecting Veronique's unusual and seductive scent in your bedroom and bolstered by the presence of identically patterned wedding bands pinned inside the frames of your chests of drawers.'

The handle broke between my fingers.

'But you said you found nothing surprising,' I reminded him crossly.

'And nor did I,' he replied. 'What is surprising about a young couple in love getting married and keeping their union secret from an employer who refuses to have married servants and has designs on the maid himself?'

'He was a filthy swine,' Easterly burst out.

'Is that why you murdered him?' I asked. 'Did Veronique get him to open the door for you to kill him between you?'

'And then hid the razor under her pillow?' Sidney Grice batted my idea away with the back of his hand. 'The French are a dull-witted nation – which is why they keep declaring republics – but even they are not quite that stupid. Besides which, Easterly is too much of a milksop to carry out such a task. Why, he swooned like a schoolgirl when he realized he had confessed to murder, and at the sight of that wretched woman.'

'And they were genuine faints,' I confirmed.

'Which only leaves two other likely suspects.' My guardian popped the binoculars away. 'Hesketh...'

Hesketh opened his mouth, closed it, then said, 'I believe I have already proved that I was far away on that night, sir.'

'There is only one difficulty with your alibi, Hesketh,' I said. 'On the night in question, the fourth of January, there was a problem with the line and the trains terminated before Nuneaton at Coventry.'

I landed my bombshell but it failed to detonate, for the valet only looked puzzled and said, 'I am sorry, miss, but you must be mistaken. I went there directly myself and back again the next morning. I am sure the railway authorities will be able to confirm that the trains ran normally – that ticket inspector, for example.'

'For somebody so practised at lying, Miss Middleton makes a poor fist of it,' my godfather said.

'Who is your second suspect?' I tried not to look too morti-fied at my bluff being so easily called.

'Why, the lovely Miss Charity Mortlock, of course.' Sidney Grice bared his clean white teeth, but he was far from smiling.

------◆◆◆◆◆------

93

The Possession of Corpses

HESKETH AND EASTERLY sat down together.

There was a new steeliness in the valet's manner. 'But Miss Mortlock was not here and I have no doubt she can produce witnesses to prove it.'

'Hi cannot believe my mistress would do hanything so cruel, hespecially to her own father.' Easterly scratched the nape of his neck.

'But how could she have done it?' I objected.

'Let us suppose that she hid in her father's wardrobe before he went to bed. He hung his clothes over a chair at night, did he not, Austin Hesketh?'

'He did,' Hesketh confirmed. 'But his wardrobe would have been full with clothes.'

'Which she carried through to the next room,' Sidney Grice postulated, 'dropping a stocking, which the gimlet eye of Miss Middleton discovered.'

'A dropped stocking is hardly proof of anything,' I objected.

'Not by itself.' Mr G dipped into his satchel. 'But this provides some evidence.'

He held something red in his hand. At first I thought it was a neckerchief, but when he dropped the object on the table I saw that it was a silk glove.

'And where did you find that?' I asked coolly, for he had never shown it to me.

'In Nathan Mortlock's wardrobe,' he replied. 'Fallen behind a boot. Its counterpart was in his daughter's room.'

'That still proves nothing,' Hesketh insisted. 'Miss Charity may have had disagreements with her father, but she loved him.'

'Under normal circumstances it would be difficult to secure a conviction against such a pretty and personable woman.' Sidney Grice kept talking. 'But when the jury find out she is living with an artist, their only dispute will be whether they need to listen to the whole case before they find her guilty. Nothing arouses the righteous indignation of an Englishman like seeing a beautiful woman giving herself out of wedlock to an oleaginous alien rather than to him.'

'But Miss Mortlock does not even have a key,' Hesketh objected.

'Any one of you could have let her in,' I proposed. 'You probably did not even know what her intentions were. Perhaps she just said she had come to collect her things or that she was going to surprise her father. No court would convict you of being deceived by a fallen woman.'

Hesketh brought the side of his fist down so hard that the table tilted. 'You go too far, miss, sir.'

'Shall we let Inspector Quigley decide?' Mr G suggested. 'I am sure he would love to meet Miss Mortlock on a more intimate level.'

Hesketh unfurled his fist, but let it lie on the table, like a man with a pint of beer.

'I believe, if I may be so impertinent, that I have the measure of you, sir. I think that you expect me or Easterly to confess to something we have not done in order to save our mistress.' The hand contracted, squeezing that invisible ball again. 'But you are a rare creature, Mr Grice – a man of honour. Are you really telling us that you would submit Miss Charity to such an ordeal?'

'Fettered by my own truthfulness, I would not.' My godfather tugged his right earlobe ruefully. 'What happened to your upper-left incisor, Austin Anthony Hesketh, ageing, but not yet senile, retainer?'

Hesketh ran a finger over the edge.

'Gypsy James Mace saw to that for me,' he replied. 'I was lucky he did not knock it out.'

'I'd give a month's wages to have watched that fight,' Easterly said wistfully.

'I would not,' Mr G said. 'But what spellbinds me in some of my apparently idle moments is my observation that, although the edge has been chipped off, it is no shorter than its counterpart and so...'

'It must have been longer to start with,' I completed his sentence.

'I suppose it was a bit,' Hesketh admitted guardedly.

'Miss Middleton has some experience in medical matters,' my guardian declared, 'and I have written an amusing dissertation on the classification of bite marks, but neither she nor I have ever come across such a thing before we met you.'

Easterly felt his teeth. 'But my lower front teeth stick up and down a bit.'

'That is because they are crowded for space,' I told him. 'But the teeth themselves are all the same length. We have seen another case since then, though.'

Hesketh spread his fingers. 'So it is not so rare after all.'

'Daniel Filbert,' I said.

The name flicked through Austin Hesketh.

'Mr Nathan's friend? What about him, miss?'

I paused to give him time to mull over that name. 'I believe you paid for his funeral.'

'Then you are mistaken, miss.'

'*God shall know you,*' I quoted, to no response.

'Snushall told us that the man who arranged the funeral spoke in a feigned French accent.' Sidney Grice slipped his little finger through the jackal ring on his watch chain.

'And Veronique told me that Easterly sometimes imitates her speech,' I recalled.

'Like an indigenous arboreal rodent, Miss Middleton discovers information, secretes it and promptly forgets where she has hidden her hoard,' my godfather remarked sourly.

'But hi do not know anything about it,' Easterly protested, at a loss as to what he was being accused of.

'I do not suppose you do,' I agreed. 'On the subject of accents, you told me that you taught yourself how to speak by copying a *toff*, Easterly. Which toff was that?'

'Mr Mortlock, of course,' he told me.

Hesketh patted his colleague's arm affectionately.

'Mr Nathan did say *Hi*,' he agreed. 'But he was not really a toff.'

'We had Filbert's body exhumed,' Sidney Grice declared. 'Dug up, in layman's language.'

Hesketh's lips worked each other. 'What of it?' he managed at last.

'Daniel Filbert was murdered,' Sidney Grice said. 'Strangled and lowered into a pit of lime.'

'The body that was found in the north wing?' Easterly asked eagerly. 'Hi heard about that.' He poked a teaspoon handle up and down his left arm.

'It occurred to us that he might be related to Hesketh,' I declared, 'having the same dental abnormality and being found so close by.'

'I have no family, miss,' Hesketh protested, 'except my mother and my brother who is childless.'

'Then you will not care what happens to his body.' Sidney Grice cupped his face in his hands.

'I am not sure I follow you, sir.' Hesketh's voice was getting husky. 'Surely it will be reburied now that it has been examined.'

'Professor Duffy plans to keep the corpse as a specimen for his lectures,' I said. No amount of self-control could have masked the horror unleashed in Hesketh by that statement and I had to harden my heart to continue. 'Normally, a dead person is the property of the next of kin to dispose of lawfully as they wish. But, in the absence of any relatives, anatomists can take possession of a body for medical teaching and research.' Hesketh put a hand to his collar with a faint choking noise, but I forced myself to carry on. 'They can remove and pickle any part they choose. I expect his head will end up on display in a jar.'

Hesketh loosened his cravat a fraction. 'Is that really the case, sir? With all due respect to Miss Middleton, I will only believe it from your lips.'

'For once Miss Middleton speaks the truth,' Sidney Grice confirmed. 'Professor Duffy is thinking of putting Filbert's naked cadaver on display in his new museum of pathology.'

Hesketh closed his eyes and swallowed. He cupped his brow in his right hand, put his elbow in a puddle of tea and exhaled noisily.

'Very well,' he decided. 'I am sure that you suspect it already, but I shall tell you. Daniel Filbert was my son.'

94

The Snowman

I LOOK IN on *Danny. There shouldn't be much left by now, but something feels heavy as I pull on the rope and, when it breaks though the surface, his face is still intact. Even his eyes. They are open and looking up at me, white as frost in the moonlight.*

Danny sits up.

'Sorry about this,' I say.

He's covered in snow.

'But it's your own fault in way.'

Danny looks at me blankly.

'You were the one who had a go at me,' I tell him. 'You told me I was too kind, helping people who don't help me back. Where were they when you had Hanratty on your back – you said – or when you had to take your family to Paris? Who put their hand in their pocket then? Why not do something for your-self for a change? There's an idea – do something for Nathan.'

And so I did. I did it all for Nathan.

Danny nods, I think.

'What a couple of pickles we are,' I say, 'me a murderer and you not even able to rot down there in that cesspit.' I feel quite chatty now. 'It was Lionel who first called me Nutty,' I remind him. 'I was always Natty to the Garstangs, but he got it wrong. I didn't mind. He meant no harm by it. But then it became a family joke and I hated it. I was always a joke to them.

'They had all the money and they fed me crumbs. I deserved better; my mother told me that once. And so I took better.'

Danny looks puzzled and so I explain, 'They kept threatening to disinherit me and they did for a while, after they found out about the picture and the gambling. I couldn't risk them doing it again.'

Danny seems about to say something but he changes his mind.

'If I had tied Lionel tighter, he wouldn't have been able to loosen the cord enough to strangle himself,' I tell Danny. 'It was kindness, not me, that killed Young Lion.'

Danny tries to stand up but the rope snaps. It has rotted, even if Danny hasn't, and he flops back into the quicklime as if he's had one too many, but he doesn't sink and I have to get a long broom. He looks frightened as I push him back under, as if I'm killing him all over again, and then I'm frightened too.

I shut the trapdoor.

I'll never go back.

If only I could.

95

The Viewing of Bodies

IT WAS EASTERLY who spoke first.

'Hi am very sorry to hear that, Mr Hesketh. No one should suffer such pain alone.' And, not being so presumptuous as to pat his superior's hand, he patted his own consolingly.

'The agony is no better for the sharing of it.' Hesketh hid his face in both hands. 'Danny was my only child. I saw him the day before the murders. We would meet for a drink sometimes when I went out on an errand. When it came out he had been arrested for affray, I was shocked. Danny was so good-natured and sensible. He had never been in trouble with the law. Mr Nathan explained that it was not their fault and that he had paid Danny's fine, for which I was truly grateful. It saved my son from a prison sentence. Then Mr Nathan said that Danny had decided to make a fresh start. The idea of having a criminal record upset him greatly and he was determined to work his passage to America,' Hesketh recounted. 'I was obviously very perturbed by this news. Danny was a delicate young man. He had been weakened by severe bouts of pneumonia and had never set foot on a ship. I could not imagine what work he would do on board or in America.'

'A nation of savages colonized by savages,' Mr G declaimed.

'I thought it was probably just a whim – he was always a bit of a dreamer – and that I could easily talk him out of it.' Hesketh pressed a thumb and second finger on to the corners of his eyes. 'But I never saw or heard from him again.'

'Were you not suspicious?' I asked.

'Anxious,' Hesketh told me. 'But suspicious of what? Of whom?'

'So how did you find out it was him?' I saw a sparrow land on the window sill.

Hesketh twiddled the top button of his waistcoat. 'A father knows when his son is dead. Danny was such an affectionate son, I knew that if he could contact me he would. I began to frequent the city morgue. There is a disgusting man called Parker who let me view the bodies for a shilling a time.'

'You know that is against the regulations?' I watched another sparrow join the first one.

'Only for Parker.' My guardian seemed edgy. Perhaps he could hear the sparrows squabbling twenty feet behind him. I could only see their tussle.

'Hi cannot himagine what you must have gone through every time.' Easterly went pink.

'I only went when there were reports in the papers,' Hesketh said flatly. 'Unidentified males, often dragged out of the Thames, anyone estimated to be between Danny's age when I last saw him and what he would be now. And then, when I saw that a body had been found after many years in the north wing, I knew.'

Hesketh drew his fingertips repeatedly over his brow.

'And you traced him to Snushall's undertakers,' I remarked, contributing to my godfather's annoyance, 'where you covered your face and spoke in a French accent.'

'It is the only accent I can do.' Hesketh looked abashed.

I paused before adding, 'And there you saw Danny.'

'My boy.' Hesketh stroked his own cheek. 'He had been turned to leather but I still knew him. How could I not? He was perfectly preserved. Mr Snushall took every penny I had – my life savings – but what did I need the money for?'

'Hi bet you did him proud,' Easterly said.

'He did,' I agreed.

'If only that were an end to it.' Sidney Grice rubbed his shoulder. 'We all know what was found on your son's body.'

'Danny was not a pickpocket.' Hesketh's neck muscles bulged.

'But what did Mr Mortlock say to the policeman who brought it?' I pressed.

Hesketh tugged at his hair. 'I do not remember exactly.' He let go. 'But he was horrified.'

'*So you have found him*,' I quoted.

Hesketh shied away from the words. 'I think he said found *it*.'

'Him,' I insisted.

'And with that one word – Austin Anthony Hesketh – it all fell into place.' Mr G punched his own shoulder to drive away the pain. 'Mr Mortlock – the boy with whom you had played and the man you had served so devotedly – slipped his own watch into his friend's pocket to give him an excuse to start a fight. Your son, loyal to the end, tried to help him, and Nathan made sure they were both arrested. The nearly perfect alibi.'

'I never knew how he got out, until I made him tell me,' Hesketh stated matter-of-factly.

'And how did you do that?' I asked.

'Don't answer that, Mr Hesketh,' Easterly urged. 'They are trying to trick you.'

I changed tack.

'Those wooden wedges interest me,' I announced. 'They were all dented – except for yours.'

'I was probably more careful with mine, miss.'

'It was not used,' I insisted. 'If you had told me you did not use it because you trusted your friends, I might have believed you, but why pretend you had used it when you had not?'

'Mr Grice has taught you well,' Hesketh said without rancour.

'But not how to share information,' Mr G remarked sourly.

'I learn by example,' I told him. 'Did you mention the rings or Hesketh's release form?' I did not wait for a response but resumed my pressure on the valet. 'Answer the question please, Hesketh.'

'What does it matter if Mr Hesketh used his wedge or not?' Easterly protested.

My godfather watched me with something vaguely approaching a smile.

'Because only the killer would know that he did not need to lock himself in at night,' I reasoned.

Hesketh pondered my statement. 'I did worry when I saw you examining it,' he admitted at last.

'Don't say any more, Mr Hesketh,' Easterly burst out. 'They don't know anything.'

'Take your junior colleague's advice by all means,' Sidney Grice agreed. 'And let me tell you exactly what went on.'

*

The coal-hole lid is still off. I slide it back into place and stand up and, as I glance back at the house which is mine now, the curtain moves on the second floor, just as it did when I wedged the lid, and I think, who the hell can that be? And then I realize it's only a breeze. I would have just got rid of the Garstangs if that curtain hadn't twitched and made me think I had been seen. So the others all died because of a draught.

But I don't have time to think about that now. Is that somebody walking their dog? At this time? It's that woman from number 4 across the Crescent. I put my head down and run.

96

The Last Day

SIDNEY GRICE FOLDED his arms.

'You were never on that train,' he said. 'As soon as you realized what had happened, you wrote to your brother to send you a telegram. I imagine you said that you wanted an excuse to visit home. There is always a weak link in every story and it usually centres on the over-abundance of evidence provided. Most people asked to prove where they had been would have some difficulty in doing so, unless they were with a large group of acquaintances. They do not usually get pretty French maids to purchase their tickets and cause confusion about the price, ensuring that the seller remembers the transaction. Nor do they stagily draw attention to themselves with the guard on both legs of the journey. Nor do they manage to retain their tickets on a morning when the barriers were fully manned by inspectors. There is so much filling in the sandwich of your story that the bread cannot contain it. John Smith.'

Hesketh looked blank. 'Who, sir?'

'The West Coast Railway guard,' I reminded him, though I suspected I did not need to do so.

'A common enough name,' Mr G remarked. 'But, armed with the information that his parents were Alfred Smith and Mabel Smith née Lineker, the unsung Birth Certificate Investigators, Serpett and Fritt of Goodge Street, were able to ascertain that the Smiths were cursed with five children – the irksomely named

John and two other boys, Harold and William, who according to their simple headstone at Nunhead Cemetery were taken by the angels in infancy.'

'I am not sure where this is going.' I stretched my back.

'Then listen and learn.' My guardian brought out his snuff-box. 'Their firstborn child was a girl, as was the third, and the Smiths let their imaginations run amok with their selection of feminine names. The first was registered as Angela Smith, born on ninth of April 1837, and the second as Ann, who became a seamstress. Angela, on the other hand, went to work as a maid with her mother in the house of a Mr and Mrs John Weaver. To pander to the impatience of my audience, I shall reveal that Mr Froume, the Marriage Detective, has discovered that Miss Angela Smith gave herself in wedlock to a Signor Juan Innocenti, newly escaped from the dreary backwater of Madrid.'

Hesketh was clutching the table edge, his fingerplate beds squeezed crimson with blanched tips.

'This marriage was fruitless, however, and Mr Innocenti's fancy was taken by Angela's sister, the more youthful and buxom Ann, who, falling prey – as foolish girls are prone – to the ole-aginous unctuousness which passes for charm in Hispanic quarters, eloped with him to vilest Paris of all places, some five months and two days after his wedding to Angela.' Sidney Grice opened the box and tipped it upside down, but nothing fell out of it. 'What could the hapless Angela do? She decided to use her one skill, capitalize on her marital name, imitate her recently departed husband's accent and present herself as Senorita Angelina, there being an unaccountable craving for Spanish maids amongst an alarming proportion of domestic employers.'

'But she was the mad woman who came through the ceiling,' Easterly realized at last.

'She was not mad,' Hesketh insisted fiercely.

'She was certainly unusual,' I remarked.

'After a brief employment with Mrs Thum, the wife of an engineer, Angelina Innocenti found employment with Mrs Peters, a widow of number 32 Burton Crescent. It was while working there that she met a handsome young valet by the name of Austin Hesketh,' Sidney Grice narrated.

'How can you know that?' I asked.

'By looking through what you found too tedious with which to trouble yourself, Mrs Garstang's household accounts. She slipped various pieces of paper into it – some of the larger receipts, a few recipes for her cook to try and a note on the back of Angelina Innocenti's character reference that she was also vouched for by Hesketh.' Mr G spread his hands. 'You cannot vouch for someone who you do not know.'

'She was a good maid,' Hesketh said. 'Mrs Garstang was always very happy with her and thanked me for my recommendation.'

'To skip merrily backwards a few paces,' Mr G walked his first two fingers in mid-air, 'nearly a year after taking employment with Mrs Peters, and some months after meeting Austin Hesketh, Angelina Innocenti left, only to return six months later to the same household.'

'Do you know why Angelina left number 32?' I asked, and Hesketh rubbed his jaw.

'To look after her sick mother, as I remember it.'

'A mother who was so sick that she was still working for the Weavers and did so until the day she died some five years later.' Grice's fingers twirled a polka.

'I can think of only one other reason young girls disappear temporarily,' I said carefully, and Easterly scratched his armpit.

'It was to have a child,' Hesketh confessed. 'My son, Danny. But I am sure Mr Grice has seen the birth certificate. I could not have him registered as a bastard and so I put both our names on it.'

'But she was married to hanother man.' Easterly edged away as if he thought adultery might be contagious.

'Only in the strictest letter of the law,' Hesketh assured him. 'There was nothing we could do about that. But we took our marriage vows and exchanged rings in a quiet side chapel of

St George's, and I truly believe that we were man and wife in God's eyes.'

'Hi knew you would do the right thing, Mr Hesketh.' The footman settled back towards him.

'But how did you and Angelina manage to meet?' I tried not to sound prurient.

'When she was here it was easy,' Hesketh admitted. 'There were ladders into the roof space and we could meet halfway or sometimes take the risk of going into each other's rooms.' He avoided my eye. 'Before she came to work for the Garstangs she would climb in through the cellar at the back of the north wing.' Hesketh puffed up his cheeks. 'I got keys cut for the side gate and the cellar and hid them behind the ivy in the garden wall.'

'Where some time after her escape last December, Angelina Innocenti discovered Daniel Filbert's body,' Sidney Grice surmised. 'The cellar had a false floor to raise it clear of the old cesspit and lime was poured through a trapdoor to get rid of the stench, but the planks had rotted away by the time the fugitive climbed in there.'

'So that was why he was found so soon after she had escaped from Broadmoor,' I speculated. 'She must have panicked and run out, leaving the gate and cellar flaps open and Danny's body on display to that family who went seeking shelter.'

'Senorita Innocenti was a determined woman,' Mr G narrated. 'She may have been frightened but that didn't stop her from returning, and getting into that loft.'

'Dear lord in heaven,' Hesketh breathed. 'She must have been coming back for me.'

'But why did she not approach you?' I asked.

'For the same reason that she abused Veronique – because she saw Hesketh with her and assumed the worst,' Mr G expounded. 'On top of which she had unfinished business with me.'

'The old woman who threw a horse dropping.' I wriggled my toes. 'Do you think she caused the gas explosion to try to kill you?' I had an itch in my left foot and it would not go away.

'It would be pretty to think so.' Sidney Grice fluttered his long eyelashes. 'But our senorita was not in the house at the time and it is difficult to conceive how she could have timed the explosion to coincide with our appearance.' He clacked his teeth as if trying a new set out. 'More likely she fractured a pipe on one of her visits whilst getting out of the cellar. The stairs would have been in a very poor condition and she may have grabbed it to steady herself.'

I kicked the sole of my left foot with the toe of my right but it did not help. 'And your son,' I asked Hesketh, 'what happened to him?'

'Danny was brought up by a Mr and Mrs Filbert in Woodcutters Road,' Hesketh said. 'We gave them money towards his keep, but it must have cost them more than that to look after him. They were good foster-parents or we should not have left him there. They lent him their surname but kept his Christian name.'

'But how did you get the money for his funeral?' I wriggled my toes desperately. 'That was an expensive coffin and headstone.'

'Angelina came into some money from a relative,' Hesketh replied. 'She gave five hundred pounds to me to look after because I could keep it locked in my pantry.'

'When was that?' I asked.

'About thirty years ago,' he told me. 'We were saving it for when we could live openly as man and wife.'

'How very convenient.' My godfather tapped the bottom of his snuffbox but nothing fell out.

'It is the truth,' Hesketh contended.

'I have small doubt that you believe it to be so.' Mr G put the box back into his waistcoat pocket. 'But – as the auditing of his accounts shows – on the fourth of May anno Domini 1855, Mr Holford Garstang paid five hundred pounds cash to an undisclosed recipient.'

'Just before Danny was born,' I remembered.

'But why would he do that?' Hesketh looked truly bewildered.

'One only maintains a child through love or duty,' Mr G said. Hesketh made as if to rise. 'He was *my* son,' he insisted fiercely.

'Oh, Hesketh,' I said sadly. 'It is not difficult to imagine why Mr Garstang might believe a child was his and have paid to avoid a scandal.'

'No!' Hesketh's face drained with fury. 'Angelina was not like that. She was a good girl.'

'So good that she never gave herself to you before you underwent that sham of a ceremony?' Mr G persisted.

'That was different,' Hesketh raged. 'We were in love and our marriage was not a sham, unlike the one Angelina went through with her so-called husband.'

'Who would have thought it – other than I?' Sidney Grice adjusted his eye. 'Beneath this courteous, calm and dignified valet's polished veneer of polite servitude seethes a molten magna of passions.'

'You are making vile accusations against the woman I loved, the woman I have just seen die violently and...' Hesketh's voice trailed off.

'There are some indisputable facts,' I pointed out as evenly as I could. 'Mr Garstang gave five hundred pounds to somebody just before Angelina gave the same amount to you.'

Hesketh hung his head. 'I did think it odd about the money,' he admitted eventually.

'That would mean Daniel was –' I did a quick sum – 'only seventeen when he died.' I checked my maths and could not quite believe it. 'But he looked so much older.'

'Death and quicklime do not flatter the complexion.' Sidney Grice touched his cheek. 'Daniel Filbert's body was unwittingly preserved by his *friend* Nathan and then partially burned by the lamentable Crepolius Snushall. He was not going to keep his youthful freshness.'

'Stop it.' Hesketh fought for breath. 'Please, Mr Grice.'

'So when you realized that Nathan Mortlock had murdered your son you decided to kill him,' I surmised.

Hesketh swallowed. 'I sent Veronique to purchase a train ticket when I was supposed to be packing a bag, and misled her about the cost so that she would make a fuss and be remembered, then nobody could accuse her of lying about getting it for me,' he admitted.

'So John Smith, the guard who gave you your alibi, was your common-law wife's brother,' I recapitulated. 'What happened next?'

'While Veronique was at her task, I took Mr Nathan's clothes from his wardrobe and hid them in Mrs Mortlock's room, but the wardrobe was still half full with her clothes so I took the rest to Miss Charity's room. Then I went downstairs and smelled the stew, saying what a pity it was I did not have time to enjoy it and pouring a bottle of Mr Nathan's laudanum in.'

'Which is why Easterly overslept,' I recollected, 'and Constable Harris fell asleep after he had eaten some.'

Hesketh nodded. 'Mrs Emmett was serving up when I went down to say I was leaving. I had a spoonful to check and the opium was undetectable. The alcohol evaporates and nobody could have tasted the residue, with Mrs Emmett's fondness for salt and pepper. The others were settling down to eat, so I arranged I would put the keys through the letterbox for Mrs Emmett to collect when she had eaten. It was against Mr Nathan's strict instructions but I told her to enjoy her dinner and persuaded her he would never know, but that I would take responsibility if he ever found out.'

'You never left the house,' I realized. 'You put the keys in the letterbox and sneaked back upstairs.'

'I stropped the blade to make it as blunt as possible. He was not going to have the clean death he had denied the Garstangs. Then I put on one of my master's shirts and a pair of trousers, and hid in his wardrobe with my own clothes folded beside me and a laundry bag.'

'You don't have to tell them this, Mr Hesketh,' Easterly protested.

'They know, Easterly.' Hesketh patted the young footman's arm. 'If I deny it much longer Inspector Quigley will decide to question Miss Charity, and I cannot allow that.'

'How did you feel as you waited for Mr Mortlock to go to bed?' I asked and Mr G huffed. He was not keen on feelings.

'In a turmoil.' Hesketh clamped his right hand to his temple. 'My mind was spinning. I could not believe I had gone that far, and I had almost decided to give up and rush to put everything back when I heard him come in and get ready for bed. I could see his bedside lamp through a crack in the woodwork and by the rustling I think he was reading in bed. Then the oddest thing happened. I dozed off.'

'It happens sometimes in times of extreme stress,' I recollected. 'I have heard of a cavalryman falling off his horse because he went to sleep just before a charge.'

Hesketh put his other hand up to his head. 'When I awoke it was quiet and I had no idea how long I had been like that. I waited and listened until I heard a snore but, when I pushed the door open a crack, it creaked. It had never done that before.'

'Probably your weight distorting the frame,' I suggested.

Sidney Grice had his pencil in his hand but the notebook stayed closed.

'Mr Nathan woke up as I climbed out.' Hesketh was clutching his temples. 'He sat up and called out *Who's there?* And then, in great relief, *Oh, it's you, Hesketh*, and lay back again. He must have been confused with his night draught or he would have wondered why I was there. I just said *yes* and climbed on to the bed, and he said sleepily, *What are you doing?* And that is when I nearly ran away. He trusted me. It never occurred to Mr Nathan that I could mean him any harm.' Hesketh released his temples and took a draught of cold tea. 'But then I remembered the Garstangs, who had treated him like their own child, and the servants, who had adored him, and my son who thought they were best friends. I do not suppose it ever occurred to any of them that this man would be their murderer. I swung my leg over and pinioned his arms under the sheets. The pain of that woke him up and he cried out *Hesketh!* in alarm. *Be quiet*, I hissed.'

'One cannot hiss words which have no sibilance,' Mr G contributed usefully.

Hesketh shook that information away. 'I made a fist in his hair and dragged his head up, wrapped the cord twice round his neck and pulled it tight. Mr Nathan went puce almost immediately; his eyes bulged and his tongue protruded, and I thought I had killed him too soon. But, when I relaxed my noose, he sucked in the air with a huge gasp. *Listen*, I said, *very carefully. If you tell me the truth I shall let you live. If you lie, you will never see the dawn. How did you kill the Garstangs?* He denied it at first, of course, but I became expert very quickly in applying just the right amount of choking pressure to make him think he was going to die. It must have taken an hour or more, but I got the truth out of him eventually.

'*And what about Danny?* I asked.

'*Oh, him.* Mr Nathan obviously thought I only really cared about the household. *I strangled him in the basement and pushed him into the quicklime they were trying to clean the old cesspit with.* And it was then that I told him. *Daniel Filbert was my son.* I showed him the razor and he opened his mouth to scream for help but I put my hand over his mouth and nose, forced him back into his pillow and dug the edge of the blade in just below his Adam's apple.' Hesketh mimed the actions, unconsciously, I suspected. 'When I took my hand away, his scream wasn't muffled any more. It just came out as a hiss.'

'Correct use of the voiceless fricative that time,' Sidney Grice approved.

'Where did you learn that from?' I asked and Hesketh screwed up his nose.

'When I was a child I had a dog called Sally. Her barking vexed a neighbour so he stabbed Sally in the neck. She lived another three years, but the wound didn't close and she never barked again.' He pulled a wry face. 'Except when I covered the hole to torment him.'

'What next?' I asked, fascinated that Hesketh could almost smile at his memories in the middle of his confession.

'That was the first cut,' he said with as small a display of emotion as a man might describe pruning his roses. 'But there were six stabbings to avenge and I did them very slowly, being careful not to go too deep. And every time I hacked into his flesh I told him: this is for Nancy Seagrove – this is for Brian Watts. Mr Nathan struggled and writhed from side to side, but he was not a strong man and I still am for all my sixty years, and heavy. I nearly killed him too soon with my fourth cut, but it pulled apart just in time for me to see the vein throbbing under the surface. There were two strangulations to account for too – Lionel and Danny. That was why I wrapped the cord round twice. I throttled my master until he almost passed out. His tongue began to swell and his eyes to bleed as they bulged in pain and terror. Then I stopped. I loosened the cord and let him fully regain consciousness. He was mouthing like a landed trout and his lips were saying *Hesketh, no, please.* I let him see the razor once more. *And this is for Angelina, the cut that will kill you*, I said. He was hissing and writhing like an injured snake now, and pleading, he was pleading with me. *I will show you the same mercy that you showed them*, I vowed, and set to work. The razor was really blunt by now and I had to saw hard to get through all the flesh and gristle. I went through the middle as deep as I could because I know the big veins are in the side. He was starting to pass out so I stopped again, but then there was this look. I don't know what it was – it might just have been the way his hair fell over his forehead – but something in it reminded me of the young Master Nathan and how we used to be, and I was sickened by what we had become. *This is it*, I told him. *Any last words?* And I put my finger over the hole but he couldn't really speak. His throat must have been too damaged by then. But he said something and – between what I thought I heard and what I thought I could read on his lips – it seemed he said *Do it.*

'I went through the side and the blood exploded out of him. *I loved you*, I said, and I think he heard me before the hissing stopped.'

Hesketh's expression recomposed itself, and he might have been the valet that I had first met, less than two weeks ago, as he spoke on. 'The shirt was soaked as I knew it would be, and I did not want to ruin Easterly's clothes as I know how much care he takes with them.'

'That was very thoughtful of you, Mr Hesketh.' Easterly brushed his own lapel to support his mentor's statement.

'In the midst of savagery is benevolence born,' Sidney Grice opined but, if that were a quotation, I did not recognize it.

'So what did you do?' Was I the only one who appreciated the horror of what we were hearing?

'I had already prepared a shirt by pouring blood from a joint of beef over it and letting it dry in the butler's pantry,' Hesketh revealed. 'I am the only one who goes in there.'

I could not help but feel a mild satisfaction when I remembered how I deduced that in Quigley's office.

'I undressed, washed in Mr Nathan's stand, poured the slops on to the bed and dried the bowl on the corner of a blanket. Then I put my own clothes back on.' Hesketh put a hand over his heart. 'The bloodstained clothes I put into the bag and left them outside the door to be disposed of in the range later on.'

'Which is why Mrs Emmett smelled burning the next morning and accused Veronique of being careless with the flat iron,' I remembered.

'Then I went round the house,' Hesketh said, 'putting the shirt in Easterly's room, the razor in Veronique's and the key in Mrs Emmett's. Everybody was fast asleep.'

'Were you trying to hincriminate Veronique, Mr Hesketh?' Something sparked inside the footman.

'No, Easterly,' Hesketh vowed.

'Or me?' Easterly shied like a kicked puppy.

'I was trying to provide evidence against all of us, including myself with the curtain cord.'

'All of us?' Easterly gaped.

'I thought, if the finger of guilt pointed at everybody, it would point at nobody.' Hesketh held his brow in his right hand. 'Anyone accused could rightly point out that there was just as much evidence against everyone else.'

'And then?' I pressed.

Hesketh rubbed his forehead. 'I put the clothes back in the wardrobe. I must have picked up Miss Charity's glove with the clothes and dropped that stocking in the dark.'

'You pulled the bolts across with a ribbon, a sample of which snagged on the doorpost.' Sidney Grice produced an envelope and tipped its contents on to a white page of his notebook. 'Miss Middleton was not the only one to leave threads on the jamb.'

And I saw that there were three green threads that must have come from my dress and a longer saffron thread curled into an elongated S.

'I knew you would work out how it had been done when I saw you take that,' Hesketh admitted. 'But I still hoped you would not be able to prove it was my doing.'

I could not help but remember another saffron thread, found under the nail of a murdered girl the day I came to London.

Easterly rubbed his eyes with the knuckles of his first fingers like a sleepy child. 'But what hiv Mr Grice decided it was me, Mr Hesketh?'

'I would not have let you even go to court, Easterly,' the valet vowed. 'I have written a full confession and placed it in the hands of Forrester's, the solicitors at number 16, with instructions that it should be opened in the event of my death or be used as evidence if anyone should be brought to trial for Mr Nathan's murder.'

'But surely, if they thought your letter contained evidence, they would be bound to go to the police,' I objected.

'I told them it was just character references for all the staff, should they need those,' Hesketh explained. 'I would never have let anyone take my place in the dock. You must believe me.'

'Must we?' My voice rose. 'The word of a murderer? I expect Nathan Mortlock believed you when you said you would let him live.'

'He had no right to the truth,' Hesketh insisted. 'And I did not murder him. It was an execution for his many crimes. I shall face my maker with a clear conscience on the last day, while Nathan Mortlock shall roast in hell.'

'*Vengeance is mine. I will repay, saith the Lord,*' I quoted. 'How did you get out of the house?'

'Through the front window.' Hesketh leaned back towards it. 'I unlocked it and scrambled out.'

'Hence the scraping of boot polish on the front wall,' my guardian observed.

'I thought your shoe was slightly scuffed,' I recalled.

'The coalman's wagon was making a delivery to number 28 Burton Crescent, the house next door,' Hesketh resumed his account, 'but he had to park outside Gethsemane because of a trench in the road. I remembered that we were due a delivery too and I couldn't risk him seeing me, so I took a sharp stone and put it under the horse's tackle. The animal reared up and bolted. It was something we used to do as boys in Nuneaton and what I think Mr Nathan did the day before the slaughter.'

'There is an agreeable symmetry in that act,' Mr G approved before reminding me, 'I instructed you to note water mains repair.'

'I rang the doorbell and Mrs Emmett let me in,' Hesketh said. 'I told her my mother had just had a turn – she had faked one for the doctor, thinking Mr Mortlock might demand proof. Then I went into the sitting room, saying I was checking the decanters.'

'Hi ham sorry for that, Mr Hesketh,' Easterly apologized. 'It was only the occasional nip.'

'It hardly matters now,' I reassured him.

'I put the padlock back on,' Hesketh recited, 'and went about my duties. The rest you know.'

'Indeed.' Sidney Grice sucked on his pencil as a man might on a cigar. 'Remember how I said I might give you time with the murderer?' He tapped off the imaginary ash. 'Well, Austin Anthony Hesketh, it transpires that you shall be spending the rest of your life with him.'

—◈—

97

The Last of the Grices

SIDNEY GRICE CLOSED his notebook with great deliberation.
I had not noticed him open or write in it.

'Oh, Austin Hesketh, once faithful and almost ancient
retainer, if only death were as simple as life. Life has a beginning
and an end but death has only a beginning, and what end can
there be to that of Nathan Roptine Mortlock?'

'Hi do not understand you, sir.' Easterly spoke tremulously
for all of us.

Mr G drummed the tabletop with his fingertips. 'Are you,
with your absurd affectation of an accent, going to inform your
beautiful, tall and slender young mistress that her late father
was a savage slaughterer of the household that loved and sheltered him?'

'Hit his not my place, sir.' Easterly looked away.

'What about you, Hesketh?' Mr G swung round. 'Are you going
to relate the history of Miss Mortlock's father's actions to her?
Or are you going to wait for it all to come out at the trial to be
tacked on to the knowledge that the valet she trusted, and of
whom she is undisguisedly fond, tortured and killed her father?'

Hesketh rotated his right hand as if remembering what he had
done with it.

'I do not see how Miss Charity can be spared the knowledge
unless,' he chose his words carefully, 'I confess to the crime but
give another motive. I could say he was going to dismiss me

about the stolen drink or some other pretext. If I plead guilty it will be a very short trial.'

'But you can't do that, Mr Hesketh.' Easterly was aghast. 'You can't let Miss Mortlock think you did that to her father for such a…' he struggled for the bon mot, '*silly* reason.'

'Better she hates just me than me *and* her father,' Hesketh said calmly.

'An almost noble sentiment.' Sidney Grice pressed down on the table as if stopping it floating away. 'But I cannot permit myself to permit you to do that.' The table rocked. 'I would be called as a witness and I shall not perjure myself for you or any man, not even for money.'

'Then the truth must out,' Hesketh said simply.

'The truth has myriad manifestations,' my guardian expounded. 'It can be the great healer and bring consolation. It can rampage like the foaming sea, destroying all, indiscriminately, in its path. I could reveal things that would rock this world of ours to its rotten foundations, but I would prefer to have a nice cup of tea.'

'Shall I make it, sir?' Easterly offered.

'Perhaps later.' I signalled for him to stay seated.

Sidney Grice stretched like a man awakening. 'If you had a child, Miss Middleton – repulsive though that concept is – what would you do with the man who murdered him, her or it?'

His eyelids were looking bruised as they fought to retain his new eye.

I ignored the insults he was heaping upon me for the time being. 'I should want him hanged, I imagine.'

'Of Miss Middleton's forty-nine most virulent faults –' my godfather touched his new eye – 'the worst is her gentle nature. It corrupts her mind with generosity and poisons her heart with kindness.' He dabbed a pink tear from his cheek. 'If I had a splendid son, which I shall never have, and he was cold-bloodedly killed by a man posing as his and my friend – though I hope never to have one of those – I should be devastated to see that man hanged.'

'Hi do not—' Easterly began and we all knew what it was he did not.

'I would devise an ingenious method of killing that murderer, preferably over many years, with the most sophisticated methods of inflicting exquisite pain that I could devise,' Sidney Grice announced, as if discussing a shopping expedition.

'This is all hypothetical,' I pointed out. 'What are you saying?'

'What I am saying is of little importance.' He rubbed his injured shoulder. 'What I am about to say is monumentally significant.' My guardian stood up. 'I cannot judge you harshly, Austin Anthony Hesketh, and, if our two companions are of the same mind, I shall not heap further miseries upon your mistress. I do not intend to point the finger of guilt in your or anybody else's direction.'

'I shall never tell a soul,' Easterly vowed, his hand clamped over his heart.

'And you?' Sidney Grice inclined his head towards me.

'I cannot agree to this,' I said.

98

Broken Glass

SIDNEY GRICE RAISED a quizzical eyebrow.

'Has the milk of human kindness finally run dry?'

'I am astonished that you have so much in you,' I retorted.

My godfather bridled. 'My decision is pragmatic. On what grounds would you hand this man over to the police?'

'First, we would be breaking the law which we are sworn to uphold,' I began.

'I have never made such a vow,' he demurred, 'and I was not aware that you had. Perhaps you could remind me when and where that was.'

'It is our job,' I persisted.

'Our job is to discover the truth and we have done so.'

'Also,' I avoided Hesketh's eye, 'what this man did was cruel in the extreme and premeditated.'

'You would prefer he acted stupidly and impulsively?'

'I would have understood it better,' I replied.

'Mr Mortlock was a very wicked man, miss,' Easterly contributed. 'He deserved what he got.'

'The decision was not Hesketh's to take,' I argued. 'My father was murdered—' how easily that sentence escaped my tongue – 'by a man he was trying to help. And I had his killer in my power. I admit I toyed with him but I did not use that opportunity to take such extreme revenge.'

Hesketh upturned his palms. 'As Mr Grice has told us, you are a kind lady.'

I riled at this. 'Do not presume upon my kindness to think it gives you the right to commit such a savage deed and walk away as if nothing had happened.'

Hesketh considered my words. 'I can't be so mealy-mouthed as to fake repentance, Miss Middleton. I have never hurt a soul before and do not believe I shall again.'

'He won't, miss,' the footman vowed desperately.

'You cannot guarantee that, Easterly,' I disagreed. 'You would have sworn that he would never have hurt your master in the first place.'

'Miss Middleton is right,' Hesketh agreed wearily. 'Only God can see into another man's heart.'

'Do you ask him for forgiveness?' I hunted for straws to clutch at.

'For the great harm I have done Miss Charity,' he admitted at last. 'She was so badly estranged from her father that I did not think she would take his loss so hard.' He breathed heavily. 'You are a good lady, Miss Middleton, and you must do your duty.'

'And put a noose round your neck?' I found myself saying. 'I cannot bring myself to do it.' Hesketh's lips parted but I burst out, 'And do not *dare* to thank me.' I jumped to my feet. 'Do *not* say another word, Austin Hesketh, nor you, Easterly Nutter, and especially not you, Mr Sidney Grice.' I went to the sideboard, poured myself a huge gin and gulped it down in three draughts. 'Terrible, *terrible* things have happened here and you – all three of you – have made me a party to that.'

Easterly opened his mouth.

'Do *not* say it,' I shouted as I stormed towards the hall.

The glass was still in my hand. I spun and hurled it over them and, to my great satisfaction, it shattered on the wall.

99

Characters and the Vixen

CHERRY CAME LATE that afternoon, pale but as tall and slim and lovely as Sidney Grice kept saying she was.

'I have spoken to the Trust committee and they have agreed, in view of events, that I should not be expected to live at Gethsemane. I may keep up my allowance if I restore the house to its former glory and promise not to sell it,' she announced as she kissed me. 'Oh, and thank you for looking after Veronique.'

'Molly will miss her,' I forecast. 'I have never seen her so happy. She has just been teaching Veronique how to spit sideways.'

Cherry smiled distractedly. 'I hope her new employer finds a use for that skill.'

'You are not keeping her?'

We walked to the window.

'I will have no need of her.' She tidied her veil. 'Veronique is a good maid and pretty. She should have no difficulty in finding work. Easterly may have more difficulty – he is not really cut out to be a footman. But I shall give them both excellent characters.'

'They are unlikely to find positions in the same household.'

'I am sorry about that.' And, to do Cherry justice, she looked it.

'I thought you were very keen to keep them,' I protested, 'and, if you are to get your income—'

'And so I was,' she interrupted me. 'But there has been a change of plan. Fabian despises the servant–master relationship.

He and I are to be wed as soon as I am out of mourning and we shall lead a simple life.'

'And what of Hesketh?' I could not be bothered to argue that Fabian supposedly despised marriage.

A performer was walking on his hands up the street, begging bowl balanced on his feet.

'We shall keep him,' she declared, a little too casually, I thought. 'Fabian could do with a man to save him from the mundane tasks and allow him to concentrate on his genius.'

It struck me that part of the great Fabian Le Bon's genius might be in hooking and landing a wealthy heiress and persuading her to dump her servants whilst retaining one for himself, but I only said, 'I see.'

'Hesketh would not find it easy to get a new position at his age,' she continued. 'He has served my family for nearly forty years and stayed loyal to my father when everyone else deserted him. I think that deserves some reward, don't you?'

'Indeed.' Sidney Grice materialized in the room. 'People say that loyalty is its own reward. They are fools. I have run up enormous expenses on your behalf, pretty Miss Charity Mortlock.'

'And you shall be reimbursed plus ten per cent, as we agreed, when my father's murderer has been convicted,' she confirmed.

Mr G puffed his lips. 'Then I have tidings to gladden the heart of any young lady wishing to remain financially continent.' He cupped his right ear. 'I am writing those expenses off, Miss Mortlock, for I have come to an end of my investigations.'

A trace of colour invaded Cherry's complexion. 'Then you can tell me the name of my father's murderer?'

'I deeply regret to inform you that I cannot.' My guardian stood before Cherry Mortlock, all at once small, in a way I had not seen before.

'So you are just giving up?' she asked incredulously.

Mr G met her gaze but his was far from comfortable. 'I do not wish to proceed when I am confident that I shall know no more of significance about this case tomorrow or this time next year than I do today.'

'So all that talk about how you always get your man—'

'I fear you are confusing me with the Northwest Mounted Police Force of Canada,' he broke in as she drew breath, 'an uncommon though not a unique mistake. I was once mistaken for Rumpelstiltskin, a fictional character from the pen of the brothers Grimm.'

'So you are admitting defeat?' She took hold of the unclosed drape to steady herself. 'Sidney Grice, the great private—'

'Personal,' he demurred.

'Detective,' Cherry carried on without a pause, 'cannot find the man who murdered my father.'

'I am unable to reveal his identity,' he admitted.

'That is the same thing.' Cherry gripped the drape so hard I feared she would bring it and the rail down.

'I find it difficult to condemn you for reaching such an irrational conclusion,' Sidney Grice told her.

'You... find...' Cherry wrenched the drape and something creaked. 'This is unbelievable. I hoped your eccentricity might be a product of your genius, Mr Grice, but I have come to realize that it is only something behind which you hide your incompetence.'

'I forgive you for that remark,' he told her magnanimously.

'I know what you are up to.' Cherry jabbed a finger in his face. 'You are hoping I shall increase your outrageous charges.'.

'He is not, I promise you,' I assured Cherry.

'And this from the same plain girl who promised me he would find the murderer?' she mocked, and I did not know how to reply to that. But I did not get the chance, for she had leaped to another conclusion. 'You have another more lucrative case and you are dropping me in favour of it.' She threw up her arms. 'I should have listened to Mr Cochran's warnings about you two – the one-eyed poseur and his deranged vixen, he called you, amongst other things.'

Mr G almost frothed as he chewed his mouth. 'I shall not

stoop to insulting that posturing, vainglorious, publicity-seeking, self-opinionated, jumped-up, inobservant, illogical, ineffectual, grasping braggart,' he retorted, and I was much impressed for these were exactly the words he had used to describe his rival almost two years ago. 'I shall not even mention his crass incompetence, the extreme anxiety he caused you and your servile minions with his incitements to false arrest, nor even seek to remind you that an escaped Broadmoor prisoner was granted ingress to your house by his demolition of your late father's protective wall, and that as a result of this she died bloodily and in great agony, not to mention dramatically, in that hitherto unexplored netherworld twixt loft and bedroom and thereby giving your architecturally uninteresting and shoddily constructed house a reputation that would be the envy of the Tower of London. I shall now permit this tirade to expire.'

'I shall sue for breach of contract,' Cherry threatened.

'And be the poorer for it,' Mr G warned. 'Clause five states that the provider of the service – *id est me* – may terminate the agreement without notice at any time. The contractor for my services – in this case you, Miss Mortlock – may not do so without my consent.'

'But that is not reasonable,' she protested.

'It puts you at a disadvantage,' he conceded, 'though I did particularly draw your attention to that clause before you signed the document.'

Cherry crushed her handbag to her breast.

'So that is it?' She looked from my guardian to me and back to him incredulously. 'This is not some kind of game?'

'To answer your enquiries in reverse order – no and yes.' Mr G smiled thinly. 'Goodbye, dear lady, and fare thee well. I would ring for Molly to show you out but I have formed the impression that you do not wish to tarry.'

Cherry went crimson.

'You walking pile of...' she drew back her arm, 'excrement.' And Cherry's open hand lashed out.

Sidney Grice had the reactions of a cat but he did not even attempt to draw back or fend off the blow that slapped sharply on to his left cheek. Mr G blinked and his right eye fell into his open palm, but he did not move as she readied to bring the back of her hand on to him.

'In case you are under any illusions –' the marks of her fingers sprang to the surface – 'I would prefer you not to.'

And Cherry drew her hand quickly but harmlessly down.

'Oh,' she said and touched her own cheek as if hers, not his, were stinging. Cherry Mortlock sniffed convulsively and rushed away.

I hurried after her but what could I say? I could not tell her that we knew who had killed her father and why. I only said, 'I am sorry, Cherry.'

'*Miss* Mortlock,' she corrected me. 'Well, open the door, girl.'

I did so meekly and was glad to see a hansom pull over almost immediately.

Cherry paused on the threshold. 'I should not have spoken to you as I have, for I believe you mean well.' She pulled her cloak around her. 'But that man has betrayed my trust, March.' She almost turned on the top step. 'And to think I thought he and I...' Cherry Mortlock shook herself in disbelief at the feeling she had almost expressed. 'Goodbye, March.'

She hurried down and into the hansom, and was hardly seated before it was away.

'What a delightful woman.' My godfather came into the hall, his socket staring into the street. 'Though I doubt she will engage my services again or recommend me to her friends.'

'I cannot help but wonder,' I said in the doorway, 'how accurate her description of you was.'

'I *am* walking.' Mr G whipped out his patch like a circus act. 'The rest cannot be literally true.'

'I do not understand you.' I stepped back. 'I always believed that your hunt for the truth was implacable and ruthless, but you have let Horwich go free – I can accept that he was duped – and

I know you are protecting Cherry, but Hesketh's crime was cruel in the extreme. In heaven's name!' I slammed the door. 'How can you let Cherry employ her father's murderer?'

Sidney Grice tied the string behind his head. 'Because there is no need to hang him.' And went back to his study.

I went upstairs to visit my three friends – Spirit, who was sleeping on my pillow, a Turkish cigarette and a bottle of gin. I poured a tumbler and drank it in one and felt ill, but at least I felt something.

100

Clockwork Soldiers and the Three Eyes of Sidney Grice

UNWILLING TO DISTURB Spirit, I had sat in my chair by the window, looking down into the courtyard garden with its tortured willow hanging over the bench.

I had only one picture of my mother, a miniature painted for her eighteenth birthday. She was a true beauty and I searched in vain for any resemblance between us. My father used to say I took after him, but I could never see it. *You must have been bought from gypsies*, my friend Barney used to tease me.

I thought I heard the front door close and then, a whole cigarette later, I heard it close again, and, before I had lit another, Molly clumped up and laid siege to the door in a series of thunderous blows.

'Are you asleep, miss?'

I threw the door open. 'No, but Spirit was.'

'Oh, bless.' Molly clasped her bosom. 'She looks like you've startled her.'

Spirit arched her back.

'What is it?' I asked.

'A cat.' Molly rolled her eyes at my stupidity.

I knew better than to ask what she wanted. The last time I had done that, she had started with a list of presents and ended with what kind of prince she would prefer to marry.

'What have you come to tell me?'

'That Easily man is here and wishes to speak to you.' She sucked her hair as if the memory were stored in there. 'Hurgently, he said.'

'What can he want?' I wondered foolishly.

'He wants a good woman, I should think,' Molly replied as I brushed past her. 'And a drop of Mr Grice's mendical brandy by the look of him.' Molly followed me down. 'Oh, and Mr Grice said to tell you he has been called out for his mother's funeral.'

I stopped on the first landing. 'But he never said anything to me.'

'He said it wasntn't not worth bothering you about.' She hopped round in front of me.

'But his mother—'

'Oh, she's always having funerals,' Molly said dismissively. 'Last year, when you were mad as a clock, she had one for her pet crockingdile. This time it's one of those birds that speaks – not a raving, a pirate.'

Easterly stood in the hall and, as Molly had intimated, he did not look well.

'Oh, miss,' he cried in his best Yorkshire, 'I am so fretted. Mr 'Esketh gave me this 'ere note to give Mr Grice tomorrow, but he's gone and shut 'imself away and won't come out.'

'Not even if you tickle him?' Molly asked.

'"E 'as locked the door.' Easterly flapped his hands. 'And I am sure he 'as been drinking, which is something Mr 'Esketh don't never do.'

I snatched the letter off him.

'It is confidential, for Mr Grice's eyes only,' Easterly protested.

'Mr Grice has three eyes.' I ripped the letter open. 'And I am two of them.'

'I 'ave kept a cab waiting,' Easterly said anxiously.

And I read:

Dear Mr Grice
I do not know how to thank you and Miss Middleton for what
you have done and I know that you have done it for the best of

THE SECRETS OF GASLIGHT LANE

*reasons but, the more I think about what I did, I was like a man
possessed and now the demons have fled, leaving me with a void
that can only be filled with horror and guilt.*

*How could I possibly serve Miss Charity, knowing what I
have done and what kind of man I have become?*

*This is for the best and I can only proffer my gratitude for the
great kindness you have both shown to me and my mistress.*

With kind regards and the deepest respect,
Austin Hesketh

'When Mr Grice returns, you must tell him we have gone to
Gaslight Lane,' I instructed Molly, who wrinkled her nose.

'Cantn't not I come? I left some things there what I need.'

'What?' I looked at her miserable attempt at an appealing
expression. 'Oh, very well.' I dashed to the study and scribbled
Gone to Gethsemane, added *Emergency,* and rushed back.

Easterly had the front door open. 'But you'll never fit hin with
hus, Molly.' He reverted to his own accent.

''Course I will,' Molly gave Easterly a nudge that nearly had
him spilling down the steps, 'if we snuggle up.'

I have always found that, in a squeeze, I am the one who gets
squeezed the most and, with Molly's bulk between us, this was
no exception to that rule. My legs were numb and the breath had
been forced out of me.

'Well, that was cosy.' Molly levered herself up with a hand to
my breast and trampled over my legs.

'Near bust me 'orse,' the driver complained as I paid him with
a generous tip, 'and me axle.'

Easterly struggled out on the other side – both of us walking
like clockwork soldiers as the blood flowed back into our limbs
– and unlocked the door.

''E his hin 'ere.' Easterly Nutter's accent was lost somewhere
between his mouth and Ilkley Moor as he touched the front sit-
ting-room door.

'Well,' Molly perched her hands on her hips, 'he will just have to hopen hup then.' I prayed that she was not going to adopt Easterly's way of talking permanently. "Cause hall my stuff his hin there.'

She rattled the handle. 'Come along, Mr Pesker, open up.'

'Whoever you are, push off.' I could hardly recognize the intoxicated slur as emanating from the dignified man I had known.

'Hesketh,' I called, 'this is Miss Middleton.'

'I told Easterly—' Something unintelligible and then, 'Why are you here? You are not meant to be here.'

'We are worried about you.'

'Shall Hi break the door down, miss?' Easterly whispered.

'I can do that,' Molly said eagerly. 'I aintn't not never brokened a door down but I'm good at it.' She bunched up ready for the charge.

'You will not,' I said sternly, and considered the matter. 'There is no keyhole in the door and I do not remember any bolts.'

'Hi believe he his using one hov those wedges,' the footman told me.

'Then run to the kitchen, Molly, quick as you can,' I whispered, 'and fetch the longest knife you can find.'

'Why are you whispering about getting a knife?' Molly boomed out. 'Are you going to stab Mr Pesker to death like you did that dog woman when you were mad as an egg?'

'I am not going to stab anyone,' I rounded on her, 'except, perhaps, you if you do not go and do as I say at once.'

I tapped on the porcelain fingerplate. 'Are you all right, Hesketh?'

I heard a crash – an occasional table being knocked over, I decided – and then, 'Is Mr Grice with you?'

'No.' I put my ear to the woodwork. 'It is just me and Molly and Easterly. Mr Grice is away on other business.'

There were more grunts and I made out a glass clinking noisily.

'I know you mean well, miss, but there is nothing you can do. Please leave me in peace.'

I turned the white porcelain handle a few degrees just in case Easterly and Molly were wrong. 'You do not sound like a man at peace.' The latch bolt clicked out of the strike plate.

'You cannot get in,' Hesketh warned, 'not without a battering ram.'

'I have read your letter,' I announced.

'That was addressed to Mr Grice.'

'Mr Grice has given me authority to open all his mail,' I lied. 'What do you intend to do, Hesketh?'

'What I should have done the moment I killed my master,' he replied hoarsely. 'Join him in hell.'

'Come out, Mr Hesketh,' Easterly pleaded, 'and we shall never speak of this again.'

'Look after your mistress,' the reply came gently, 'for I cannot.'

Molly galloped back, holding a wicked-looking carver in her raised fist like a Mahdist warrior launching into battle. I put my finger to my lips and, for once, she understood and crept the last few steps at a pace that would have done her proud in a game of musical statues. I took the knife gingerly from her before she tripped and impaled me. As quietly as possible in several layers of rustling material, I got to my knees and peered under the door, but the slit was so narrow and the light so poor I could not make anything out. I slipped the blade through the gap near the jamb and inched it towards the other end.

'What are you doing?' Hesketh must have seen it.

I moved quickly now until I felt an obstruction, pulled the knife back, then along half an inch, and rammed. The wedge flew away. I felt it give and heard it skitter away as I struggled up.

'Let me go first, miss.' Easterly helped me to my feet.

Something struck the door. A chair?

'He will not hurt me,' I said, with greater aplomb than I felt, and turned the handle. 'I am coming in, Hesketh. I mean you no harm.'

There were footfalls and hurried movements. I pushed on the door and a small piece of furniture fell away.

'You will both stay here, until I summon you.' I straightened my skirts and tucked a hanging tress behind my ear.

'I hope he aintn't not found my granddad's old blundlebust that I brought to frighten ghosts,' Molly said anxiously.

'Don't go in there, miss,' Easterly pleaded.

But I opened the door fully, took a deep breath and stepped inside.

'I am so sorry, miss, so very sorry,' Hesketh croaked. 'I am sorry, Mother.' And I heard the snap of a hammer.

101

His Last Bow

THE SHOCK SLAMMED into me, knocking the air out of my body and smothering me in smoke. Far away I coughed silently, choking on the acrid fumes. I banged my ear like a swimmer getting water out, but there was nothing except a dull thud.

The shutters swung apart.

Standing with his back to the jagged window was a man, but not a man – a mannequin in Hesketh's uniform. A ragged stump jutted from the collar, still neatly encircled in a cravat, a small volcano spewing darkly from its core.

I walked though the clouds towards death and Hesketh made his last bow. He bent at the waist, his torn neck vomiting the final pump of his heart over me. I wiped my face on my sleeve and Hesketh crumpled, toppling, chest first at my feet, a bottomless lake of his life flowing over the rug and around my boots.

The knife fell – I had forgotten I had it – skewering the rug to a floorboard. It quivered.

There was an upright chair on its side. The tracery had been smashed out and the stock of a musket jammed between the vertical slats, its butt wedged against the seat and the barrel pointing outwards, which would have been upwards when the chair was on its legs. Greyness curled lazily out of its flared opening and settled like morning mist over the lake, the pale sun hovering on the surface, no more than reflection of the naked flame in the shattered mantle.

And all around – on ceiling, walls, floor and shards of glass, on the fallen chair, the saturated rug and the copper vase – was the hair, skin and splintered bone that had made the man I had known. And sprayed carelessly through this was the bloody pulped meat that had formed every thought, stored every memory, felt every sensation, known love and loathing, laughter and fear, and harboured every secret that made but finally destroyed Austin Hesketh.

I was aware of somebody touching my left arm and somebody else at my right, and I allowed myself to be led from what I knew to where I knew not, as if they thought that by turning me they could stop me seeing it or that by walking, dragged foot after dragged foot through the sticky liquid death, I could somehow leave it all behind.

Easterly enthroned me in his footman's chair.

Molly was talking. 'That was my granddad's blundlebust,' came through fuzzily. 'I brought it to frighten ghosts.'

'And now it has created one,' I said or thought.

She was going back.

'No!' I heard myself. 'Do not disturb the evidence.' And she stopped and closed the door.

And I thought about it. Was that what the man who killed the master he loved had become? And what of his son and the household he had served all those years ago? Was that what they all were now – evidence?

*

'I told you there was no need to hang him,' Sidney Grice reminded me when I had given him an account of what happened. 'Give me your handkerchief.'

'You could not possibly have known.'

I handed it over and my guardian rubbed something from the tip of my nose.

'It is only necessary to know three things to know a man.' He shaped my handkerchief into a cone. 'And I know fourteen about

Hesketh.' Sidney Grice placed his creation on the hearth. 'You write people's words for them. I write their deaths.' My handkerchief toppled over and the cone came apart. 'Well, that was a napkin-folding lesson wasted,' he said.

102

The Wants of Women

OTTORLEY CRITCHELY LET me in reluctantly and I noted with a twinge of guilt that the ornamental pottery pedestal was still missing its vase.

'Have you come to return my stolen property?' he inquired without conviction.

'If I were to give that journal to anyone it ought to be the police,' I told him, and the doctor buried the fingers of his left hand in the grizzled confusion on top of his head.

'A patient's records are confidential,' he protested weakly.

'It is a criminal offence for anyone, even a doctor, to conceal a criminal offence,' I told him as sternly as I could, fully aware that I was committing exactly the same crime myself.

'They were dreams.' His fingers worked through his hair as if searching for wildlife.

'Remarkably detailed dreams.' I sat down uninvited.

'People can imagine all sorts of things under the influence of opiate medication.' Critchely massaged his scalp. 'And survivors often feel guilty and blame themselves. It happens all the time after shipwrecks.'

I did not tell him that I had had personal experience of poppy dreams in the dens of Cabool.

'You knew that those so-called dreams were based on fact, Dr Critchely,' I argued. 'They had far too much detail in them.' He was making me feel itchy. 'How you must have revelled in having a patient who might one day become notorious.'

My host set to work with his right hand. 'I could have dragged the study of nervous diseases into the nineteenth century,' he declared, but with a curious lack of fire. He mopped his brow with his sleeve and peered at me from under his arm. 'Women always want something, Miss Middleton. What do *you* want?'

'For you to make recompense.' I straightened a crease in the rug with my feet and wondered if I were turning into my godfather. 'The Jews' Deaf and Dumb Home in Burton Crescent is looking for a doctor who will give his services for free.'

Critchely extracted his fingers. 'I suppose I could spare a morning a month.'

'Two days a week,' I said firmly.

'Two?' he shrieked, staring into his hands as if they held his innards. 'With deaf Jews?'

'Three,' I said, 'and do not provoke me to insist on four.'

'I would be ruined.'

'Not as much as a spell in one of Her Majesty's—'

'Stop.' He crinkled up. 'You will return my notes?'

'We most certainly will,' I assured him, 'not.'

'You will at least destroy the journal?'

'I never do things *at least*,' I responded, not quite sure what I meant but satisfied with its Gricean ring. 'But it shall be kept confidential for so long as you infest this world.'

'Infest.' He repeated the word as if it comforted him.

'For heaven's sake,' I burst out. 'Did you really think he would have let you live, with everything you know?'

103

The Unity of Death

I PAID CREPOLIUS snushall a visit. He was not pleased to see me either and even less so when I explained that I had never promised not to talk to my Fleet Street *friend* Traf Trumpington, but would hold my tongue on one condition: Daniel Filbert was to be reburied in a new plot along with Angelina Innocenti, his mother, and Austin Hesketh, his father, and with a headstone of my choosing.

Inspector Pound came to the funeral.

'I had a soft spot for Hesketh,' he admitted.

'You had one for me once.' I watched the long-bladed spades plunge into the mound of clay.

He touched my sleeve. 'This is not the time, March.'

'This is *exactly* the time.' I heard earth thump on the oak lids. 'They spent their lives apart but at least they are united now. If you have your way, we will not even have that small mercy.'

'It is not that simple, March.' Pound's voice dropped urgently. 'And people are listening.' He had a hold of my wrist.

'If only you were one of them.' I tried to jerk my arm away but his grip tightened. 'You shed your life's blood for me and mine runs through your veins. Did it poison you?'

I was fully aware that I was making a spectacle of myself but I was past caring. I twisted round and took his face in my left hand. It felt so big and I felt so tiny.

'It is not that,' he replied.

From the corner of my eye I saw the vicar start towards us, lifting his cassock clear of the dirt.

'What then?' My right hand clutched his shoulder.

'You know what it is.'

The vicar approached behind the inspector, caught sight of my face, hesitated and hurried away.

'For the love of God!' I cried out. 'Do I have to fall on my knees in the mud and beg you?' He looked down, but I dipped to hold his gaze. 'What does it take to make you follow your heart, George Pound?'

The diggers had stopped their work and were leaning on their shovels to watch the entertainment, but I do not think that Pound was even aware of them any more. He pulled off his glove to touch my cheek and I felt him tremble. His eyes darkened and his face paled.

'I don't know, March,' he said desolately and it was not just our hands that fell away.

—◆◆◆—

104

Judgment Day

O NE DAY I *will have to meet them again, all the people whose lives I took, when I wasn't me. And I shall have to tell them why they died, though I can't remember* now. *Was it really for this rotting house that became my prison or the allowance policed by sanctimonious vicars nosing over my shoulder all the time? Or was it for the wife I couldn't keep or the daughter who loathes me?*

She told me once. 'I love you, Daddy, but not as much as I hate you.'

They will all hate me.

Mr and Mrs Garstang will preach at me.

Mrs Emmett will give me a good ticking off.

Brian will ask for a rematch, a fair fight this time, and beat the innards out of me.

What of the maids, Angelina, who might outlive me, and poor Kate, whom I hurt the most? I can't even begin to imagine how they will be.

How will Danny greet me – my friend, who tried to protect me in a fight I started, whose last night was one of torment because he was terrified of being trapped – my friend, whom I throttled and lowered into that cesspit because he saw Sergeant Horwich letting me back in?

And how will I face Lionel, whom I brought back into the world when he was shut away? Lionel will still love me. He will want to hug me and forget all about it and I could not stomach that.

And Mrs Samuels, whom I brained and mashed with a rolling pin, I had quite forgotten about her.

Hell will be a release after all this.

And Fortitude, my sweet Forty, as I used to call her. She put up the biggest fight of them all. She kept saying, 'Don't do this, Natty. Think of Charity.'

And I scream back, 'But you are trying to take her away from me.'

And afterwards I do think of my darling little Cherry, still tucked up in her bed, so lovely, and I can't help but wonder. Will there ever come a day when I am forced to murder her?

105

Crumpets and Catmint

T HE FOG LAY heavier than ever, suffocating the city. It seeped into the house, making everything cold and damp, but at least we had a blazing fire to huddle beside and hot crumpets with butter melting into the holes of mine.

'Is it not wonderful how the symmetry of fourteen encompasses recent events?' Sidney Grice took a box of safety matches from the hearth as a connoisseur might an *objet d'art*.

'How?' I asked blankly.

'Beginning with the three major non-lethal criminal violations I have solved.' He slid the box open. 'Crepolius Snushall's illegal disposal of corpses, the corruption of Sergeant Horwich and the withholding of evidence by Dr Ottorley Critchely.'

For every offence Mr G listed he laid a match on the edge of the table.

'And what about our sheltering of Hesketh?' I demanded.

'You cannot harbour a dead man and Austin Hesketh was all but dead the moment I exposed him.'

'Was Angelina's attempt to assassinate you not a crime?' I was surprised he did not mention it first, but my guardian was busy marshalling his fragments of food.

'Under the rules formulated in the wake of the M'Naghten case in 1843, a person certified as being insane cannot be guilty of a criminal offence.' My guardian delved into the box. 'Add to those the deaths that can be laid at Nathan Mortlock's door

– Holford and Augusta Garstang, Brian Watts, their footman; Kate Webb, their maid; Lionel Engra, their godson; Daniel Filbert, Nathan's friend; Mrs Samuels from number 4 Burton Crescent, Angelina Innocenti—'

'He was already dead when she had her accident,' I objected.

'And whose spikes killed her?' And, seeing that I was not going to reply, my guardian recited, 'Nathan himself and Austin Hesketh.' And dealt out two more matches.

'You must be very proud to have solved so many crimes in one case.' I did not trouble to ask him for the eleventh death, for that came to light in the last entry of Nathan Mortlock's journal.

'One of my fourteen finest achievements.' Sidney Grice nodded happily as he aligned the last match. 'In fact there have been so many fourteens in this case.' He sliced open a plain muffin. 'If ever you come to write it up, why not entitle your account *The Sign of Fourteen*?'

'That is a dismal title.' I spooned out some cherry jam.

He nibbled round the edge of his muffin thoughtfully. 'For once you are right.'

I thought again about that last death.

'Why were you surprised that Fortitude Garstang's letters were written in the same hand?' I asked, and Sidney Grice put his ragged muffin back on the plate.

'I was not.' He trimmed the rim with the point on his knife. 'I observed that it was remarkable how identical they were. Every word common to two or more missives was written in exactly the same style and size on every occasion. Nobody's hand is consistent. It varies according to which pen one uses, one's temper, whether one is sitting at a bureau or writing in a railway carriage, et cetera, et cetera. If you add to this the knowledge that Signor Agostino Cristiano Montanari is a notorious forger—'

'You said you admired his work,' I remembered.

'And so I do.' He reassembled the muffin. 'I have never seen so good a counterfeiter of Dürer.'

'So Nathan's drawing—' I began.

'A skilful fake, which would doubtless deceive a lover of so-called art, but one who loathes such nonsense views it with a more dispassionate eye.' Sidney Grice tapped his glass prosthesis to imply that he had used it to view the picture. Absorbed in his thoughts, he poked at his muffin and told me, 'One of Montanari's favourite ways of getting a work on the market was for one accomplice to lose it to another in an illegal game. How else could Nathan explain his ownership of a valuable work of art? And a greedy collector is not going to look too closely at the provenance of a work acquired in such an illicit manner.'

'Then why did Nathan never sell it?'

'Montanari was greedy. He produced too many Dürers in too short a space of time and aroused suspicions. He fled and would have been grateful for any commissions, including forged letters purportedly from dead wives.'

'Artwork at twenty pounds a time,' I remembered. 'So that was why the last letter said that they were moving. The money has dried up and poor Cherry will wait for ever for another communication.'

Sidney Grice stabbed his muffin and held it up like a speared fish. 'Unless Montanari decides to send begging letters in Fortitude Garstang's name.'

Spirit came out from under the desk.

'Roll over.' Mr G twirled his fingers and she lay down at his feet. 'At last a trainable female in this house,' he declared triumphantly.

'She is just resting,' I objected.

'Nonsense. Watch this.' He curled his fingers and commanded, 'Sit up and beg.'

And Spirit, I was proud to see, merely yawned and closed her eyes.

'That reminds me.' I wiped my fingers dry and delved in my handbag for the catnip mouse. Something glinted underneath, the silver locket that I had picked off the pavement. I had forgotten about it with all the other events. It was beautifully worked in interlocking hearts, with a tiny catch on the side, and when I unclipped it there was an oval photograph of an extraordinarily beautiful young woman.

'What the devil!' Sidney Grice exclaimed.

'I thought she had dropped it,' I whispered, more to myself than him.

My guardian stood up, his plate clattering on to the hearth, his muffin depositing into the ashes.

'This is what you were looking for when you were leaning over the railings complaining that you hated going into the moat,' I accused, and I suddenly realized that the locket was so small because it was designed to hang on a watch chain.

There was a message engraved in the left hand. The letters were tiny and intertwined but legible: *To my darling Siddy with all my heart*. The glass was cracked, but I did not need to read the signature *Constance* to know that the picture was of my mother and – not for the first time – I wondered that I did not look like either of my parents.

'Give that back.'

I hardly heard the words but, when I looked up, I saw the curl at the corner of his mouth that I had seen in our twin reflections.

'Dear God in heaven,' I cried. 'Are you my father?'

Postscript

I SWORE AN oath to Sidney Grice, and he reminded me of it before he died, that I would not tell a living soul what he told me over that broken plate for at least sixty years, and so I must wait – if God spares me – until 1944 before I am relieved of that vow.

*

Shortly after this I had a letter from George Pound. He was being transferred to Ely in Cambridgeshire. They needed reorganization and a more sedentary job with fresh air might benefit the inspector's health. He would like to say farewell before he left.

*

I never saw Cherry Mortlock again. The following year she married Fabian Le Bon and they went to live in France where his genius might be appreciated better. It has yet to be recognized.

They were visiting his brother in Belgium in August 1914 when the Germans invaded. Fabian fled, leaving Cherry, who had gone to meet her niece from school, to fend for herself. He got a boat to England. She stayed behind to help in a clandestine hospital for wounded British soldiers trapped behind enemy lines. In 1917 she was denounced by a neighbour, arrested by the Germans and shot as a spy.

There is a small memorial to her in what is now Cartwright Gardens. Sidney Grice paid for it and decided upon the words.

CHARITY 'CHERRY' MORTLOCK
1859–1917
A SEEKER OF TRUTH

And once a year I tend it. Two years ago I saw an elderly man step out of Gethsemane with an easel under his arm. He did not glance at the plaque and I do not suppose for one moment he understood the little old lady, who looked into his sallow soul as he shuffled past, when she whispered, 'Murderer.'

I almost added *Just like her father*, but by then I was the only person alive who truly knew the secrets of Gaslight Lane.

M.M., 1 September 1943
125 Gower Street